THE WINNERS OF NINE BOOK AWARDS transcending the genres of science fiction, environmental fiction, and action-adventure, ***The Girl Who Rode Dolphins*** and ***Dolphin Riders*** have proven themselves thrillers with a labyrinth of spellbinding twists, turns, and thunderous action that takes readers on a roller coaster ride of nail-biting suspense and explosive adventure.

Upon its original debut, ***The Girl Who Rode Dolphins*** received the following multiple awards:

- ***Winner of Best Epic Adventure of 2008***
  BooksandAuthors.net
- ***Winner of Best Science Fiction Epic Adventure of 2008***
  BooksandAuthors.net
- ***Winner of Science Fiction Genre***
  2009 Green Book Festival
- ***Finalist in Action Adventure Category***
  2009 National Indie Book Excellence Awards
- ***Winner of Environmental/Green Fiction Category***
  2010 International Book Awards Competition
- ***Winner of the Talking Category***
  2015 Animals, Animals, Animals Book Festival
- ***Honorable Mention Awardee in Science Fiction Category***
  2015 London Book Festival

Dolphin Riders, the sequel to ***The Girl Who Rode Dolphins***, is an ensuing adventure combined with political intrigue that promises to captivate readers with enthralling action and mysticism on a scale every bit as intense if not greater than the first book.

- ***Official Selection Winner of Action/Adventure Category***
  2016 New Apple Summer eBook Awards
- ***Finalist In Action/Adventure Category***
  2016 Beverly Hills Book Awards

Following their original debuts, both books were re-released in 2026 by Seaworthy Publications, Inc. as a five-part cliff-hanger series as follows:

The Girl Who Rode Dolphins, 3rd Edition

- Part 1 - Gaia's Intervention
- Part 2 - Gaia's Heartbeat
- Part 3 - Retribution

Dolphin Riders, 3rd Edition

- Part 4 - Creation
- Part 5 - Survival

Gaia's Heartbeat

Part 2
of
The Dolphin Riders Series

The Girl Who Rode Dolphins
3rd Edition

Gaia's Heartbeat

Part 2
of
The Dolphin Riders Series

The Girl Who Rode Dolphins
3rd Edition

by

Michael J. Ganas

SEAWORTHY PUBLICATIONS, INC. • MELBOURNE, FLORIDA

Gaia's Heartbeat
Part 2 of the Dolphin Riders Series
The Girl Who Rode Dolphins, 3rd Edition

Paperback ISBN 978-1-966191-06-3
eBook ISBN 978-1-966191-07-0

Published in the USA by:
Seaworthy Publications, Inc.
6300 N Wickham Rd.
Unit #130-416
Melbourne, FL 32940
e-mail orders@seaworthy.com
www.seaworthy.com

Library of Congress Cataloging-in-Publication Data

Names: Ganas, Michael J., 1946- author | Ganas, Michael J., 1946- Girl who rode dolphins
Title: Gaia's intervention / by Michael J Ganas.
Description: Third edition. | Melbourne, Florida : Seaworthy Publications, Inc, 2026. | Series: The dolphin riders series ; part 1 | "The girl who rode dolphins 3rd edition" | Summary: "Former Navy SEAL Jake Javolyn, a part-time smuggler by necessity and dive boat operator by profession, has come to Haiti in search of something. Hiring his boat out to Dr. Franklin Grahm, a renowned marine zoologist, Javolyn sets course for Navassa Island, only to stumble across a beautiful girl in the open sea. Encircled by a pod of six white bottlenose dolphins, the girl is found riding a seventh, much larger but similar creature. Upon rescuing the girl from the nets of a tuna trawler crewed by vicious members of a drug cartel, Javolyn soon discovers the girl has strange and unusual powers. Even more amazing are her companions, for they are unlike any sea mammals he has ever encountered. They possess forelimbs with hands, super-intelligence, and can speak in human languages. From then on, he is plunged into a world of the supernatural and confrontation with iniquitous forces bent on vengeance and the capture of nature's most recent miracles. A stunning rollercoaster ride of epic adventure, Gaia's Intervention is the first book in this blockbuster series, an ecological saga that will leave readers spellbound and enthralled with its superb mix of intense action, environmental issues, and mysticism"-- Provided by publisher.
Identifiers: LCCN 2026000755 (print) | LCCN 2026000756 (ebook) | ISBN 9781966191049 v. 1 paperback | ISBN 9781966191056 v. 1 epub
Subjects: LCSH: Dolphins--Fiction | LCGFT: Ecofiction | Action and adventure fiction | Fantasy fiction | Novels | Fiction
Classification: LCC PS3607.A4385 G35 2026 (print) | LCC PS3607.A4385 (ebook)
LC record available at https://lccn.loc.gov/2026000755
LC ebook record available at https://lccn.loc.gov/2026000756

Dedication

To my gemstone, Harriet.

Table of Contents

Facts

Haiti is currently the poorest country in the Western Hemisphere, a Caribbean nation beleaguered by economic strife, dismal squalor, and political instability, a land of defoliation and ecological ruin. It is a place with a violent past, punctuated by a succession of bloody rebellions and previously governed by a long line of statesmen and dictators whose policies were either inept, ineffectual, unpopular, corrupt, or oppressive. The Duvalier dictatorships of father and son, however, proved to be the most corrupt, oppressive, and violent, and under their brutal regimes Haiti suffered deeply.

Francois "Papa Doc" Duvalier ruled Haiti from 1963 until his death in 1971 when his son Jean-Claude "Baby Doc" Duvalier took over the reins of power. Under the Duvalier governments, the population was kept in a state of fear, terrorized by the regime's secret police force, the Tonton Makout. They were also known as the VNS, Volunteers of National Security, and Papa Doc referred to them as his "civilian" military, while the citizens called them "the bogeymen." They were recruited mostly from Haiti's slums and were used to crush all opposition, often imprisoning without trial, torturing, and even killing individuals considered enemies of the state.

An estimated 60,000 Haitians were murdered at the hands of the Tonton Makout, which had a standing force of roughly 10,000 loyalists. Papa Doc made sure his secret police outnumbered the Haitian army by a factor of two in order to assure that he did not get overthrown in a coup. Both Francois Duvalier and his son also took advantage of the people's strong belief in voodoo to control the population. Consequently, much of the citizenry believed them to be voodoo spirits. To this day, voodoo, merged with Catholicism, is the religion of choice embraced by most Haitians.

Misappropriation of government funds amounting to hundreds of millions was common practice under Baby Doc's tyrannical rule, and in the wake of intense political unrest and pressure from the United States to step down, he was finally forced from power in February of 1986, whereupon he fled to France. A wealth of evidence shows various drug cartels to be firmly entrenched in present-day Haiti, where the political climate, endemic poverty, and a breakdown in civil rule makes it an ideal staging area for the transshipment of illegal contraband, where public officials are often threatened or corrupted by bribery to keep a blind eye to drug trafficking.

Navassa Island is a small, uninhabited island, which lies in the Caribbean Sea between Haiti and Jamaica. The island originally belonged to Haiti before being claimed in 1801 as an unorganized, unincorporated territory of the United States, which currently administers it through the U.S. Fish and Wildlife Service.

Malique is a fictitious fishing village that lies roughly midway between the real cities of Saint-Marc and Gonaives along Haiti's western coastline. It has been created solely for the purpose of this novel.

Al Qaeda is an actual present-day organization of Islamic extremists bent on the destruction of the United States and its allies. To this day this terrorist group continues to flourish despite the loss of its originator and leader, Osama Bin Laden, who was killed by a team of U.S. Navy Seals when they stormed his hideout in Pakistan during a bold raid that occurred in 2011.

All mention of Haiti's former leadership and historical events, both past and modern day, are based on documented history and are used as a backdrop for the writing of this novel. In this way, history has been merged with fiction.

All characters, creatures, and unusual settings that play a key role within the novel's plot are entirely fictitious and have been created solely for the reader's intrigue and entertainment.

Michael J Ganas

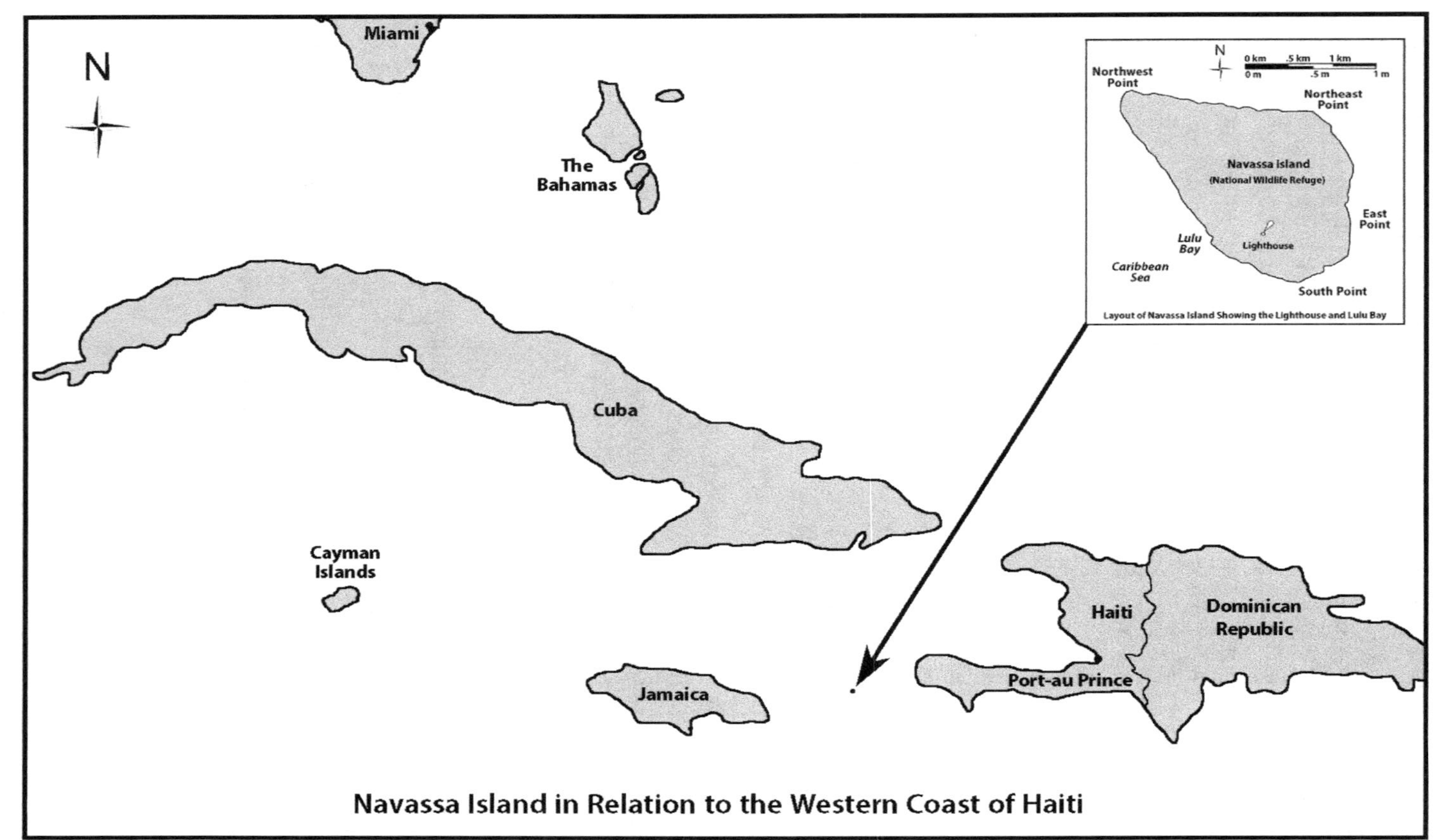

Navassa Island in Relation to the Western Coast of Haiti

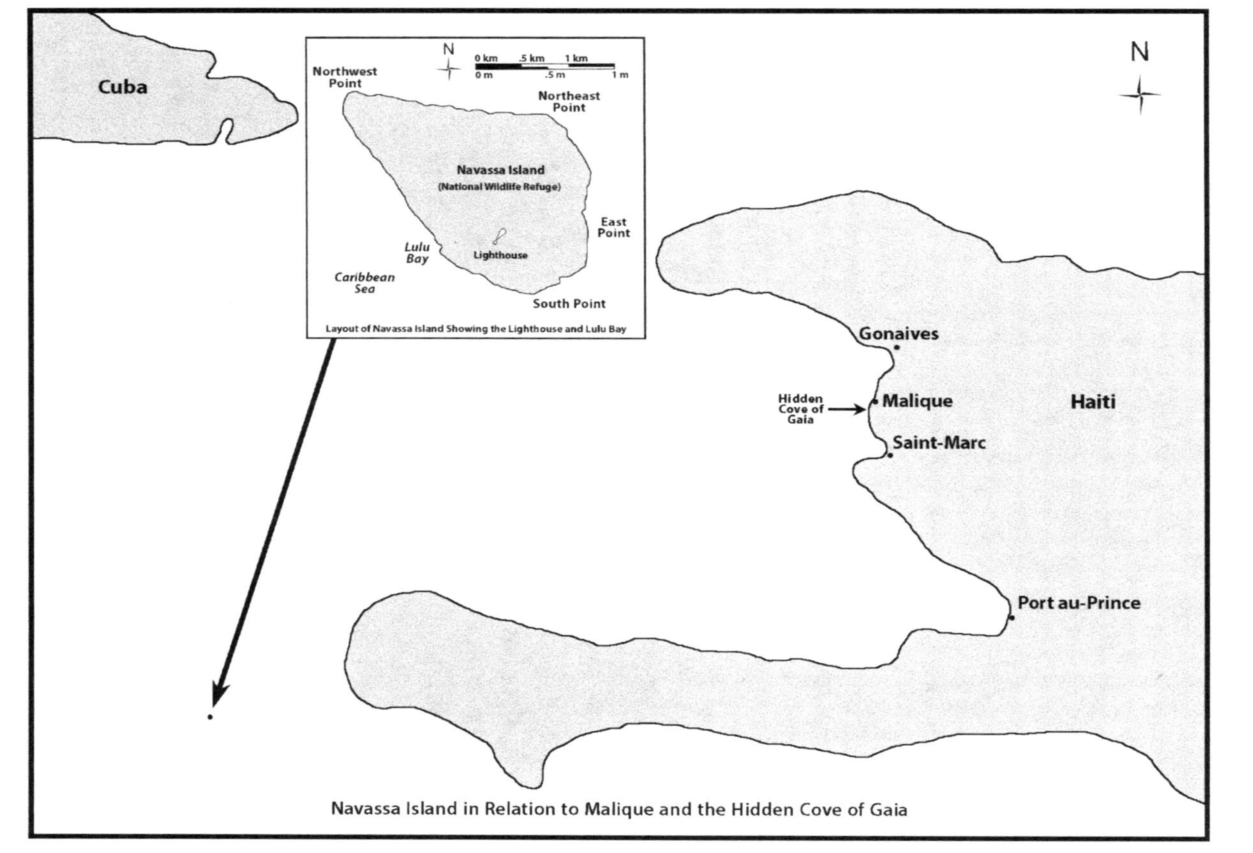

Navassa Island in Relation to Malique and the Hidden Cove of Gaia

Introduction

In Book One of the series, the story opens up in the year 1986 with a woman stranded in a tumultuous sea. Relentlessly battered by churning waves, she is clinging to a piece of flotsam as she fights for her life, and it is revealed she is pregnant. With her will to survive beginning to flag, she is ready to surrender to the sea's embrace. But finding herself painfully entangled in the stinging cells of strange, oblate jellyfish, something from behind pushes her back to the surface where an angry, thunderous sky awaits, and her prayers for a quick and merciful death are quickly answered as a lightning bolt streaks down upon her.

The scene changes, and it is twenty-two years later. Former Navy Seal Jake Javolyn, a part-time smuggler by necessity and dive boat operator by profession, has come to Haiti to fulfill a solemn promise made to a comrade-in-arms killed in the mountains of Tora Bora four years earlier. Javolyn is sitting across from his Jamaican first mate, a giant of a man called Zimbola, both of them sipping ale from frosty mugs in a sleazy tavern situated along the waterfront of Port-au-Prince. Their hushed conversation about locating something they had been seeking for some time now is suddenly interrupted by Chester Hennington, a broker who Javolyn has been dealing with for all his business, both legitimate and otherwise. Javolyn is not too pleased with Hennington because of a recent smuggling gig that had gone sour. Begrudgingly, he agrees to take on another risky smuggling assignment, one that promises a major windfall of monetary reward, but before that happens he must first take on some charter diving work the broker has also arranged with a professor from the University of Miami and the two assistants accompanying him.

Hiring his boat out to Dr. Franklin Grahm, a renowned marine zoologist, Javolyn is instructed by the congenial Grahm to sail for Navassa Island where he believes a sloop owned by him went down in a storm twenty-two years earlier. Confiding to Javolyn that his pregnant wife, a marine zoologist, had perished along with the vessel, Grahm is still unable to get over the loss of his spouse after all this time.

Setting a course directly for the island, Javolyn stumbles across a beautiful young girl in the open sea. Encircled by a pod of six white bottlenose dolphins making their way toward Navassa Island, the girl is seen riding a seventh much larger but similar creature. Following the pod, he eventually catches up with the girl to discover her name is Destiny. She is on a rescue mission aimed at saving other dolphins injured by the crew of a Colombian fishing trawler harvesting tuna. Having had an earlier run-in with the ship's crew back in Port-au-Prince, Javolyn knows them to be a mean, pernicious bunch that will have no scruples about harming the girl. Launching a custom-tailored waverunner armed with weaponry, Javolyn opposes the trawler crew in a blazing gun battle, zipping the highly maneuverable watercraft among other small vessels sent out to intercept him. The action is fast, furious, and explosive, and Javolyn eventually comes out victorious, ultimately preventing Destiny and several dolphins from becoming trapped in the trawler's immense purse seine. He is soon introduced to Jacob, a grizzled Haitian fisherman who arrives in a rickety pinnace to tow the wounded dolphins back to their home using makeshift floats. Javolyn is left stunned by what happens next. A gunshot wound he suffered during his firefight with the Colombians is completely healed in a matter of moments by Destiny's touch. His amazement escalates further when he notices the albino dolphins are nothing like any sea mammal he has ever before seen. They possess forelimbs with what amounts to hands and are able to speak in human languages. And he is soon to learn they possess an intellect that dwarfs anything on a human scale.

As one of the leading dolphin experts in the world, Dr. Grahm is especially excited by this spectacular find, and through his persistence he and Javolyn are invited by Destiny and Jacob to follow them back to a hidden cove along the Haitian coast.

Chapter One: The Thurentra

The Haitian coastline rose up like a distant storm cloud looming over the eastern horizon, dark and towering as the sun began its final descent toward the sea. Sunset was less than two hours away. The pinnace continued on its slow trek until it was less than three hundred meters from the craggy escarpments lining the shore before it turned ninety degrees and headed south, skirting an outer barrier reef. The *Avenging Angel* kept pace behind it until the operator of the smaller vessel suddenly threw the engine into idle, letting the craft drift lazily in the gentle swells.

Jake could see Grahm nodding in acknowledgment to something Jacob was pointing at in the water. The scientist exchanged a few more words with the man before turning and signaling the larger vessel to come abreast of the pinnace's starboard gunwale. Jake stepped to the *Angel's* port railing as Zimbola steered them alongside and reversed the prop.

"Jacob tells me there's a break in the reef here, but that it's too narrow for your boat to get through," Grahm shouted. "He wants you to anchor your vessel farther out and come in by dory. One of the dolphins will guide you in. I'll be going on ahead with these people."

Grahm turned back to Jacob again, attentive to something else the Haitian was telling him. Jacob pointed to the water south of where the pinnace now drifted, seeming to be deeply concerned about the seabed directly under his craft. At the conclusion of the brief discussion, Grahm pivoted his head around to face Jake once more. "Jacob says to make sure you set your anchor at least one hundred meters south of this location. He'll explain why later."

Jake scanned the nearby bluffs and nodded, then climbed up into the pilothouse to give Zimbola instructions. Monitoring the depth sounder, he could see the bottom was dropping off quickly as they moved away from the barrier reef. When they were in sixty feet of water, he had Phillipe drop the Danforth. Turning, Jake caught a glimpse of the pinnace just as it disappeared from sight behind a rocky outcropping north of the channel through the reef. He blinked in surprise at the deceptiveness of the coastline here. From his position, no inlets, bays or openings in the craggy escarpments were visible, giving him the impression that the shoreline was impenetrable.

Jake looked back at Zimbola. "I'll make sure we're hooked onto something solid," he said. "I don't want our sweet girl slipping her anchor in the middle of the night and ending up on the reef. That coral comes too close to the surface for my taste."

Zimbola nodded in agreement as Jake headed below to grab a mask, fins, and snorkel.

Less than a minute later, Jake jumped from the *Angel's* prow and began to follow the anchor line to the ocean floor. Underwater visibility was close to a hundred feet, and as he dipped under the surface, he was astounded at what he saw. In place of the dead zones he had grown accustomed to seeing when diving close to the Haitian coastline, the sea floor was rife with life. Interspersed over a sandy bottom, a wide assortment of corals bloomed in thick clusters where various species of small tropical fish hovered in dense clouds.

As he descended, the longer wavelengths of the visible spectrum were quickly filtered out, causing the majority of colors exhibited by the different flora and fauna to be suppressed. Red tinctures were the first to get absorbed by the water, followed by a sequence of other rainbow gradations the deeper the remaining light traveled. At a depth of ten fathoms, such a condition tended to give most of the sea life a pale blue or pale green tinge with the reduced amount of sunlight penetrating to the seabed. Some dull yellows were also in evidence. He knew, however, that the place was actually abounding with an explosion of color, a fact that could easily be confirmed if the corals and fish were to be exposed to artificial light at close range. Such a thriving environment was not typical of the local waters where heavy pollution and excessive runoff from deforestation had devastated marine ecosystems immediately adjacent to the land. As Jake pulled himself deeper along the line, he wondered what had caused such a startling rebound in the ecology at this particular place.

Reaching the bottom, he removed the anchor from where it had snagged onto an outgrowth of healthy brain coral. Locating a nearby stand of dead coral barely protruding from the sand, he repositioned the anchor flukes so that they hooked under the lip of one of the outcroppings. He tugged hard on the line to test it, making sure the anchor held fast. Satisfied that it would not come loose, he spun around and inspected the first cluster of coral he had come upon. While the upper portion was alive and robust, its base displayed patches of dull calcareous growth long dead. As best he could surmise, the coral had begun to revive and bounce back within the last ten or fifteen years.

Lingering longer than originally intended, Jake could feel the strain on his lungs as the urge to breathe started to grow stronger. At that moment, a dark shadow glided over him, making him look up sharply. With relief, he realized the huge albino Destiny had ridden was nearby and was watching him intently.

Another torpedo shape, substantially smaller than the giant bottlenose, shot out from behind a nearby coral head and began to circle Jake. Achilles greeted him with that peculiar plastered on smile so typical of his species. Although the juvenile was perhaps only a few inches longer than him, Jake knew it still had a ways to grow judging from the size of the adult albinos.

Upon orbiting Jake a few times, Achilles suddenly came to a hover less than a foot away. On impulse, Jake reached out and grabbed hold of the albino's dorsal fin, certain it was being proffered. He had the strange notion that the dolphin understood his growing need for air and wanted to hasten his ascent to the world above.

With a flick of its tail, the juvenile took off for the surface with Jake in tow. In that instant, Jake got a sense of the raw power typical of these creatures as the young albino pulled him along with relative ease. Suddenly filled with euphoria, he stared ahead as the boundary separating hydrosphere from atmosphere rushed closer, its surface dancing like quicksilver under the glowing light of the evening sun. No more than a few arm lengths away, the giant albino matched Achilles' speed, holding to a parallel course. In unison, both creatures breached the surface at exactly the same time, giving Jake the opportunity to refill his aching lungs.

Not wanting to overstay the courtesy of the ride given him, Jake released his hold on the smaller dolphin. Abruptly, Achilles spun around and faced him. The juvenile's mouth opened slightly as the creature emitted a high-pitched chirp. Jake looked back in confusion as the dolphin repeated the sound, an odd, almost rhythmic lilt. Then remembering what Grahm had told him about this incredible new breed, he realized the creature was trying to communicate with him. Listening carefully, he was able to cut through the poorly spoken diction, isolating each syllable and word and getting to the gist of what the young dolphin was telling him. "Hold on, Jake Javolyn," it said. "To Destiny and Jacob I will take you."

Though Jake had already witnessed Natalie speak in such a human-based tongue, the albino's utterance of such words flabbergasted him, nevertheless. The fact that it even knew his name also astonished him. But then he realized that Grahm had previously introduced him and other members of the *Angel's* crew to Destiny when they had provided assistance to the girl back near Navassa Island. Either the girl had disseminated this tidbit of information to the rest of the pod, or the dolphins had heard his name mentioned during the introduction.

Finally overcoming his awe, Jake removed the snorkel from his mouth, then looked into Achilles' dark liquid eyes. "I'll go with you," he responded. "But first I must give instructions to the people aboard my boat."

Achilles replied with more garbled speech, but Jake quickly found meaning in the prosody of words as he translated the lilt of the inflections. "I will take you when you are ready."

Jake turned in the water and found the *Angel* at anchor less than twenty meters away, its starboard stern closest to where he now floated. Zimbola was hugging the railing, watching his interaction with the dolphin.

Jake called out to him. "I'll be going on ahead, Zimby. Have Hector and Phillipe stay aboard and mind the store. You and the others can come on in when you're ready."

As an afterthought, Jake turned to the larger albino floating next to him. "What's your name?" he asked curiously, placing a hand on the dolphin's huge beak. He was clueless about the creature's name, remembering that neither Destiny nor Jacob had mentioned it.

The giant bottlenose regarded him with black inscrutable dark eyes before speaking. "I am called Hercules."

To Jake, the words of the larger dolphin were more clearly enunciated than those of its smaller counterpart. As he reflected on this, he realized it made sense that Hercules would articulate air-based speech better than the younger dolphin. Hercules was an adult of this marvelous new species, or so he assumed. Being much older than the juvenile, the huge albino would have had many more years in which to develop such a skill. Even human children had trouble pronouncing certain words.

Jake addressed the giant bottlenose again. "Hercules, will you stay here and wait for my friends? They'll need you to guide them through the opening in the reef."

"That is why I am here," Hercules said, appearing to nod his head in an almost human-like manner.

Satisfied with the albino's reply, Jake was about to reach out for Achilles when another thought struck him. "Tell me, Hercules, how old are you?"

"My essence has existed since the beginning," Hercules answered.

The statement confused Jake. Wondering if he had understood the words correctly, he tried another question. "No…I mean how many years have passed since the time of your physical birth?"

When Hercules did not immediately respond, Jake had the impression the dolphin did not understand the query. He was about to restate the question differently, but before he could do so, Hercules spoke. "This planet has completed fifteen point three four orbits around its star since the time of my physical conception." The permanent smile etched on the dolphin's face seemed ridiculously incongruous with the depth of intelligence the statement implied.

Jake took in the words, continuing to ponder the creature's unique affiliation with the girl. Something Grahm had told him suddenly came to mind. Making sure to phrase the question precisely, he queried Hercules again. "Tell me, Hercules, what do you believe your fate will be?"

Hercules did not hesitate. "The ultimate course of my life has already been predetermined."

"By whom?" Jake pressed. He was getting good at how quickly he was able to understand the dolphin's garbled singsong speech.

"By the great creator."

Jake tried another approach. "Does your fate reside in the hands of the girl who you carry on your back?"

Hercules exhaled sharply before refilling his lungs. The albino bull seemed to turn the question over and over before providing Jake with the information he sought. When the answer finally came, though, it was more than Jake had expected. "Up until today, all those of my pod believed that Destiny held the key to our proliferation. But now we are certain this world cannot survive without her."

Jake found it difficult to comprehend the full measure of what this strange creature was telling him. He had to keep reminding himself he wasn't dreaming, that the conversation he was having was not some surrealistic figment of his imagination. "What exactly do you mean when you say this world cannot survive without her?" he found himself asking.

"Without Destiny, all life on this planet will perish."

A feeling of uneasiness began to take hold of Jake. Under normal circumstances he would shrug off such a doomsday comment. He had heard this type of claim before, usually entwined in the rhetoric of a noted scientist or acclaimed ecologist. But there was nothing normal about the creature he was conversing with. To ease his mind, he decided to get additional clarification. "Does that include humans…mankind?"

"Humans are a part of this planet's biosphere. Humankind would also perish."

Jake was dumbstruck. Dazed by the context of the words, he found himself groping for something appropriate to say. "We will speak again, Hercules. I have enjoyed your company immensely."

"And I have enjoyed yours as well, Jake Javolyn."

Like a man in a stupor, Jake refitted the mask to his face and placed the snorkel in his mouth. Absently, he reached out and grabbed hold of Achilles' dorsal fin. The juvenile gathered speed quickly, moving north along the water's surface. Using only one hand to maintain his grip, Jake lowered his face into the water to observe the seabed as it swept past.

The break in the reef soon came into view, and as they approached it, he noticed thick vine-like strands that wound their way through the sand and stands of coral. They littered the bottom haphazardly, many of them crisscrossing and appearing to extend from the deeper water toward the barrier reef. He could see no beginning and no end to them, each strand seeming continuous in length. In all the dives he had made throughout his relatively young life, he had never seen anything like them before. Greatly puzzled, he kept his eyes riveted on the strange rope-like growths as Achilles pulled him through the narrow channel.

Once through the reef, Achilles turned to his left by almost ninety degrees, parallelling the cliffs looming high above them. Along the inside of the reef and less than twenty feet down, a white sandy bottom predominated the seascape adjacent to the shoreline. As Jake hung on, he was surprised to find the strange vine-like growths still beneath him. Stationary and intertwined, they continued to wend their way along the sand like cables strung out on the seabed. From Jake's perspective, it seemed as if Achilles was following the trail they made. The odd organic strands appeared to be segmented, forming a chain, and as best he could tell, each segment was about eight to twelve inches long and roughly two inches in diameter. In the shallower water they appeared bright green in color.

With the organic chains now much closer to him, he became aware of something he hadn't noticed before. They pulsed. Though subtle to the naked eye, each segment comprising the chain billowed incessantly, swelling and contracting at a rate slightly out of sync with its immediate neighbor. The way the chainlike strands rhythmically palpitated reminded him of arteries pumping blood. Scrutinizing one of the strands carefully, he could see the pulsations go rippling along its length, each pulsation separated by approximately one second and heading off in Achilles' direction of travel.

Achilles suddenly veered hard right, following the path formed by the vine-like projections. Jake took the opportunity to get his bearings.

Looking above him, he noted the escarpments jutting high overhead on each side. They were entering a wide cleft in one of the rock walls lining the shoreline, actually a crevasse that was perhaps thirty feet across. As the juvenile tugged him along, he observed a slight dogleg to the rocky inlet. Within moments they traveled down the length of it before it opened into a large cove, and as he glanced around, he was amazed at what he saw.

The place was a veritable Garden of Eden.

Aside from a lush and healthy coral reef, it was one of the most beautiful places he had ever seen. The cove was set in a chasm with steeply tiered sides that funneled down to the water from high above, giving it the shape of a crude amphitheater. Off to one side and farther back, a waterfall threaded its way down from a natural spring located at the highest section of the gorge, cascading in a series of cataracts before making its longest and final plunge to the pristine water trapped within the basin.

With the sun now low on the western horizon, much of the vista was bathed in shadow, but where sunlight did fall it revealed an eruption of color. Along the tiered sides, various types of fruit trees abounded along with flowering bushes in full bloom. The slopes were alive with flora, and flitting among the lush vegetation Jake could see substantial throngs of multi-hued songbirds and butterflies representing a variety of species. At the base of the gorge, a white sandy beach ringed the cove by about two-thirds of its perimeter, providing balance to the strange but breathtaking vista. The place had an unreal quality to it, as if constructed by the brush strokes of some gifted painter who had seen such a panorama on another world at the far end of the galaxy.

As Achilles pulled Jake across the placid water, the scene before him was made all the more surrealistic by the two thatched structures that adorned the opposite shore. Though crude and set back from the beach, their rustic appearance seemed to harmonize well with the setting. It was the pod of white dolphin milling near the beach, however, that instilled a profound depth to the picture, the eye-drawing focal point that gave the backdrop a dimension like something out of a fairytale.

Out of curiosity, Jake dipped his head below the surface again, wondering if his gaze would fall on any other unusual sights. The green organic chains were still under him, twisting around one another in a thick concentrated bundle, throbbing with ceaseless micro-pulsations that shot forward toward the shore.

No more than thirty feet from the beach, Jake's expectation of seeing something else strange was suddenly met. The dense cluster of vine-like strands abruptly terminated in a huge bulbous node lying on the bottom, a squat mound of living matter that rose and fell at regular intervals as if periodically inflated and deflated. As Jake studied it, he realized it was pulsing at a frequency roughly equal to the rate at which the segmented strands palpitated. It reminded him of a beating heart. The mass of organic tissue had the approximate shape of a pumpkin and swirled with a mix of contrasting colors, mostly deep reds, rich greens, and vivid yellows. He judged it to be nearly twelve feet in diameter.

Knowing the way the tide had been running, Jake was almost certain the water level had reached its lowest point for the day. Where the beating node presently sat, he estimated the water depth to be no more than ten feet. Fully expanded, the highest portion of the organism came to within two feet of the water surface. Emanating from the top of it, a continuous stream of bubbles rose upward.

It was then that Jake noticed the inverted metal funnel positioned directly over the unusual mass. Flaring wide, the funnel currently dipped a foot below the water, held firmly in place by a cantilever steel frame connected to several pipes embedded vertically in the bottom and located closer to the shoreline. The pipes also supported a hose that attached to the apex of the funnel and extended horizontally over the water to the beach where it eventually became buried in the sand. Though the exact purpose of the rudimentary setup was a mystery to Jake, he knew the system had been designed to collect the gas streaming forth from the pumpkin-like node.

As Jake took in the odd sights, he realized Achilles had been hovering close to the strange organism for several seconds. Dropping his face back into the water again, Jake scrutinized the colorful object once more. At its base, a thick carpet of glittering material, granular in texture, caught his eye. It sparkled and shimmered with a dazzling radiance as it reflected rays from the fading sunlight, nearly hypnotizing him with a mix of yellowish and grayish-white lusters.

Not quite believing what he thought he was looking at; he released his hold on Achilles and dove down to examine it more carefully. Scooping up a heaping handful of the stuff, his suspicions were quickly confirmed as he brought it close to his face.

The material was composed of metallic grains, a rich mixture of gold and platinum.

Jake was stupefied. Letting the grains slip from his hand, he rose to the surface with his mind reeling. The weird occurrences he had been exposed to on this day were too much for any sane man to be subjected to in so short a time. As he thought about it, he knew he had to be either dreaming or hallucinating. This couldn't be real. Sometime during the voyage to the Haitian coast, he had crossed the boundary of reality and fallen asleep. There was no other explanation. He was currently having a lucid dream. And in a dream, you could do anything, maybe even fly. In a dream there were no limits as to what was possible.

Staring at the throbbing organic mass before him, he reached out to touch it, but before his fingers made contact, Achilles interceded and nudged him away. Somewhat taken back, Jake raised his head above the water and looked questioningly at the juvenile albino.

Achilles phonated a string of garbled speech, sounds to which Jake was rapidly growing accustomed. "Touching the *thurentra* is not advised, Jake Javolyn. To do so may injure your anatomy."

Jake thought he heard Achilles pronounce the word *thurentra*, whatever that meant. "What is a *thurentra*?" he found himself asking, having some difficulty rolling the sound off his tongue. He thought it rather distracting to carry on a conversation with a creature that continually smiled back at him. He wondered what it was truly thinking.

"It is a hybrid life form, genetically related to both holothuroidea and coelenterates," Achilles stated.

Based on the lesson Grahm had given him, Jake knew what a coelenterate was. He was unfamiliar with the other word, however. Rather than attempt to pronounce it, he simply nodded his head as if in understanding. "I see," he said. "What does it do?"

"The primary function of the *thurentra* is to produce hydrogen gas. Other byproducts come from it as well."

"I assume gold and platinum are some of these other byproducts," Jake said, finding it difficult to restrain the smile working its way onto his features. "Are you aware of the worth and benefits such metals bring to whoever is fortunate enough to possess them?"

"The *thurentra* produces the substances you speak of, yes, but no true benefit is derived from the production of such elements."

Jake eyed the juvenile in confusion. "Platinum and gold are considered to be some of the most valuable metals on earth," he intoned, practically gasping out the words. "Things of great value are always beneficial."

"Jacob has taught us such elements have been the cause of many wars among mankind."

Such a simple yet irrefutable statement caught Jake momentarily off balance. How could he possibly debate the concept of precious metals as a medium of exchange with a creature that had no use for such commodities? He looked around the cove in frustration, searching his surroundings for the people who had led him here. Jacob had moored his vessel off to one side of the cove's center and was still aboard it along with Grahm. Both men appeared to be awaiting the arrival of an aluminum dory currently being towed over to them by one of the albinos. The floatation mats carrying the ailing dolphins were no longer tied behind the pinnace. As Jake took in the scene, he couldn't help but assess the condition of the Haitian's boat. To Jake it just didn't add up. The pinnace was in a deplorable state, exceedingly rundown and in need of repairs. With the amount of wealth lying on the cove floor, Jacob could be the owner of a modern mega-yacht.

Turning his head, Jake located Destiny and the remainder of the pod. They were still attending to the injured dolphins at the north end of the cove. Several of the albinos were currently slapping the surface with their tail flukes, sending a heavy spray of water onto the stricken grays still cradled on the floatation mats. Apparently, periodic dousing was still necessary.

Lifting his eyes to the lush slopes forming the gorge, he was suddenly struck by the contradicting nature of the place. There was a luxurious poverty here, a majestic splendor that somehow seemed to be in conflict with an underlying privation. There were riches to be had, substantial accumulations of gold and platinum that had the potential of greatly improving the lifestyle of the mysterious people living here. Yet those riches went unheeded, completely ignored as if such wealth had no meaning. To his way of thinking it just didn't seem logical that Jacob would consider precious metals to offer no benefit.

Jake returned his attention to the juvenile. "Achilles, if Jacob were to collect some of the precious metals below us, he could use it to buy himself a new boat." Shifting his gaze to the two structures set back from the shore, he added, "He could also repair the cottages on the beach. Aren't such things beneficial?"

Though Achilles had no control over the grin permanently cemented on his features, to Jake it seemed absurdly out of place with the juvenile's response. "To use these elements in the manner you speak of would only bring harm to Gaia."

"Who is Gaia?" Jake asked, greatly perplexed.

"Gaia is the name of this place."

Jake surveyed his surroundings again. "Gaia, you say." Although the name had an oddly familiar ring to it, he couldn't quite remember where he had heard it before. Strangely enough, though, it seemed quite appropriate.

Chapter Two:
The Gaia Theory

The red dusk heralding the setting sun was soon replaced by an inky blanket sprinkled with a spectacular array of twinkling dots. A yellow lunar disk hung high overhead within their midst, bathing most of the gorge in a gentle wash of pale golden light that shimmered off the calm waters. In close proximity to one of the structures fronting the beach, a stone grill of sorts glowed brightly with a steady flame as fillets of grouper sizzled softly at its center. Between the grill and the abode, six men clustered, some sitting on boulders while others stood, the combination of light cast from the heavens and the nearby flame causing their features to undergo weird transformations as they intermittently turned faces in conversation.

"...a most amazing place," Grahm said, lifting another morsel of grilled fish to his mouth. "Having a perpetual supply of free energy is something most people only dream about. When and where did you first discover this strange new organism?"

Jacob turned another slab of grouper over the flame. "It was many years ago. The *thurentra* came into being right here in Gaia."

One of the other men turned his head toward Grahm, light flickering off his eyeglasses as they reflected the flame from the grill. "Are we to accept this man's claim that this so called *thurentra* is a crossbreed between a sea cucumber and a jellyfish?" Nick Henderson interjected sarcastically. Pivoting his head, he looked back at Jacob. "How can you be so sure of this? You're not a marine biologist."

Jake turned his head sharply to look over at Grahm's upstart computer whiz. The scientist's assistant had a definite tendency to annoy.

Jacob smiled back, ignoring the barb. "The *thurentra* did not just spring into existence by the natural processes that drive evolution." He hesitated briefly, apparently deciding what he was willing to divulge about the organism. "Rather it was the result of an experiment."

Henderson's eyebrows shot up questioningly behind his glasses. "Then you do profess to be a marine biologist?"

A small laugh escaped Jacob's lips. "Hardly. But I am well read and can tell you many things about the biota contained within these waters."

"So, what led you to perform this so-called experiment?" Henderson continued to press, his tone exceeding the bounds of politeness.

Henderson's rude manner was beginning to piss Jake off, but before he could set the man straight on what constituted good manners, Jacob expounded further.

"Whether you are aware of it or not, Haitian waters abound with holothuroidea, more commonly referred to as sea cucumbers outside scientific circles."

"Exactly just what is a sea cucumber?" Grahm's other assistant asked, giving Henderson a look that suggested he better stem his abrasiveness. Jeff Parker seemed much more friendly than his peer, displaying an infinitely calmer temperament and better social graces than Henderson.

"A sea cucumber is a type of animal that most often resembles its namesake, but it is best described as a slug with warts," Jacob answered. "It lives on the sea floor. Over fourteen hundred varieties have been classified worldwide, with various species inhabiting nearly every marine environment known to man. They are most diverse in the tropics where shallow-water coral reefs are in abundance, but they also have been discovered at the bottom of the deepest oceanic trenches. Their body sizes range from two to two hundred centimeters in length, attaining a thickness of between one and twenty centimeters. Their colors vary, with many species exhibiting a dark green or dark red-brown pigmentation." Jacob halted his discourse to remove some more cooked grouper from the grill.

Jake noted the metal hood situated above the brazier, paying particular attention to the tubing that rose from the top of the contrivance and extended to one side where it dropped back down in a series of spirals. The tubing ended in a large flask.

"I've seen them," Parker blurted. "They're usually scattered over the sand or lying under boulders." A frown seemed to materialize on Parker's face in the semi-darkness, partially revealed by the fire dancing on the grill. His eyes were suddenly concealed in shadow as he turned his head to gaze out over the water. He seemed to be searching for something. "But don't they also like to burrow down into the sea floor?"

"They especially like rich organic mud," Jacob said. "Here in Haiti, they like to graze on the bountiful organic snow that drifts down from above. This probably explains why they are so plentiful off our coast. There is an abundance of food to sustain them. As I think you are aware, the ecosphere in and around Haiti has been severely damaged by runaway pollution. To a small degree, these scavengers tend to counter the effects of nutrient pollutants on our environment. The fact that they consume organic waste helps to cleanse our waters, but unfortunately, not enough to overcome the vast amount of garbage and toxins that is rapidly overwhelming the marine habitats adjacent to our coastline."

Jake looked over at Grahm to get a read on how the scientist was reacting to all of this. As far as he could gather, the man appeared content to just sit back and listen, letting his assistants do the talking. On impulse, he scanned the cove, wondering what had become of Destiny. The last he had seen of her, she had been at the north end of the cove with the dolphins, occupied with the injured grays. Though the moon was full, there was insufficient light for him to see any activity in that direction. He assumed she was still out there.

"The reef outside this cove looked healthy enough to me," Parker countered. "On our way in I could see no damage to the corals. As a matter of fact, the habitat appeared to be thriving."

"Yes, that is true," Jacob agreed. "What you saw, however, is not typical of what you will find farther along the coast. The teeming marine habitat here is an anomaly, not characteristic of the overall marine environment that exists around Haiti."

"You mentioned an experiment," Henderson interrupted, his tone slightly less abrasive now.

"Ah, yes, the experiment," Jacob said. He sighed deeply and glanced out over the water. "Over the years, the excessive pollution in our waters has caused a huge bloom in the number of jellyfish, causing them to flourish and propagate. Currently, there is sufficient scientific evidence to support such a correlation, but that is another subject I will forego for the time being. With the proliferation of such huge numbers, it is hypothesized that some mutations will occur, causing new varieties to emerge. There are still a lot of species out there that we have no knowledge of. Some of the first organisms to appear on the planet at the beginning of animal evolution were jellyfish and corals. Jellyfish and corals are closely related and are both classified as coelenterates."

Jacob took a ponderous breath as if preparing for a lengthy discussion. "Anyway, about twenty years ago one of my associates, a person very knowledgeable on the subject of coelenterates, began to notice an influx of a type of jellyfish she had never seen before."

"A mutation?" Parker asked.

"If it was a mutation, she had no way of proving it. But she was certain it was a new species; something never previously cataloged in scientific journals."

"Most of the things I've read on mutations show them to offer no favorable benefit to the new species," Henderson stated. His tone was testy again.

Grahm, who had previously chosen to remain silent, suddenly chimed in. "Pardon the interruption of this old scientist," he said apologetically, directing his gaze at Jacob, "but I'd like to offer my two cents on what I know of the subject… that is, for what it's worth."

Jacob nodded. "Please go on."

"There are four primary things I know about mutations. Number one, mutations happen. Number two, they happen with great frequency. Three, almost all mutations are neutral; that is, they offer no benefit or harm to the species or the environment. And four of the mutations that aren't neutral, the benefit or harm they offer depends on circumstances."

"How can you tell if the mutation is favorable?" Henderson queried.

"Normally you can't," Grahm said. "But it's important to realize that mutations do not as a rule occur in response to the environment. They simply happen. A mutation is a change in the genetic material that controls heredity. The average human being has between fifty and one hundred mutations occurring in his body over the course of a lifetime, primarily because most cells are constantly being regenerated. If the typical mutation were harmful, life would go extinct in short order. The more reproductions of a species that occur, the greater the chance a mutation will take place. Bacteria evolve very rapidly, mainly because they reproduce at a rate many times greater than other organisms. This increases the chance for mutations. Because of this, it is not surprising that they often develop a resistance to antibiotics over many successive generations."

"So what do you mean when you say the benefit or harm of a mutation depends on circumstances?" Parker asked.

In the flickering light of the fire, it was hard to tell if Grahm was smiling when he answered the question. "The English peppered moth provides a perfect example of how circumstances come into play. English moths come in two varieties, light and dark. Prior to the Industrial Revolution, dark moths were very rare, mainly because birds eat the kind of moth they can see most easily, and that was the dark moth. During that period, light moths were more difficult to see since they blended in better with the light-colored lichens that often covered the trees in England. However, during the worst years of the Industrial Revolution, the air became very sooty, causing the trees to become darker from the soot. This resulted in a reversal of the circumstances, which had previously favored the light moths. The environment had changed. Now it was the dark moths that had become more difficult for the birds to see against the darker background, whereas the light moths stood out like sore thumbs. This situation ultimately led to the dark moths becoming more common, while the light moths became rare."

Parker was the first to respond. "I get it. What you're telling us pretty much coincides with Darwin's theory on natural selection, something I'm somewhat familiar with. As I remember, Darwin postulated that any trait which allowed a member of a species to survive more easily in a particular environment would give that member an edge, allowing its progeny to proliferate and multiply. Conversely, the ones lacking such a trait would gradually die off or have their numbers greatly diminished." In the flickering light, Parker looked down as if in deep thought, then looked back at Grahm. "But something you said just doesn't seem logical to me."

"What's that, my boy?"

"You said that mutations do not occur in response to the environment. Has this been proven conclusively? Isn't it true that plants exposed to nuclear radiation will undergo abrupt mutations?"

"Hmmm, that's true. Such mutations are usually deleterious to the organism. Rarely does it survive for very long following such an event. But I see your point."

Henderson suddenly fidgeted uncomfortably as if being pestered by some unseen insect. Turning his head, he stared condescendingly at Parker. "Aren't we beginning to stray from the original topic of discussion?" he said in annoyance. He glanced over at Jacob. "This man was telling us about an experiment."

Henderson's words hung in the air like noxious gas from a sewer, leaving everyone momentarily speechless in the way one might avoid opening their mouth for fear of breathing in the bad air.

Jacob broke the silence by first clearing his throat. "As I was saying, about twenty-two years ago, an unknown type of jellyfish started appearing in the waters just beyond this cove. While they were small in numbers, they began to have a strange impact on the local marine habitat."

"What kind of impact?" Parker wanted to know.

"Every living organism they came in contact with would be injured, but shortly thereafter the organism would rebound and function in a more robust state. During that time, most of the corals that were still alive out on the reef here were in very bad shape, and there were very few fish. But I started to notice little subtle changes in the immediate marine environment that made me wonder about what was taking place. Within several months, the reef began to teem with life. Fish populations began to soar and numerous corals started to bloom in lush, heavy growths."

"So you attributed these changes with the arrival of these strange jellyfish?" Parker said.

"That is correct. It was too coincidental not to postulate some sort of correlation between the positive changes to the ecosystem and this unknown organism. It was my associate who suggested we expose other life forms to one of these jellyfish to see what would result."

Jacob stopped talking to retrieve several chunks of grilled fish from the brazier. Placing them on a dish, he handed it over to Zimbola who had been standing nearby listening to the conversation.

"So what happened?" Parker asked eagerly, unable to contain his interest.

"The organism that lives in the cove is what happened." Jacob let the statement hang, suddenly becoming quiet.

Henderson jumped back in, his tone now fully chafing. "Would you mind elaborating on that? We'd all like to know exactly how that thing out there came about."

Jacob kept his eyes on the fillets cooking on the grill, as if deciding to continue. Finally, he said, "Six of these unknown jellyfish entered the cove on a day much like today, coming in with the tide in a tight group. They were very large oblate organisms, heavily covered with stinging tentacles. On average, they were about two meters in length and one and a half meters in width. They floated just below the surface of the water. My associate suggested we drop an injured grouper from the fish pen on top of one of them to see what would happen. We also had a Yellowfin tuna that was barely alive. Attaching both specimens to a fishing line, we lowered them into the water. Each fish was stung and quickly became paralytic. Following that, we retrieved them and placed them back in separate bins within the holding pen."

Jacob plucked additional morsels from the brazier, then turned to Jake. Handing him a plateful of grilled tuna, he regarded the former Seal with appraising, curious eyes, as if up close he might see something he hadn't seen before.

"Thank you," Jake said appreciatively. "The fish smells great."

Jacob acknowledged the comment with a nod before turning to meet the cold stare Henderson gave him. "Upon penning the two fish, my associate gathered some sea cucumbers from the floor of the cove, leathery muscular specimens with spines jutting from their skin. These we simply dropped on top of one of the oblates. Although the specimens became caught up in the tentacles, nothing unusual occurred. For the rest of the day, we gave little thought to the experiment, leaving the cove for a day of fishing at sea. It was not until the following day that a huge surprise awaited us. The strange oblates had vanished from the cove, that is, all but one. It had undergone a startling change. The texture of its body had transformed, becoming less gelatinous. It had also become anchored to the sandy bottom in much the same manner holothuroidea do. The sea cucumbers were still visible, but they had also changed... and grown. They became elongated, extending outward in segmented rope-like growths, working their way slowly toward the cove's entrance. These extensions were also doing something else unusual. They were undulating with pulsations. In researching holothuroidea, I found that they breathe by pumping seawater in and out of an internal organ called a respiratory tree, but under normal circumstances such a process is not very pronounced, and therefore, not usually noticeable. These new coils, however, were alive with what appeared to be visible pulsations. Each day that went by, the extensions became longer, gradually making their way out of the inlet. For reasons unknown to my associate or me, the extensions followed the inside of the barrier reef, continuing to grow still longer. Once they had reached the break in the reef, they altered their direction, winding their way through the opening. Beyond the outer reef, they began to spread out more, snaking and coiling their way among clusters of coral and working their way toward deeper water."

"How fast did they grow?" Parker asked.

"As time went on, the rate of growth began to accelerate," Jacob said. "For a while I monitored the coils on a daily basis, noting that the extensions were elongating by as much as twenty feet a day once they had reached twelve meters of water."

"When did the organism begin to produce hydrogen gas?" Grahm asked.

"Six months went by before the main part of the organism began to vent off the gas."

"A most interesting story," Grahm said.

"So for the past twenty-two years you've been using the gas from the *thurentra* to cook with," Parker added.

Jacob nodded. "Yes."

Grahm suddenly arose from the boulder he had been sitting on. "You seem to believe this *thurentra* is one new organism, but have you considered it may actually be comprised of two new mutated organisms that exist in a symbiotic relationship?"

"Such a possibility has occurred to my associate. Although she has not been able to substantiate such a relationship, she believes an exchange of DNA between the two organisms occurred which caused the mutations."

"I assume she was referring to what is known as a horizontal transfer of portions of the genome," Grahm said.

Parker looked puzzled. "I'm not following you."

Grahm scratched his head. "Well, most mutations take place through vertical transfer. These occur when the genome is copied during reproduction and transferred from ancestor to descendant through vertical lines of descent. In the original work on population genetics, it was assumed that all mutations were propagated through vertical transfer. But then it was discovered that genes could be propagated much more quickly through horizontal transfer. If evolution were to be represented by a tree, vertical genetic movement is the transmission of genes along branches as opposed to horizontal genetic movement, which is the transmission of genes between branches."

Parker looked to Jacob for confirmation. "So, your associate surmised that a horizontal transmission of DNA material took place between the jellyfish and sea cucumbers?"

Jacob nodded. "She did."

Grahm appeared thoughtful as light from the brazier flickered off his face. "Has your associate figured out how the organism is able to produce hydrogen?"

Jacob turned to stare out over the cove, then looked back at Grahm. "She has developed a hypothesis, but again, she has no way of verifying it conclusively."

When Jacob failed to elaborate further, Grahm prodded him gently. "And that is?"

"There is some kind of delicate interaction that she does not fully understand, but she believes the ropelike coils from the *thurentra* reach thousands of feet down to the deeper parts of the ocean where they become buried in the organic sediment. Within the sediment these coils somehow interact with microbes called archaea. Such microbes are found in the deep mud along cold seeps where methane gas bubbles up from faults and fissures covered in organic mud. The archaea govern the earth's methane cycle, which is really one loop of the planet-wide carbon cycle. One form of archaea microbe living deeper down in the mud produces methane gas from hydrogen and carbon extracted from organic sediments. Other species of archaea in concert with other microbial partners consume the methane for energy and reduce the sulfate contained in the mud to hydrogen sulfide."

Jacob paused, taking another deep breath. "My associate has theorized that the *thurentra* extensions are able to free up the hydrogen within this compound through some kind of biochemical process."

Everyone remained silent for several seconds, trying to absorb Jacob's explanation. Henderson, however, was still intent on doing battle. "The whole thing sounds ridiculous to me. For one thing, your theory assumes the *thurentra* extends its tentacles for thousands of feet to reach the depths you speak of. It seems rather absurd that a living organism can grow to the incredible lengths you infer. Secondly, how would the organism be able to nourish so much body mass?"

"My associate believes that such a thing is possible," Jacob rejoined. "Jellyfish do not have much of a nutritional need, and therefore, do not require much in the way of food to survive. All they consist of is a nervous system and a gut that is bell-shaped in most species. They have tentacles with stinging cells that stun their prey. One percent of their body mass is made up of organic matter and the remainder is water. And even though the original organism has mutated, my associate contends that most of the basic protein structure remains the same."

"Who is this associate you keep mentioning?" Henderson demanded testily. "And what are her credentials?"

"Nicolas!" Grahm chastened sharply. "I remind you that we are the guests of this man. How dare you show our host such disrespect?"

Grahm's chastisement was like a forceful slap in the face to his young assistant. Henderson's look of shock was quickly replaced by one of sullen withdrawal.

Jake thought it best to intercede. "Tell me, Jacob, why do you call this place Gaia?"

Jacob appeared eager to distance himself from the embarrassing scene. "Gaia is a term used by the ancient Greeks. It embodies the idea of a Mother Earth, the source of the living and non-living entities that make up this planet. The name was adopted by a renowned atmospheric chemist to describe a revolutionary hypothesis he originally developed over forty years ago known as the Gaia Hypothesis. Formulated by James Lovelock and published in a book in 1979, it has become one of the more controversial ideas of our time."

"I thought the name sounded familiar," offered Jake. "The hypothesis states that the Earth is alive, doesn't it?"

A happy smile crossed Jacob's face. "It seems you have read up on Lovelock's work, or at least some of the concepts spawned from it."

"Ah, yes," Grahm chirped in. "Lovelock saw our planet as a single living entity, an idea that has tended to rankle many noted scientists."

"The concept was really nothing new," Jacob amended. "In the latter portion of the eighteenth century, James Hutton, a man considered to be the father of geology, once described the Earth as a kind of super organism. But the key point these men were trying to make was that the Earth acts as a single system, a coherent self-regulated assemblage of physical, chemical, geological and biological forces that interact to maintain a unified whole, balanced between the input of energy from the sun and the thermal sink of energy discharged from the planet into space."

"I've always been a fan of Lovelock's," Grahm said. "He viewed the Earth as a complex entity involving the interaction of the planet's biosphere, atmosphere, oceans, and lithosphere, a totality that constituted a feedback or cybernetic system seeking to optimize a physical and chemical environment conducive for life."

"That is true," Jacob agreed. "Through Gaia, the Earth is able to sustain a kind of homeostasis, a maintenance of relatively constant conditions that would best support life. In its strongest form, the Gaia Hypothesis states that life creates conditions on Earth for its own purposes, basically to suit itself."

"There is a growing body of evidence that both supports and detracts the concept," Grahm said. "Overall, it appears to have gained a toehold in the scientific community. In its weakest form, the hypothesis still holds merit. The idea that life has an influence on planetary processes is now generally accepted."

Parker's head pivoted back and forth like a man watching a tennis match as he listened to the conversation. "Forgive my ignorance," he interjected apologetically, "but I'm not sure I completely understand how life can bring about a balance that is optimal to its own survival." He glanced at Grahm. "Can you provide an example?"

The marine zoologist looked to Jacob. "Is there any case you can think of that would enlighten this bright young mind?"

Jacob smiled, more than happy to comply. "To a large degree, phytoplankton, single-celled plants that are abundant in the world's oceans, contribute significantly to controlling the temperature of the earth."

"How?" Parker persisted.

"Given that the oceans cover more than seventy percent of the Earth's surface, it is relatively simple to conclude that anything that causes the formation of clouds over the water will have a major impact on the global temperature. The formation of clouds affects the amount of sunlight being reflected away from the earth. Solar energy is blocked and therefore cannot be absorbed by the oceanic thermal reservoir. The greater the cloud cover, the more solar energy is bounced back into space. This causes the planet to cool. With less clouds, the planet warms."

Parker's eyebrows rose up sharply in surprise. "So you're saying phytoplankton are responsible for producing clouds? I find that difficult to comprehend."

"Phytoplankton is only one of a number of factors that affect cloud formation," Jacob stressed. "The interaction between sea and atmosphere is another major factor. Weather fronts are another since they also contribute to cloud cover."

"So how do phytoplankton produce clouds?" Parker wanted to know.

"You have to examine the mechanism behind cloud formation to understand how these plants are able to do this," Jacob explained. "Clouds form when water vapor in the atmosphere condenses or freezes, but for this to happen a particle or nucleus must be present to collect the water into a droplet. Such particles are called cloud-condensation nuclei. Certain types of phytoplankton, particularly coccolithophoroids, are known to release trace quantities of dimethyl sulfide into the atmosphere. It is these particles of dimethyl sulfide that provide sufficient nuclei for clouds to form out over the ocean. When there is little cloud cover, phytoplankton will grow rapidly as do most plants when they receive an abundance of sunshine. This leads to the production of dimethyl sulfide and a corresponding increase in the amount of cloud cover. This increase blocks sunlight, causing less energy to be absorbed by the oceans and therefore a temperature reduction of the planet. With more cloud cover, the incidence of sunshine reaching the Earth's surface is lessened, causing the phytoplankton to grow more slowly and release lower amounts of dimethyl sulfide."

Jacob let out a satisfied sigh. "This self-regulating cycle continues to repeat in a balanced manner, tending to keep the temperature of the planet in a state of equilibrium."

"The type of phytoplankton you mentioned…coccolithop," Parker stammered, having trouble pronouncing the name. "What did you call them?"

"Coccolithophoroids. England's White Cliffs of Dover are the fossilized remains of such organisms. Their beautiful calcareous skeletons are revealed under a microscope."

"I find this most amazing," Parker said in awe. "Imagine that! Tiny single-celled plants regulating the Earth's thermostat by maintaining non-equilibrium conditions in the atmosphere." He turned to Grahm, then pivoted his head back to Jacob. "But I see one major flaw in this so-called Gaia Hypothesis."

"What is that?" Jacob asked.

"If the concept suggests that the Earth is alive, how come the planet lacks the ability to replicate itself like other living organisms? I was taught to believe that one of the hallmarks of life was its ability to pass on genetic information to succeeding generations. How does the Gaia Hypothesis account for this inability?"

"Your argument is nothing new," Jacob admitted. "Critics of Lovelock have used it to reject his idea, for if the Earth were truly alive it should be able to reproduce. Some proponents of the hypothesis, however, believe that man is the means by which the planet will reproduce."

"Huh?"

"It is inevitable that sooner or later, the dominant sentient species on Earth will develop the means to leave this world and colonize other planets. If the species is honorable and unselfish, if it is morally upright and respectful of life in all forms, we can assume that this species will only seek worlds where life has not yet begun to evolve or where life has long since died off. In doing this, all their technology and knowledge will be used to transform the dead planet into a place of beauty, a living, evolving entity which will have a self-regulating environment optimal for the survival of the life it will support."

Jacob looked as if he was seeing something far away. "Imagine... a place previously static and hostile to life as we know it slowly being changed forever, a place of frozen desolation and barren waste miraculously transmuted, blossoming. Healthy oceans and thriving forests will spring up in once sterile environments, places where life can flourish in a delicately balanced ecosystem undisturbed. No longer will nature be viewed as a primitive force to be subdued and conquered, stranded on a planet without purpose and endlessly traveling around an inner sun. This is indeed the power of Gaia, and one of the more compelling reasons to consider her existence and to speculate about the consequences of our own presence here."

"Why do you use the term 'dominant sentient species'?" Parker puzzled. "The way you say it makes it sound like the species can be something other than man."

Jacob shrugged, his manner hinting frustration. "For those of us who believe the Gaia Hypothesis to be true, we can no longer think of the Earth as a thing with separate distinct components. We can no longer believe man's actions in one part of the planet will remain independent from some other part. Anything that occurs on the planet will ultimately affect the entire organism, whether it be an increase in the emissions of carbon dioxide, the pollution of the oceans, or the deforestation of the land. If the Earth is indeed self-regulating, then it will eventually adjust to the negative impacts of man…maybe-." Jacob abruptly looked away, suddenly appearing uncomfortable. He seemed reluctant to expound further.

"Yes," Parker encouraged. "Maybe what?"

Jacob took a deep breath. "Maybe introduce something completely new to counter man's destructive tendencies."

"I'm not sure I get your drift," Parker said slowly.

"If Gaia is going to achieve replication, she must first insure the survival of the home planet. She will require an agent to carry out such a task, an instrument of her choosing."

A small gush of flame licked up from the grill as Jacob flipped one of the fillets, the sudden wash of light revealing Parker's deepening puzzlement. "Such as?"

Jacob lifted his gaze to study Parker's face momentarily before continuing. "Whether it be the Homo sapiens or another evolved and clever species will only bear the test of time."

Jake noticed that Henderson had moved closer to the fire, and in his eyes Jake could see a lust for battle growing steadily in the flickering glow. "So you think man is too stupid to undertake such a burden?" Grahm's freckled assistant said. His tone was just short of outright ridicule.

"Are you familiar with the writings of Friedrich Nietzsche?" Jacob replied patiently.

"Wasn't he a nineteenth-century German philosopher?" Parker said quickly, cutting Henderson off before he could interject further.

Jacob nodded soberly. "Yes, a very wise philosopher who displayed a fondness for aphorism. But among his writings, one profound idea stands out." The Haitian paused introspectively, scanning the faces all about him. "Nietzsche saw mankind as something to be surpassed."

Jake searched his memory, remembering something he had once read. According to Nietzsche, man will travel through three stages of evolution: ape, present-day man, and…a strange feeling took hold of him as he reflected on the word…and destiny. He rolled the concept over in his mind with newfound understanding, shifting his gaze back in the direction where he had last seen the girl. Man was destined to be replaced by a higher intelligence, much the way the ape had been superseded by man's superior intellect.

Jacob surged on before anyone could interrupt, the rapidity of his words swiftly gaining momentum. "So far, man has shown himself to be an irresponsible life form, placing too many demands on too few resources. Food and energy are the primary commodities that support mankind. In obtaining these staples we have disrupted the ecological balance of our world, causing such problems as the greenhouse effect and the ozone hole. Once mankind made the transition from the nomadic wanderings of hunter-gatherers to creatures that used agriculture to increase food production, he began to extract a huge toll from the planetary ecosphere. To keep pace with our expanding population, agriculture demanded that we clear forests, subject grasslands to the plow, and appropriate vast tracts for grazing our herds. Human numbers surged exponentially, and with it a growing need for energy. Strip-mining of timber beyond its sustainable yield began to occur in many parts of the world, resulting in substantial clearing of forests and runaway erosion of landscapes. Over-reliance on fossil fuels became our biggest problem, however. Burning coal and oil unleashed enormous amounts of carbon dioxide and acids into the atmosphere, doing untold harm. Accumulating buildups of carbon dioxide has created a potential for global warming that threatens to melt the polar ice caps. Already this is happening. Acid rain is increasingly killing off timberlands. Urban blight is another growing problem. Immense numbers of poor people in search of employment keep flocking to already over-congested cities that continue to expand like slime molds, spewing out mountains of garbage, sending torrents of toxins into our seas and casting an umbrella of smog into our skies. Overall, the rapacious demands of mankind are overtaxing the environment and bringing Gaia perilously close to the brink of extinction. If the human race is to be judged in its entirety, it is apparent that man has proven himself unfit to live in harmony with his environment. As such, we cannot rule out the possibility that Gaia will take proactive measures against the chief source of her problems, maybe introduce a species-specific plague to eradicate all of us and let another species evolve to take dominion over the Earth, a species that has the potential for a greater show of sapience than does the Homo sapiens. But then again, maybe the human race will be given a chance to atone for its sins, to redeem itself for past mistakes by correcting the wrongs it has inflicted on the ecosphere. Either way, Gaia will have the opportunity to heal herself. Who's to say what options Gaia will choose?"

Parker seemed taken back by Jacob's rhetoric. "Assuming your argument were true, why would the planet follow a course of action that would eliminate man? If we adhere to the definition that Gaia is the sum total of all the things that comprise the Earth, why would it eradicate a portion of itself?"

"A logical question," Jacob said, "and one that deserves a logical answer. From Gaia's perspective, perhaps mankind is perceived as a tumor harmful to her health, a group of cells that have somehow gotten out of control and become an intrusive growth, cells that have malfunctioned and strayed from the purpose for which they were originally intended. Either the tumor must be removed entirely from her body, or it must be shrunken to a small enough size so that her bodily processes can attain a state of equilibrium once again. If she does this, her tissues will eventually be restored to a condition of vitality, allowing her to reproduce at some future point in time using an alternate group of cells to carry this out."

"This is preposterous," Henderson railed, unable to contain himself any longer. "You speak of the Earth as if it is some super organism capable of making rational decisions."

"Whether it can be described as a cell, an organism, or a super organism is merely a matter of semantics, a topic best left to the philosophically minded. I am not claiming the existence of a sentient intelligence behind Gaia, but then again, I cannot refute it. But even organisms lacking a brain possess various defense mechanisms. Certain types of coelenterates such as fire corals have stinging cells with which to discourage attack in order to avoid being damaged. However, if in fact Gaia does harbor an intelligence of some kind, perhaps it resides in the conscience of man. After all, man is one of the organisms comprising the biosphere, and as such, is therefore a part of Gaia."

Henderson was beginning to seethe. "For better or worse, life has evolved man as the only species with the intelligence and digital extremities to build machines, the one species destined to make the jump into space. It is only a matter of time before he gets his act together and stops bringing harm to the environment."

Jacob gave him a lingering stare. "For all our sakes, I hope you are right. But time is the very thing working against Gaia. A recent report by the Millennium Ecosystem Assessment concluded that human activity is putting such a strain on the natural functions of the Earth that the ability of the planet's ecosystems to sustain future generations can no longer be taken for granted. According to this report, man has caused ecosystems to change more rapidly and extensively over the past fifty years than any comparable time in human history. This has resulted in two-thirds of the planet's resources being heavily polluted or depleted over this time period. This includes energy sources, fresh water, and clean air. There is little doubt we are destroying the Earth. If mankind fails to take immediate and assertive action, it may be too late for all of us, assuming it is not too late already. The longer we delay, the more inevitable it will become that the Earth's ability to rebound will reach a level that is irreversible. The way I see it, time is quickly running out."

"You're talking about one report," Henderson countered smugly, "the opinions of a few scientists."

"The report was prepared by thirteen hundred and sixty experts from ninety-five nations," Jacob shot back.

"Humans are the most successful species in the history of life on Earth," Henderson said in exasperation. "If anything, we are an ingenious, resilient, stubborn lot, without equals on the evolutionary scale. We'll figure out a way to avert disaster."

Jacob mulled this over for several seconds, his face suddenly hidden in shadow as he turned his head away from the fire to look up at the tiered precipice rising high above them. As if making up his mind about something, he swung back around and met Henderson's glare. In the dim flickering light cast by the brazier, Jake was certain he detected a strange, shrewd smile in the Haitian's expression.

"Perhaps it will be Gaia herself who will provide man with the way," Jacob finally said, his voice now carrying a mysterious cryptic quality.

Chapter Three: Submarine Alert

The damp sand felt cool under Jake's bare feet as he strolled along the beach, making him revel in the comfort it gave him. There was something about wet sand between his toes that always seemed to give him a sense of serenity. No, serenity was not quite right, he thought, reflecting on the word. Freedom. Yes, that was the lemma that stuck in his mind now that he rolled it over introspectively.

Some distance behind him, the intermittent glow of a fire added enchantment to the fragrant night air, rich with the sweet scent of wildflowers and hibiscus. As he walked, he became aware of the cataracts pounding the water at the far end of the cove. At his present distance, the sound was reduced to a dull roar that hung in the background, ceaseless and soothing to the soul. Sometime in the last hour, spray from the falls had caused a cloud of vapor to go swirling across the cove, shrouding the waters in fine mist.

Continuing to follow the shoreline, Jake angled slightly left of where the brine met the sand, inexorably drawn beyond the juncture. He loved the water and hated being away from it for very long. Water was an elixir, invigorating and mind cleansing. As he entered it, tiny wavelets rife with moonbeams swashed a golden luminescence around his ankles. The strange place entranced Jake, blanketing him with a gentle yet powerful embrace, giving him a sense of unfathomable peace that reached down to the farthest recesses of his being. Filling his lungs, he took in more of the pervasive atmosphere, unable to get enough of it. Thoughts of Shangri-La raced through his mind, an imaginary idyllic hideaway depicted in James Hilton's classic novel, Lost Horizons. If ever such a place existed, this was it, he reckoned.

Though his spirits were greatly uplifted, there was something missing, an empty place within him that was unfulfilled and yearning for something more. He couldn't put his finger on it. Earlier on this evening he had become restless. Growing weary of the endless discussions and debates that continued to persist around the brazier, he had needed to get away. At least that was the excuse he had given himself.

Jake had deemed it best not to mention the gold he had seen lying at the bottom of the cove. He had heard stories about what gold could do to some men. Gold was an alluring temptress, a beckoning seductress that tended to twist and corrupt weaker souls. The abundance of wealth he had seen residing beneath the water was enough to make the man called Jacob one of the richest men in Haiti. Yet Jacob appeared to ignore the enormous potential it offered, preferring to live a simple existence here in this place. Jake had not allowed himself to be misled by Jacob's grizzled outward appearance. He had seen the stacks of books and periodicals piled high inside the man's cottage. The brief contact he had made with the Haitian had shown the man to be exceptionally intelligent, possibly one of the smartest individuals he had ever run into. Like the girl, Jacob was an enigma. The fact that Jacob saw value in the hydrogen gas rather than the gold only added to the mystery the Haitian posed. And though Jake could only speculate, he sensed that Jacob harbored some well-guarded secret, something that would make the *thurentra*'s ability to produce gold and platinum appear insignificant by comparison.

The girl had failed to join the gathering, continuing to remain missing. He looked out over the water in the direction he had last seen her, wondering if she was still there. It was darker in that part of the cove, the moon's golden disk eclipsed by one of the chasm's towering walls. Where he now stood, the sandy shelf of the beach had ended, merging with some rock outcroppings.

Without giving it conscious thought, he waded out into the water and began to pull himself along in an easy sidestroke, trying to see through the veil of mist. Swimming out into deeper water, a soft chittering came to his ears, and as his eyes probed the shroud of darkness, he could make out two wraith-like objects moving toward him.

A warbling gently cut the air, whistling softly like a hushed whisper being forced between the teeth. Jake immediately recognized the sound and the entity emitting it. "We have been waiting for you, Jake Javolyn," Achilles said.

Jake stopped stroking, peering at the shapes before him. As his eyes adjusted to the dim light, he was able to discern the huge head of Hercules floating beside that of the juvenile albino. "Is Destiny still out here, Achilles?" Jake asked.

"Yes, Jake Javolyn," Achilles trilled back in that strange signature lilt, speaking more quietly than when Jake had first conversed with the young dolphin. "Come, I will take you to her." Achilles abruptly turned, presenting his dorsal fin. "As before, I offer myself as an object of conveyance, Jake Javolyn," the juvenile added.

Jake latched onto the proffered fin, letting himself be whisked forward. Liquid tendrils tugged at him as the dolphin transported him across the water, and as he looked into the foggy dusk, the mist abruptly parted to reveal the outline of the floatation mats. Destiny was on one of the floats, her body stretched out horizontally beside the gray bottlenose lying adjacent to her. She was stroking the dolphin gently as the other dolphins hovered nearby, her head resting against the side of the injured creature. As Achilles pulled Jake abreast of the float, the girl continued to run her fingers gently along the gray's flank.

"Is there anything I can do to help?" Jake asked, keeping his voice low in the same manner as demonstrated by Achilles. He had no way of knowing it, but he was certain the young dolphin had not wanted to disturb the sanctity of this place.

Destiny shook her head slowly, turning her face slightly to acknowledge Jake's presence. "Thetis must decide to help herself. There is nothing more any of us can do for her. We have done all that is within our power."

Jake released his hold on Achilles and grabbed the float. "What's wrong with her?"

"She is unhappy and confused. She does not understand why humans would bring harm upon her and the others."

Jake himself was confused. "Then she is not ill?"

"Physical damage still resides within her, but it can be healed. She chooses to block our efforts."

"But why?" Jake asked, not knowing what else to say.

"She is not sure whether she belongs in this world any longer and feels that perhaps now is the time to make the spiritual transition to the next realm."

Jake recalled the scene when the *Avenging Angel* had first come upon the injured dolphins, remembering how distraught the juvenile albino was about one of the grays in particular. He posed another question. "Is Thetis the mother of Achilles?"

Destiny answered with a small nod.

"These dolphins…I've never seen anything like them," Jake said. "Are they all able to speak?"

The girl continued to stroke Thetis. "Only the white ones have developed such an ability. They are fluent in several languages."

"And do they all possess what some people would consider the equivalent of hands?"

"Thetis is the only gray here at Gaia who has such appendages, though all of the whites are endowed with them."

Jake looked over at the other two floats tethered to the one he was holding. "How're the others doing?"

"They are still weak but will recover." Destiny seemed preoccupied with something as she said this. "Thetis has been waiting for you. She would like you to place a hand on her."

Jake was perplexed. "She's never met me. Why would she be waiting for me?"

The girl peered intently at Jake, holding back a response. She suddenly sat up, letting her legs dip into the water. "Thetis wishes to discover who you are. Your touch will give her this knowledge."

Jake found the request unusual. "Getting to know someone takes time. How can a person's nature be perceived from a touch?"

"Thetis will know," the girl said softly.

Jake hesitated with uncertainty, but not wanting to refuse the girl he reached out and placed the palm of his right hand on Thetis' flank.

Keeping it there for several seconds, he noticed that the creature's skin was smooth and rubbery.

As Jake did this, Destiny watched him closely, her eyes boring into him as if searching for something. "Thetis believes you are the one," she said at last.

Jake stared back, unable to discern her meaning. "I don't understand."

The girl turned her gaze to the heavens, then met Jake's eyes again. "Thetis had a dream, what some would call a vision. In it there was a man. She is now certain you are the man she saw, a person the pod can trust, the one to which her offspring will bond."

This was all getting to be too much for him to handle. "Offspring?" he uttered, a bit off balance. "Does she mean Achilles?"

"Yes."

Jake shifted his eyes to Thetis. The dolphin's right orb, the eye facing him, was scrutinizing him with a deep abiding interest. Taking in the moment, he turned back to the girl. "Thetis is not well," he reminded her. "Perhaps she's mistaking me for someone else."

Destiny was not to be dissuaded. "We have all experienced moments of inexplicable connection when events in a dream spill over into real life," she said. "There is an inner vision that exists in all of us that is often blurred, buried beneath daily stresses so that it is not readily apparent. Search yourself, Jake Javolyn. You must honor the wisdom of your inner voice, that part of yourself that knows what you are meant to do. If you deny it, you will destroy your spirit."

Jake was unsure as to what the girl alluded. The events that had taken him to this unusual place were strange enough. Attempting to make sense of the things Destiny was trying to communicate to him was like trying to unravel a riddle. And yet he had to admit there was a mysterious affinity that drew him to the juvenile albino, some genuine sense of connectedness that seemed to be awakening something deep within him.

Destiny came back at him with more words. "Thetis sees an inner conflict raging within you, an unfulfilled harmony between your conscious and subconscious states of awareness. If you are to reach the invisible worlds that lie just outside of ordinary reality, you must learn to access your own divinity and spiritual light to discover who you truly are beyond your own skin."

Though this bit of guidance continued to confound Jake, there was no need for him to dwell on it. He knew himself very well. He was a soldier of fortune, plain and simple, a person willing to accept whatever cards fate dealt him. And if per chance those cards threw hardship and suffering his way, he would meet such obstacles head on and without complaint. Whatever Thetis was seeing in him was clouded by her physical state, a condition that needed immediate rectification. "Thetis must overcome her fear of living and stop blocking your attempts to heal her," he snapped, surprised at the anger he felt. "She must engage in the direct experience of life regardless of how it may disappoint, frighten, or pain her."

Destiny looked away, unable to meet Jake's choleric eyes. "Thetis is not afraid for herself," she said, her voice almost a whisper. "She fears for the survival of this world. She does not wish to see the pod perish with it."

"Some creatures choose to die because they are too cowardly to live," Jake argued, his words coming out harsher than intended. Realizing this, he softened his tone. "Thetis must learn to fight back against the men that did this to her."

"Fighting back is not in her nature," Destiny gently asserted. "Her species lacks a willingness for aggression. She is incapable of harming or destroying, of striking back in anger."

The girl went back to stroking the injured dolphin. In the subdued light, Jake could see a faint glistening on one of her cheeks. When she finally spoke again, her voice was close to a sob. "She will not let us heal her."

Jake tried a new line of reasoning. "If that's how she's going to repay you for risking your life for her, then I will forego bonding with her calf," he threatened.

Thetis visibly flinched over this sudden declaration, letting out a loud squeal of protest. "Thetis begs you to reconsider," Destiny implored, speaking for the dolphin. "Failing to bond with Achilles will place the pod in immediate danger, setting it on an irreversible course of imminent doom."

"Why should this trouble her?" Jake asked irritably. "She's already told us she doesn't want to stick around for fear of seeing her pod perish along with the rest of the world."

Destiny stared at the gray as if listening to something. "She believes there is still hope, but only if you remain linked to Achilles. Without this link, the pod will cease to exist."

"Then the responsibility for such an outcome rests with her," Jake replied stubbornly. "I'll be leaving now." He pushed away from the float and began to swim toward the shore.

"Wait!" the girl called after him, her tone suddenly joyful. "Thetis will comply with your wish. She will allow us to heal her."

Jake stopped in mid-stroke. Turning, he stared back at the girl and her charge, the smile on his face concealed by the near darkness. "Then I will bond with her calf," he said, still unclear about what that meant.

Now that Thetis no longer blocked them, the combined efforts of Destiny and the eight albino dolphins quickly healed the internal injuries the gray had sustained. From Jake's perspective, the albinos formed a tight circle around the float, lifting their rostrums above the edge of the mat and making contact with Thetis' prone form. Less than a minute had gone by when the girl finally raised her head from the gray's back, appearing satisfied with the outcome of their ministrations.

"You haven't eaten anything all day," Jake said, feeling deep concern for the girl.

"Jacob will prepare something for me when I go ashore," Destiny replied wearily. "He always...," Stopping in mid-sentence, she spun around abruptly, directing her gaze to the cove's inlet. In that instant her manner changed, becoming tense and alert. "It approaches the reef," she stated sharply. "It nears your boat!"

Jake sensed an acute warning in her tone. "What nears my boat?"

"A submarine."

"How do you know this?" Jake asked incredulously, taken completely off guard by this sudden revelation.

"Apollo and Artemis are still out there watching it. It followed us most of the way from Navassa."

The two missing albinos, Jake thought. "Why didn't you tell me this before?" he demanded.

The girl read Jake's flash of anger, searching his eyes closely before answering. "The vessel stayed far enough away, presenting no danger at the time," she explained demurely. "But now the pod sees it as a threat."

With all the other strange things Jake had seen of late, the possibility of a mental link between the girl and the missing albinos did not surprise him at all. "Zimbola must be alerted to this," Jake said hurriedly. "Please go ashore and let him know what's going on. Tell him I'm on my way to the *Angel*." Jake knew that if Destiny followed through on this, Zimbola would give Hector a heads up about what was going on via the walkie-talkie he kept with him.

Jake turned and began to swim for the inlet leading from the cove, but before he had made more than half a dozen strokes, Achilles was at his side. The young albino squealed out in that odd warbling lilt of his. "I will help you, Jake Javolyn. Grab hold."

The speed at which the juvenile hauled Jake through the water amazed him. It was as if Achilles sensed Jake's immediate wishes and automatically responded to them. Without Jake even having to mention it, the young dolphin appeared to understand that, as of now, every second counted.

Jake needed to formulate a plan, and quickly. But before he could come up with one, he needed to know what he was up against. Unfortunately for him, he had left his mask, fins, and snorkel on the beach and, as far as he was concerned, taking the time to retrieve them was not an option.

In less than a minute, Jake was transported across the cove to the inlet leading to the sea. Keeping his head above the water, he watched as the rock walls flashed by, sporadically illuminated where moonlight was reflected off the craggy surfaces. Hanging on by one hand, he looked behind him and spotted the brazier still glowing eerily on the other side of the water. To his relief, he could see the silhouette of a person emerging onto the beach and moving quickly toward the fire.

As Jake was towed along, he focused his thoughts on the problem at hand. A submarine, the girl had said. What was a submarine doing here? A string of questions began to race through his mind, none of them having answers. Managing to take a quick glance at his luminous wristwatch, he saw that it was a few minutes past midnight. He could only hope that either Hector or Phillipe was still up and keeping a vigilant watch to discourage possible intruders from boarding the *Angel*.

The moonlit panorama of the northern Caribbean Sea opened up before Jake as Achilles sped past the final outcropping of rock. A short distance to the southwest, the outline of his boat lay at anchor, undisturbed on the other side of the reef. Scanning the shimmering waters, he could see nothing that would indicate the presence of another vessel.

Jake was about to tell Achilles to stop swimming when the juvenile suddenly slowed and came to a halt. "Do you see any large objects under the water, Achilles?" Jake asked.

"I do not, Jake Javolyn," Achilles ululated back.

The albino's response made Jake wonder if Destiny had been wrong about the submarine. If no such vessel was currently lurking below them, he had to be sure. Perhaps he had not phrased the question correctly. "Does the reef block you from seeing what lies in the deeper water?"

"Yes, Jake Javolyn.""

Jake felt like kicking himself for not initially considering something so obvious. If a large enough sub were skulking about, it could not possibly get through the reef. And the reef would interfere with dolphin biosonar, preventing speak-see signals from breaching it. "Are other members of your pod on the other side of the reef?" he continued to probe.

"Artemis and Apollo are there," Achilles squealed. "They are watching a large metallic vessel below the water surface.""

Jake assimilated this. "Achilles, are you able to communicate with Artemis and Apollo right now?"

"Yes, Jake Javolyn," Achilles confirmed.

"Take me to my boat, Achi-"

Before Jake had even completed the sentence, the albino shot away like a torpedo rapidly accelerating toward a target, and it was all Jake could do to maintain his grip and hold on.

Chapter Four: The Hijackers

The bearded man lowered the periscope, the prominent scar marring the cheek just below his right eye giving him a sinister appearance in the console's greenish glow. He had not planned on crossing the body of water shown to be the Windward Passage on the nautical chart he carried. Troubled by his own rashness, he chastised himself for being so foolish, for letting his desire for revenge divert him from his primary mission. He had a rigid timetable to adhere to and he now ran the risk of messing it up. Normally he wouldn't have even considered helping the Colombian called Ortega, but he had seen something he had not expected, and a vendetta had to be satisfied.

When he had first spotted the individual riding the waverunner, there had been something vaguely familiar about him. It was when the helicopter had come within striking distance of the small watercraft that an old memory had re-surfaced, making him squint his eyes to get a better look at the man skimming the water below him. As luck would have it, he had been deprived of seeing the man clearly. The fusillade of tracer rounds screaming up at him had made him duck his head back into the aircraft, but not before he had gotten a glimpse of the machine gun mounted on the small vessel. It was the way the waverunner had been configured with weaponry that had made him think of his old nemesis Jake Javolyn.

It was Javolyn who had come up with the idea of mounting machine guns and small torpedo launchers to waverunners, turning them into highly mobile attack vessels. He remembered how Javolyn had tried to sell the brass on developing such a concept. Yeslam recalled how happy it had made him when Javolyn's brainstorm had been brushed aside, scoffed at by Captain McPherson as being absurd. As far as he knew,

Javolyn was the only man who would have followed through on the idea and taken the time to construct a working prototype.

Yeslam had gotten several more glimpses of the attacker shooting up at them during the ensuing skirmish, but never one that could positively confirm the identity of the man. By the time he had landed aboard the *San Carlo*, however, he had been certain their assailant could have been none other than Jake Javolyn. That was when he had decided to present Ortega with the offer. If Ortega would ferry him over to the island, Yeslam would use his resources to follow the two boats to their ultimate destination. In exchange for providing the Colombian this information, Ortega would supply him with one hundred 55-gallon drums of diesel fuel. He had purposely refrained from mentioning the submarine he now rode in. For the time being, he would keep that a secret.

In the confined quarters, Yeslam Raduyev looked up at one of his subordinates crowding the sub's command console. Kalid was not smiling.

"Have you fixed the problem?" Raduyev asked testily in Arabic.

"The launch tubes continue to show an electrical problem and will not fire," Kalid said. "Perhaps Allah is giving you a sign. Perhaps he prefers you kill the infidels with your own hands."

Raduyev nodded slowly, studying the religious fervor burning deep in Kalid's eyes. Kalid's interpretation of the situation at hand gave him cause to reflect. "Yes…yes," he conceded begrudgingly, the irritability he felt towards his crew rapidly subsiding like a spent wave sliding back from shore. "Maybe you are right, maybe Allah must be satisfied another way."

Six other crew members turned to look at him as he gazed distractedly about the interior of the modified P-130 submarine. Although still fairly new, the sub had a few annoying bugs, one of them being the malfunctioning of the torpedo tubes. The 90-foot vessel had been purchased less than a year ago at a sum of $12,000,000 from Rosoboronexport, a huge Russian arms dealer. Other than the vessel's current inability to fire torpedoes, it had so far performed admirably. With a depth capability of 200 feet and a range of 2,000 miles, the diesel-electric powered submarine ran silently on batteries when submerged, making it virtually impossible to detect using passive acoustic measures.

With a maximum underwater speed of twenty-six knots, the P-130 was designed to carry up to ten people, and as Raduyev had learned, had proved itself to be a most reliable vehicle for smuggling cargo and insurgents in and out of unfriendly coastlines.

After Ortega had ferried Raduyev back to Navassa Island, the Chechen had found his way back to the craggy fissure located inland among a concentrated cluster of poisonwood trees. The fissure lay well hidden within the thicket and led to a subterranean chamber deep under the island.

Raduyev and his crew had first discovered the chamber during their initial reconnaissance of Navassa in the hopes of finding a suitable base of operations. That had been six months earlier. Cruising the P-130 at a depth of eighty feet, he had spotted a huge gaping hole in the coral reef that ran along the island's southern perimeter. The reef had grown outward on both sides of the hole, cantilevers of calcareous rock precariously overhanging a deep vertical drop-off. As best he could judge, a massive buildup of coral had collapsed under its own weight, falling away into the depths to expose a dark yawning pocket beneath it. Intrigued by the possibilities it presented, he had brought the sub to a halt and swam out the airlock, accompanied by two of his men. Dressed out in diving gear and carrying powerful underwater flashlights, they had entered the opening in the reef, each of them riding a DPV. Letting the DPV headlights illuminate the way, they had discovered a wide tunnel that penetrated deep into the interior of the island. Following it back, they had eventually emerged into a spacious air-filled cavern of sufficient size to accommodate the sub. Shining their lights around the underground chamber, they had observed a profusion of sharp-pointed stalactites hanging down from a high-domed ceiling. It hadn't taken them long to discover a shelf of rock that provided enough space for fuel drums and other supplies to be stored.

Upon climbing from the water, they had shed their air tanks and knelt on the limestone floor between several stalagmites, giving thanks to almighty Allah for leading them to this hidden place. As far as Raduyev had been able to tell, it was the perfect staging area for carrying out their mission.

Subsequent explorations through a forest of stalagmites soon revealed several passageways extending through the bedrock forming the chamber's back wall. Upon following one of them, Raduyev noticed that it gradually wound its way upward. Squeezing himself through a few narrow places, he had ultimately gained access to the surface. In the ensuing weeks, he was to learn that the subterranean portions of Navassa Island were extensively honeycombed, literally riddled with what seemed like an intricate and endless labyrinth of tunnels and caves.

Through his Yemeni contact in Kingston, Raduyev had arranged several pickups at sea of various items and provisions to make the underground chamber more livable and better suited to carry out his mission. Generators and floodlights had been brought in, as well as thousands of feet of electrical cable and ventilation hose. In order to widen the passageways and to clear away stalagmites, compressors for powering pneumatic jackhammers and dynamite had also been mobilized. The magnitude of the work Raduyev and his crew had endured in carving and clearing hundreds of tons of rock had taken its toll, leaving them physically exhausted most of the time. Yet there was still a staggering amount of backbreaking work that remained. Though tracking down Javolyn had taken the Chechen away from these labors, it was a welcome respite from the demanding toil that still lay ahead.

By the time Raduyev had met up with his crew in the underground cavern and launched the sub, the two-boat convoy had vanished over the horizon. Following what he had perceived to be their last known heading, he had steered the sub at full speed just below the ocean surface, every so often raising the periscope to scan the sea in all directions. Within an hour, he had spotted two vessels and, quickly closing the gap, confirmed the boats to be the ones he had been seeking. Keeping well to their rear, he had shadowed them for the remainder of the day, annoyed and bored at the snail-like pace they maintained. During that time, he had been tempted to sneak up closer to the trailing boat, hoping to get a clear look at the occupants aboard it. He needed to confirm once and for all if one of them was Javolyn. Such a move, however, would have been all too foolhardy, he finally reasoned. Knowing the ex-Navy Seal's proclivity for vigilance the way he did, the potential for compromising his position would have been too great a risk.

When they had eventually reached the Haitian coast, Raduyev had hung back at a distance and watched the smaller vessel disappear among the cliffs as the larger boat set its anchor. It was only after the sun had set that he had crept up close to where the anchored vessel now sat. From the air he had counted a total of nine people among the party he had pursued. In trailing the vessels, he had reconfirmed this count over and over through the sub's periscope, mostly out of boredom. Having observed most of the people go ashore, he was now certain that only two crew members remained aboard the boat that now floated before him. After weighing his options, he had originally decided to sink the moored vessel. But now that he thought about it, firing a torpedo into the boat's hull might alert authorities to the possibility of a rogue sub plying Caribbean waters, a fact that could jeopardize his mission. That his torpedo launch system was suddenly inoperable was surely a sign from Allah not to carry out such a foolhardy move.

Raduyev looked over at the Palestinian contingent of the sub's crew. Azzum and Bashir were watching him intently, awaiting his next command. He had trained both men as divers and found them to be marginally competent. And although they each had the desire to learn amphibious commando tactics, neither possessed the qualities or skills that came anywhere close to Navy Seal caliber, particularly Bashir who was the weaker of the two. Bashir, Raduyev knew, had a tendency to overestimate his abilities in the water, a man that would surely come apart at the seams if pushed too hard. Azzum, on the other hand, was easily distracted, unable to keep his attention focused on an objective for very long. As Raduyev studied the men, he was struck by the fact that they were the only divers he had available to him for the time being. That, however, would change in the near future. A group of highly skilled mujahedeen fighters would be joining up with him by tomorrow, holy warriors that were cut from the same cloth as he, jihad crusaders that would form the backbone of an elite group of frogmen currently coming out of the Middle East. He was confident this little diversion of his would not offset his schedule, certain he could still reach the prearranged rendezvous point in time.

"Suit up," Raduyev ordered. "We will board the vessel."

"Are we to kill anyone encountered?" Azzum asked, his eyes gleaming hungrily in the greenish light.

Raduyev weighed the question for several seconds before replying. "No. We will take prisoners for interrogation. I want to know who these people are and why they were near Navassa Island."

Chapter Five:
A Brewing Disaster

Using both hands to grasp Achilles' dorsal fin, Jake's forearms ached miserably from the strain of holding on. The juvenile was all muscle and seemed tireless, cutting through the water with powerful, arm-wrenching flicks of its tail. Jake was sure the albino was capable of achieving a faster pace, but perceived Achilles was purposely holding back in an effort not to dislodge his rider, staying just short of exceeding Jake's physical limit.

Through eyes reduced to slits, Jake watched the outline of the *Avenging Angel* grow rapidly larger in the moonlight as the dolphin moved diagonally across the reef. The water had risen in the last several hours, allowing Achilles to stay above the razor-sharp coral that grew to within inches of the surface at low tide. As Jake neared his vessel, it became evident that none of the cabin or deck lights were on. Within the span of a minute, the juvenile had him at the side of the dive platform that jutted from the *Angel's* stern. As expected, the platform ladder that could be lowered into the water was in the up position.

As Jake let go of Achilles and reached for the platform, the marine mammal turned and faced him. "Beware, Jake Javolyn," the juvenile ululated, keeping the vocalization just loud enough for Jake to hear. "Others approach."

Jake gave a quick scan of the darkened water all around him. Not seeing anything, he stared back at Achilles. "Do you mean people from the submarine?" he asked, careful to whisper out the question.

"Yes, they come from beneath the water and will be here shortly."

"How many?"

"Three."

Jake hauled himself from the water as quietly as possible, letting the platform support his weight. Leaning out over the edge, he placed a hand on the albino's beak. "Swim away from here, Achilles," he whispered. "If I need you, I'll call you."

Achilles complied with Jake's instruction, submerging quickly.

Rising into a standing position, Jake turned and silently climbed the three steps that ascended to the vessel's rear transom. Opting not to unlatch the gate, he hopped over the railing. Almost immediately, something loomed up out of the darkness and came straight at him. Instinctively he ducked, sensing the air being cleaved by an object swung in his direction a split second before it grazed his hair. Thrown off balance by the near miss, the assailant stumbled forward and collided heavily with Jake, the man's body having the rigidity of a block of wood.

"Easy, Hector," Jake blurted, clamping an immobilizing bear hug around the shorter man. "It's me, Jay Jay."

Hector let out a short, shallow breath. "You're crushin' the shit outta me," he wheezed painfully.

Jake released his python hold. "There are strangers coming to board us," he warned in a low voice. "You got the message from Zimby?"

Hector nodded, shifting the baseball bat he carried between hands and rubbing one of his biceps. "He called on the radio and told me about the sub."

Jake looked over Hector's shoulder. "Where's Phillipe?"

"Keeping watch up on the bow," Hector said.

"Go below and get me my backup mask, fins and snorkel," Jake ordered, reaching out and taking charge of the bat in Hector's hands. As Hector turned to retrieve the items, Jake grabbed him by the shoulder. "I'll also need my bang stick and MP-5."

Hector nodded again and scooted away. A moment later, Jake heard something bump lightly against the dive platform. He reached to his thigh, feeling the hilt of his K-Bar. Satisfied that it still rested firmly in its Kydex sheath strapped to his leg, he slipped the retaining ring off the knife's haft to make it readily available should he need it. Sidling up to the stern railing, he crouched behind it and peered through the crack in the gate.

The head of a diver suddenly poked above the platform and glanced furtively around. Jake held his breath and tightened his fingers on the handle of the bat. The diver looked back down at the water, appearing to gesture at someone else. As Jake watched, he could see two other hands grasp the upper edge of the platform. An instant later, the diver came to rest on the platform, boosted above the water by his as yet unseen comrades. A flag immediately went up in Jake's head. The maneuver involved teamwork and was similar to those practiced by Navy Seals when gaining access to overhanging structures without the aid of a ladder.

Jake remained motionless and well hidden in the semi-darkness, continuing to observe the scene as it unfolded. The dark figure on the platform removed his swim flippers and placed them aside, rising in a low crouch. Reaching back down, the interloper grabbed hold of something handed up to him from the water. In the dim moonlight, Jake could see the man remove an object from a sealed plastic bag. The outline of a submachine gun suddenly came into view as the man turned to climb the small stairway. Jake knew the man was seeking to secure the aft end of the *Angel* before he would give the all clear sign to his accomplices to come aboard. It was a standard commando tactic.

Thinking quickly, Jake groped behind him, feeling the lip of a bucket normally kept there. The bucket had lead weights in it, the kind that fitted to a diver's weight belt. Grabbing a three-pound weight, he waited until the intruder was almost to the top of the steps, then tossed the weight over the side as he kept his eyes locked on the man. The lead piece hit the water with a noticeable plop, making the man spin his head to investigate. Timing his move perfectly, Jake rose up at the exact instant the intruder looked away and swung for the bleachers, catching the man squarely on the side of the head with the sweet spot on the bat. With buckling knees, the man fell to one side of the steps, bounced off the platform and tumbled into the water with a loud splash.

His position of concealment now compromised, Jake slid back from the railing and faded into the darkness close to the *Angel's* rear cabin, keeping low. As he had anticipated, a bout of gunfire erupted a moment later as the felled man's companions realized what had happened and opened up with their weapons, raking the stern transom with small arms fire. Without having to look, Jake knew the remaining two interlopers were lifting their weapons over the dive platform and firing blindly, only putting their arms at risk. It was the type of move used by professional soldiers. Because the enfilade was coming up at an angle, none of the rounds had any chance of hitting Jake, who was now too far back to be in the line of fire.

In the midst of the din, Hector scurried back to Jake's side and handed him his Heckler and Koch MP-5 DPW. The other requested items were also in the shorter man's possession, including spare clips for the automatic weapon. Almost as quickly as it had started, the gunfire ceased. Jake removed the magazine from the submachine gun, checking to make sure the clip was full, then snapped it back into place. Grabbing the sleeve holding the bang stick, he strapped it to his left thigh. A moment later, he had the mask and fins strapped on.

Reaching out, Jake placed a hand behind Hector's head and pulled him close. "Stay right here and keep low," he instructed. "Be ready to take the gun and keep these guys from coming aboard."

With that said, Jake stood up and, now wearing the swim fins, frog-leaped to the railing where he unleashed several short bursts of suppressive fire into the sea. A heavy spray of water kicked up to one side of the dive platform, which remained vacant of any would-be boarders. Putting the gun's safety on, he tossed the weapon back to Hector and jumped over the side, keeping the dive mask pressed firmly against his forehead and removing the assault knife from its scabbard before hitting the water.

Plunging below the surface, Jake lowered the mask into place, cleared the water from it with a partial exhalation through his nose, and inserted the end of the snorkel into his mouth. He quickly oriented himself, directing his gaze aft along the *Angel's* hull. A subdued glimmer of moonlight penetrated into the depths, revealing little, if only shadows. Straining his eyes into the darkness, sudden movement caught his attention, then vanished. Glancing behind him, Jake made sure his six was clear before kicking off toward the stern. As he made his way below the swim platform, he peered around in search of the diver he had clouted but saw nothing.

Jake evaluated the present conditions. The tide had now gone slack, having reached its peak. With little current to carry the interloper away, the man should have floated close by, assuming that he was still unconscious or dead and that his dive equipment provided sufficient positive buoyancy to keep him afloat. As he analyzed the situation, only a few things were possible. Either the man had sunk to the bottom, or he had regained consciousness and swum away. Jake dismissed these two suppositions and went with a third possibility, the one he deemed most likely. The other two intruders had taken their wounded comrade in tow and were now heading back to the sub.

Rising to the surface, Jake blew water from the snorkel and recharged his lungs. On instinct, he kept swimming forward, moving downstream of the *Angel's* stern. He was about to turn back to his vessel when a sudden flicker of light gleamed dully below him. A moment later it disappeared. Something was agitating the algae in the water, causing it to give off a phosphorescent glow.

Taking a huge gulp of air, Jake shot into the depths, descending upon the disturbance like a pelagic predator on the scent of prey. Again, he perceived movement, and as he swam deeper he caught sight of a diver's flipper no more than five feet away. Kicking hard in an effort to catch up, his right swim-fin suddenly met resistance. Something was tearing at it, attempting to grab hold. Jake immediately spun, pulling his knees to his chest as he did so and preventing whatever it was from grasping his flippers. The silhouette of another diver was outlined in a wash of effulgent bioluminescence. Jake could distinguish the faceplate of the diver's mask as the man reached up for him. The glint of steel in one of the diver's hands galvanized Jake further and, reflexively, he smashed the heels of his feet into the oncoming face as it came within range, gratified by the solid impact. His assailant abruptly floundered, stunned from the blow, and Jake took advantage of the moment, sheathing his own knife before pulling the bang stick from its scabbard. The diver slashed out in agitated madness, unable to see through a flooded face mask. Swimming under the frenzied blade, Jake thrust upward with the bang stick, jabbing for the man's chest. As luck would have it, the man raked back with the knife in that instant, his forearm intercepting Jake's own weapon. The bang stick exploded with brutal force, and the gleam of polished metal fluttered before Jake's eyes as the blade spun away beneath him.

Jake was not about to take any chances, knowing the man could still be dangerous. He re-inserted the spent bang stick into its sleeve and pulled the K-Bar from its sheath once again. Reaching up, he ripped the regulator from the diver's mouth, his adrenaline flowing fast and furious. A split second later he severed the regulator air hose, cutting the line where it connected with the yoke mated to the scuba bottle valve. An explosion of air immediately erupted behind the diver's head and the man jerked around in desperation, fumbling with panicky hands in a futile bid to locate the gushing hose. Maintaining his advantage, Jake slammed his balled fist into the diver's midriff. Through the water, he heard a distinct grunt, and in the crepuscular light he could see a rush of air stream from between clenched teeth. Though greatly incapacitated, the man somehow found the strength to claw insanely for the surface. Maneuvering behind him, Jake remained clear of the man's flailing arms and tore free the dive mask sitting lopsided on his face.

Completely disarming the intruder was Jake's next priority. As the diver struggled for the surface, Jake stayed with him, looking for other weapons he knew the man carried. Re-sheathing his assault knife and groping with both hands, he located the submachine pistol holstered to the man's right thigh. Lifting the holster's Velcro flap, he pulled the gun free. From its feel, he recognized it to be a Colt 633HB 9mm. Based on the staccato din the weapon had made earlier, it did not surprise him that the gun's muzzle lacked a suppressor. Although the weapon was no longer protected in a watertight plastic wrapping, he knew it might still be capable of firing in the watery environment. Releasing his grip on the submachine pistol, he let it fall away. The gun left a sprinkling of phosphorescence trailing behind as it dropped harmlessly to the bottom.

Jake was amazed at how easy it had been to subdue the diver. The man was rather clumsy in the water, appearing insufficiently trained to attempt hand-to-hand combat in the open sea. Latching onto the neck of the scuba tank strapped to the man's back, he let himself be towed upward, riding his charge as if the man were a loggerhead sea turtle. Jake could sense the diver's escalating panic. It was apparent the man had become aware of the additional drag restraining his ascent, causing him to go completely over the edge, caught up in the throes of a maddening frenzy focused only on reaching atmosphere. The man coughed convulsively when he finally broke the surface, his body coming halfway out of the water and, as chance would have it, practically landing in the *Angel's* skiff recently taken ashore.

Jake was surprised to see Zimbola and Grahm looming above him as both men leaned over the boat's gunwale. "I'd appreciate you taking this guy off my hands," Jake huffed mightily upon spitting out the snorkel and steering his captive the short distance to the side of the skiff.

Zimbola reached down and hefted the man from the water, tank and all, careful not to upend the small boat as he did so. Bleeding profusely from an open wound on his right arm, the diver was now weak and lethargic, still gasping painfully for air and too physically exhausted to put up any fight.

Inhaling deeply to catch his breath and resting his chest on the opposite end of the skiff, Jake counterbalanced the additional weight being put aboard, watching Zimbola deposit the diver in the boat's stern. Grahm flicked on a flashlight, shining it in the man's face. Jake was immediately struck by the man's features, which suggested a Middle Eastern heritage. Though debilitated, the man looked over at him with smoldering, hateful eyes.

"I've taken away his gun and knife," Jake wheezed, seeing a deep frown form on the black giant's face in the faint moonlight, "but it wouldn't hurt to check him for other weapons."

"Who is this man?" Zimbola asked, kneeling down to search the diver.

"I'm not sure," Jake said hurriedly, getting his wind back. "But he's got a few companions roaming around below us, and they're not very friendly. I suggest you put him aboard the *Angel* and tie him up."

"This man needs medical treatment," Grahm stated, reaching for a length of rope lying on the floor of the skiff. He looped the rope around the man's injured arm and cinched it tight in an effort to stem the flow of blood.

"Where you going?" Zimbola questioned as Jake pushed away from the skiff.

"There's a sub lurking somewhere below us. I'm going to see if I can locate it."

Jake was about to dive down again when a sudden idea came to him. "Achilles!" he shouted. The name had barely left his lips when the juvenile albino appeared at his side as if by magic. "Achilles…the channel through the reef, the one Jacob uses to get his boat into the cove. I need the other members of your pod to position themselves along both sides of the channel," Jake petitioned. "I need them to show the *Angel* the way through the reef. Can they do this, Achilles?"

Achilles appeared to ponder the question, not making any detectable sounds and regarding Jake with that permanent, unwavering smile. "They will do as you request, Jake Javolyn," the dolphin finally answered.

Jake turned back to the skiff, noticing the special interest both Zimbola and Grahm were taking in his exchange with the dolphin. "Get back to the *Angel* and pull her anchor fast as you can, Zimby," Jake ordered. "I want you to bring her through the reef and into the cove. The dolphins will show you the way."

"What you ask is too dangerous," Zimbola objected hotly. "We risk opening her hull."

"Better that than the sub holing her," Jake argued impatiently. "Do as I say or we won't have a boat at all."

Zimbola wavered, then gave a defeated shrug. "As you wish," he said gravely, engaging the skiff's tiny electric engine and grabbing hold of the tiller. As the big man headed off in the direction of their boat, it was clear that he did not relish the prospect of having to steer the *Angel* through so narrow a gap in the reef.

Jake reached for the juvenile's dorsal fin. "Take me to the sub, Achilles!" he instructed.

Achilles gave Jake just enough time to place the snorkel between his teeth and fill his lungs before submerging. The sea tugged hard against him as the dolphin accelerated quickly into the depths. Swallowing hard, Jake felt his ears pop in protest to the rapidly increasing pressure. A moment later, Achilles leveled off. Without a depth gauge, Jake had no way of knowing precisely how deep they had descended, but from the way his dive mask was pressing against his face he sensed he was now below fifty feet. Exhaling slightly through his nose, he equalized the pressure within the mask against that of the surrounding water. The discomfort the mask squeeze caused him abruptly vanished.

As his eyes adjusted to the reduced light, Jake suddenly caught sight of something huge and dark against the backdrop of hydrospace. Achilles raced along its entire length before turning and traversing its opposite side. Making yet another pass, the dolphin suddenly slowed and came to a stop near the object's midpoint, hovering within arm's length of it. The water's exceptional clarity in conjunction with the moonlight filtering into the depths made the object visible in the night sea. Through the murk, Jake perceived something sizable protruding above the rest of the structure and immediately identified it to be a conning tower.

Looking into the near darkness, Jake's attention was drawn to a greenish lambent aura further back from the sub's tower. Something was stirring the water, causing the microscopic algae to flash like fireflies, an eerie sight in the surrounding black void. Jake knew such bioluminescence was common to marine environments, typically caused by single-celled dinoflagellates that emitted light when their cell walls were deformed by mechanical agitation. And although it was a biochemical phenomenon he had grown used to, never before had he seen it so pronounced as he did now.

Jake released his hold on Achilles and kicked off toward the flickering radiance, feeling the first tinges of discomfort in his lungs. Checking the luminous dial on his dive watch, he saw that he had been submerged for nearly three minutes. If he didn't overtax himself, he might last another two before having to come up for air. He had been gifted with an exceptional pair of lungs and had the ability to stay underwater for prolonged periods when diving without the aid of scuba. Coming within ten feet of the glowing green pinpoints, he discerned movement. A diver had his back to him and was entering an airlock through a hatchway on the sub's deck, moving into the opening feet first.

Pulling his knife, Jack finned forward quickly, attempting to catch the diver off guard. By the time he reached the opening, however, the diver was pulling the cover into a lockdown position. Jake caught the lid just before it sealed, getting the fingers of his free hand under the rim opposite the hinge and bracing both feet against the deck. Yanking hard, he rotated the hatch cover back up a quarter of the way before he met resistance. The diver pulled back furiously, attempting to batten down the hatch, and a tug of war instantly ensued, with each man trying to gain the upper hand. Effectively stalemated, Jake's lungs began to burn from the strain, but he was not yet ready to give up. Managing to reposition his feet and getting the fingertips of his knife hand under the lip of the cover, he threw his back into the task and applied more leverage. Now tugging with both hands, the lid began to come up again. In his current position, he knew he held the advantage, able to exert superior force over his opponent. Slowly, the lid continued to rise.

Jake was suddenly thrown backwards as resistance from the lid's opposing side abruptly ceased. The diver, carried upward by the motion of the hatch cover rotating on its hinges, rushed out of the airlock and came straight at him. Much less encumbered with equipment than his opponent, Jake recovered quickly, moving aside and just barely avoiding the tip of the blade thrust at him. Turning, the diver came at him again. Jake met the man's charge amid a swarm of sparking fireflies, parrying the blade that stabbed for his chest with the K-Bar and nicking the assailant's arm with a slashing riposte. The superficial wound seemed to freeze his adversary for one fleeting moment, giving Jake the opportunity to catch the wrist of the man's knife hand. Kicking hard with his flippers, he drove the diver backwards, reaching for the man's face with the other hand. The man seemed to anticipate the move, snaring Jake's free hand with a countermove of his own. Both men locked up, performing a strange undersea ballet, pirouetting and twirling and forming a pinwheel of bioluminescent radiance that spiraled away from the twosome as each vied for advantage.

Jake was surprised at the strength of his opponent. Unlike the diver's two accomplices, the man was proving himself to be a seasoned warrior. In the midst of the struggle, Jake discerned the conning tower looming above them and quickly changed tactics. He extended his legs laterally and kicked powerfully, spinning his opponent and driving the back of the man's head into the rigid metallic structure. Seemingly stunned, the man released his hold on Jake.

His lungs now screaming for air, Jake had no choice but to make a hasty retreat for the surface. Almost dizzy with a need for oxygen, he knew unconsciousness was not far away. With blackness rapidly eating away at the fringes of his awareness, he had trouble orienting himself, vaguely perceiving the nearby conning tower extending up from the submarine deck in the darkness. Using it as a guide to the surface, he swam above the structure and continued on, feeling his strength rapidly dwindling. In anticipation of gulping the sweet air he hungered for, he spat out the snorkel mouthpiece. He was certain he had been submerged for close to five minutes now, pushing himself to the max. The thought that he had stayed below too long and exceeded his physical limits crossed his mind, and though he could now discern the sea's upper boundary, the silvery sheen of moon glow upon it suddenly seemed unreachable, as if it were several light years away. He felt himself beginning to black out.

The sound of a diver's regulator hissed somewhere close, momentarily providing Jake with something to focus on, a point of reference for him to hold onto in the midst of his growing predicament. He looked below him, fighting off the fugue that was swiftly descending upon him like a dark cloak dropped from above. A swarm of air bubbles agitated the water just below his fins, highlighted by a twinkling of luminescence that somehow made him think of stardust. Through the expanding cloud, he could distinguish the aura of the diver dogging him, rising up to finish him off. He tried to kick away, unable to avoid swallowing water as he struggled for the surface. He had gone over the edge, way beyond the physical threshold of normal men. He had pushed himself too hard and desperately needed oxygen.

With delirium quickly enfolding him, Jake barely perceived something clutch both his armpits. He had the sensation of soaring, accelerating, and rising swiftly like a gliding bird of prey caught in an updraft. An alpine breeze seemed to flow all around him, gently washing over him before finding a corridor to his soul, the center of his being.

And then reality spun back as he realized Destiny was hovering over him, her lips pressed firmly against his, her breath warm and sweet like the fragrant tropical flowers within the cove. Seeing his eyes flutter open, she pulled her mouth away and sat back astride Hercules, her expression showing deep concern and overlaid with a hint of disbelief. Strangely revitalized from the resuscitation he had just received, he began to clear his lungs, gagging up water and filling his chest with deep, satisfying gasps. He became aware of another creature behind him, propping him above the water's surface. Achilles was under him, floating on his back and using those strange grasping appendages to hold him snugly under both arms and elevate him.

Jake felt his strength returning as he continued to inhale greedily. "I'm okay, Achilles," he finally rasped. "You can release me."

The juvenile lowered him into the water and let go, spinning around to look him over. "You are still weak, Jake Javolyn," Achilles ululated in that lilting speech characteristic of his unique species. "You may rest your body on mine."

Jake hooked an arm over the albino's back and stared back at the girl.

"The man chasing you has gone back to the submarine," Destiny informed him. The childlike timber of her voice was gone, replaced by a husky tightness that made him look at her more closely. In the soft wash of moonlight, her face appeared taut, and her eyes slightly glazed.

The context of the girl's words suddenly registered, jarring him back to full awareness. Yes, the submarine, he was reminded. His recent encounter came flooding back all at once, making him spin his head to locate his vessel. The *Angel* had pulled her anchor and was now churning the water, heading in the direction of the nearby cliffs. Scanning the water forward of the vessel, he could just make out the dorsal fins of other dolphins leading the way. Already Destiny had moved off toward the pack, preparing to assist Zimbola in negotiating the reef. If the *Angel* could squeeze through the narrow channel, she would be safe, beyond the reach of the sub. Having seen the size of the undersea vessel, Jake was certain it could not possibly follow his boat through such a constricted passageway where fangs of heavy coral lay in wait to tear open a passing hull.

But if the sub had a torpedo capability, it might very well launch such a projectile at the *Angel*, reef or no reef. Because the tide was up, a torpedo had the potential of traveling right over the coral, possibly clearing the highest calcareous projections by as much two feet.

"Where is the submarine, Achilles?" Jake asked anxiously.

"The metal vessel is coming to the surface as I speak, Jake Javolyn," the juvenile answered. Achilles turned almost ninety degrees. "There!"

The nose of the sub suddenly breached a short distance away, angling high above the sea before sending out a heavy spray as the rest of the vessel followed. In the pale moonlight, Jake had a broadside view of the thing, seeing that its overall length clearly exceeded the *Angel's* by at least twenty feet. As he looked on, a hatch opened atop the conning tower and the silhouette of a person poked out. Within moments the sub began to pick up speed, coming about quickly and pushing a bow wave before it.

Though the water was warm, a chill shot up Jake's spine as he realized where the sub was heading. "They're gonna ram the *Angel*," he yelled out in horror, feeling completely helpless for the first time since his stint in Afghanistan.

Raduyev's Hatred

Raduyev's cheeks ticked with hatred as he kept a malicious gaze locked on the vessel plodding the water, its port broadside presented vulnerably to him as it made a run across his bow. Now that the sub was no longer hidden under the mantle of sea and was clearly on a heading that would intercept the watercraft, he was surprised that the boat before him did not waver from its present course. "Three degrees left!" he growled into the lip mike, speaking Arabic.

To confirm the order, a voice came back over his headphones, repeating the command in the same language. "Turning left by three degrees."

Raduyev listened to Kalid with annoyance. His second in command sounded a little too nervous for his taste. A brief moment elapsed before he sensed the P-130 swing slightly as the helm responded to his command.

As he closed the gap separating the two vessels, the other boat appeared to increase its speed. "Bring us left another three degrees!" he snarled. He would have his satisfaction with these infidels. By the grace of Allah, he would have it. The sub would be used in the manner it was intended. Allah's Sword would live up to its name.

"We have no more room to maneuver left," the helm warned, the voice in the headphones now urgent with a pleading edge to it. "We risk going aground on the reef if we do so."

Kalid's words fueled his growing rage. It was apparent the vessel before him was presently scrambling for the same passage through the reef taken earlier by the smaller boats. With the sub's diesel currently churning at maximum rpm, he could only hope to catch the wooden vessel before it made the channel, and that meant adjusting the sub's heading just a little more. Three more degrees would ensure that his prey did not escape. By his estimation, three more degrees was conservative enough not to put the sub in any danger. He knew exactly where the reef began to rise.

"Do not argue with me, Kalid," Raduyev screamed. "You will turn left by three more degrees. Do you think Allah will not protect one of his instruments?" Raduyev's words seemed to pacify his comrade-in-arms, for the sub turned to port a moment later, now perfectly aligned to intercept the vessel he was determined to destroy.

As Raduyev looked beyond the sub's bow, he became aware of the fins cleaving the water directly ahead of the target he was rapidly converging on. There were six of them. No, he suddenly corrected himself. He could now discern a person propped above the surface just forward of a seventh, much larger fin. He assumed it was that same girl he had seen earlier. The people the girl was associated with were an irritating lot. He could well understand Ortega's need for vengeance against these people. From all outward appearances the Colombian should have been able to crush them, and rather easily at that. But somehow they were proving to be an elusive, resourceful lot, having the means to block and foil both overt and covert attempts aimed at vanquishing them. And now these mysterious white creatures were adding to the mix of unforeseen factors, seeming to contribute to the problems he was experiencing. Perhaps there was more to these seagoing mammals than met the eye. The thought made him think back to Ortega. He remembered the unusual interest the Colombian had shown toward the strange albino dolphins, including the girl accompanying them.

Whoever the girl was, the sight of her made Raduyev's blood boil all the more violently. She had rendered aid to the man he had fought, her and one of the dolphins accompanying her, denying him his quarry. He had almost caught up to the man, perhaps a second away from stopping him from reaching the surface. His adversary had gone without air during their struggle, a most foolish yet extraordinary feat. The man had not only thwarted him from boarding and taking command of the vessel he was now pursuing but had taken both his comrades out of the fight. Azzum was still out cold, and Bashir had vanished without a trace. Plunging his knife between the man's ribs would have given him tremendous satisfaction, making his foolhardy and time-consuming voyage across the Windward Passage ultimately worthwhile despite the obstacles thrown in his path. His foe had been deprived of oxygen far too long and, from what Raduyev had been able to surmise, would have been easily defeated in such a weakened condition. Raduyev would have put an end to his adversary once and for all if not for one of those irksome white dolphins rushing in and carrying the man away beyond his reach. Driven on by the overpowering rage that had gripped him, he had nevertheless continued on and popped his head above the surface, only to witness the girl administering mouth-to-mouth resuscitation on the man no more than fifteen meters away. Running the incident over in his mind, Raduyev was convinced that only one man could have given him such a fight with such limited resources at his disposal, and that man was Jake Javolyn.

But now retribution was at hand. The sub's steel bow would crush the infidel vessel's flimsy wooden hull, staving through it with little effort. If the owner of the boat was indeed Javolyn, Raduyev would at least reap some gratification at knowing he had put a valuable possession of his longtime nemesis on the bottom. And it was only befitting that Allah's Sword would deliver the lethal strike. A sense of elation began to build within him in anticipation of the moment of impact.

He tried to recall the name of the vessel converging with his own. What was it called? Ah, yes, now he remembered. *Avenging Angel.* That was it. When he had followed the watercraft, he had elevated his periscope and gone to maximum magnification, getting close enough to read the words emblazoned on the boat's stern. It had struck him as blasphemous that an infidel would presume to identify his vessel with that of a spiritual entity created for smiting God's enemies. If there was avenging to be done, it would come through the power of Allah's Sword.

As Raduyev surveyed the scene unfurling before him, his eyes came to rest on the group of dolphins escorting the vessel he was about to turn into a mass of splinters. They had all stopped and were now spread out at even intervals from one another. Somewhat puzzled, he turned his attention back to the *Avenging Angel*, bracing himself for the impending collision. A malevolent giddiness began to take hold of him as the P-130 charged ahead, its bow about to smash amidships on the boat looming before him.

The expression on Raduyev's face quickly turned to shock as a screeching shudder reverberated through the sub's hull, and he gritted his teeth as his body was jarred sideways with unexpected violence. Suddenly slowed, Allah's Sword broke abruptly right from its intended target, deflected by some unseen obstruction. Dumbfounded, Raduyev could only watch as the sub's prow skirted past the *Angel's* stern, missing the vessel's dive platform by mere inches. Wide-eyed, he stared in disbelief as the *Avenging Angel* swept away from him unscathed, its hull plowing between the two lines of dolphins floating stationary on each side of it.

Chapter Six: Safe Haven

It was well past 1:00 a.m. by the time the *Angel's* crew had dropped anchor on the south side of the cove, well away from where the *thurentra* nestled. Miraculously, the North Sea trawler had made it through the confined opening in the reef without so much as a flake of bottom paint being scraped from her hull. What had made the feat even more remarkable was the fact that Zimbola had traversed the incommodious passage at full throttle, something the Jamaican would never have attempted had not the submarine sought to ram him. Jake knew, however, that had the dolphins not been so precise in their alignment or had the tide been so much as two inches lower, the outcome might have been far different. It was Achilles who had informed him of this, as conveyed to the juvenile by other members of the pod who, acting as channel guides, had perceived just how close the *Angel* had come to disaster.

Following the perilous episode, Zimbola had been able to squeeze the vessel through the second channel leading to the cove, clearing the rock walls on each side by less than a foot where the passageway was tightest. Not knowing what armaments the sub carried, Jake felt it prudent to bring the *Angel* into the safe haven the cove provided, certain that the sub could not follow. Even fully surfaced, the sub would have drafted too much water to clear the highest protuberances of coral lining each side of the reef channel. And while the sub had a beam approximating that of Jake's vessel, it lacked a hull tapered to the degree of the *Angel's* to adequately negotiate the narrow width the opening through the reef afforded. Though Jake had been relieved to learn the sub had left the area based on what the dolphins conveyed to him, he couldn't be sure it would not return. According to Achilles, the metal boat had sustained some damage, brushing up against a huge mass of brain coral on the outside portion of the reef. In the end, it had been the submarine captain's insane desire for retribution that had come back on him full circle, almost leading to the destruction of his own vessel.

Shortly after the incident, Jake had asked Achilles if members of his pod could follow the submarine to its next destination and report back this information. Upon communicating with the other albinos, the juvenile assured him that his request would be carried out. By arrangement, Hermes and Aphrodite would fulfill this task.

Although Jake's near drowning had left him with a severe headache, he deferred getting some rest until the man he had captured was properly treated and secured for the night. He had looked for Destiny to see if she could heal the man's wound, but the girl had vanished again. The last thing he needed was for the man to get free and become a danger to the *Angel's* crew or the other parties currently in the cove. Assuming his captive was willing to talk, he might learn something about the objective of the submarine crew. In the morning he would put in a call to Mat Daniels and apprise him of what was going on, but right now he was just too damned tired.

As he lay down in his bunk aboard the *Angel*, a jumble of snapshots depicting recent events danced through his mind. Tenaciously they followed him as he plunged through the barrier separating reality from the realm of dreams. Only one image seemed to dominate his thoughts, however, and that was of a raven-haired girl with doe-like eyes.

Chapter Seven: The Ambitious Colonel

Colonel Ternier sat at his desk, idly scratching the scar marring his lower jaw. Omar's request puzzled him. If he followed through on it, he risked reprisals from a host of human rights groups, and even worse, prosecution by the International Criminal Court at the Hague. But then again, a leak would have to occur within his network of acolytes and spies for him to get implicated, and that possibility was extremely remote. Fear and greed were the primary motivators he used to keep his people in check, and over the years he had come to realize the full magnitude of their effectiveness. Fear, however, worked best for him, and the use of such an incentive was much more to his liking.

Weighing his options, Ternier looked across the desktop at the fat little man sitting opposite him. It was already past three in the morning, an hour when his quarters would seem most ominous to anyone brought to such a place, a good time to conduct business. "Twenty able-bodied men, you say?"

Hennington appeared uncomfortable, dabbing the sweat streaming profusely from his brow with a handkerchief, a habit Ternier had grown used to seeing. "Ortega was very specific on that point. These men must be fit enough to withstand hard physical labor over a period of months."

Ternier got out of his chair and strolled around his desk, his hands clasped stiffly behind his back, his posture rigid. The Colonel knew the effect such a regal bearing had on people. He saw himself as a man destined to lead, and not just on the level he currently commanded. The winds of change were fast approaching and it was important he did not impede them.

"You may tell Ortega I will honor his request," he said, not bothering to look at the chubby broker. "How does he propose to take delivery of the merchandise?"

"He has arranged to have them put aboard the *San Carlo* when she makes port by week's end," Hennington said, his voice betraying the tenseness he felt.

Ternier stopped in mid-step, showing his surprise. "So you have followed through on my suggestion. Good…very good."

Hennington fidgeted nervously in his chair as Ternier moved behind him. The Colonel enjoyed making the broker nervous. It only served to keep him in line, to make the man do his bidding.

Ternier glanced over at the wall behind his desk, his eyes singling out one photograph in particular, a scene showing a smiling Rene Preval, president-elect of Haiti, shaking Ternier's hand at a recent state function. As he stared at the picture, he had to remind himself that Preval was the current head of state of the strife-torn country. So many leaders, he thought amusedly. To him, they were all becoming a blur.

Scanning the wall further, Ternier located another photograph. Prior to Preval's national election victory in February of 2006, another man by the name of Gerard Latortue had provided interim leadership to Haiti, functioning as Acting Prime Minister during that period. Latortue had been one of the latest in a succession of Haitian leaders who had enjoyed U.S. backing, placed in power as a short-term remedy by United Nations mandate for quelling the chronic political unrest that afflicted the impoverished nation. Ternier knew that Latortue had been nothing more than an international business consultant who had previously served as Foreign Minister in 1988 under former President Leslie Manigat. Manigat had only lasted three months in office before being ousted by a military coup.

From Ternier's perspective, Latortue's appointment had been motivated primarily by U.S. and French interests assembling multilateral support for humanitarian intervention. A subtle sneer formed on Ternier's features as he mused over the politics that had always seemed to surface throughout the history of his nation. Restoring order in Haiti through the meddling of international economic giants like the United States was becoming commonplace these days. To Ternier, it was just another example of the rich imperialist countries exploiting the poor under the guise of nation building. In actuality, Latortue had manipulated his way to power, calling upon the Americans to remove President Aristide in the midst of mounting political strife that threatened the stability of the country. Sworn in under heavy security before a tiny gathering of only two hundred people, Latortue was simply another manifestation of illegitimate leadership thrust upon the Caribbean nation by outside influences who thought they knew what was best for Haiti. In essence, the interim government under Latortue had been a surrogate regime almost totally dependent on Washington for its survival. And from experience, Ternier had no misconceptions about what that meant. It had been a complete failure.

Being a student of modern history, the Colonel knew that, to date, no American-supported regime had ever made the full transition to democracy following the withdrawal of military support. Events since the fall of Baby Doc had shown him that once U.S. or U.N. military forces withdrew from Haiti, the same problems that had previously plagued the country would resurface as they always did, and the transition to democracy would flounder yet again. From 1986 to 1991 the country had experienced as many as four military coups. Like his predecessors, Latortue had been forced to resort to repressive measures to maintain power, imposing martial law on the citizenry and relying on the Haitian National Police to enforce it. As in the past, this always led to some strongman rising to the forefront and seizing power to advance his personal ambitions. Botched nation building efforts historically produced undesirable consequences for the local population, with dictators always emerging from the wreckage. Ternier was convinced that the creation and maintenance of surrogate regimes always mutated into military dictatorships or corrupt autocracies, with the cycle endlessly perpetuating itself in the face of imperialist meddling.

Perhaps under the current president the country stood a chance at becoming more progressive, but Ternier strongly doubted it. Highly popular among the poorest members of Haitian society, Preval proclaimed himself to be a nonviolent anarchist, believing power should flow from the government to the people. A former Aristide protégé, Preval had shown less than stellar performance in the past when he had tenured as Haiti's president once before, serving from 1996 to 2001.

Perhaps it was the never-ending array of internal problems that made stellar performance impossible to achieve. Preval had his hands full with Haiti's current state of affairs, incessantly facing a demanding schedule at resuscitating international assistance. Already many manufacturers within the country were closing up shop because of the growing gang violence. Shortly before being inaugurated as president for the second time over a year ago, Preval had addressed the U.N. Security council, citing the enormous challenges he faced in the form of widespread poverty, unemployment, dilapidated infrastructure, and chronic national insecurity. Preval, it seemed, appeared to be on a crusade at saving the land, proclaiming that Haiti needed more than just an influx of money to correct its problems. The country also needed expertise brought in from abroad in order to upgrade its electrical power generating facilities and improve its infrastructure, health, and education sectors, all of which were his top priorities. Preval had been careful to stress that even if the nation got both the finances and expertise it so desperately needed, it would take at least twenty-five years before real progress would be seen. Therefore, his people should not have unrealistic expectations for an immediate solution to the critical woes afflicting the nation. With such a long timetable in the works, Ternier was certain that political unrest would soon boil over once again, manifesting itself in more riots and bloody rebellions.

And that kind of atmosphere was just fine by the Colonel. He loved political instability, a situation that allowed him to cultivate his own aspirations. Without it, he could not possibly enjoy the power he exerted. He was one of the true power wielders behind the scenes in Haitian society. But he would not allow himself to make the same mistakes all the others had made before him, lured by the desire for overt ascendancy over a nation only to be dethroned by American might shortly thereafter. No, he was too smart to make such a futile grab for power in the face of looming imperialism; that is, unless the time were ripe. Without some cataclysmic upheaval to divert its attentions, the United States was currently far too strong to let its core security and economic well-being go undefended.

Ternier held down the laugh beginning to take root in his belly, for he knew the time was now very close for that upheaval.

At heart, Ternier was a true cynic, believing that the American goal of building democracy in Haiti was merely a pretext for advancing its economic interests. He was privy to much information and from what he could gather, the coup that had ousted Aristide in 1991 had been orchestrated by the U.S. Though Aristide had gotten sixty-seven percent of the popular vote in a democratic election, he had not been acceptable to Washington. With corruption and mismanagement of government funds by past Haitian leaders seemingly out of control, the U.S. had counted on Marc Bazin being elected, a man Washington deemed as having considerable integrity. Bazin was a former World Bank official who had been assigned to the post of Finance Minister in 1982 under the Baby Doc regime. Although Duvalier had officially appointed Bazin, Ternier knew that the arrangement had been a stipulation of the U.S. if Haiti was to continue receiving foreign aid. But Duvalier had not anticipated the extreme zealousness of his newly appointed Finance Minister, and Bazin had uncovered case after case of corruption. In the end, Bazin had determined that at least thirty-six percent of government revenue was embezzled, and as a consequence he had declared the country to be the most mismanaged in the region. And though Baby Doc had quickly replaced him, Bazin had given credence to the world that Duvalier had overstepped the traditional accepted boundaries of Haitian corruption where leaders had a history of self-enrichment.

The Colonel continued to reflect on those earlier years. Under intense internal as well as U.S. pressure, Baby Doc had fled the country on February 7, 1986, taking exile in France and absconding with millions in government funds. Back then, a real Haitian army had existed and although Ternier had been part of it, he had felt it prudent to keep a low profile, remaining in the background as the National Council of Government took charge of the country. After Aristide had been elected in 1991, it was General Raoul Cedras who had been responsible for deposing the people's choice of leadership. Rumor within the intelligence network had it that Cedras was a long-time agent of the U.S. Central Intelligence Agency. With Aristide temporarily out of the way, the U.S. had again pushed for a return to democracy in Haiti while supporting a half-baked embargo that exempted American-owned factories and demanding increasing concessions from the nation's government. If Haiti failed to comply, Washington would withhold badly needed economic aid to its beleaguered neighbor. Somewhere in the midst of political maneuvering, the U.S. had managed to weaken France's privileged position in Port-au-Prince politics and initiate sweetheart deals for American corporations. Even under Jean Claude Duvalier the U.S. had sought to make the Haitian economy more like an extension of its own. In implementing this, Haiti's tariffs had been cut, making the country a market for U.S. agricultural surpluses and a source of inexpensive tropical produce. Unable to compete with cheap American staples such as corn and beans, many peasant farmers failing to make ends meet began cutting down fruit trees to make charcoal, while others left their land and migrated to the burgeoning slums surrounding Port-au-Prince and the other cities, forming an immense pool of cheap manual labor for U.S. textile and electronics assembly plants. Already Haiti had become known as the Taiwan of the Caribbean. Whereas the nation was nearly self-sufficient in food in 1970, importing only ten percent of its needs, by 1993 that figure had risen to forty-two percent and was still rising.

Ternier suddenly thought of the rice trade. Haiti was currently the largest consumer of U.S. rice in the Caribbean, and the seventh largest in the world, importing well over two hundred thousand tons a year.

The Colonel felt no malice toward the U.S. or the de facto Haitian regimes that had favored American interests. That was the way the world worked. It was only natural for the strongest or smartest members of humanity to exploit the weak, either using them or pushing them aside for personal or national gain.

And as Ternier well knew, Haiti had fallen victim to exploitation throughout its turbulent history. Haiti had officially declared her independence in 1804 following the slave rebellions more than half a century earlier. Subsequent to much internal struggle to rid itself of slavery, the country saw Jean Jacques Dessalines, a black general, emerge as the new leader of the Haitian Revolution. But Dessalines' reign was short-lived. Two years after his crowning as Jacques the First, Dessalines was assassinated in an ambush. At first, the French government refused to recognize the new republic as an independent state. Through diplomacy, Louis XVIII tried in vain from 1814 to 1823 to regain Haiti as a colony. As a concession, Haiti's President Boyer signed an ordinance, agreeing to pay the French government an indemnity of 150 million francs to recognize the country's independence and to compensate for the loss of the plantations owned by the white colonists. Boyer's submission to that ordinance not only emptied the national treasury, but ultimately mortgaged the republic's future to the French. France did not recognize the country's independence until 1825, while the British did not accept it as a sovereign nation until 1833. Nevertheless, Haiti became the second republic in the Western Hemisphere and the first independent black nation in the world at a time when all the nations around it still resorted to slavery. The Spanish, French, English, Dutch, and Americans had all seen Haiti's successful revolution as a threat to their national interests and their status quo as slave owners, causing them to boycott, manipulate, isolate, and refuse to recognize Haiti's independence until it was deemed that the small Caribbean nation was impoverished and made weak enough militarily so that it could not pose a threat to anyone.

The violent history of Haiti intrigued Ternier. Following Boyer's administration, the country went through twenty-two heads of state between 1843 and 1915, a period before occupation by the United States occurred. Of these, only one had been able to serve out his term in office. Among the others, three had died horribly while still serving. One was presumably poisoned, another was hacked to pieces by a mob, while a third was blown up with his palace. The Colonel refrained from laughing aloud as he thought about the fate of the others. Except for one who had prudently resigned from office, all were deposed by revolution after incumbencies ranging in length from three months to twelve years.

A sigh escaped Ternier's lips as he thought about Haiti's heyday, a bygone period in history when the land was surnamed the pearl of the Antilles because of its wealth in gold and other precious metals and stones, a place noted for its natural beauty. Unfortunately, too many occupations and interventions by outside nations had taken place since that time. He could not deny that Haiti was a country of seemingly unending turmoil, a land whose heritage and resources had been exploited and mismanaged by its sons, daughters, and foes alike. But he had seen a dramatic change in world affairs as of late, something that, under the right circumstances, could be taken advantage of to restore the nation to its days of international prominence.

It was all proving to be so easy, he thought. The idea he had come up with was extremely simple at its core, in many ways not much different from that of a seed. In the right environment, a seed took root, tending to grow and flourish if properly nourished. In many ways, ideas mimicked seeds, often starting out as a tiny pip before germinating into something colossal, and with very little nurturing. As a small boy he had been quite fond of the fairytale Jack and the Beanstalk, liking how a very small bean had transformed itself overnight into a thing that stretched up into the clouds where a strange kingdom existed and where incredible riches abounded. Unaware of the power held in his hand, Jack had planted the bean only to find it towering into the heavens the next morning.

Unconsciously, a pompous little smile spread across the Colonel's face as he continued to stare at the framed picture on the wall, a vision of the giant falling to his death coming to mind, the ruler of the kingdom in the sky usurped by the diminutive Jack stealing the golden goose. His plan was rapidly gaining impetus, driven by forces requiring only a minimum of tweaking and tending on his part in order that a pathway to ultimate glory be paved for him. Yes, his beanstalk was now growing swiftly, sending out a multitude of shoots that spiraled and twisted about one another, each and all taking him ever closer to the realm of treasures and power he so desperately sought, a place where he would be the undisputed king, unchallenged by anyone.

Ternier did not perceive any aspects of the world about him as being evil. In much the same way, he did not see himself as being an evil man. It did not matter to him that philosophers and religious scholars alike denounced greed as a wicked human failing, an undesirable flaw in man's inherent makeup. The quest for power was the natural order of life, and wealth translated to power. Like energy and matter, the two were interchangeable and equivalent. Human nature being what it was, greed was a good thing. It tended to motivate humanity, advancing it toward bigger and grander stages of existence where it would otherwise remain stagnant. It was mankind's way, a standard the human race had no trouble conforming to. The fulfillment of greed often remained cloaked under the guise of demagoguery and altruism, false political posturing frequently used in placating the downtrodden. Humanitarian causes were popular these days among democratic superpowers with hidden agendas. From where Ternier stood, democracies were nothing more than hypocrisies, led by big business and the most affluent through the use of lobbyists and special interest groups to get what they wanted.

He saw free elections as shams, designed to delude the masses into thinking they were somehow in control and guiding their own destinies. Things were rarely what they appeared to be. It all boiled down to survival of the fittest, nature's plan to discard the weak and ensure the proliferation of only the strongest among a species. This view was one of the cornerstones of Ternier's personality. If he refrained from going after the potential spoils he envisioned lying before him, there would always be another that would come along and seize what he could have taken himself. Timing was everything and he had to work quickly if his seed was to continue to sprout.

Ternier's smile abruptly disintegrated, turning into a frown as the thought of a seed taking root made him think back to that mysterious cove near Malique where he had almost lost his life many years ago. The place had teemed with plant life, providing a backdrop of beauty unlike any landscape he had ever seen. And it was there that he had his last and only glimpse of the ancient amulet, a treasure in itself. The power of that talisman was something that would have ensured his destiny.

Shortly after his encounter with the cheval in that strange place, he had lost contact with the one and only spy he had planted in Malique. Rumor had it that the man had died at sea, but he could never be sure. In any event, Erzulie had advised him against going back there, believing the cheval to be much too powerful for either of them to confront. Continuing to dwell on the subject, he could not dismiss the possibility that the cheval was now gone and would not return.

On impulse, Ternier took his eyes from the picture on the wall and lowered his gaze to the back of Hennington's head. "Perhaps you can do me a little favor," he said.

"Yes?" Hennington replied hurriedly, eager to please.

Ternier could not help but smile. Hennington's obsequious manner gladdened him to no end. "I would like you to take a trip for me." Pausing for effect, he added, "Have you ever heard of a fishing village called Malique?"

Chapter Eight: An Ailing Captive

Jake was on one knee cradling Myers in his arms. The light in Myer's eyes was fading fast, now faint as a flow of blood black as ebony in the pale moonlight bubbled up from his open mouth. Mat was beside him lending support.

"Promise me!" Myers gasped, choking up more blood and focusing glazed eyes on Jake.

Jake could only nod, not trusting how his own voice would sound.

Myers groped for one of Jake's hands and squeezed, the grip surprisingly hard. "Say it!" he blurted, as if trying to speak from under a column of water. "Promise me!"

"I…I promise," Jake vowed, trying desperately to keep his tone strong. "You have my word."

Said aloud, the words seemed to satisfy Myers, for a smile transcended his face. "You are the big brother I never had," he uttered weakly. With that his grip went slack.

Jake stared dazedly as Myers' head lolled to one side. "No!" he found himself yelling. He glanced quickly at Mat. "We're losing him," he cried. Lowering Myers to the ground, the two men went to work, applying CPR to their fallen comrade. Jake was tenacious, refusing to give up, periodically blowing air into Myers' lungs and spitting away the blood that obstructed his effort.

After a while Mat clutched his shoulder. "He's gone, Jake," he said quietly. "There's nothing more we can do for him."

Extending a hand, Jake ran his fingers over Myers' eyelids, giving him the look of a man sleeping peacefully. Slowly, he became aware of the sporadic gunfire disturbing the night. His M4 lay on the ground next to him and he reached for it, beginning to rise in a semi-crouch.

A hand suddenly clutched his shoulder. "No, Jake!" Mat screamed. "You'll only get yourself killed."

Ignoring Mat's plea, Jake pushed his hand away and began to move forward. He could feel the tears streaming down his face, something he had never let show. They would pay for this. By God, they would pay. The hate he felt was overwhelming, taking on a life of its own and consuming him.

The hold on his shoulder was there again, restraining him, stopping him from doing what had to be done. "Jay Jay!" Mat persisted.

Jake shrugged the hand away a second time, vaguely aware of the name by which Mat addressed him. Mat never called him Jay Jay.

"Wake up, Jay Jay."

Jake reached up, grabbing the throat of the person jostling him and simultaneously pulling the K-Bar from its sheath.

"No, Jay Jay," the voice pleaded, the tone full of fright.

Reality slowly flooded Jake's consciousness as he became aware of Phillipe hovering over him, the boy's arms pulled back to fend off the blade. Lowering the knife, Jake removed his fingers from Phillipe's throat and sat up. Realizing his own cheeks were damp, he took a moment to wipe away the wetness, looking away to cover his embarrassment. "What is it?"

"You were yelling in your sleep," Phillipe said, rubbing his windpipe.

Something bumped the *Angel's* hull just below the bunk upon which Jake rested. Lifting the curtain that draped over the porthole overlooking his bed, Jake brought his face close to the Plexiglas. The head of Achilles poked above the water and stared back at him. A quick peek at his watch told him it was a few minutes past 9:00 a.m., an hour of the morning he rarely slept past.

"Where is everybody?" Jake asked, trying to shake off the remaining grogginess that continued to cling to him like a cloud of mist.

"Zimbola is repairing the damage made by the men who tried to board us," Phillipe said. "Hector guards the man you captured, and the scientists are all ashore with Jacob and the white witch."

Phillipe's use of the last term made Jake look sharply at him. "She's not a witch," he countered in annoyance.

Phillipe appeared puzzled. "If she is not a white witch, then what is she?" the boy asked innocently. "Zimbola tells me only a witch of the vaudun possesses the power each of us saw her use."

"Zimbola is wrong," Jake said quickly, wanting to change the subject. He arose from the bed. "Has our uninvited guest given Hector any trouble?"

When Phillipe did not immediately answer, Jake scrutinized him closely. "Well, has he?"

"The man says we are all dead men."

"Does he now?" Jake could not help but notice Phillipe crinkling his nose. "What?"

"You do not smell very good, Jay Jay."

Jake became aware of an unpleasant odor assaulting his nostrils. He was sweating profusely under the Farmer John wetsuit he still wore, realizing he had failed to remove it the night before. In the limited confines below the trawler's main deck there was little ventilation.

A wry little snicker escaped Jake's lips. "In the Seals, we drank in each other's sweat all the time. It's part of being a soldier." Without warning he reached out and pulled the teenager to him, squeezing him in a bear hug. "Just think of this as part of your training."

Phillipe giggled mirthfully, trying to squirm away, and after a few seconds Jake released the boy. Jake knew Phillipe loved the show of affection he gave him. Growing up on the streets of Port-au-Prince, the Haitian lad had been starved for attention, learning to fend for himself for most of his young life. Jake had changed all that and had adopted the role of a protective older brother for the boy. In taking Phillipe under his wing, he had inadvertently rescued the boy from a life of despondency and crime. And without even realizing it, he had imparted solid core values to the former street urchin. In more ways than one, Jake had become someone Phillipe could look up to, a role model for him to emulate. Phillipe was now under his care and Jake took the responsibility seriously.

"What be all this ruckus?" a deep voice boomed. Zimbola's massive frame spilled into Jake's quarters. The big man rarely smiled, but from the look on his face Jake could tell he was amused by the horseplay that had just ensued.

"Just indoctrinating the lad in the way of the Seals," Jake stated glibly.

"I don't think this boat can handle more than one reekin' like that. What you trying to do, split open her keel?"

"Not the *Angel*, Zimby. Never."

"The good doctor called from the beach. He asks if you can come ashore to speak with him."

"Tell him I'll be there just as soon as I get cleaned up."

Jake took the better part of ten minutes to shower and shave, scrubbing himself down good using some of the *Angel's* limited fresh water supply and also taking the time to wash and rinse off the shorty wetsuit. He found it strange the suit stank the way it did, though he suspected it had something to do with the bioluminescent microorganisms that abounded locally. The suit had obviously picked up substantial amounts of plant and animal life that began to decompose once leaving the water.

As a rule, Jake was very conservative with the vessel's potable water reserves, particularly since uncontaminated drinking water was considered a commodity on the Haitian market, a substance in short supply. But the seemingly endless stream of fresh water cascading down the nearby falls afforded him the luxury of topping off his tanks. He would do that before he left the cove.

After freshening up, Jake used the satellite phone to put in a call to Mat Daniels. He was fortunate enough to get a signal, and Mat answered on the third ring.

"Daniels here."

"Any changes on the local front since I last saw you?"

"Is that you, Jake?"

"Last I looked in the mirror it was."

Mat laughed. "Always the jester. No, nothing's changed, good buddy. What gives?"

"I've got a present for you."

"Oh!"

"Yeah. I think you'll like it. It's the kind of gift you've been looking for."

A moment of silence followed as Mat absorbed this. "Where can I pick it up?"

"Keep your phone handy, Mat. I'll call you later and let you know." With that said, Jake ended the call.

Jake's next course of business was to pay a visit to the man he had captured. Hector appeared bored with the MP-5 straddling his lap as he sat across from the prisoner who lay in a small bunk in the forward part of the vessel. One of the man's ankles was chained to an eyebolt jutting from a bulkhead at the foot of the bed. The man gave Jake a baleful glare as soon as he entered the compartment. In spite of his defiance, the man appeared pale and weak.

"Has our guest been behaving himself?" Jake asked.

Hector shook his head. "According to him, we'll all be dead by tomorrow. He has already promised at least ten different ways we'll be murdered, but I'll avoid elaborating on how he intends to do it."

Leaning on the edge of the bunk, Jake studied the man closely. He had the skin tone and features of a person indigenous to the southern Mediterranean. A dark, close-cropped beard lined the lower part of his face. He was fairly young, no more than twenty-five in Jake's opinion.

"If I were a betting man," Jake said, " I'd lay a thousand to one that sub of yours is operated by Islamic extremists bent on hurting a lot of innocent people."

The words appeared to strike a chord, for the man's eyes flared subtly, just enough for Jake to confirm what he had suspected ever since encountering the submarine. "I suggest you avoid ever playing poker," Jake jeered, "though I doubt such a game would interest you."

The man turned his eyes away and stared at the ceiling in silence. Grahm had treated the man's injury, and from what Jake could see, the wad of gauze wrapped tightly around his right forearm was stained heavily with dried blood where it covered the wound. The man's wet suit jacket had been removed, leaving him bare-chested, and where the man's upper arm was exposed above the dressing, the skin was bloated severely and starting to manifest a greenish tinge. A mild stench hung in the air, making Jake wonder if the odor emanated from the injury or the lower half of the wet suit, which the man still wore.

Jake turned to Hector. "He speaks English, doesn't he?"

"All his threats were in English."

Jake faced the man again. "Knowing what I do of the kind of person you are and the people you represent, I find it strange that you would go out of your way to attempt boarding my vessel." Jake paused, looking for the man's reaction. "The question is, for what purpose?"

Jake's captive continued to ignore him.

"You followed us here…why?"

The man offered nothing, keeping his eyes focused on the ceiling.

"That arm of yours doesn't look too good. Guessing, I'd say the bone is shattered and gangrene is setting in. If we don't do anything about it, you'll probably die. And even if we're able to treat it, you could very well end up losing the arm, anyway."

"I will welcome death," the man suddenly blurted, addressing Jake for the first time. "Allah will embrace me in paradise."

"And I suppose you'll look forward to those seventy-two virgins the mullahs keep promising."

"Yes."

Jake sighed sadly. "Those religious misfits have been conning you all along. I'm told that nowhere in the Koran will you find any such reference. It's just a ploy concocted by radical Muslim clerics to coax guys like you into doing their bidding. I think you'll be greatly disappointed in the afterlife, my friend, but then again, I doubt heaven will be your final destination."

The man abruptly let out a string of gibberish, babbling in a language incomprehensible to Jake. Although he didn't understand the words, he knew it was Arabic, having heard it on numerous occasions during his tour in the Middle East. He could see the man was beginning to sweat heavily and that his eyes were beginning to glaze over.

Reaching out, Jake placed a hand on the man's forehead. Turning, he looked at Hector. "He's burning up." Pondering the situation, he made a decision. "Keep an eye on him while I see about making him healthy again."

Hector shrugged. "Maybe you should save yourself the trouble and just dump him over the side."

"Not on my watch," Jake said, striding from the compartment. Making his way to the main deck, he scanned the water off the starboard side. He was about to call for Achilles when the young dolphin suddenly reared his head above the surface.

"What do you wish of me, Jake Javolyn?" Achilles ululated.

How does he do that? Jake could not help but wonder. "Achilles, I need you to bring Destiny to me. It's very important. Can you do that for me?"

"I will do as you ask, Jake Javolyn," the dolphin replied.

Jake expected the juvenile to turn and head for the beach, but that didn't happen. The albino remained stationary instead, continuing to stare up at him.

After a few seconds, Jake arched a brow. "Achilles?"

"Destiny will be here shortly, Jake Javolyn," Achilles stated.

"Uh, do me a favor, Achilles," Jake said, doing his best to conceal the annoyance he felt.

"What is that favor, Jake Javolyn?"

"I prefer you call me Jay Jay, Achilles, and you don't have to use my name each time you address me."

"As you wish, Jay Jay."

Destiny showed up five minutes later, letting one of the other albinos tow her out to the *Angel*. As she climbed up onto the dive platform, Jake's breath came up short. He could see she was no longer wearing the white full-body wet suit that had fit her like a glove. Also missing were the strange goggles she had worn. Attired only in a skimpy white bikini, her skin had the smooth golden luster of sunlit honey, enhanced all the more by the sheen of water bejeweling her body. Though the girl was tiny, her limbs were long and lean, graced by a muscular suppleness often exhibited by swimmers. A silky mane of glistening black tresses partially hid her face, draping down past both her cheeks and reaching to her waist. Arching her back and grabbing her hair with both hands, she wrung the water from the thick mane, sweeping it back so that it fell to her buttocks. Her eyes lingered on Jake momentarily before speaking. "Achilles said you needed to see me."

"I need a favor of you," Jake answered, fighting back his arousal and nearly croaking out the words. "I need you to heal the man I captured last night. His arm is badly infected, and I think it's broken."

"I'll do what I can," the girl said. Her voice was soft and euphonious, further meliorating her attributes.

Jake led her below deck to where the injured man lay. The man's delirium had now escalated, and his incoherent jabbering had gotten louder. Hector's jaw drooped noticeably as Destiny stepped past him, his gaze befalling the girl as if in worship.

Destiny looked the stricken man over briefly before placing a hand on his brow. The man flinched suddenly, his eyes bulging wide like a person caught in the grip of some unseen force. Letting out a low startled gasp as if in pain, Destiny reeled slightly before regaining control of herself, then placed her free hand on the man's injury. After several seconds, she turned to Jake. "We must place him in the water where the others can help," she said, her tone hinting strain and weariness. "I cannot do this by myself."

Jake looked at Hector. "Give me a hand with this guy."

Moving the man topside proved awkward and cumbersome in the restricted quarters below deck, but after several minutes of struggle they had him on the *Angel's* rear platform. By then Zimbola joined in to assist. Before placing the man in the water, Jake took the time to strap a life vest securely around his torso. The captive seemed suddenly aware of his surroundings, and in his eyes Jake saw the look of a man being led to the executioner's block.

"I go to Allah willingly," the man uttered weakly, staring at Jake as Zimbola lowered him into the water.

"We're not going to drown you," Jake said.

Numerous wakes rippled the water as all the albinos converged toward the *Angel's* stern. One by one, they nosed up to the man on all sides, crowding in and forming a tight circle with Destiny positioned to the man's front. Even Achilles joined the group of adults. Surrounded by the sea mammals, the man looked clearly frightened. Jake could see it in his eyes.

As Jake watched, his captive stiffened noticeably when Destiny placed a hand on the wound. The conjoining of minds did its magic, however, and after a minute the girl lifted her eyes to Jake who continued to gaze down in wonder from the rear platform. "The infection is gone," she said, sighing deeply. "His arm is mending quickly."

Jake smiled and nodded his thanks as Zimbola hauled the man back up onto the platform and sat him down. The Jamaican then peeled off the remaining portion of the man's wet suit, allowing Jake to hose off his charge with fresh water. Once this was done, Jake gave the man a dry pair of coveralls to wear.

Prior to donning the coveralls, the man unwrapped the bloody strip of gauze from his arm and stared incredulously at Destiny's work. The swelling was now completely gone and only a tiny pink scar remained. "What form of…of madness is this?" he stammered, moving his fingers to test them. The full use of his arm was rapidly returning. He looked first at Jake, then eyed the girl with disbelief. His expression slowly hardened into a scowl. "Miracles such as this are not possible among non-believers. This can only be the work of a demon."

"No," Jake corrected. "This is the work of an angel. You should be grateful to her for saving your miserable, worthless life." Jake was suddenly besieged by a brainstorm, a possible way to breach the fanatical mindset of the man. "Could it be that this miracle is a sign from God for you to rethink what those deceitful Islamic mullahs have been preaching to you all along? Did it ever occur to you that this girl is one of God's servants, a messenger sent from heaven to show you the true path to enlightenment?" He let that sink in before continuing. "Look at her helpers. Are they not all white like angels?"

Jake's skewed logic seemed to have the desired impact, for the man seemed to mull his words as he turned back to face the girl in silence.

Even as the man was led away, Jake could see he was in deep thought. With Zimbola's hulking presence discouraging any resistance, the man was taken back to the bunk in the *Angel's* forward section where he was shackled to the bulkhead as before and left under Hector's watchful eye once again.

When Jake went back up on deck, he saw that Destiny had climbed back aboard. She sat at the end of the dive platform with her back to him, her feet dangling in the water and almost touching Achilles. With the exception of only one other dolphin floating next to the juvenile, all the albinos had dispersed to various parts of the cove. Jake identified the second dolphin as Natalie. Through the crystalline water, he could discern the long lateral scar running along her flank.

"It seems I owe all three of you a show of gratitude for saving my life," Jake said, sitting down beside Destiny. He pointed to the scar on his forearm. "This little souvenir could have been much worse, Natalie. You kept that big nasty Mako from having me for lunch."

"Certain things are meant to happen, Jake Javolyn," Natalie trilled back. Her voice had a slightly different pitch than that of Achilles. "There is no need to thank me. My actions on that day ultimately led you here where you were able to bond with Achilles."

"Please call me Jay Jay. All my friends call me…tha…," Jake's words trailed off as he eyed the flustered expression on Destiny's face. She looked deeply troubled, staring down into the water as if seeing something repulsive beneath the surface.

"Why does that man hate you?"

Jake shrugged helplessly. "It's a long story, one you shouldn't concern yourself with."

"I have plenty of time to listen."

Jake studied the girl's face up close. She was a complete mystery to him, her and these extraordinary creatures floating at his feet. "I'll make a deal with you," he offered. "Tell me a few things about yourself and I'll tell you anything you want to know."

"There's not much to tell."

Jake restrained himself from laughing. "On the contrary, pretty damsel, but you're dead wrong on that count. It's not every day I come across a beautiful girl with a remarkable ability to heal life-threatening injuries, a girl who lives with talking white dolphins possessing hands. Either I'm having one incredible lucid dream, or they've got me locked up in some psycho ward where I'm hallucinating all this."

Destiny smiled shyly at Jake's humor. "I can assure you I'm a real person."

"Then tell me how you came to live in this...," Jake looked around to take in his surroundings, "this most unusual place."

The girl swashed the water with her feet. "I was born here."

"You mean right here in this cove?"

"Yes."

"And these dolphins?" Jake looked down at Natalie and Achilles. Both creatures stared back at him intently, seemingly interested in every word he uttered. "How did they come to be here?"

"They were also born here. This is their home."

Jake nodded contemplatively, then glanced around. "A hidden paradise, I'd say. You're lucky to have grown up in so peaceful a setting. Do any others know about this place?"

Destiny seemed to withdraw into an abrupt silence over the question, dropping her eyes reticently to the water.

"I'm sorry," Jake apologized. "You don't have to answer the question if you don't want to."

The girl continued to gaze at the water. "Some of the locals have knowledge of this place, but they understand our need for solitude and leave us alone. With the exception of a few villagers, you and the other men with you are the first outsiders to set foot here ever since I can remember."

"What about Jacob?" Jake asked, spying the Haitian over by the fish pen at the far end of the cove. "How does he fit into all this?"

Destiny followed Jake's gaze. "Jacob raised me."

Jake lifted an eyebrow skeptically. "He's your father?"

The girl shook her head. "No. Jacob is my dear friend and teacher. He taught me everything I know about the world we live in. He saw to my education." She paused momentarily and indicated the albinos. "He educated all of us."

"Jacob seems to be a most extraordinary man. Not your run-of-the-mill fisherman, I'll grant you that. What did he teach you?"

"Lots of things."

"Like what?"

"History, philosophy, languages, geography, mathematics, genet…"

"Whoa! Slow down!" Jake interjected, impressed by the diversity of subject matter. "Did you say mathematics?"

"Yes. Jacob taught us such things as number theory, set theory, geometry, logic, algebra, trigonometry, calculus, and statistics. He's gradually taken us into higher mathematics like differential equations, linear algebra, and topology."

Jake looked dumbfounded. Having earned a college degree in mechanical engineering, he was quite familiar with higher mathematics and knew how convoluted the subject could be to the average person. He especially found it difficult to believe the albinos understood such abstract concepts. Nevertheless, he decided to put what the girl was telling him to the test. Turning to the juvenile, he asked, "Achilles, what is differential calculus?"

"It is a branch of mathematics concerned with studying the rates of change of functions with respect to their variables, Jay Jay," Achilles replied without hesitation.

The quick, unrehearsed response almost caused Jake to fall off the platform. To be sure he wasn't being misled, he tested Achilles again. "What about integral calculus, Achilles? Do you know what that is?"

"Yes, Jay Jay, it is a branch of mathematics that focuses primarily on advanced methods of finding lengths, areas, and volumes of spatial objects."

Jake's head began to spin. "Tell me, Achilles, are you able to solve a differential equation?"

"Yes, Jay Jay. If the equation has a solution, I am able to solve it."

Jake was growing more perplexed by the moment. "But how? Don't you need something to write on in order to do this?" An image of Achilles scribbling out and then reducing an equation in the wet sand lining the cove's shore flashed briefly in his mind.

"No, Jay Jay."

Destiny suddenly chimed in to clear up Jake's bewilderment. "Unlike Jacob or most other humans, Achilles does not require the use of paper or pen to solve a mathematical problem. He's able to perform the calculation in his head."

Jake looked at Natalie. "What about the others? Do they also have this ability?"

"All of the albinos can do it."

Jake was awestruck yet again. "What about you? Can you also do this in your head?"

"In a way, yes."

"I don't understand."

"It's hard to explain. Usually, I see the equations being reduced, but most of the effort is carried out by the others."

"You mean the other albinos?"

"Yes."

Jake shook his head. It was all starting to make sense. It certainly explained why he never witnessed any verbal exchanges between the girl and her companions or between the albinos themselves. "I find this most amazing. You actually see and feel what the others are seeing and feeling?"

"Yes, but it works best when I'm mentally conjoined with them at close quarters. The number of minds involved in the conjoining also makes a difference. I don't know why it works, it just does. Jacob thinks we somehow create a synergy that becomes greater than any one of us. The more of us that are conjoined, the more powerful the effect. But the bond weakens when great distances separate us."

Destiny suddenly grew quiet again, as if wondering how much she should reveal.

Jake sensed she was holding back on something. "So you use this conjoining to heal?" he prodded.

The girl seemed to overcome her reticence. "Yes. But when we're linked this way, we sometimes get insights or visions of things that aren't readily apparent. It's…it's as if we're looking beyond time."

"When did you learn to do this?"

"I've always been able to do this, ever since I can remember. I grew up thinking this was normal, to be able to see and feel what the others were thinking and feeling."

Jake mulled this over, intrigued by it all. "Where are your parents?"

"I never knew my biological father, only my mother. She lives here, too, but she's away."

"She must be a most unusual person to produce a girl like you. When-"

A dark shadow suddenly fell across the platform as a heavy load landed behind Jake and the girl, making Jake look over his shoulder. Zimbola loomed above him. "Excuse me, Jay Jay, but Doctor Grahm grows impatient for your company," the big man reminded him.

Jake realized he had forgotten. "Tell him I'll be with him in a minute." He shifted his gaze back to Destiny. "Can I have a rain check on this conversation?" he said apologetically.

"If you'd like."

"How about you and I have some lunch over by the falls at twelve noon?"

"Alright."

"I've been very selfish asking all the questions and not giving you a chance to ask anything about me," Jake said as he began to rise.

"I already have all I need to know about you, Jay Jay."

Jake was taken back. "How's that?"

Destiny looked out over the water, seeming to grope for the right words. "In healing you, I was given a glimpse of your inner being."

"Now that's a scary thought," Jake chuckled. "There's a lot of junk and loose baggage banging around in there. I'm almost embarrassed to ask what you found."

"You have nothing to be ashamed of."

Jake stood up, suddenly feeling uncomfortable. "See you by the falls at noon," was all he could think to say. With that he dove from the platform and began to swim for the beach. Achilles stayed with him, executing a series of quadruple somersaults on the way in.

Chapter Nine: Keeping Tabs on the Enemy

Franklin Grahm greeted Jake with a warm smile. The scientist was with his two assistants and had various equipment set up close to the base of a steep bluff located at the northern end of the cove. In the deep confines of the gorge, it was here that Grahm would have the best chance of receiving an unobstructed telemetry signal relayed from an orbiting satellite.

"Quite a show you put on last night, my lad," Grahm praised. "I find it rather impressive the way you were able to stop those men from boarding and then destroying your vessel."

Jake's eyes drifted distractedly over the water, locking on the albinos closest to where he stood. He could see that Achilles was still shadowing him. "These dolphins played a large part in preventing a disaster."

"Yes, they did," Grahm effused. "Magnificent creatures they are. This trip proved more fruitful than I'd ever imagined. How's the man you captured doing?"

"Healed," Jake said. "The girl and the dolphins did it. Kept the man from losing his arm, probably saved his life. A severe case of gangrene had already set in."

Grahm shook his head in wonder. "Most amazing."

Jake thought it best to get down to business. "Any feedback from those dolphins?"

The scientist pointed to a computer screen manned by Henderson. "See for yourself," he said ecstatically. "Your idea to fit Hermes with the Dee Bee Tee was a good one."

Looking over Henderson's shoulder, Jake caught a glimpse of a submarine's stern as viewed from behind underwater. Grahm had termed the small metallic device Jake had recovered off the seafloor following his encounter with Natalie as a DBT, a Delphine Biosonar Transmitter. As Jake watched, he realized he was observing the hear-see signals of the two albinos sent out to follow the sub that had attacked them. Remembering what Grahm had told him about the way the device operated, he knew he was not looking at a real-time transmission since the unit could only send a signal when the dolphins breached the ocean surface. "What's their current position?"

Henderson manipulated a few computer keys, then checked the lower part of the screen where several numbers where displayed. "Seventeen degrees, fifty-eight minutes, thirty seconds north latitude, seventy-five degrees, twenty-six minutes, four seconds west longitude," he said, enlarging the global coordinates on the digital monitor.

"Where's that with respect to Navassa Island?" Jake asked.

Henderson changed screens, pulling up a map of the Caribbean. A small dot flickered midway between Kingston, Jamaica, and the tiny teardrop of Navassa. "About twenty nautical miles to the southwest," Henderson said.

This was not where Jake had expected the sub to be, way off the direct route between the cove and Navassa Island. Although this bit of information came as a surprise to him, he refused to let go of his conviction that the sub had tracked them here all the way from Navassa, shadowing them unseen on their tail during the trip. To him, it was simple deduction to conclude a connection between the people manning the sub and the *San Carlo*. This was getting interesting, he thought, Islamic frogmen with hints of Seal-like training at Haiti's doorstep. Mat had said the DHS had reason to believe Al Qaeda was currently operating in the Caribbean and that something was coming down. A partnership between Colombians and Muslim terrorists was something he never would have anticipated, however. The colluding parties had sent the sub after him, of that he was certain. There was no other explanation as to why he would have been followed across the open sea. As far as he could see, his vessel offered no strategic value to these men, nor did Jacob's. And he refused to let himself believe the encounter was purely coincidental. So what was the objective of these men? Had immediate retribution been their goal for

Jake's attack on the Colombians, they could have easily used the sub to ram the *Angel* long before they had reached the Haitian coast. It wasn't adding up. Some key piece of information was missing. It was only after he had repelled the boarding party that they had sought to ram him. That part of the incident made sense to him. He had pissed them off and they had sought revenge. But try as he might, he could not pin down their motive for tailing him to this place.

As Jake pondered all this, the thought that this hideaway was now compromised greatly troubled him. He could not dismiss the possibility that these people would return with vengeance in mind.

Jake became aware of Grahm staring at him. "Something on your mind, lad?"

"I'm trying to figure out why that sub followed us here."

Grahm's brow crinkled briefly. "What makes you think we were followed?"

"Just look at the evidence. We had an encounter with a hostile force in the aftermath of our conflict at Navassa. It's only reasonable to assume that sub was sent by the same people who attacked us. There's just too much coincidence. What I don't get is why they didn't try to even the score long before we got here? We were a sitting duck on the open sea, particularly since we weren't even aware we were being tailed."

Grahm nodded gravely. "I see what you mean. But in science, the explanation that ultimately turns out to be true doesn't always match the one that seems most obvious, no matter how much circumstantial evidence tends to support the initial assumption. Putting it more simply, what sometimes tastes like a rat and smells like a rat doesn't always turn out to be a rat."

"Alright then, give me another possibility."

Grahm suddenly appeared sullen, a look that did not suit his face. Turning in the direction of the waterfall at the far end of the gorge, he remained silent for several seconds before pivoting his head to glimpse the computer screen once again. "Could it be that last night's intruders have an interest in the dolphins as I do, that they came here with the intention of capturing a few of this incredible species? We cannot rule out such a possibility."

As Jake listened, he sensed something in Grahm's manner to suggest this was more than mere speculation. "Who else would know about these dolphins other than those people who tried to blow us up from the air? According to the girl, we're the first outsiders to gain access to this place."

The scientist placed a hand on Jake's shoulder and steered him away from his assistants, walking him towards the water. "I think it's only fair I come clean with you," he said after they had taken half a dozen steps, his voice reduced to a low murmur. "When I gave you my reasons for releasing Natalie back into the wild, I left out something."

Grahm paused, a tinge of anguish in his expression. Jake could see that the doctor was having difficulty in divulging what he was attempting to tell him. "Go on," Jake urged.

"When Natalie was under my care back in Miami, I thought it prudent to keep her amazing attributes under wraps, knowing that if such information ever reached the wrong ears, she could be taken from me and possibly end up under the care of people who would not have her best interests at heart."

Jake could not stop the cynical grin that crossed his face. "You mean like the government."

Jake's utterance caused Grahm to look at him in wonder. "Great guns, my lad, you continually amaze this old scientist. You have a keen perception of the way the world around us works."

"I've been around the block a few times."

Grahm went back to being serious. "Anyway, I felt it important to keep quiet about Natalie's unusual digital extremities and the fact that she could speak fluent English for fear that the government would enter the picture. After all, it was Uncle Sam who was subsidizing the major portion of my research."

"Weren't you concerned that Natalie's abnormal skin tone would draw attention?" Jake interrupted.

Grahm shook his head thoughtfully. "No. Although albino bottlenose dolphins are rare, they're occasionally sighted in the wild. So, the fact that I had one in my laboratory would only have elicited mild curiosity at most. Anyway, in order to protect Natalie, I had conveyed my concerns to her, making her understand that whenever anyone other than myself or my two assistants were near her that it was crucial she never spoke or exhibited her prehensile appendages."

"Did she follow your advice?" Jake asked.

"Yes, she did. She was good at keeping a secret. But in spite of the precautions, I received a visitor one day, a man who claimed he knew all about Natalie's peculiarities and that he was willing to pay big money if I would relinquish her to his care."

"I assume this man was from the government."

"I suppose you could call it that since the military is considered to be a branch of the government. The man was a captain in the U.S. Navy."

This did not surprise Jake. He knew how interested the Navy would be in such a creature. "So what happened next?"

"I told him Natalie wasn't for sale, that she deserved to be free as soon as she was healthy again." Grahm unleashed a huge sigh, a far-off look dominating his face. "In no uncertain terms, he told me I had better reconsider his offer or there'd be hell to pay, that he'd pull the right strings within the government and create all kinds of problems for me."

Jake could almost guess at what those problems would be, but he wanted to hear them anyway. "Like what?"

"Like dry up my funding and discredit my research in the eyes of the scientific community. He even threatened to get me fired from the university. And on top of that, he could have one of the covert branches of government just waltz in and have Natalie taken away on the grounds that she was a potential threat to national security if she ever fell into the wrong hands. He said it'd be a colossal mistake for me to underestimate the amount of clout he could exert."

"How do you suppose this man found out about Natalie?" Jake asked. "Surely you must have your suspicions."

Grahm looked dejected. "I just don't know. Graduate students and a host of other people often visited the lab. Some of them had clearance to use the Mac G4 where most of my files were contained. My staff and I were not the only users of the computer. Though the system was encrypted and secured with special access codes and passwords, a clever hacker might find a way to breach it. There's probably a myriad of possibilities."

Jake said nothing for the moment, mulling this over carefully. "So you think that submarine may have been sent by the government to apprehend Natalie and others like her?"

"I think it would be a mistake to dismiss such a possibility."

"What did you do after this man left?"

"I made hasty arrangements to get Natalie back into the environment where she was first discovered before he could follow up on any of his threats. In less than a day, I had her aboard the university research vessel I always used and sailed for Jamaica. I realized how selfish I'd been, keeping her holed up in the lab far too long in carrying out my research, way past the time she had needed to recuperate from her injuries. I was happy to free her, but I still harbored a strong desire to observe her in the wild, hoping to come across others of her kind." Grahm shook his head glumly. "Unfortunately, my enthusiasm to fulfill this desire seems to have gotten in the way, and now it appears I may have inadvertently compromised the secret of this beautiful sanctuary forever."

Jake studied Grahm's downcast demeanor before commenting. "Would it ease your conscience, professor, if I told you the man I captured is in all likelihood a-"

A loud shout suddenly cut Jake off. "Professor!"

Jake noticed Parker beckoning wildly from a distance. It was only then that he realized just how much ground he and Grahm had covered walking along the water engrossed in heavy conversation.

"What is it?" Grahm yelled back.

"You better come see this. Hurry!"

Grahm and Jake plodded back through the sand at close to a run, finally coming to a halt close behind Henderson again and staring at the picture Parker was pointing to on the laptop screen. The sub had surfaced and was now berthed against the side of a ship. As Jake continued to watch, two men were currently on the sub's deck steadying a rope ladder draped down the ship's side. Above their heads, a man could be seen clambering down the rungs.

"I don't get it," Jake blurted, unable to contain his confusion. He shot a quick glance at Grahm. "If the DBT is designed to catch and record bottlenose dolphin biosonar within a hydrous medium, how is it we're getting a visual of something out of the water?"

Grahm watched in astonishment, the look on his face seeming to mirror Jake's bewilderment. "I have to admit, I've never seen anything like this happen before." He let his eyes follow the imagery on the screen. "But while what we are witnessing is most unusual, I would have to venture it is not altogether impossible," he added after a moment of reflection.

"What are you saying?"

"Perhaps we're seeing a mental recreation of what Hermes' twin sister has observed above the water. By sending out a series of picture-speak signals aimed at her brother, the DBT will pick up the sounds as if they were speak-see signals on the rebound and relay them each time Hermes comes up for air."

"But these albinos don't communicate with each other the way normal bottlenose do," Jake shot back. "They have the ability to see and feel what the others are seeing and feeling."

The marine zoologist appeared dumbstruck, his mouth agape. "How do you know that?"

"Destiny told me."

Grahm hung onto Jake's words as if not believing what he was hearing. "Well, I'll be," he finally said. "If what the girl told you is true, it explains an anomaly I noticed yesterday."

"What's that?"

"On the way back from the island, I had Jeffry drop two hydrophones into the sea to record the acoustical interaction of these creatures," the scientist said, suddenly finding it difficult to contain his growing excitement. "When I failed to get the usual degree of delphine chatter, I thought the units were malfunctioning."

"So you weren't picking up any sounds from the pack."

"I wouldn't go so far as to say that lad, no. Every so often a member of the pod would emit a speak-see pulse in order to scan the surrounding hydrosphere. Probably making sure no pelagic predators were in the immediate vicinity. But the level of noise was far below what I've come to expect over the years."

"Maybe it was the few grays accompanying the pod that emitted the sounds you picked up. From what Destiny tells me, the grays don't have the same abilities as the albinos. It stands to reason that without such unique capabilities, the grays would rely on echolocation and sound-based communication to a much greater degree than the albinos."

Grahm elicited his signature smile once again. "You're close to the mark on that one, lad. We were able to isolate the sounds and identify which member of the pod each emission originated from. While some chatter did come from the albinos, the grays had them beat by at least a factor of ten on that score."

Jake suppressed a smile of his own and let his eyes drift back to the computer screen. Somehow it gave him great comfort in knowing there was some evidence to support what Destiny had revealed to him, even though that evidence was marginal at best. "Know what I think?" he found himself saying, not waiting for an answer. "I think the two albinos trailing that sub are smart enough to comprehend the principle upon which your little contrivance works." He paused, attempting to get a read on how the scientist was taking this.

"Keep going," Grahm encouraged.

"I think they've figured out its shortcomings and found a way to help us back here by using your device in a manner for which it was not originally intended, performing what you described a few moments earlier to reflect conditions out of the water. In the case we are currently observing, Hermes remains quiet, letting his sister, Aphrodite, convey what she has seen in the form of picture-speak signals."

Grahm immediately sobered. "As I've stated before, my lad, you should have been a scientist."

"Maybe now we'll get a clue as to who these people are and what they're up to," Jake said hopefully, returning his eyes to the screen where he observed a second man climbing down the ladder to join the first. Almost immediately, the image began to break up, fading in and out before disappearing completely. "What just happened?" he asked, turning to look at Grahm.

"I suspect the satellite transmitting the signal just passed beyond our line of sight." The scientist lifted his gaze to scan the tiered walls of the chasm towering high above him. "In a place like this, our window of opportunity for receiving signals will be rather short in duration."

Jake directed his next question at Henderson whose fingers flew rapidly over the keyboard. "Has any of this been recorded?"

"It has," Henderson said tartly. "Give me a moment and I'll have it retrieved."

Within the span of a second, Jake found himself observing a replay of what he and Grahm had initially missed during their earlier conversation. Looking upon the aft section of the sub as if he was swimming behind it, he watched as the line of the hull suddenly tilted upward and broke the surface. In moments it plunged downward again in the midst of a billowing wash of whitewater as seen from below. The scene abruptly shifted. With its conning tower and upper deck now perched above the waves, the vessel came into alignment with the stern section of a huge seagoing freighter stacked high with boxlike cargo containers. Jake hoped to catch a glimpse of the letters painted high on the vessel's stern, but the sub's elevated superstructure blocked them from view. A hatch suddenly lifted atop the sub's conning tower and the head of a person abruptly protruded from the opening. Though the individual was too far away for Jake to discern much, it appeared that the person's attention was focused on the ship. The perspective of the ship changed as the sub swung its bow hard to port in a maneuver that drew it alongside the freighter. For one brief instant Jake was able to catch sight of more lettering adorning the ship's port side. Unfortunately, the lettering was presented for too short an interval and at too oblique an angle to be read. Subsequent imagery showed two individuals climbing down from the sub's conning tower onto the deck where they proceeded to grab hold of ropes flung down to them from the ship. Upon securing the ends of the rope to the sub's forward and aft sections, the men then steadied a rope ladder after it unfurled from above. Jake had already seen what came next before the picture broke up and then vanished again.

"Any chance of enlarging some of these images so we can get the name of that ship?" Jake asked, directing the question at Henderson.

The computer whiz turned his head and stared up at Jack as if annoyed by his presence. "Maybe," he spat gruffly. "It may be possible, but it'll take time, and right now I have other things to do."

Jake turned to assess how Grahm was taking this open display of testiness. The scientist gave a lackluster shrug as if to apologize for Henderson's abrading behavior, choosing to remain silent but moving his lips in a quiet gesture, one that conveyed to Jake that his request would be taken care of. Locking eyes once again with the freckled grad student, Jake flashed a congenial smile, fighting back the urge to wring his scrawny neck. "Well, do us all a favor and be sure to let me know if you make any progress in that direction once you get around to it," he said, keeping his tone pleasant. With that, Jake gave Grahm a wink and walked back towards the water.

Chapter Ten: Jacob's Explanation

Jake strolled along the water's edge, deep in thought yet vaguely aware of the proximity of the juvenile albino less than fifteen feet away. He could not get over the exotic lushness of the tiered walls overlooking the white sandy beach. The sand on which he walked had the consistency of fine sugar, and the gorge was like nothing he had ever set eyes on, a place that exerted a profound pull on his soul, its essence seeping into his inner being like twisting, vaporous tendrils drifting on the edges of time and space. He could not explain it. An indefinable, unseen force seemed to play all about him. Like an ethereal cloud of pure energy, it pulsed in measured cadence to the beat of the cosmos, sending out rhythmic vibrations that breathed life into everything within its grasp. There was magic here, a delicately balanced flux between air, water, and earth that seemed to be just as alive as the very flora and fauna it sustained, keeping him in constant awe of this idyllic hideaway.

Inhaling deeply of the smorgasbord of sweet aromas permeating the air, he could not help but wonder if he had found Gaia or Gaia had found him. Either way, he could not shake off the guilt he felt. He had made an assumption, and by doing so, he had unintentionally endangered Destiny and the albinos. Based on Phillipe's run in with the Colombian fishermen along the waterfront back in Port-au-Prince, he knew these men were a bad lot, but then again, they had been drunk at the time. In retrospect, he had no way of knowing the ultimate intentions of the *San Carlo* crew towards the girl and the three dolphins back near Navassa Island. As he continued to walk, the feeling of culpability nagged at him like a deeply embedded thorn. Had he not interfered, the outcome might have been quite different than what had actually ensued, with the girl and her companions still safe, but without the threat of requital that now hung over their heads like a cloud of poisonous gas. In mulling these thoughts, he had no way of determining whether his rashness had been the best course of action, and it was this that troubled him to no end.

The sound of metal grating against sand caused him to break from his reverie, and he lifted his eyes to observe Jacob coming ashore, pulling his small dory up onto the beach. "Good morning," Jake greeted him, managing a smile in spite of the guilt clinging to him.

Jacob regarded him with an intense, calculating air, then glanced at Achilles floating nearby. "You must be a very special person," he said. "Achilles is drawn to you like a hummingbird drawn to the scent of nectar."

Jake's smile turned rueful. "I'm not sure I deserve his friendship. I think I may have put your little realm here in great jeopardy. If the men operating that sub are who I think they are, they or their associates will most likely be back, and if that happens, this peaceful haven of yours may end up becoming a battle zone."

A trace of humor showed in Jacob's face. "Gaia is not my realm. Even though I live here, I do not own it." He glanced around for emphasis. "I, like all the creatures and plants you see about you, belong to her. In any event, Gaia will take care of herself."

Jake was momentarily speechless, unable to immediately respond. The Haitian seemed totally unconcerned with such dark speculation. "Then you are not afraid of what could happen, of what I may have brought upon you, of the possible danger I've put Destiny and these dolphins in?" he finally said, somewhat flabbergasted at Jacob's indifference.

Jacob grew serious. "Fear is like a toxin that can paralyze and poison if you let it. It is good to be aware of the danger it poses, but it cannot harm you if you do not react to it."

This bit of philosophy came as a surprise to Jake, and he studied the Haitian with newfound admiration. He would have expected a man who lived in seclusion the way Jacob did to be especially fearful of the outside world. "Maybe you've never had to deal with the kind of men I'm talking about," he found it necessary to say. "Only through killing is their bloodlust satisfied."

Jacob merely smiled, seemingly unperturbed. "Perhaps that is why Gaia has embraced you. Maybe she has chosen you to defend her."

"Come again?" Jake puzzled, not understanding what he was hearing.

Jacob placed a hand on Jake's shoulder and pointed to Achilles. "Look around you. These unusual creatures are new to this planet, far more sentient in many ways than anything that ever came before them. They are extremely intelligent and very particular about with whom they develop attachments, yet they must sense something unique within you to have chosen you. They have connected with you through Achilles, bonding with you in much the same way they have bonded with Destiny. They are an extension of Gaia." The Haitian looked at Jake closely. "Tell me you have not already felt her pulse as all of us have who dwell in this place, the peace, serenity, and joy of her blessing. Gaia is real. By denying her existence, you will not experience yourself, you will not discover your own pulse."

Jake felt strangely moved by Jacob's words. "What makes this place so different?"

"It is the very soul of this planet, the one refuge uncorrupted by the ravages of man."

Jake looked for outward signs of madness in the person standing before him but could find nothing that would indicate lunacy. Jacob's eyes were bright and alive with intelligence. Here was a man at peace with himself. "How long have you lived here?" Jake found himself asking, wanting to learn more about this strange personage.

"Long enough to know that a change is coming," Jacob said, his manner suddenly light and cheerful.

"What do you mean?"

Jacob smiled cryptically. "Some things are best left unsaid until they actually occur."

Jake could see that Jacob was not the type of man to be pressed. "Destiny tells me you helped raise her," he said, steering the conversation in another direction. "Is your associate you mentioned her mother?"

A moment's hesitation ensued before Jacob answered. "Yes."

"This ability of Destiny to heal, was she born with it?"

"She acquired it from her mother, yes. I'm sure you have also noticed that all the albinos possess such a talent."

Jake shifted his gaze along the gorge above him. "You planted all those fruit trees?"

"Some of them. Most were already here before I came to know this place. Gaia existed long before I was born."

Jake pivoted his head, continuing to scan the layout of the orchards lining the tiered ledges. The intervals between trees seemed to be too uniform to be natural. Seeing this, he posed another question. "Then somebody else must have planted them?"

"Perhaps," Jacob said. "Long before Columbus set foot on these shores, a race of people called the Tainos inhabited this land."

Jake tested the word, rolling it off his tongue. "Tainos, huh! Sounds Spanish." He suddenly realized he had heard the word before, for Phillipe had claimed a portion of his bloodline as belonging to the Tainos based on what his grandmother had led him to believe. Whether this was actually true he had no way of knowing.

Jacob smiled at Jake's ignorance, deciding to give him a condensed history lesson. "The word Taino stems from the Arawak language spoken by the original natives who settled here. The word meant 'men of the good.' The Tainos lived throughout the greater islands of Cuba, Haiti and Puerto Rico and had migrated from South America more than one thousand years before the arrival of Columbus. The culture that developed here in Haiti was said to be the most advanced of their race, and according to early Spanish historians, their population on this island numbered somewhere between three and four million people when Columbus first arrived in fourteen ninety-two."

"Why were they called men of the good?" Jake asked curiously.

"By all accounts, they were a gentle people. Generosity and kindness were dominant values within their culture, a culture that was geared toward a sustainable interaction with the natural surroundings. They had a great respect for nature and reflected this in their ceremonies. Their way of life prescribed a spirituality that cherished their primary food sources, as well as the natural forces of climate, season, and weather. Edible food sources were in abundance back then. The land and nearby seas were rife with plants, fish, and animals. Because the Tainos lived in harmony with a bountiful environment, their core nature was bountiful. Bounties from the earth were to be shared and they strived to feed all the people."

For no particular reason, Jake was greatly fascinated by what Jacob was relating to him. "The way you describe them, they sound like they were a very giving society. What else do you know about them?" he said, ambling leisurely beside Jacob as the Haitian began to move off in the direction of his tiny abode. He could see that Jacob did not mind giving him a history lesson, noting the smile he continued to wear.

"Actually, very little is known about these people, and what I do know about them is based mostly on accounts compiled by historians from the records of early explorers venturing into the Caribbean. I remember reading about entries taken from the ship's log of Columbus during his first voyage into the Americas. Translated into its English equivalent, one quote in particular summed up quite succinctly the way Columbus perceived the Tainos: 'They are so ingenious and free with all they have that no one would believe it who has not seen it; of anything they possess, if it be asked of them, they never say no; on the contrary they invite you to share it and show as much love as if their hearts went with it.'"

"Too bad more people didn't follow their example," Jake said wishfully. "The world would be a much better place."

"To the Spanish, their world was like a tropical paradise," Jacob went on, "a veritable heaven on earth. The Tainos lived in the shadows of a diverse forest so biologically remarkable as to be almost unimaginable to the average person in this day and age. They enjoyed a peaceful way of life that modern anthropologists now call 'ecosystemic'." Jacob stopped walking, stooping to pick up a shell that had washed up on the beach.

"I'm not familiar with the term," Jake said.

Jacob examined the shell momentarily before tossing it back in the water. "Envision a human population living in complete harmony with its environment, an environment where ecological degradation is non-existent, a habitat constantly nurtured and respected by its human counterpart. Now contrast that with the Haiti you see today, a place where extensive pollution, hunger and deforestation abound. In the wake of recent scientific revelations concerning high impact technologies upon the natural world, a culture that could feed several million people without permanently wearing down its surroundings is now viewed as much more practical and far less primitive than the way the first arriving Europeans perceived the Tainos civilization. Comparison of the lifestyle described by the early Spanish chroniclers and today's standard of living of the average Haitian indicates the Tainos were better fed, healthier, and better governed using so-called primitive methods than the modern populations of today. The Tainos lived in small, clean villages of neatly appointed thatch dwellings along coastal regions and inland rivers. They were an ocean-going people who took pride in their courage and navigational skills on the open seas. They visited and traded with one another constantly and fished for countless varieties of fish, turtles, and shellfish. Columbus was frequently astonished to find a lone Tainos fisherman sailing in the open ocean as he made his way among the islands. These people appear to have practiced a rotation method in their agriculture, harvesting nuts, corn, yucca beans, cassava, and other roots, and according to Columbus, they hunted fowl from flocks that darkened the sky. They were a handsome people who had no need of clothing for warmth. Their fondness for bathing was often frowned upon by the Spanish who invoked a royal decree forbidding the practice, thinking it did them much harm." Jacob paused to let Jake absorb all this.

"What ever happened to them?" Jake asked.

Jacob's demeanor suddenly saddened. "Most of them were wiped out. Columbus reduced the Tainos to slavery shortly after his arrival, exploiting them to work the limited number of gold mines that existed within the land. Within a single generation, their population was decimated. A large portion of the Tainos died off through the hardships imposed on them as slaves, while organized massacres and diseases contracted from the Spaniards took its toll on the rest. To the Spaniards, the life of a Taino had little value other than to perform grueling work in the mines. The wanton cruelty and disregard for human life by the fifteenth century Spanish in the conquest of the Indies is darkly legendary, and Taino miners often died of starvation, though food was easily obtainable. By 1515, just twenty-three years after Columbus first set foot on this land, only a few thousand Tainos were left. The genocide of the Tainos was one of the most brutal in history."

"So," Jake said shaking his head, "just as it happened with the Incas and the Aztecs, it was primarily greed which led to their annihilation."

Jacob nodded. "Virtually all expeditions conducted by the European powers of that age were motivated by greed, and Columbus' venture was no different. Columbus was quick to size up the local real estate and its inhabitants, doing it with a banker's eye. He was financed by powerful investors who wanted a return on their investment, and his ship's log betrayed the things he was most interested in finding: a trade route to the East, gold in great quantities, and valuable resources such as slaves, precious woods, and land. It is rather obvious that Haiti satisfied the last two."

Jake hated cruelty in any form, and he wanted to know more. "You mentioned massacres. Why would the Spaniards resort to this if such an act would kill off potential sources of labor for their mines?"

"Such cruelty stems from the type of people who came to the Americas during that era. Columbus brought fifteen hundred men to the Caribbean during his second trip, a mix of adventurers, ex-prisoners, and former soldiers who came seeking their private fortunes. They were transmigrants looking to end their state of poverty, a situation that was widespread in Spain and plagued all social classes within the homeland. Many of this first wave who came here were poor Spanish noblemen with parasitic ways. These men had swords, steel armor, harquebuses, crossbows, trained attack dogs, and cavalry. Haiti rapidly became overrun with a lawless band who increasingly demanded women, took captives by surprise, and announced their hunger for the yellow metal. As a result, the Tainos quickly lost their good will for the Spanish. The first actual clash broke out when a Spanish attack dog killed a Tainos chief. After the chief's subjects retaliated a short time later by killing a few conquistadors, the Spaniards perpetrated a massacre of the local village. The conquistadors enjoyed testing their swords on Tainos flesh, cutting off hands and heads at the slightest offense. Minor skirmishes often broke out and swiftly escalated into pitched battles. Sometimes the Tainos were able to rout Spanish soldiers, but unfortunately, these people ultimately proved to be no match for the cannon, steel swords, horses, and dogs used against them. Retribution became first and foremost on the Spanish agenda, and one by one, the tribal leadership of the Tainos was crushed. The conquistadors were a treacherous lot, often suing for peace just before luring the Tainos into a trap. When the Tainos would put on a large feast following negotiations as a show of good faith, the Spaniards would attack."

Jake continued to walk beside Jacob, mulling the harsh history of this strange land. Something Jacob had said earlier came to mind and he asked another question. "This change you mentioned...the one you believe is coming. Do these dolphins have something to do with it?"

Jacob stopped abruptly, taking in a deep breath. "Mankind has mastered many things. Unfortunately, our species has failed miserably in mastering its own human nature. In general, man has used his abilities incorrectly, causing terrible damage to our world and its inhabitants, destroying more than we are creating. Many want to gain at someone else's expense, often poisoning the planet's air and water just to satisfy their wanton greed. As a species it is obvious we are not fully developed. Some scientists believe man was created to supervise and protect this planet, to take care of this world in this dimension we perceive as reality. One has only to look at history and study the world around us to know that humans have fallen miserably short of this responsibility."

Jake's eyebrows went up at Jacob's reference to this dimension, but he held off asking what he meant. "So where do these dolphins come in?"

"On this planet, high intelligence has evolved in two contemporary life forms, one that lives on land and one that lives in the sea. One of the greatest neurophysiologists of the twentieth century, Dr. John Lilly, argued that dolphin behavior indicates a very intelligent, creative, and self-aware mind at work. He maintained that, compared with humans, dolphins are at least equal or perhaps even greater in intelligence. With humans, tool production and other technological advancements are possible because humans have hands with opposable thumbs and fingers. Assuming that dolphins possess a comparable intelligence with that of man, without such an anatomical feature they cannot build machines even though they are capable of inventing with their minds."

"So with this new breed, you think man no longer has such an advantage?"

Jacob hesitated before answering, staring in the direction of the falls. "Only the test of time will be the judge of that."

Thinking back to some of the things Jacob had mentioned during the fireside discussions the night before, Jake looked behind him to note Achilles and some of the other albinos floating languidly on the water. "You were referring to these dolphins when you spoke of Gaia introducing something else to counter man's destructive tendencies, weren't you?"

Jacob merely smiled, choosing to remain noncommittal.

"Based on what Destiny told me, these albinos are incredibly intelligent, a major jump above your ordinary bottlenose dolphin on the evolutionary scale. From what I can gather, they're capable of communicating with one another without resorting to high-pitched clicks and whistles normally used by cetaceans. Preliminary findings by Dr. Grahm seem to support this. The girl sees and feels everything they see and feel through some kind of mind link. Most scientists refer to this kind of ability as telepathy. A creature that can solve a high order mathematical equation in their head has to be much smarter than even the most intelligent humans."

"I don't profess to know everything about these creatures," Jacob said. "How or why they have come into existence, I do not know. And although I have so far spent twenty-two years of close association with them, I can only speculate about their true purpose on this planet."

"You schooled them, educated them on a wide variety of subjects only a small percentage of human beings will ever get to learn. As far as I can see, there would be no need of such knowledge in a place like this. A man of your apparently exceptional intelligence doesn't strike me as a person who would do this without some purpose in mind. I believe you're holding back on something."

The sigh that escaped Jacob's lips seemed to suggest a great weight being lifted from his shoulders. "Over the years I have devoted a great deal of thought about man's shortcomings, his irresponsible behavior, and I keep coming back to one inescapable conclusion, one logical explanation as to why this occurs in so sentient and intelligent a species."

"What's that?"

"Most human beings are not yet fully developed." Jacob noted the way Jake's face clouded before adding more. "I am referring to the way humans use their brains. The brain of man is comprised of two hemispheres, but only one of these hemispheres typically dominates the thinking and actions of the average person. For most people it is the left side, and though they have developed their left-brain hemisphere to an extraordinary degree, they have not yet learned how to use their right-brain hemisphere effectively to think with and to obtain information that they can use to make better decisions and correct problems."

"I'm not following you."

"Following their biological birth, the average human has spent a lifetime developing the left side of their brain, the part that governs the five physical senses. Unfortunately, it is the right hemisphere that has remained underdeveloped, the part that some scientists believe to be responsible for subjective intuition, extra sensory perception, and precognition. Among other things, there seems to be supporting evidence that the right hemisphere gives us a sense of spirituality. However, to categorize each hemisphere with certain abilities would be a gross oversimplification. But as a species, if we were to learn how to think with the less dominant hemisphere and then act with the more dominant one, we would function in the balanced manner nature intended, not in the unbalanced manner by which we are presently killing one another and destroying our planet. Learning to use the infinite capacity of the less dominant side of the brain to solve problems will help us to know one another better, allowing us to get all we need for ourselves without taking anything from anyone else, without hurting anybody. If used correctly, it will convert our entire planet into the paradise it was intended to be, ultimately ending the desire to fight and kill one another. Before the arrival of the Europeans to this land, I believe the Tainos were well on the road to this type of development."

"I still don't see how this ties in with these dolphins," Jake said.

Jacob noted Jake's perplexity and grinned again. "Unlike the human brain, the two hemispheres of the dolphin brain work independent of each other."

"Dr. Grahm mentioned something about that."

"While scientists like Dr. Grahm have not yet figured out what this means, we cannot rule out the possibility that dolphins are capable of complicated thought well beyond the way humans think, thought that is highly abstract in nature."

"Please go on," Jake encouraged.

"This may take some time," Jacob forewarned, "but if you are willing to listen, I will do my best to explain it."

Jake nodded. "You have my complete and undivided attention." There was something unique and intangible about Jacob's intellect that drew him to the man, something pure and noble.

Jacob stopped walking and sat down in the sand, prompting Jake to do the same. "Maybe our perception of the three-dimensional universe is the result of the way the human nervous system is structured. Perhaps it is merely an illusion, created by some limitation imposed on our consciousness. Maybe there are many more dimensions the human brain is unable to interpret because of this limitation."

Jake sat quietly, taking in the words.

Jacob continued his explanation. "This very limited three-dimensional interpretation by normal humans in this universe may actually be only a very small slice of a much greater reality that is simply beyond the detection of the neural hardware we possess. Recent advances in mathematics pertaining to string, fiber bundle, and group theory seem to support the existence of higher dimensions, giving credence to the supposition that matter is really hyperdimensional in nature. In essence, there may be an infinite number of spatial dimensions, each one vibrating at a different frequency pattern that may be out of phase with this specific universe, or for that matter, any other universe. As such, the dimension we perceive is simply a subspace of a much greater realm. If such a theory is true, the space-time continuum of this universe may be only one of an infinite number of co-existing dimensions that are interconnected via a hyperspatial energy grid." Jacob paused, looking for signs of comprehension in Jake's face.

"I've read about some of these theories," Jake said. "In a roundabout way you're talking about the unified field theory. A physicist by the name of Michio Kaku presented a lot of what you're describing in a book he wrote called Hyperspace. Kaku discussed how mathematical use of higher dimensions provides a logical means for building a model that unifies all the known forces within our universe."

Jacob nodded with eyes widened slightly, apparently surprised at Jake's sagacity. "Yes, that is correct. I, too, have read his work. Assuming there is a cycling of energy between an infinite number of dimensions along this hyperspatial energy grid, different universes could be separated by the specific frequency at which this flowing energy vibrates in space, allowing separate dimensions to simultaneously co-exist within the same three-dimensional space our brains are wired to perceive. It is these specific frequency patterns that determine the parameters through which matter can form and the physics that govern it, and although these different forms of matter do not normally interact, maybe it is possible that strange or unusual circumstances may cause exceptions to this."

It was obvious to Jake that Jacob was laying the foundation for something even more esoteric than what he was presently describing. "Like the formation of interdimensional wormholes or vortexes that might connect with our own space-time subspace?"

"Well, yes, I suppose such anomalies in the fabric of our own space-time can cause such interaction. But what I am about to tell you goes far deeper than that. It is what mystics have affirmed throughout the ages, that human consciousness is not merely a passive perception or awareness of the universe. It is an active force that we can exert upon the universe to affect our individual or, if need be, our collective trajectory through four-dimensional space, assuming we use Einstein's premise that time is the fourth dimension."

"It sounds to me like you're talking about the power of prayer and wishful thinking to affect our destinies," Jake interrupted.

"In a way I am," Jacob asserted. "But as human beings, we tend to identify ourselves with our three-dimensional shadows, namely our bodies, and the matter we perceive around us are actually the projections of energy vibrating at a higher dimension. There is a connectedness. If we start with the assumption that hyperspace in its full context is an infinite-dimensional space, then there are an infinite number of energy projections and sub-projections, each extending or stepping down from a higher to a successively lower dimension. With each step down, something gets left out and is unable to be perceived by the sentient beings within that dimension, and yet those unseen things are very real."

"So, what you're saying is that this realm, this universe, depends on a higher dimension for its very existence."

"Yes." Jacob gave a slight shrug. "The concept is really nothing new. For thousands of years man has conceptualized the existence of a spiritual realm, indoctrinating it into various religious beliefs. But now mathematics and physics seems to be proving that a higher realm actually exists, a realm that theologians have instinctively pondered about throughout history. The mathematical proof of hyperspace corroborates such conviction, revealing to us that the ordinary world around us is only a partial view of reality, a reality that is encompassed by a much richer realm that we cannot normally see."

Jake felt a mild touch of disappointment at what Jacob alluded to, and the tone of his response reflected this. "As sophisticated and scientific as you make it out to be, isn't this simply another view of the supernatural?"

"Yes, but one where consciousness comes into play. You see, consciousness and hyperspace equate to one another in much the same way that matter and energy do. In this day and age, most people accept Einstein's matter-energy equivalence since it has already been proven. Unfortunately, no one has yet solved the unified field theory, and until that happens, there will be no way of showing how consciousness fits into the multi-dimensions of reality."

"You're getting way above this limited human intelligence of mine."

"Throughout the history of physics, scientists have pursued finding a relationship between the forces of nature, attempting to unify them into a singular, all-encompassing force. So far, only four known forces have been discovered - gravity, electromagnetism, and the strong and weak nuclear forces. Isaac Newton unified celestial gravity, the force that keeps the planets in their orbits and binds the galaxy, with the force that makes objects fall here on earth. Later on, James Maxwell unified the various forms of electromagnetism, including electricity, magnetism, and light, into a single, beautiful theory. And very recently, physicists have been able to link electromagnetism with the weak nuclear force responsible for radioactive decay. The strong nuclear force that holds the nucleus of an atom together against electrical repulsion is another force science is on the verge of integrating with these other forces. The biggest hurdle, however, is finding the relationship between gravity and the other known forces. In using fiber bundle theory to unify all these forces, mathematicians may ultimately find that there is another force lurking within the overall scheme of things, one that needs to be considered in order to make a working model of a unified field theory complete."

"And you believe consciousness is that missing force?"

"Yes," Jacob said. "But my viewpoint is only mirroring the same notion of a growing number of eminent physicists and mathematicians who now take the concept very seriously. In using the tools of modern physics, they have come to the conclusion that in attempting to fathom the structure of hyperspace and multiple dimensions they are actually looking at the very structure of the human mind itself. As they delve deeper into the mysteries of the physical universe, matter appears to be taking on mind-like qualities more and more."

Jake frowned heavily. "So in trying to develop a unified theory, these scientists see the human mind as one of the missing pieces of the puzzle, another component comprising the structure of creation?"

A sly, impish grin lit Jacob's face. "In a way, yes, but the human mind is only a small part of it. Sooner or later, it might be mathematically proven that our own minds are actually projections from a much greater mind, a collective mind residing at a higher dimension. Working our way up through successive dimensions, each collective mind can be considered another projection of an even higher mind until the ultimate consciousness is reached. And that is the cosmic mind, the very essence of hyperspace, and the basis of all reality. Most scientists who support this idea believe this collective cosmic mind is actually consciousness acting on itself. The proof of this will most likely happen when a theory is finally derived that simplifies and unites the laws of nature. When this happens, it will lead to major changes in the way we as human beings think."

Jake spotted Achilles near the shoreline watching him, then swung his eyes back to Jacob. "The problem with conceptualizing higher dimensions is that they are impossible for us to visualize."

Jacob gazed idly in the direction of the *Avenging Angel* at anchor. "That is true. In many ways we humans are like blind men trying to conceive the grandeur of a sunset or a clear night sky littered with stars. Though a sentient being with sight may describe them to us, even the most eloquent words will fail to convey the utter beauty of such vistas. But there is a symmetry in using higher dimensions to simplify and merge the laws of nature. It is very much like looking down from the heavens to note that the earth is actually a spheroid rather than a flat surface. Only then does the planet become fully integrated into a coherent three-dimensional picture against the backdrop of space and the other celestial bodies rather than the two-dimensional landscape we normally perceive when standing upon it. By retreating into the abstract domain of mathematics, however, we are at least able to get a shadowy glimpse of higher dimensional space."

"Earlier you mentioned that our perception of the three-dimensional universe all around us may be an illusion concocted by the limitations of our brains. Are you implying that we live in a dream world?"

Jacob sighed even deeper than before. "From the standpoint that we are not seeing the entire fabric of everything that pervades our surroundings, yes. Things are being left out that our brains normally fail to perceive. All our experiences are based on our awareness of both the world in which we live and our inner thoughts and feelings, yet this personal awareness remains mysterious. Though we experience such things as imagination, emotion, creativity, reason, intuition, and instinct on a daily basis, few of us can give a fully satisfying explanation as to what these things are. Within us is a cognizance that goes radically deeper than the thoughts and feelings we usually identify as ourselves. The consciousness that comprises the root of our being is identical with the core of every other being, connecting us with each and all because it is also the root of their existence as well. As human beings we generally fail to grasp this given that we are ordinarily overwhelmed by the intensity of our own senses and our mental interpretation of them. Although modern cultures have instilled in us that mind and intellect are the arbiters of reality, these things have not always enjoyed such high prestige. Older cultures based on spiritual philosophies held different views. A basic tenet of Hindu philosophy, for example, holds that the mind, when unilluminated by the spirit, condemns us to inhabit a largely deceptive self-made world, a realm of illusion. Because most human beings are limited in roughly the same way, these misconceptions and self-imposed restrictions are collective and widespread. In most academic fields of today, the vast majority view consciousness from a materialistic perspective, believing it to be a byproduct of the biochemical and neurological complexity of the brain. In contrast to such narrow thinking, a growing contingent of scholars and scientists studying the subject are amassing a substantial body of evidence that points to a very different conclusion, that there is a grand purposeful design underlying all of creation and that all of existence is permeated by a superior intelligence."

"But it is our five physical senses that gives us a reference," Jake insisted adamantly. "It's hard to deny the validity of what we see."

"I think you will agree that a mirage is not real, yet we see it. And while a hologram appears three-dimensional, we cannot deny that it is actually flat. In a darkened room we may see a twig and mistake it for a snake, but when there is enough light, we realize it was a twig after all. It is the way our brains interpret what we are seeing that determines reality. The world exists for us only when the mind and senses are directed towards it. Once we silence the senses and close our mind to it, we open ourselves to a fuller awareness."

"No offense, but I'm finding it difficult to buy into this argument of yours," Jake persisted.

Jacob gave the impression of a man with limitless patience. "Everything is in the mind. What we experience in dreams can sometimes be taken for reality. During deep sleep when your physical senses are not active, can you prove the reality of this world? After you wake up and another person tells you that the world existed while you slept, can you truly demonstrate that it was real while you dreamt? The life we live and the world we experience are actually based on the thoughts we project. No two lives are the same. Depending on what we see, hear, and feel, a world is created. In order to experience a different reality, we must change our thoughts. In doing this, are we not really creating an illusion that appears real? It is only when we shut down all conscious thoughts that the world we know loses its reality, and that is when our awareness seems to shift to a new dimension."

Something weighed heavily at the back of Jake's mind and instinctually he threw another query at Jacob. "Where do you think the consciousness of these dolphins lies?"

From the look on the Haitian's face, he could tell the man had not expected such a question. Jacob sat quietly for a long moment before answering, and when he finally did, the words came slowly. "I believe they see the world much differently from the way humans do, that their sense of reality is much more profound than what we experience."

Jacob abruptly fell silent, and Jake looked at him closely before pursuing the subject further. "Assuming everything you just described to be true, do you think they can see higher dimensional space?"

"Yes." The word came out of Jacob's mouth as if it was sacred and his face suddenly took on the expression of a man lost in deep thought. "The forerunners of these albinos held a marvelous advantage over the human species by not possessing prehensile extremities."

"How do you mean?"

"Without the ability to build machines, they were able to avoid becoming grounded in materialistic pursuits like most of mankind, allowing them to develop inwardly over the last fifty or sixty million years. It set the stage for the new breed to make the evolutionary transition that would transcend the dimensional gap we humans have trouble getting past. Dolphins were well on the way to learning how to control and repair their energy bodies, the true essence of all sentient beings that pervades the universe and hyperspace. But these new creatures appear to have taken it a step farther, somehow learning to master and draw upon this unseen power rather easily."

Bafflement lifted from Jake's face like fog burning off under a hot sun. "So that explains how these creatures are able to heal others so quickly." He mulled this briefly, then said, "But how do you account for this ability in Destiny? She seems even more adept than the others in this capacity."

"Destiny's mother is endowed with such a gift. Through genetics she has passed this trait onto her daughter."

"Are you telling me Destiny also sees beyond three-dimensional space?"

Once again, Jacob responded slowly. "Destiny is very unique. She may very likely represent a newly evolving class of human with senses that give her the means to interact with the fabric of hyperspace. But her thoughts and emotions are so intertwined with the pod, it would be too difficult to determine if she actually possesses such an ability alone and by herself."

Jake nodded at the logic. "So you're saying she may only see higher dimensions through the minds of the albinos."

"Not exactly. Separately, the consciousness of each of these albinos may not be able to see higher dimensions. But when linked with each other in a kind of synchronous mind meld, they can. It may very well be that only together are they able to achieve such an expanded state of awareness."

"You mean like forming a supermind."

"Very much so."

"But each of these creatures seems to possess their own distinct personality. What you're suggesting sounds as if each of them would lose their individual identities."

"Then you have a good grasp of what I am saying with the exception of one point that seems to be confusing you. True individual identity and the ultimate reality of hyperspace are not separate concepts. Each is something infinitely greater than what we may ordinarily conceptualize, and both are actually one and the same. Yes, on an individual basis each of the albinos is unique in their own right. In much the same way as humans and other sentient beings, each of them is characterized by common yet varying abilities and traits. It is their individual thoughts and skills that give each of them their identity. But in combination they seem to form a synergy that goes well beyond the sum total of their individual skills and abilities. Collectively they are able to forge a state of awareness much greater than any one of them by themselves, and in so doing every one of them has a loss of ego while this is happening. Although hyperspace is theorized to be outside the physical body, the only way of arriving there is to go inside oneself. Only by dissolving the boundary between inner and outer events in a collective manner are they able to view and act upon reality from a single, unified perception."

"And I assume that includes Destiny."

"Yes. Destiny's consciousness, as best I can determine, seems to be the pivotal point about which the delphine minds revolve."

"Which brings you and I back full circle to one of my earlier questions. But I'll rephrase it. What do you think is the purpose of these creatures?"

Jacob grabbed a handful of sand and let it spill from between his fingers as he pondered the question. "I believe the history of this planet is really an evolution of consciousness. If we chart this evolution, we see a tree with increasingly complex life forms coming into physical being and branching out in order to express more fully the consciousness behind existence itself. Perhaps the true definition of life is the physical linkage to its energy body residing in higher dimensions. As you look around this cove it is quite evident that a new species has emerged and, in the face of the dominant life form on this earth, is asserting its right to live. In the process of doing this, it is awakening to its cosmic calling and is mobilizing to resist the intelligence gone wild of the biggest threat to this planet, the irrationality of the Homo sapien. The disease called humankind, in all its combative, ego-oriented, divisive, exploitive, and technological madness, has brought such pressure to bear on nature that the life force behind creation has brought a higher life form onto the planet to save it. While mankind threatens all life and unconsciously is bent on self-destruction through its materialistic addictions and the unseen effects of these addictions on the biosphere, the emerging species is life-embracing and seeks to live in harmony with the dominant species, guiding it toward a collective change in its cultures, transforming its present temperament and showing it how to live in balance with the living world. In essence, the collective exertion of consciousness by these creatures will become an active force that can be used to alter what may appear to be our irrevocable destiny, bringing forth a new order founded on love and wisdom."

Jake found himself strangely touched by Jacob's words, sitting quietly and staring out over the water for a long moment. "Then you feel that these creatures are not here to replace man?" he finally asked.

"That may or may not be. As I said before, only the test of time will prove whether my assessment is right or wrong."

Jake kept looking for a contradiction to some of the things Jacob had mentioned and he suddenly thought he had found one. "What about the Gaia Hypothesis? How does it tie in with hyperspace?"

"Just think of it as another aspect of higher-dimensional consciousness, one that embodies this planet and all living things on it as being one single organism, a projection of a collective intelligence residing in hyperspace."

Jake struck again. "Why have you tutored these dolphins in so much knowledge? What use will mathematics be to them in a place like this?"

"In order for them to transform the conscious state of the human species they must be enlightened about the world humankind dominates. If they are to understand the underlying nature of man and the way he thinks, it is necessary for them to study the history of this planet and the foundations of all knowledge acquired by him, the very extensions of his mind. Are not such things as physics, philosophy, and mathematics conscious interpretations by man of the world in which he dwells? Whether or not there is any fundamental truth in these subjects, they are still creations of his own awareness and are therefore his reality."

For some inexplicable reason Jake found himself growing impatient. "Is Destiny to be a key player in all of this?"

Jacob scooped up another handful of sand and let a stream of grains drop back onto the beach slowly. "She is the bridge between the two species, the salvation of both."

"I'm not following you."

Jacob brushed off his hands and stood up, staring back down at Jake with eyes that seemed to bear the weight of the world. "Without her, everything we know will cease to exist."

Chapter Eleven: Behind the Waterfall

At precisely 12 noon, Jake stood near the base of the waterfall awaiting Destiny. Phillipe had recently taken him ashore in the skiff, dropping him off with a tiny charcoal hibachi, a pot full of fresh water, a few dinner plates, and a small ice chest packed with various provisions. Already he had the coals on the hibachi burning and the pot of water atop it close to a boil.

Forty minutes earlier, Achilles had towed him out beyond the outside reef and, using his cetacean biosonar, helped him locate and then retrieve the 9mm Colt 633HB submachine pistol he had removed from the man he had captured. During the short excursion, several other albinos had accompanied him, including Hercules. The weapon had lodged among some elkhorn coral at the base of a large coral head, and it was there that Jake had spotted the antennae of three medium-size lobsters protruding from a crevice. Wearing only a bathing suit, his K-bar, mask, fins, and snorkel, he had reached in and snared the prizes one at a time, stuffing them into the catch bag strapped to his waist. Now as he waited for the girl, he had the lobster tails laid out side by side on a plate in preparation for boiling them.

As Jake scanned his surroundings looking for the girl, something abruptly broke the water's surface close to the beach, quickly followed by more than a dozen sleek objects. All of the dolphins within the cove were there floating before him, including the previously injured grays. Rising within their midst, Destiny's head suddenly poked above the ripples, her black mane shimmering in the sunlight. Jake stared in astonishment as the girl waded gracefully ashore, her slim figure glistening with beaded water clinging to golden silken skin. It was only a few minutes ago that he had observed the entire pod floating and frolicking at the cove's north end, a distance of perhaps sixteen hundred feet from where he now stood. Although he had no way of knowing for sure, he was almost certain the girl had traversed the entire stretch underwater, staying submerged with the group during the time it took them to reach the falls.

"I'm glad you could make it," Jake said happily, unable to pull his eyes from such a vision of innocence and beauty. He had to speak loudly for his voice to carry above the thundering water. "I hope you like boiled lobster tails."

Destiny smiled demurely, arching her back and wringing the water from her hair in the same manner Jake had seen her do before. "Lobster is my favorite seafood," she murmured, walking up the sandy incline.

Pleased with the girl's response, Jake dropped the tails in the pot, which was now at a full boil. Reaching behind a nearby rock, he pulled a small bouquet of wildflowers from where they lay hidden. "Please accept these as a small token of my appreciation for what you did this morning."

Destiny stared at the flowers briefly before lowering her eyes. "Doing what I did does not merit a reward," she demurred. With her naturally soft mellifluous voice, Jake barely heard her above the roar of the water.

"Helping others always merits a reward," Jake countered, placing the flowers in her hands.

Destiny turned and looked back at the dolphins watching them. She regarded the creatures for several moments before pivoting round to face Jake again. "I was only doing what I am meant to do, just as you are doing what you are meant to do. Each of us has a responsibility to fulfill."

The girl's response caused Jake to scrutinize her closely. There was something in her expression just below the surface. "And what am I meant to do?" he asked, completely mystified.

Destiny held his gaze, staring searchingly up at him before replying. "You are meant to protect. I would think that deep down you already know that."

Jake felt his jaw go slack and he quickly caught himself. Though well intentioned, the girl's words brought back a painful memory. "Your perception of me is all wrong," he said uneasily, looking away to conceal the guilt he felt. "I've already failed in that department."

The sound of the pounding water seemed to suddenly recede, and for an awkward moment Jake found himself with nothing else to say. He could feel the girl's eyes boring into him as if probing for something. "We all carry pain," she finally said, placing a hand on his shoulder. "Pain is joy turned upside down, inside out. Both are our companions, but we are truly in harmony with our purpose when we experience an inner state of joy. Certainly, a man like you is no stranger to such a state."

Jake was amazed by the girl's depth of insight. He would never have expected something so profound coming from someone seemingly so sheltered from the harshness of the outside world. "I know the life I prefer to live, if that's what you mean," he replied, turning back to face her.

"Why don't we eat," she suggested, her face lighting up in a smile. She dropped down and sat cross-legged on the blanket Jake had spread out on the sand prior to her arrival, placing the flowers off to one side. "I have something I want you to see, but not until we've eaten."

"What's that?" Jake asked curiously.

Destiny became solemn. "Some things have to be seen and felt rather than told. You'll find out soon enough."

Jake nodded slowly, studying her closely to gather the meaning behind the words. Destiny's large brown eyes held the same inscrutable quality as the albinos, though he sensed something troubling her just below the surface. "Alright," he said. "I can wait."

It didn't take long for the outer chitinous layers covering the lobster tails to turn red and swell as the succulent underlying meat began to cook. Both Jake and Destiny dug in, dining on the tasty meal with gusto and washing it down with several cans of coke from the ice chest. Driven by hunger, conversation between the two was kept light. All the while the dolphins stayed close, watching the two of them with those frozen smiles.

Finally, Destiny stood up and looked down at Jake, her expression solemn once again. "There is a hidden cavern behind this waterfall," she said. "Let me show you what I've discovered." With that, she turned and strode toward the nearby rocks.

Suddenly intrigued, Jake rose up quickly and followed. With surprising agility, Destiny worked her way up a craggy wall, climbing onto a stone ledge that wound behind the plunging water. The roar of the falls became deafening as Jake moved along the same path. Moss clung to the rock in many places, making the going slippery and treacherous, particularly where handholds and toeholds had to be negotiated. Jake was astonished at how easily the girl handled the difficult climb, displaying the nimbleness and balance of a mountain goat and showing no fear at all.

Pulling himself forward, Jake became aware that Destiny had vanished around an outcropping jutting close to the opaque curtain of dancing water. Turning the corner, a dark recess in the rock became visible, yawning wide and revealing only shadows in the subdued light penetrating the waterfall. As his eyes adjusted to the semi-darkness, he caught sight of the girl further back within the confines. She was hunkered down, removing something from a box stationed along one wall. A small burst of flame suddenly erupted, and he realized Destiny had struck a match, which she then used to ignite the head of a torch protruding from a nearby crevice. Grabbing the handle of the torch, she dislodged it and advanced deeper into the cavern, casting an eerie flickering light on the cavern walls as she went.

An assortment of artifacts became visible to Jake as Destiny led him further back, all of them situated along the cavern floor on both sides. Walking behind the girl, he noticed dozens of pottery vessels and small wooden carvings adorning the base of each wall. Destiny stopped momentarily to point something out. The rock walls to each side rose higher here, and as Jake looked at what she was indicating, he recognized the narrow face of a Spanish conquistador peering out from beneath a metal helmet.

Destiny turned to gauge his expression. "It's one of several murals within this cave," she shouted, her words almost drowned out by the thunder of the falls as they echoed within the chamber. "It shows the first contacts between the Spaniards and the people that inhabited this land back in the fifteenth century."

Jake nodded, letting his eyes sweep the full limits of the painting, which stood nearly eighteen feet high. "Jacob gave me a history lesson about the locals from that era," he shouted back, continuing to study the layout of the mural. In the background behind the peering Spaniard, the painting showed a galleon at anchor and a scene of the Tainos giving offerings of bread to men with beards.

Moving deeper into the cavern, Destiny rounded a bend and brought Jake to another painting, this one larger than the first. It depicted a heavy wooden beam supported by timber columns on each end. Suspended from the beam were more than a dozen naked men and women hung by the neck, their arms tied behind their backs. Off to one side, two large mastiffs were shown tearing apart another naked man while several armored soldiers looked on. Destiny's torch revealed other inhumane horrors as she traversed the mural, and although Jake had been previously apprised of such horrors by Jacob, the skill of the unknown artist seemed to bring life to the images, making them far more revolting than anything the Haitian had described. It was as if Jake was observing scenes from hell. Bearded Spaniards armed with lances were portrayed chasing a band of Tainos through a forest. A succession of montages revealed how these men used swords to lop off various body parts of their captives. Decapitations and other grisly examples of human depravity were made all too real.

Destiny continued to lead Jake deeper into the cave, her torch now showing another mural, this one showing a cluster of Spanish galleons grouped tightly together in a pristine bay with boatloads of men coming ashore and forming a tightly packed river of humanity venturing inland. Further on, Jake perceived what were supposedly the roads to the mines, appearing like ant hills with an incessant march of new world arrivals prodding along captured natives burdened with heavy loads on their backs. A blow-up of several Taino slaves toiling under the whip of a nearby Spaniard in what seemed to be a mine came into view under the flickering light, their bodies severely emaciated from grueling work and starvation. Another picture showed several natives being burned to death as other Tainos were forced to witness the execution under the watchful eyes of armed conquistadors. Jake was observing human suffering at its peak, and it both sickened and enraged him.

As Jake moved still farther into the cavern, the sequence of horrors finally ended. Destiny slowed and turned toward Jake, her eyes reflecting a subdued mournfulness under the glow of the torch. "I grew up with these paintings," she said pensively. Where they now stood, the roar of the falls was much less severe, and Jake could hear her more clearly. "I rarely come in here anymore, but when I do, I usually avoid looking at what's shown on these walls. Both Jacob and my mother don't think it's very healthy for me to see what atrocities men are capable of-" Her voice suddenly broke and it took her a moment to gather herself. "-of... of what men will sometimes do to their fellow man."

Destiny paused again, as if searching for the right words, and Jake could see that she was fighting back a tear. "But while these murals show a hopelessness, the person that painted them seems to have seen something in the future that gives hope."

Jake saw nothing in the paintings that suggested hope of any kind. All he saw was bloodlust and greed, the victimization of a gentle and giving nation. The brush strokes of the unknown artist depicted a segment of mankind at its absolute worst. He looked closely at the girl, trying to comprehend her meaning. "If hope is reflected somewhere in these paintings, please point it out to me," he said gently. "I just don't see it."

"Come," Destiny urged, her voice suddenly taking on a strange cryptic tone. "There's more for you to see."

Destiny lifted the torch and began walking again, taking Jake still farther into the dark recesses. The cave narrowed a short distance beyond, and under the torchlight he made out a jumble of fallen rock. The girl stepped carefully between some boulders and slipped sideways into a fissure, seeming to disappear, and leaving Jake in near darkness. Jake realized her smaller frame worked to her advantage in the reduced confines and he had difficulty in following, struggling to squeeze his body through the tight opening. Once through, the cave widened to a width of about four feet, and Destiny stood awaiting him.

Jake discerned a narrow passageway with a series of steps that appeared to have been carved in the rock. The passageway rose sharply upward. With a barrier of rock now behind them, the din of the falls was now much quieter, reduced to a dull susurration that became subordinate to the sound of dripping water emanating from somewhere close by.

As Jake stepped up to the girl, she abruptly turned and led the way up the stone stairway. The climb was short, and moments later they emerged onto a landing. Destiny swung the torch around her to indicate the new surroundings. They were standing near the center of a fairly large room with smooth walls, ceiling, and floor. The torch wasn't burning as brightly as it had before, leaving most of the room in shadow, but from what Jake could see the chamber appeared to be a perfect square. Like the corridor they had just ascended, it was too smooth and uniform in configuration to have formed naturally. He assumed it to be man-made, chiseled out of solid rock.

"About five years ago, this extension of the cave became accessible after a section of rock at the bottom of the stairway collapsed," Destiny said, pointing to the top of the steps Jake had just negotiated. "What I'm about to show you came as a great surprise when I first discovered them."

Extending the torch off to one side, Destiny walked up to one of the rock walls, bringing light to bear on its surface. Jake judged the wall to be about twelve feet high and about twenty feet long. A mural covered its entire surface and depicted on it was a woman in a storm-tossed sea, a cascade of whitewater rushing toward her as a towering wave crested nearby. The woman clung to the dorsal fin of a gray bottlenose dolphin to keep from going under, her face raised toward the heavens and clearly showing anguish as a jagged streak of lightning struck the water just behind her. A tangle of thin luminescent tentacles entwined both the woman and the creature supporting her, raising a series of heavy red welts on the woman's exposed skin. As if viewed through the glass of an aquarium, the scene gave perspective to the ocean below, revealing the source of the tentacles. A cluster of strange looking oblates floated just below the surface, and as Jake studied the painting, he noticed the distinct bulge of the woman's belly.

Destiny held the torch steady for several moments, giving Jake the time to take in all the details of the artistic work. Then without saying anything, she moved counterclockwise down the length of the mural to the adjacent wall where another scene had been painted. This one showed the same woman cradling a newborn infant in her arms as she stood waist-deep in water. Next to her floated a gray bottlenose with a newborn of its own, the calf completely white and focusing its gaze on the human child. In the background, a waterfall could be seen gushing a stream of whitewater emanating from the side of a steep chasm. From the perspective of the painting, the scene was one from the cove, the place Jacob referred to as Gaia.

Continuing on to the third wall, Destiny revealed yet another painting under the glow of her torch. A pod of six albino bottlenose dolphins charged through the sea. At the pod's center was another albino, considerably larger than the others, and riding on its back just forward of its dorsal fin was a girl. The girl was hunched forward and attired in an all-white body suit, her coal-black hair shimmering under a dazzling sun and billowing backward as if windswept. Jake immediately recognized the girl in the painting to be Destiny.

Stopping short of the fourth and last wall, Destiny seemed hesitant to move on, speaking for the first time in several minutes. "When I first saw the painting I'm about to show you, I didn't know what it meant until yesterday."

Jake raised an eyebrow, trying to assess what she was getting at, but as the girl swept the torch toward the final wall it all became clear. The mural displayed what could only be described as a modern-day whirlybird hovering high above several albino dolphins, a dark-haired girl riding the largest one.

Destiny walked the torch off to one side of the mural, shining additional light on something there, and as Jake's eyes found what she wanted him to see, his blood suddenly ran cold. It was a man riding a waverunner. From all appearances, the watercraft looked suspiciously like the model he rode, a Kawasaki STX-12F, and mounted on its forward section was an over-under machine gun combination similar to what Jake had mounted on his own craft. The artist had shown both guns belching lightning directed up at the whirlybird, as if the rider of the waverunner was in pursuit of the helicopter. Although the man firing the machine guns was shown to be too far away to be clearly identified, the way the man was attired, and his choice of personal weapons strapped to his body looked to be exactly the way Jake was normally outfitted when running the Kawasaki.

Jake stared transfixed, knowing it would have been impossible for someone to paint the mural in less than a day. The detail of the artistry was just too precise. As if to confirm this, he ran a finger over the wall's surface, checking to see if any paint came off. Rubbing his thumb and forefinger together and looking closely for any signs of wet paint residue under the torchlight, he determined that the wall was dry.

Destiny finally broke the silence. "When I first saw this painting, I didn't know what to make of it. It wasn't until our encounter with that ship yesterday that I knew the man in this mural was you." She turned to face Jake. "You are the protector, the reason why Achilles has chosen you for bonding."

Jake could only stare back, unable to voice any words.

Chapter Twelve:
Esoteric Art

Hennington was exhausted. After leaving Ternier's compound he had traveled the remainder of the night through the coastal and mountain roads that wound northward from Port-au-Prince. So far the journey had been arduous and painfully slow due to the poor condition of the roads they were forced to negotiate. Using a beat-up jeep provided him by the Colonel, the ride had been uncomfortable and bumpy most of the way once they had left the main thoroughfares of Haiti's largest city. The roads were nearly impassable in numerous locations, covered with heaping amounts of debris from rock falls and mudslides.

Accompanied by the same undercover police previously assigned to both protect and keep watch over him, he couldn't help but feel like a prisoner on a long leash. But he figured that was better than the alternative, and that was ending up in one of Ternier's congested and filthy jail cells harboring the numerous poor souls currently being incarcerated.

Although the early afternoon air was hot and humid, a chill ran through his body at the thought of the shadowy woman that lurked within one of the darkened chambers deep within the prison walls. He fully understood now the source of Ternier's deep-seated depravity, for here was a prime example of the apple never falling far from the tree. The woman was a sorceress and the colonel's biological mother, a highly skilled practitioner of the black arts and the apotheosis of pure wickedness. He was nearly certain the woman was Erzulie, Baby Doc's former voodoo witch.

Sitting in the right front passenger seat of the vehicle, Hennington was jarred again as the driver tore over another pothole in the unpaved road, this one quite deep. The jeep bounced hard and veered momentarily out of control, coming precariously close to the edge of the high mountain road and seemingly about to plunge into a yawning abyss far below. Hennington felt his heart leap into his throat as he stared breathlessly at the dizzy drop lying in wait on his side of the open vehicle. The jeep careened wildly as it teetered for one split second on two wheels, and one of the men in the back seat let out a cry of alarm as the driver fought for steerage. The airborne side of the jeep slammed back down a moment later, and Hennington let out a shallow breath as all four tires found purchase once again.

"You trying to kill us all!" the other man in the back yelled in Creole. "Slow down."

Speechless, the driver could only nod, clearly shaken by the near mishap. He rounded a bend in the dirt road and seconds later the town of Saint-Marc came into view. The town sat on the sea at the base of a large hill where the ruins of an old fortress perched.

Hennington had never much cared for Haiti's fourth largest city, finding the place to be hot, dusty, shadeless, and rather uninteresting, but he also knew the current calm could be deceptive. He found it hard to believe that more than four years earlier anti-government uprisings had stirred most of the city's population of 100,000 to revolt against President Jean-Bertrand Aristide's regime. As he remembered it, opponents of the now ousted Aristide had attacked the main police station, burned down the courthouse and thrown up a maze of blockades to thwart the police from taking back the town. Hundreds of frenzied looters had ransacked shipping containers along the harbor, stripping them of their cargoes and setting the empty containers ablaze.

As Hennington thought about these things the driver descended the steep road, occasionally beeping his horn and screaming obscenities at those who blocked his path, mostly people leading horses, mules, and donkeys laden with various goods and produce. He became aware of the heavy erosion marring the hills and knew that two years earlier, in the aftermath of torrential downpours brought on by a passing tropical storm, heavy mudslides sweeping down from the defoliated slopes had wreaked havoc on some parts of the town, killing at least 1,200 people. Gonaives, an even larger city farther to the north, had fared far worse with about 200,000 of its 250,000 residents rendered homeless in the face of catastrophic flooding and mudslides that left more than 1,500 dead and

900 missing. Decaying corpses had been scattered everywhere. To avoid the spread of cholera and other deadly diseases caused by the human carnage, the surviving locals with the aid of the Red Cross had to gather up the bodies and bury them in mass graves. Hennington could see the changes the disaster had caused since the last time he had visited the area. Many of the structures were either completely destroyed or had become dilapidated shanties, rivaling some of the slums common to Port-au-Prince. As he studied the devastation he realized that the worst damage had been confined to the outskirts of the city. The closer they got to the main part of town, the less evident the destruction became.

Rolling along through the streets in the heart of the city, Hennington became aware of the charred remnants of the police station and courthouse, stark reminders of past political unrest. A short time later the driver pulled up to one of the cantinas along the waterfront and all four men climbed wearily from the jeep.

"This place has the best food and drink in the city," the driver said. "At least it used to be. I haven't been back here in years."

Hennington eyed the cantina's façade with skepticism before entering through the front door. The driver led the way with the other two men following in Hennington's wake. The broker was glad to get a respite from the sweltering heat. Unlike many of the watering holes found in Port-au-Prince, he was amazed to discover the air inside the establishment was cool and provided much relief. This was unusual, particularly since electricity was in short supply. With all of the Haitian cities cut off from the flow of electrical power anywhere from sixteen to twenty-two hours each day, wasting such a scarce resource on air-conditioning was almost unheard of. In some of the more congested shantytowns, going without electricity for days at a time was quite common. In most places that served food and drink, the scant commodity generally went toward the refrigeration of perishables and beverages. He assumed the tavern was run on inverters that converted battery-stored DC power to AC current, and that required a sizable bank of batteries. There was a major shortcoming to such a system, however, if it was to be used on a daily basis. The batteries needed a flow of electricity for recharging at the end of each day, something the nation's power company, Electricity of Haiti, could not provide to a reliable degree mainly because the power generators were always breaking down.

As he looked around, he saw at once that at least a dozen male patrons were clustered at one end of the bar, their faces alive in animated discussion. Curious as to what held everyone's attention, he stepped casually up to the counter off to one side of the crowd and eavesdropped on what was being said.

"-healed my son completely. His paralysis is now a thing of the past and he can walk again." The words were spoken in a maudlin tone by a man with ebony skin and brooding eyes.

"She has healed others suffering the same fate," another man said reverently. "She is a powerful mambo."

"I cannot deny the truth in what you say," a third man agreed, "but I have heard she keeps her face well hidden under a veil. They say she is hideously deformed, that her face would cause most people to run away in fear."

"There is nothing to fear from this woman," the first man stated. "She has brought only good fortune to Malique. All the fishermen who live there continue to fill their boats with fish. They sell their catch here and in Gonaives and are growing rich from it. They are blessed."

"She consorts with sea creatures," another voice piped in. "She uses them in her healing rituals."

"How do you mean?" one of the others asked.

"The people who are the sickest or the most gravely injured are placed in the sea and surrounded by several dolphins which she summons."

"She calls them?"

"No, they just seem to appear without any words being spoken by her."

"You have seen this?"

"Yes. The dolphins are not ordinary dolphins. Their skin is all white. They remind me of angels."

"Too bad this woman did not use her power to keep the mudslides from destroying parts of the city and killing people," someone else interposed.

"Why not just use her vaudun to keep the heavy rains away?" the bartender quipped. "It is the heavy rains that always cause the mudslides, are they not?"

A momentary lull in the discussion ensued as everyone stopped to consider the clever logic. It was the man with the brooding eyes who finally spoke first. "Maybe her vaudun is not strong enough to control the weather."

Several men nodded in agreement but remained silent, seeming content to sip their drinks. Hennington took the opportunity to get the bartender's attention, and it was then that the others became aware of the party of newcomers. Seeking to curry favor with the locals, Hennington ordered a round of drinks for everyone, including the man behind the bar. Alcohol tended to loosen tongues and he wanted to learn more about Malique and this woman.

He hadn't realized how thirsty he was until the barkeep slid a frosty mug of ale before him, and he quickly quaffed in down. It wasn't until his glass was refilled that he struck up a conversation with the man serving him. "How often does the power company provide you with electricity?" he asked nonchalantly, starting out with some small talk to break the ice.

The bartender smiled, presenting a wide gap between his front teeth. "I have no need of electricity from the power company."

"Oh?" Hennington was mildly surprised. "You do not need it to recharge your battery system?"

The proprietor pursed his lips and shook his head. "I have no need of a battery system."

"Then how do you run the air conditioner?"

"Gas powered generator. It gives me all the electricity I need to run everything in here, even the refrigerators."

One of the locals nearest Hennington leaned in close. "You should see the system he has out back. Hydrogen gas powers the generator to produce electricity."

Hennington looked quizzically back at the barkeep. "Really." He removed the white fedora he habitually wore and placed it on the countertop, letting the tavern's cool air wash over his cranium. "Where do you get the hydrogen?"

"That is a secret," the proprietor said evasively.

"Bull!" the man beside Hennington scoffed. "Everyone knows a fisherman from Malique brings you a dozen full cylinders every other day."

Hennington feigned disinterest, directing his eyes to several framed paintings hanging on the wall overlooking the bar. Perhaps this was going to be easier than he had originally anticipated. He did his best to introduce a tinge of boredom in his tone. "Where does this fisherman get the hydrogen?"

"No one knows," the bartender readily offered.

The opening was there and Hennington took it. "I could not help but hear mention of the mambo who lives in Malique. Could it be that she creates the hydrogen gas with her magic?"

The bartender shrugged. "I have considered such a possibility, but what does it matter. I am content to get refilled bottles of the gas as often a supply is available. As long as the generator works, I have no need of the power company's electricity."

Hennington continued to let his eyes wander over the paintings. There was something in the artistry that moved him, something exquisite, and as he stared upon the imagery, some suppressed facet of his inner being seemed to awaken. Oddly, he found himself beginning to reel. Startled by the strangeness of it, he pulled his eyes away nervously like a man looking down from a dizzying height, afraid he might fall if he did not avert his gaze.

Not wanting to appear overly eager for more information on the mambo, Hennington changed the subject. "Where did you get those paintings?" he asked. Guardedly, he let his eyes fall back on the art, unable to look away.

Turning to stare over his shoulder, the proprietor followed Hennington's gaze. "They are beautiful, are they not? I never tire of looking at them."

Hennington was about to ask another question, but his driver suddenly spat up the ale he had been chugging and staggered toward the front entrance. The man didn't look right, holding a hand to his mouth and appearing to choke back a mouthful of bile. An instant later

Ternier's other two thugs bolted for the door, and moments later loud retching could be heard outside the establishment.

Someone further down the bar spoke up. "Looked to me like all three were going to upchuck right on the floor."

The bartender smiled in amusement, staring after the newly arrived patrons who had just fled the premises. "At least they kept it down long enough to leave. I hope they don't leave a puddle outside the door like the last one did. It hurts business."

The man standing next to Hennington stirred. "The paintings also come from Malique."

"Do you know the artist?"

"The artist prefers to remain nameless," the bartender said. "I have tried to get the painter's identity, but even the fisherman who gave me these pictures claims he has no idea who created them."

"He did not offer them for sale?" Hennington queried incredulously.

"No, he said he wanted others to enjoy them. If I agreed to hang them on this wall, he offered them as a gift."

Steeling himself against any more strange stirrings, Hennington studied the artistic work with the critical eye of a connoisseur. He was, after all, a broker by profession and the work of a talented artist always had the potential of fattening his pockets with profits. There was a lucrative international market for Haitian art, and the possibility of having stumbled onto the creations of another Pablo Picasso in the making suddenly crossed his mind. Several of his wealthy clients were art collectors and had a strong fetish for unusual works. He was certain he could make a hefty return on such paintings, particularly if they could be gotten free of charge or next to nothing.

There were three paintings on the wall, all reflecting a theme hovering somewhere between abstractionism and surrealism. From where he stood, it appeared that the unknown artist had used an oil-based paint. Each of the creations depicted a strange mix of geometric shapes, textures, and vivid colors intertwined with a grid of diverging and converging lines seemingly twisting back upon one another in a timeless dance. For some inexplicable reason, he let his eyes settle on the painting in the middle. It held his gaze, and the longer he stared into it, the deeper he was drawn. He could feel himself being transported to another time and place as fragmented imagery was pulled from the depths of his subconscious. A glimpse of his ancestry suddenly flashed before him, and with it a sense of infinity. The sensation of something long forgotten brushed his awareness like a faint puff of air wafting off jasmine blossoms, something obscure and buried deep within him. He tried hard to remember what it was, but it eluded him like a honeybee roving among a field of wildflowers. The feeling intensified, taking hold of him like the embrace of a loving mother.

Something clutched his arm and pulled him back. Hennington became aware of the bartender reaching over the counter and grasping his bicep, a knowing smile on his face. "You were a long way from here a second ago. I have seen others become lost in these paintings when they stare into them."

Hennington felt slightly embarrassed. "Would you consider selling me these paintings? I will pay you well for them."

The bartender's smile quickly faded and became solemn. "I am bound not to sell them. If ever I did, my business arrangement with the fisherman would come to an end. He requires that I keep these paintings on the wall for all to see who come in here, otherwise he will no longer sell me the hydrogen gas."

Hennington nodded at this, wondering why this unknown fisherman would require such an unusual stipulation. Normally he would have been more persistent in trying to acquire items representing a handsome profit, but he let the matter go. There was something purifying to the spirit at having looked upon the masterpieces hanging before him. For some unfathomable reason he felt like a man who had suddenly found himself after being lost for a very long time, but his thoughts were just too jumbled at the moment to give such a notion any credence. With regret, he pulled his eyes from the paintings, avoiding any further entrancement until he could clear his head. Try as he might, he just couldn't seem to grasp the full meaning of the mysterious symbolism exhibited within each picture, something almost...mathematical in context. The idea confounded him. Mathematics had never been a subject he particularly relished, that is, other than using it in calculating net profits and returns on investments.

He finally dismissed such weird musings and directed another question at the bartender. "How far to Malique?"

"Is that where you are headed?" the bartender asked.

"Yes."

"It is about sixteen kilometers up the coast, and only reachable by boat. The road that used to lead to the village was blocked by a mudslide long ago. It has been impassable ever since."

"Do you know where I can charter a boat to take me there?" Hennington inquired further.

The bartender swung his eyes to the man hovering next to him. "Franz here has a boat."

Franz took another sip from his drink before lowering the stein, his manner suddenly all business. "I am not a charter service," he declared.

Hennington peered back at him with the look of a man well accustomed to bargaining. "How much?"

Franz nudged his drained glass toward Hennington. "I do not conduct business over an empty glass."

Hennington pivoted his head back to the bartender. "Another round for everyone," he ordered.

Chapter Thirteen: Trebek's Disturbing Disclosure

The village of Malique finally came into view as the decrepit boat rounded a small headland. As he studied its layout, Hennington was momentarily taken back at how picturesque and peaceful the place was, noting that it did not fit the typical profile of other coastal villages. All of the structures were neat and tidy, with no piles of debris or garbage anywhere in sight. Coconut palms lined the rear of a white sandy beach, and as he looked beyond them he could make out other types of trees rife with fruit. Further upland he noticed hundreds, maybe even thousands of tiny saplings, each growing from a planter, with the planters arranged in uniform rows. His eyes darted to the shoreline. A long wooden pier, apparently in good condition, jutted out into the water with a fleet of fishing boats of varying sizes and shapes tethered to it.

Hennington glanced back at his entourage. He could see that all three men were now fully recovered from the inexplicable sickness that had come upon them earlier on, and as he watched their eyes rove over the village, he noticed they were just as surprised as he. Turning to Franz he said, "Malique appears to be doing exceptionally well for itself."

"It has for many years," Franz replied as he eased back on the throttle and scanned the pier for an empty place where he could disembark his passengers. "It is no doubt the mambo who lives here that brings such good fortune to the villagers."

Hennington decided the time was right to inquire about the man Ternier had instructed him to locate. "Do you know a man by the name of Ronaldo Trebek?"

"He is one of the fishermen who lives here."

"Can you show me where I might find him?"

Franz pointed out a tiny blue house at the north end of the village. "You should find him there. He should be home because his boat is tied alongside the pier." A minute later he dropped Hennington and his party off at the dock.

Various locals gave Hennington and his escort odd stares as they made their way to Trebek's house. As he passed them he nodded out of courtesy and wore a congenial smile, but refrained from stopping and striking up a conversation. The village was fairly small and it did not take him long to walk the short distance to Trebek's house.

The middle-aged man who answered the door was a short blocky individual with a skin tone similar to Hennington's. His eyes widened appreciably when he noticed the three men standing behind the broker. "What do you want?" The man's wariness was readily apparent.

Hennington saw no need to be overly formal and decided to get down to business immediately. "Monsieur Trebek, my name is Chester Hennington, and I am here at the request of Colonel Henri Ternier. May I come in?"

Trebek stood momentarily frozen, his face reflecting indecision over whether or not to slam the door shut. Several seconds passed before his expression abruptly drooped in resignation, and he stepped aside to let Hennington enter. "I will only speak with you," he said. "The others must wait outside."

All three men hesitated, wondering over the wisdom in complying with Trebek's request. Hennington looked back at his escort, his eyes conveying diplomacy. "Perhaps you should abide by this man's wishes if we are to get even a small measure of his cooperation. The Colonel will be very displeased if we do not."

The leader of the group finally acquiesced, nodding with a begrudging scowl.

"There are some chairs out back and an apricot tree ripe for picking," Trebek offered the men. "You may help yourselves to some of the fruit if you wish." With that said, he closed the door.

Trebek gestured for Hennington to sit in one of the three wicker chairs adorning what could pass for a living room. "What is it Ternier wants of me after all these years?"

Hennington removed his hat and placed it on the small table adjoining his chair, then proceeded to mop his brow with the handkerchief he habitually carried. "Before we get to that, please understand that I am simply an emissary sent by Colonel Ternier to obtain certain information. I have nothing personal to gain in coming here."

"So Ternier is a colonel now. The last I remember he was a captain working for Baby Doc Duvalier. His ego and ambition went well together. Both were the size of a full-grown mapou tree."

A shade covering the room's only window kept the home's interior fairly dim, but as Hennington's eyes adjusted to the dim light, he became cognizant of something on the wall facing him that caused him to sit up straighter in his chair. "That is a most unusual painting. I saw several more like it in Saint-Marc." The style was distinct, though the accompanying shapes and use of geometry by the unknown artist depicted something altogether new and different from the other creations. Once again, he could feel himself being drawn irresistibly into the geometric pattern, and he quickly averted his gaze. "Can I trouble you for the name of the artist?"

Trebek appeared annoyed. "Is this what Ternier has sent you to find, the artist behind this painting?"

"No. The Colonel wants to know why you lost contact with him all these years."

Trebek fidgeted slightly and tapped his fingertips together, appearing uncomfortable with the question. "I am no longer the same man I was during Baby Doc's reign. I gave up being a spy long ago. Life has changed for the better here in Malique since those days, and I along with it. My allegiance has shifted to the welfare of the people who live here." Trebek uttered the words like a man ashamed of his past but satisfied with what he'd become.

Inexplicably, Hennington felt invidious of the man. "I have heard much about the good mambo who lives in this village. Perhaps she is the reason behind your change of allegiance."

Trebek stiffened noticeably, his face clouding with cynicism. "If Ternier has sent you to assassinate her, it will be a waste of time. The woman cannot be harmed."

"You have nothing to fear from me. I am not an assassin."

Trebek ignored Hennington's comment. "Amphitrite cured me of a serious illness many years ago. It was she who opened my eyes to what I had become back then. I have changed my deceitful ways ever since."

"That is the mambo's name? Amphitrite?" Hennington paused, mulling the word. "The Colonel claims she is a cheval."

Trebek cast cold eyes on Hennington. "She is no cheval."

"I have heard she keeps her head covered so as not to reveal her face. Could it be that she is cursed with the face of a wild beast?" Like most Haitians, Hennington was not immune to the tenets of voodoo, holding fast to certain beliefs predicated on the folklore that pervaded the land. Back in Port-au-Prince he had gotten a small taste of Erzulie's dark power and was terrified at what an adept of voudun could do. "Is it possible that she is strong enough to keep such a dark spirit from gaining control of her mind, though it may have gotten partial control of her body?"

"I have seen the mambo's face. She is a white woman with kind features."

"Then why does she keep her face hidden?"

"Because most Haitians would perceive a white woman having such powers with mistrust. It is only when she is in view of people not of this village that she covers her features."

Hennington nodded slowly. This confirmed what Ternier had already told him, but he found it necessary to probe a little deeper. "I have been informed that the source of this woman's power is derived from a special charm she wears around her neck."

"What you speak of is an amulet that once belonged to Malique's former mambo. The white woman has taken possession of it and uses it during her curing rituals."

Hennington got right to the point. "The Colonel is very interested in acquiring that amulet. He claims it is an ancient family heirloom, one which the mambo has stolen from him. He has sent me here to get your cooperation in finding a way to take it from this woman."

Trebek stared icily at Hennington as if he were deranged. "What you ask of me is madness. I will not help Ternier."

Hennington had difficulty meeting Trebek's laser-like gaze and quickly turned his eyes away. The thought of having to go back to Erzulie's chamber of horrors sent shivers coursing through his body. Ternier hated failure and would be unforgiving. Trebek was forcing him to use harsh leverage to obtain the man's cooperation. "I think the townspeople would be very displeased to learn you were a spy for the Tonton Makout during Duvalier's rule."

Trebek did not react the way Hennington expected, though his eyes flashed with scalding menace for one fleeting second before subsiding into lugubrious resignation. "Do what you think you must, but I will no longer do Ternier's bidding."

"The Colonel has instructed me to offer you the sum of ten thousand dollars in United States currency for your services."

Trebek's face clouded with insult. "Do not try to entice me with the promise of material gain. That will only work on a selfish person motivated by greed. I no longer have a desire to be self-serving the way men like Ternier allow themselves to be. Over the years I have found that serving others in attaining a better life is much more satisfying and harmonious with who I truly am."

Hennington had trouble believing what he was hearing. In a place like Haiti the amount of incentive Ternier was willing to dole out would greatly improve the standard of living of someone like Trebek. "Are you sure this mambo has not dulled your sensibilities with her vaudun?"

The fisherman's face suddenly appeared ready to erupt with laughter, but then sobered just as quickly. "How can I expect a man like you to understand what this woman has done for the locals, myself included?" He paused wearily and rose from his chair. "She has provided a philosophy that unites all aspects of living. She has given new meaning to our existence."

As Trebek spoke, Hennington's eyes were drawn back to the painting on the wall like iron ingots to a magnet. There it was again, something indecipherable yet not altogether alien. It was almost within his grasp. It…Something loomed over him, blocking his vision, and he abruptly became aware of Trebek looking down at him oddly. "You can tell Ternier I will not help him."

Hennington stared back dazedly as if awakening from a deep sleep. "Where can I find this mambo?"

Trebek assayed him carefully, his expression reflecting indecision. "Attempting to harm her in any way will be foolish," he finally advised. "Go and see for yourself what others have discovered. You will find her with Lucette Baptiste, the wife of Emmanuel Baptiste."

Shards of some old memory surfaced at the mention of the name. Yes, now he remembered. Emmanuel Baptiste had been one of Baby Doc's staunchest enemies, a growing threat to the Duvalier regime of years past by virtue of the substantial public support he had garnered. There were some who believed that Baptiste should have assumed leadership of the floundering country following Duvalier's departure. Since the time of Baby Doc's exile, however, he hadn't heard anything of the man. That is, not until now.

"And where will I find Mademoiselle Baptiste?"

Trebek gave him directions, but before the two men parted company, the fisherman grabbed Hennington's arm. "Do not let yourself be manipulated by Ternier. He is truly an evil man without any chance of redemption. He would have destroyed this village long ago if not for the sudden arrival of the white mambo. She is the reason he will not come here himself. He fears her too much."

Hennington studied Trebek's face with newfound interest. This was something he hadn't known. "Why are you telling me this?"

"Ternier is ambitious. He is a man consumed with a need for power. Under the right circumstances he would seize control of Haiti. If that were to happen, past dictators like Papa Doc and his accursed offspring would appear like saints next to the cruelty Ternier would unleash on his people."

Hennington mulled this for a brief moment before replying. "History has shown that holding onto the reins of power in Haiti for very long is impossible."

"Call it a premonition, but Ternier may prove to be different." Trebek was suddenly radiating fear.

"How?" Hennington asked.

Trebek let go of Hennington's arm and turned away. "I am not proud of the man I used to be. As a member of the Tonton Makout, I used to torture and kill to appease the bloodlust of Baby Doc. Back in those days I had worked with Ternier on several occasions in ridding the young Duvalier of his enemies. Under orders from Baby Doc, we had captured two white men he suspected of being agents of the American Central Intelligence Agency."

Trebek paused and turned back to face Hennington, his expression detached as if seeing something from the distant past. "I never knew a man could take such pleasure in inflicting pain on another the way Ternier did. Under excruciating torture one of these men revealed himself to be a former U.S. bomber pilot and not a CIA agent. With the help of the other man, he had spent the better part of twenty-eight years searching the waters of the Caribbean looking for something very valuable." Trebek expelled a heavy breath as if relieving himself of some oppressive burden. "He had knowledge of a lost H-bomb," he finally blurted, looking gravely at Hennington for his reaction.

Hennington stared back, his mind trying to grasp the full measure of this unexpected information. "Does Ternier have possession of such a weapon?"

"I would only be guessing if I told you he did, but Ternier did learn where it could be found. That is, if what the man told us was true."

"Why was this man searching for an H-bomb?"

Trebek related everything he knew concerning the weapon, appearing not to hold back on anything he could remember. It all came pouring out like a hot, scalding liquid that had been pent up far too long, fragments of information that had been seared into his memory as though by a branding iron. Frank Jameison, a retired lieutenant colonel in the United States Air Force, had eventually died under Ternier's sadistic measures. But before he had expired, he had disclosed a most interesting story. Carrying out a simulated combat mission out of Homestead Air Force Base in Florida, a B-47 bomber under his command had become disabled over the Caribbean after colliding with an F-86 fighter jet in bad weather. The B-47 had quickly lost altitude, and with most of its instruments malfunctioning, the aircraft's crew was forced to fly blind within a cloud-strewn and darkened sky. Completely losing his bearings, Jameison was ultimately forced to ditch the plane into raging seas. The B-47 had flooded rapidly with water, and as it sank it took all those aboard with it, all except Jameison. The bomber had been carrying one of the most powerful nuclear devices of its time, a hydrogen bomb weighing close to four tons. With only an inflatable life vest keeping him afloat, Jameison floundered among tumultuous waves for several hours until a passing boat just happened by and rescued him. The boat's captain was an individual by the name of Mercades Myers, the other white man Ternier had captured and tortured.

As the sole survivor of a serious air crash, Jameison soon found himself under fire from the military. With an impeccable service record suddenly tarnished over losing such valuable military assets, Jameison was forced to resign his commission shortly after the accident. But he would not rest until he located the aircraft again and recovered the bomb. He spent the next twenty-eight years of his life intermittently plying Caribbean waters in search of the downed bomber, often in the company of Myers with whom he had established a lasting friendship. His relentless efforts had eventually paid off, and he was certain he had found the plane's resting place. Misfortune would strike a second time for the man, however. Seeking to garner the resources he would need to retrieve the H-bomb, he had foolishly made a stopover in Haiti, a stopover that quickly led to his demise.

After listening to the tale, Hennington asked, "Where is this bomb to be found?"

"The exact coordinates I cannot remember, but a small island lies nearby. It bears the name Navassa. I have fished near there on several occasions." Trebek looked closely at Hennington. "If Ternier ever gets his hands on that bomb, the Caribbean will never be the same."

Chapter Fourteen: Hennington's Cleansing

Amphitrite was well aware of the visitors long before word of mouth reached her. Though flashes of precognition would still hit her at the oddest times, they did not occur quite as often as they used to. Over the years she had found it difficult to accept such clairvoyance and some of the other unusual powers she possessed as part of the person she had come to be. The trauma of failing to remember her distant past had gradually ebbed away, leaving only a fulfilling contentment in its place. She was satisfied with her current identity, taking immense pleasure in being able to help others. The people needed her. Haiti was a land synonymous with human misery and dreadful poverty, where humanitarian crises consistently abounded, a place where a stable democratic government was about as alien as a blizzard to the beleaguered Caribbean nation.

The past twenty-two years had gone by swiftly in the face of strange happenings that no longer astounded her. It was near the beginning of that wondrous span of time that she had given birth to the only biological child she had knowledge of, a girl she had instinctively named Destiny.

She recalled the late-night hour when Destiny had emerged from her swollen womb more than two decades ago. She had been floating waist-deep within the cove's warm and comforting water as her favorite but faint constellation, Delphinus, made its way across the heavens. Lucette had been there to assist during the miraculous event, acting as midwife, with Jacob pacing nervously along the shoreline. Amphitrite's ever present and faithful companion, Athena, had also been present, giving birth at almost the same moment, spawning a healthy female calf tail-first from her uterus. Amphitrite remembered Jacob's jaw-hanging reaction when he first set eyes on the exotic young albino, its two prehensile extensions not yet fully developed and jutting obtrusively from under its pectoral fins like the wings of a baby raptor. In time the appendages had grown into retractable jointed limbs that folded back covertly into recesses under the lateral fins. At the terminus of each limb was the semblance of something that approximated the hand of a primate, exhibiting four jointed fingers supplemented by an opposable, jointed thumb. As the white dolphin had grown, it had demonstrated the remarkable nimbleness, strength, and dexterity of those amazing appendages.

It had been Jacob who had insisted on the name Natalie for the baby cetacean, this in honor of the actress Natalie Wood who had drowned off California's Santa Catalina Island five years earlier. Half-jokingly, he had said the actress was now reincarnated in the form of a dolphin. Within six months, however, Jacob found it hard to jest when Natalie began to utter her first words, so great was his astonishment. He was again rendered speechless when Destiny began riding Natalie around the cove a short time later.

In the ensuing years, Natalie had matured at a faster rate than what was typical of a bottlenose dolphin, mating and then birthing other albino dolphins with the same attributes she, herself, possessed. The albino twins, Coral and Reef, were the first of her amazing offspring, followed two years later by another set of twins, Hermes and Aphrodite. It was the union of Reef and Aphrodite that produced Hercules, and the subsequent union of Hermes and Coral that sprang forth Apollo and Artemis, the youngest set of twins. Through her telepathic connection with Athena, Amphitrite knew that the birth of twins, particularly albino twins, was extremely rare among dolphins.

Amphitrite was aware of one thing in particular, that the genetic strain of mutated albinos Natalie had birthed only mated with others of their kind, and with the exception of Hercules, always generated mixed genders among the pair of paternal twins they in turn produced. Natalie, however, demonstrated an anomaly altogether different from her direct progeny in that she had the ability to mate with any common male bottlenose dolphin, bearing either one or two calves each time she delivered. In doing this, she was capable of breeding either grays similar to Thetis or albinos like herself, with the resulting offspring being either male or female, or mixed each time she bore twins. This proved to be substantiated after she had birthed her second set of albino twins, Hermes and Aphrodite.

Over the succeeding years, Athena had also stayed busy, producing a succession of calves. Following the birth of Natalie, however, her offspring were always gray and were unable to speak in human languages, although they were all born with the same prehensile appendages as the albinos. Incredibly though, every so often one of these grays would birth or sire an albino. That was one of the strange phenomena that had always puzzled her and Jacob, the fact that Athena seemed no longer capable of breeding any more albinos like Natalie while her succeeding offspring could, even if they mated with a common bottlenose dolphin lacking prehensile appendages. Thetis was one such progeny of Athena's, who in turn had given birth to Achilles. As Amphitrite reflected on these things, she knew that, not including the six white dolphins that helped her here in Malique, there were at least another two dozen albinos currently in existence possessing the same unusual and amazing attributes, all of them descendants of Athena. And greatly exceeding that number was a rapidly growing contingent of grays with those same amazing forelimbs.

Such thoughts paraded through Amphitrite's mind as she watched the small fishing vessel head up the coast toward Gonaives, its passengers glancing back in her direction as though in worship. This was the third such boatload this day. So far, she had cured half a dozen cases of cholera and an assortment of other physical afflictions, with most of her patients ending up teary-eyed and thanking her profusely for taking away their suffering. Word of Malique's benevolent mambo had slowly trickled out over the years, sparking an incessant stream of visitors seeking relief from their ailments. But there was a price for her services. All those cured were required to make an oath vowing to plant saplings given them and to help clean up their towns and cities of garbage and waste. Finally, the rolled-up canvas each was handed upon departure must be displayed in a public place where their neighbors and others could view it.

Amphitrite gazed at the departing vessel as it gained distance from the village. Two of its occupants she had not been able to help. She had long ago learned the mystical powers she and her dolphin retinue wielded were not infallible, that there would be people with corrupted natures that came before her from time to time. Such people, she knew from experience, had naturally dark souls with little hope of redemption. It was as if their own latent evil neutralized Amphitrite's ability to heal.

And for those she was unable to help, she had noticed something they all had in common: they could not gaze upon the dolphin art without becoming ill. But the degree of illness varied from person to person, with some becoming nauseous and suffering a splitting headache, while the most severe cases became debilitated with seething migraines that usually left them writhing and moaning on the ground in excruciating agony. The paintings, she knew, affected each person differently depending on their inner natures, with those she was able to cure experiencing a kind of euphoria whenever they viewed the art. But it seemed those truly harboring evil always became debilitated by some inexplicable malady when their eyes fell upon the enigmatic dolphin creations, and these were the ones that could not be cured.

The veracity of this supposition seemed suddenly in doubt as she recalled her daughter's encounter with the men manning the tuna trawler. Destiny had felt the appalling darkness coming off three of the four men Jake Javolyn had nearly destroyed with the torpedo. Only one had been an innocent, a young man held by the corrupt strands of circumstance ensnaring him. The others, however, had been content with the raw wickedness that lay ingrained within them, and Destiny had sensed those irreversible flames. Yet Destiny had been able to save them, making the decision to intervene and heal their otherwise mortal injuries before escaping the trawler's seine.

The thought caused Amphitrite to think back to the man who had tried to kill her back in the cove years earlier. She was certain the wound the Tonton Makout captain had suffered would have been fatal if not for her intervention. Perhaps the man would have lived anyway, but she could never be sure. She had held steadfast to the belief that her touch had stopped the man's bleeding. Maybe her psychic ability to heal had been stronger then, allowing her to penetrate to the very core of the man's iniquity in order to keep him alive.

It had been just before sunrise when she had slipped quietly from Jacob's cottage while everyone else slept, coming to stand over the trussed up Ternier. To this day she still couldn't explain to herself why she had freed the man from his bonds as he lay moaning incoherently in the sand. Somehow, she had found the strength to drag him into the water, and even now the sheer magnitude of the wickedness that had pulsated from him was strong in her memory. It had been the same kind of evil she had sensed during her encounter with Erzulie, something unforgettable like the hideous stench of decay from some dank, dismal dungeon that lingered on in one's nostrils long after the experience. She had known at once that Ternier was Erzulie's son. Puzzled by her own actions, she had held Ternier's head above the water as Athena towed them both through the cove's narrow inlet and then down the coast. Eventually they had reached the Devil's Horn, and it was there that she had pulled Ternier ashore and left him on the beach. But before leaving, she had scrawled numbers in the hard-packed sand close to where he lay. Strangely, she had known the numbers represented a specific latitude and longitude, the coordinates the Colonel had demanded of her, but for reasons she could not explain, she could not fathom why she was able to remember them so well when she could not recall any of her previous life. There was no need to give the man this information, especially when weighed against the atrocities he had openly confessed. He had killed her crew and left her to die, but even to this day, try as she might she still could not remember any of it. Nevertheless, something within her had compelled her to write those numbers in the sand.

Intuitively she had known Ternier would survive and that someday they would meet again under circumstances that would be potentially much more lethal. Something deep within her caused her to believe this with arrant certainty, its inevitability woven into the fabric of time and space long ago.

The type of people Ternier and Erzulie represented did not repulse Amphitrite. She harbored no enmity toward them. Judging the moral fiber of others was not in her makeup, and although many of the villagers regarded her as an absolute moral authority, she did not see herself this way at all. She sensed only a divine objective in her existence. She was a person whose previous identity had been erased by some unknown force in order to become someone sufficiently able to follow through on a grand and noble cause. If anything was absolute, it was her purpose. For her, compromise was not an option. The plan she was a part of was far reaching in scope, an enterprise that had seemingly and gradually taken shape of its own, and one that was still evolving. In its early stages, Emmanuel had perceived it as being impossible to carry out, an unwinnable scheme that was far too ambitious to succeed. But now even Emmanuel had embraced it, casting aside his own innate skepticism. And though Jacob had played a large role in its development by expanding upon the original rudiments first conceived by the albinos, it was her daughter who was the pivotal point in how it would ultimately play out. Destiny was the key and must be protected at all costs. Inasmuch as it hurt her deeply to know that many dolphin lives had been expended with the effort, primarily at the merciless hands of tuna fishermen, she could not condone her daughter placing herself at risk by coming to the aid of injured cetaceans. Even Athena had concurred with this. But Destiny had her own mind and, try as she might to convince her progeny otherwise, Amphitrite knew that it was a losing battle of wills.

Shifting her thoughts back to the present, Amphitrite watched the approach of the four men, their leader a short pudgy individual adorned in a suit of white linen coated with dust. She had been expecting them, having seen the same exact scene in a dream the night before. From the dream she had learned that the fat little man had been motivated by greed most of his life, a vice that often sprang out of a need to survive in a nation despairing from poverty. And while the man's deeds could be perceived as dark, she sensed the underlying nature of the man to be altogether different. Here was a person trapped by circumstances, a prisoner of himself and those he associated with. Mulling this, she suddenly felt a touch of empathy for the man as he walked to within arms-length of Lucette and Louwanda, each standing resolutely blocking his path.

Amphitrite placed a hand on Lucette's shoulder. "It is all right to let this man pass," she said, letting her eyes drift over the man's clothing. "One of your ancestors was Tainos," Amphitrite found herself telling the man, speaking in French. "Did you know that?"

Hennington gawked back wide-eyed with disbelief. "How could you possibly know that? You are a stranger to me."

"We have met before, although you would not be expected to remember it," she replied loftily. "The existence you have so far lived has not been an easy one, for you have invariably made wrong choices. Not everything in life can be controlled the way we'd like them to be, but we can choose our response to the challenges we face. You are innately flexible, and that has been your strongest suit."

Hennington stared back hard, as if trying to see beyond the veil covering the woman's face. "I do not mean to be impolite, mademoiselle, but I have no idea of what you speak."

"You continue to travel the same path over and over, and in so doing you are constantly disappointed where you end up."

Amphitrite turned her head and studied the men standing behind Hennington, knowing each man carried a concealed handgun. The weaponry did little to mollify the fear registering on their faces. "Those who behave like earthworms should never be surprised when people walk over them." It was a common Haitian proverb. "Seek not destruction but rather seek change and positive ends. Those who have chosen to go against the will of the people, who chose profits over the betterment of human existence, shall soon enough discover their final wages to be oblivion. Do not abuse. Though God may often punish late, he punishes severely."

Amphitrite became conscious of the way Hennington eyed the amulet dangling obtrusively on the outside of her shawl. She had purposely let it be exposed for display before the arrival of these men. "Happiness cannot be bought or sold like goods or services. You cannot give or sell it to a person who lacks it. We often confuse happiness with pleasure, but pleasure is only a shadow of happiness, an illusion that tends to delude the inner being of a person. It is not happiness that belongs to the soul, for the soul itself is happiness, an extension of the Great Creator."

She hesitated briefly, reflecting on the words that automatically flowed from her lips with little thought. Over the years she had grown into the person she had become, and sometimes she found it strange how philosophical she must sound. Nevertheless, she continued to sermonize. "The pursuit of physical gold is for those who as yet are only children, for physical gold is merely an imitation of the true gold. There is a great deal of difference between true and false gold. It is the longing for real gold that causes man to collect the imitation gold. Because gold represents the color of light and spiritual inspiration, man has unconsciously pursued this divine light by seeking an imitation of it much the way a small child satisfies itself by playing with toys. In this way man attempts to gratify this craving of the soul by seeking the false gold, ignorant that the true gold lies like a hidden spark deep within his heart, his innermost being."

Hennington stared as if mesmerized, unable to speak for the moment. His mind tumbled restlessly among a windstorm of human vices suddenly brought before him like molten silver, running and flashing without form, and he was all at once revisiting the painting hanging on the wall in Trebek's house, pulled into its imagery like a man caught in a powerful whirlpool. He tried to focus, but concentration was beyond him. He was spinning shamefully amongst a thousand dizzying liquid drops, each drop representing a virtue of some kind. They streamed by close to his fingertips, only to go racing off before he could grasp them. A perception of humility came and went, followed by sympathy, tolerance, and unselfishness, rising and falling and taking him closer to something even more profound. His fingers abruptly located substance, and he was able to latch onto a single thought, that alchemy was possible here, that the silver might be transformed into something more desirable, something that might make him truly happy.

The intense blue light that burst forth from the amulet made the three men standing behind Hennington shrink back in fright a split second before they raced off in frenzied flight. Amphitrite was only doing what the dream had suggested, and that was helping Hennington find himself. There was something more to be done, however, something else she had seen herself carry out within the dream but did not fully understand, sensing only that the man standing before her would play a significant role in future events. She had long ago learned to trust her dreams implicitly.

She reached forward and lifted the white fedora from Hennington's head, then placed a gloved hand on the man's forehead. "Believe in the healing power of nature as your forefathers did, as your Tainos heritage cries out for you to do. The whole earth is a living organism. Our Mother Earth and all life upon it is a miraculous gift that must be treated with respect and loving care."

Removing the amulet from around her neck, she dangled it before Hennington, who looked uncomprehendingly at the offer. "I bestow this trinket onto you. Take it and do what you must with it." Amphitrite knew the charm held no real power. If anything, it was useful in focusing the strange powers she was able to invoke. In many ways it was nothing more than a placebo, acting only to reinforce the belief of the people in a woman they accepted as a priestess of the vaudun.

Playing Chess

I'm sorry, Jay Jay, but I believe your king has been checkmated once again," Achilles trilled, the dolphin's perpetually smiling face belying the apology.

Jake studied the board with a critical eye, trying to ascertain how his seemingly infallible defense had crumbled so quickly. He considered himself to be an excellent chess player, having taken either second or third place in several tournaments during his college days. But the albino juvenile had apparently found a weakness in his strategy and exploited it rather easily, sacrificing first a knight, then a pawn, and finally his black queen before driving Jake's king into a position of forced mate in six more moves. Throughout the game, each time Jake had moved one of the pieces Achilles had immediately responded with a countermove that appeared to take little effort in thought.

"Showoff!" Jake said, shaking his head in awe.

Achilles slid back into the water, retracting his left prehensile extremity as he did so. He had been using the appendage to move the chess pieces as he lay prone on the edge of the *Angel's* swim platform where he had engaged Jake in the ancient board game.

"Hey, come back here!" Jake protested halfheartedly. "I demand a rematch."

A stifled giggle next to Jake made him turn. "He's already beaten you three games in a row," Destiny reminded him.

"How does he do it?" Jake asked in mock frustration, looking to Destiny for sympathy. "Achilles plays speed chess, something this slow lumbering brain of mine is ill suited for. You should have given me fair warning."

"Achilles is still learning the game," Destiny said, trying hard not to laugh. "Some of the adults are even better players."

"If you're trying to make me feel any better, you're doing a poor job of it," Jake shot back, attempting to keep a straight face but failing. "Where did they learn such advanced play?"

"Jacob taught them the rudiments of the game, but then they just picked up everything else on their own. They're very quick learners."

Jake smiled sheepishly. "And here I thought I was going to show Achilles something new and interesting. Was I playing against Achilles only, or the whole conjoined pod mind?"

"Just Achilles," Destiny said sweetly. "He would never take such unfair advantage of you."

Upon leaving the cave behind the waterfall, Jake and the girl had somehow ended up back at the *Angel* as their conversations roamed over a number of enlivening topics. Though it became quite evident to him that Destiny was exceptionally intelligent and learned in a wide range of subjects, it also became obvious she was in many ways naïve about the true nature of the modern world, having been sheltered from its boundless iniquities her entire life. To him, this was probably the most stimulating facet of her personage, a quality he could grasp, one that he found both refreshing and aglow with unblemished probity, untainted and pure like a drop of distilled honey. Yet she continued to baffle him, making him feel like a man stranded in a dream where nothing made sense, and everything seemed unreal. And while the final painting she had revealed to him back behind the falls only added to his stupefaction, it also increased his sense of wonder over his surroundings, for if he was truly a man trapped in a dream, then nothing should make sense. Expect the unexpected, he had told himself. He did not want it to end.

He thought back to the skirmish at Navassa when he had raced back to the *Angel* to repel the attacking helicopter, fearful of the damage it could do to his crew and beloved boat. One of the albinos had leapt high into the air, snaring within its jaws a grenade dropped from the aircraft before hurling it back the way it had come. The aerial maneuver, he was sure, would have required something more than athletic prowess to pull off in the manner he had witnessed. No, it would have required anticipation at exactly the right moment, almost as if the creature had known in advance not only the destructive potential of the object it had intercepted, but also the precise moment it would be dropped in order for the dolphin to have sufficient preparation in gaining momentum and timing its leap precisely from beneath the water. He was positive something more than dumb luck would have been needed for the albino to do this, and that something was a glimpse of the immediate future, a flash of precognition. Just as the unknown creator of the cave painting had seen the future, so had the dolphin.

Certain of this, Jake had felt a nagging desire to further test the intellect of these unusual white creatures. In a subtle way he had brought out one of the two chess boards he carried aboard his vessel, asking Destiny if Achilles, who had been floating nearby, had ever been introduced to the game.

"I'll let you see for yourself," she had said, her face lighting up in a cryptic smile. Within minutes, the uncanny cleverness of the juvenile became apparent, clearly astounding Jake.

Jake dropped his reflections and brought his eyes to bear on Achilles again as the dolphin headed off to the north end of the cove where other albinos appeared to be gathering. "Where's Achilles going?"

"Art class," Destiny informed him, noting the frown that formed on Jake's features as he turned to face her. "Several times a week each member of the pod creates a work of art."

Jake looked back at the gathering with sudden interest. "Now this I've got to see with my own eyes."

"Come!" Destiny said, slipping gracefully into the water. The head of Hercules suddenly emerged above the surface next to her and she grabbed hold of the giant's dorsal fin, looking back up at Jake expectantly. "Well, are you just going to sit there or are you coming?"

Jake hopped off the platform and moved to the side of Hercules opposite Destiny before latching onto the creature's fin just above the area where Destiny clutched it. He immediately sensed the raw physical strength of the giant as the animal quickly gained speed, something several times more potent than what Achilles was capable of exerting. But this became secondary to the strange and alluring attraction exuded by the girl next to him. Already a strong friendship had grown between them, one that seemed to have existed for many years rather than a single day. Even so, she nevertheless remained a complete mystery to him. As he was pulled along, he held the girl's gaze, her eyes less than a foot away and continually roving over his face, seemingly exploring the depths of his very soul as if she might uncover something altogether new and fascinating. This was a good day, he decided, one worth living. He let his hand slide down the fin until he made contact with Destiny's. Only then did he fully enjoy the ride.

The Telemetry Expert

The telemetry specialist sat at the terminal studying the console as he sipped from a steaming cup of freshly brewed coffee. It was currently several minutes past 7:00 p.m. in Toulouse, France, and he yawned tiredly as he monitored a map of the Caribbean displayed on the computer screen. Under the guise of working later on one of his company assignments, he had stayed at his workstation more than an hour beyond his normal shift, having been given ample incentive to do so. It wasn't every day an unknown benefactor was willing to pay him so handsomely for his services. Though the firm he worked for paid him an impressive salary as it was, he was willing to risk unauthorized use of company resources in furthering his financial objectives, particularly when the money was tax-free and had already been deposited in an offshore bank account he kept in the Cayman Islands. His job description allowed him unlimited access to the hardware and software comprising the computerized system he was presently using.

The Argos system was unique, utilizing both a ground and satellite based network to collect, process and disseminate environmental data from fixed and mobile platforms worldwide. The system had been operational since 1978 and was established under a joint agreement between the Centre National d'Etudes Spatiales, better known as the French Space Agency, and two American agencies: the National Aeronautics and Space Administration (NASA) and the National Oceanic and Atmospheric Administration (NOAA). Operated and managed by Collecte, Localisation, Satellites (CLS), the specialist's employer for the past three years, the system had recently been upgraded with the addition of more advanced computer technology.

The hardware comprising the integrated system was unparalleled in its reach, incorporating well over ten thousand transmitters on a global scale that included a vast network of receiving stations. At the heart of the system were six NOAA series satellites following sun-synchronous, circular polar orbits at an altitude of 850 kilometers. At least two of these satellites were simultaneously in service most of the time, sending information to major processing facilities located in France and the United States. With such a configuration, any location on the planet could receive data from a satellite every six hours. No security clearances were necessary to gain access to the data, which was available commercially. Potential users of this data could readily purchase the necessary equipment from commercial companies for unlimited access to the satellite transmissions. In addition, there were no fees or licenses required by NOAA to receive this data. Archived data was also available from NOAA or various companies that stored it, either processed or in raw form, but acquiring such data usually incurred a reproduction fee.

This knowledge caused the specialist to smile ironically, for if such information were so easily obtainable to anyone who required it, why would some users need him? It was the intermittency of data streams received every six hours from orbiting satellites that created problems for many users, particularly when tracking ground-based signals. This was the area where he held an advantage. From where he sat, he could acquire that same data at any time from linked ground stations all over the globe by using the recent upgrades. And it was this that put his moonlighting services in demand, this, and a unique ability to customize software with programs that gave some users the same advantages he currently enjoyed.

Leaning back in his reclinable chair, he began propping his feet on an adjacent desk, but before he could get comfortable, he became aware of the blip that suddenly began pulsing on the monitor. Abruptly, he sat back up. Shifting his eyes to a corner of the screen, he checked a readout that identified the modulated frequency of the signature signal he was scanning for. Satisfied that it was the correct one, he noted the coordinates that pinpointed the source of the transmission. The incoming signal, he knew, was almost real-time in nature and that the actual position of the source would be within 1,000 meters of the coordinates shown on the screen. Such a discrepancy was typical when tracking signals emanating close to the equator where the Doppler effect would be more pronounced. Hitting a few keys, he homed in on the transmission's origination point by reducing the map scale, then changed perspectives, giving him a close-up view of that part of the earth as seen from one of the satellites at that moment. He knew that at least one of the satellites orbiting near the planet's North Pole had to be in the right position to receive a signal.

An oblique panorama of the West Indies suddenly sprang into view. He immediately recognized the northern ends of Cuba and the Island of Dominica dominating the major portion of the picture screen. For the most part, the landmasses and seas were relatively unobstructed by any significant cloud cover. Increasing the magnification by a factor of ten, he zeroed in on the area southwest of the Windward Passage between the two large islands. The enlarged view showed a sector of ocean that dazzled him, displaying a rich variegation of indigo and turquoise hues that fell away to the southern horizon. A small oblong island loomed in the left foreground, and as he scrutinized it, he could make out what appeared to be a tall man-made structure overlooking its eastern side, probably the remains of an old lighthouse. Punching a few more keys, he pulled up the name of the tiny island.

Navassa.

Several nautical miles beyond the island, a flashing red dot indicated the location of the beacon sending the signal. Enlarging the magnification further, he was disappointed when only water filled the screen. Whatever was sending the signal, he concluded, was presently submerged below the waterline. He hadn't been informed about what the transmitting unit was mounted to, but from experience he assumed it would be a marine animal of some kind. Satellite telemetry was useful in solving many mysteries, including the migration routes of various animal species. Unfortunately, orbiting satellites were still unable to detect signals originating underwater mainly due to the limitations of the sending units used in studying marine animal behavior. To consume as little power as possible from the batteries that powered them, most units were designed to generate signals intermittently and just long enough to transmit vital data. During the course of his career, he had often tracked leatherback sea turtles and knew that the transmitters mounted on their backs only switched on when the creatures were on the ocean surface. This caused him to deduce that the pulsing red dot shown on the screen was the last point of transmission and did not necessarily represent the current position of the sending unit.

He again sat back and pondered the task he had been hired to perform. He was only required to locate the transmitter's global position and track its movements subsequent to relaying this information to the anonymous party that had sought his services, nothing more. In order to gain access to this information, the unknown recipient needed a special receiver, a piece of hardware that was not available commercially. Fabricating such a unit was not for the layman, for specialized technical knowledge was required to produce one. That problem, however, had already been taken care of. The person responsible for setting up this gig had both built and supplied the hardware to the obscure recipient days earlier. All he had to do was download the data and send it off to its intended destination to fulfill his end of the bargain. His client, whoever he or she was, had retained him in good faith by paying his exorbitant fee in advance. He tried to visualize the type of individual willing enough to dole out such a hefty sum for so simple a piece of work. It had to be someone possessing considerable wealth. He had recently checked his Cayman account to confirm that the money had been deposited.

Maintaining a solid reputation for reliability in this covert line of work was important to the specialist, for it continued to set the stage for the amount of future moonlighting he could expect. Promoting himself through word of mouth had done wonders for his financial health during the last year. Precaution was paramount, for routinely exercising it protected both him and clients that didn't want their identities revealed. That was why he worked through intermediaries only, trusted individuals he had discreetly cultivated within scientific and military circles where his services were most frequently sought. One such intermediary was actually a close friend of his, a graduate student at the University of Miami and the person who had arranged this job. Unlike his friend, though, the specialist had completed his doctoral thesis in computer science three years earlier. He made a mental note to supplement his friend's Cayman account with the commission he had earned. He would make the electronic transfer of funds as soon as he concluded this business.

Swinging his eyes back to the screen he realized the current point of transmission had shifted by several hundred meters, but again nothing showed on the ocean surface. Damn, he should have been more observant, he chided himself. The carrier of the transmitter had to have breached the surface when he had looked away. It was driving him crazy to know what manner of beast carried the telemetry unit. He frowned in irritation, but an idea suddenly hit him, and the frown abruptly faded. Perhaps it wasn't an animal at all, he surmised. Maybe it was a man-made object, maybe a submarine.

Curious, he decided to retrieve other data streams from the satellite's remote sensing instrumentation, starting with thermal imagery of the waters in the immediate vicinity of the submerged transmitter. If a submarine were there, it just might put out enough heat to give him a thermal footprint. Switching over to HIRS, the High Resolution Infrared Sounder, he became disappointed when a trail failed to appear. He gave this finding some thought. The lack of a thermal signature didn't necessarily mean that a sub was not present, particularly if it was an electrically powered sub. Usually it was only the large nuclear subs that put out thermal emissions sufficient to be detected by satellite, and that almost always occurred in cold polar waters where heat emissions from a sub contrasted more sharply with lower ambient temperatures.

In frustration he widened the scale, scanning a larger field. Although most of the screen exhibited blue, it contrasted sharply with a yellow-red zone occurring near the south side of Navassa Island, an indication of heavy phytoplankton concentration. This surprised him, for such concentrations were only possible if an upwelling of deeper water had taken place, and in the Caribbean upwellings were relatively rare. Upwelling brought nutrients to the surface, causing phytoplankton to erupt into frenzied growth. He had scanned the Caribbean Basin on numerous occasions during his first two years with CLS, but not since then. He did not remember having seen a concentration anywhere close to this magnitude. Seeking to confirm this he accessed the archives and pulled up a history of sea temperature imagery covering the same area dating back over the last year. Displaying a sequence of frames in reverse chronological order, each frame separated by one month, he could see the size and concentration of the algae bloom had remained fairly consistent during the past year. Pulling up additional frames, he went back in time another year. He only had to look at the first frame to confirm a smaller plankton bloom. Shifting back through several more frames told him what he was looking for. The plankton had begun to reproduce exponentially about thirteen months ago, exploding into riotous growth with a rich supply of nitrogen-laden nutrients brought to the surface from deeper, colder water.

His interest sparked, he mulled this. With the exception of the earth's polar regions where upwelling was common, surface waters in warmer climates remained relatively devoid of nutrients containing nitrogen. This was because phytoplankton absorbed such nutrients rather quickly while capturing sunlight and, through the process of photosynthesis, converted it into proteins, fats, and carbohydrates. At sea, nutrients were not readily available and were not recycled in the same manner as on land. Marine organisms sank into the depths when they died, taking the nutrients bound up in their bodies with them. The specialist understood that nitrogen was the key nutrient for the proliferation of life, the basic building block of all amino acids, with food production dependent on it. The oceans of the world contained an almost limitless source of nitrogen from decomposed organisms, particularly in the form of nitrates, the concentration of which increased rapidly with depth before leveling off at around 3,300 feet. Because fixed forms of nitrogen were vital to plant metabolism, he knew an upwelling from the depths would have a profound effect on the local ecology, for at sea phytoplankton formed the base of a living pyramid, providing sustenance for the myriad organisms comprising the pyramid above. A substantial increase in the supply of fixed forms of nitrogen would dramatically broaden the pyramid base, rapidly expanding the rest of the biomass supported by it by quickly working its way up the food chain. The numbers of tiny crustaceans and other grazers of planktonic sea grass would escalate swiftly with a large increase in available plankton, providing food for shrimp and other small organisms. These would then be consumed by sardines and other small fish, which in turn would serve to feed schools of tuna and other more complex life forms near the top of the pyramid. As he studied the various frames, he was certain the area near Navassa had to be teeming with huge schools of fish at this very moment.

Upon learning this, he had to remind himself of his mission. Deleting the picture frames from the computer screen, he went back to real-time viewing. The monitor exhibited a new flashing dot, this one still closer to the island. Still seeing no sign of any creature on the ocean surface, he displayed the location of all three pulsing dots he had so far witnessed and projected a path of travel from them. Noticing that the spacing between transmission points was roughly equal, he focused on a spot ahead of the last point of transmission at a distance approximating the degree of separation between the preceding points.

He only had to wait less than a minute before another point pulsed where he had anticipated. It was then that he saw a disturbance on the surface, and as he scrutinized the cause of it, he realized he was observing the backs of two albino dolphins swimming side by side in perfect synchrony. Totally fascinated by the sight, he watched the creatures for one brief moment before they disappeared into the depths again. Only then did he relay the locations of the transmissions to his anonymous client.

Chapter Fifteen: Dolphin Artistry

Jake didn't remember seeing the large wooden raft at the far end of the cove, mainly because it had been tethered to the backside of the fish pen where it remained hidden from view. The raft was square in shape, accommodating one albino per side. Centered close to each edge of the raft was an easel fitted with a canvas that faced outward within easy reach of each dolphin. As Jake looked on, he could distinguish a palette containing an assortment of brushes, colored oils and other liquids situated on both sides of each easel. Already the creatures were busy, the upper third of their bodies jutting vertically above the water, their prehensile appendages fully extended and moving rapidly between canvas and palettes.

Awed by what he was seeing, Jake found it difficult to pull his eyes away from the scene before him. "They're all ambidextrous!" he uttered in disbelief, continuing to hold onto the dorsal fin of Hercules as the giant albino towed him and Destiny slowly around the small gathering.

Jacob smiled knowingly as he sat nearby in the small aluminum dory he used to maneuver around the cove. "Yes, they have the ability to compose with both hands simultaneously."

As if reading Jake's mind, Hercules ceased moving and hovered close behind Achilles, allowing Jake to observe the creation that was quickly unfolding on the young dolphin's canvas. "I don't claim to know much about art," Jake said, "but that looks to be some kind of abstract." He pivoted his head toward Destiny, then brought his eyes back to the painting. "What's it symbolize?"

"That all depends on the one doing the viewing," Destiny replied.

Jake studied the fast-developing artwork. "The viewer will only perceive as much as they allow themselves based upon the capaciousness of representation," Jacob interposed. "For most people, the forms, images, and composition will only touch what a person has absorbed throughout their existence. Works such as these will appeal to some, while invariably repulsing others. With some individuals, though, the context of what lies on a canvas may reach down to the very essence of the viewer, affecting that person in a unique and unexpected way."

Jake nodded, intrigued by what he was witnessing. "Yes, but what does Achilles want this painting to represent?" He turned back to Destiny. "Surely you must be feeling what he's trying to convey?"

The girl stared back; her eyes filled with infinite patience. "He doesn't know. Each of the artists before us is simply letting their brush strokes be guided by subconscious thoughts."

"What you are seeing is what some authorities within the art world would term 'unconscious autonomous creativity,'" Jacob added, noting the blank look on Jake's face. "From the moment of birth, the brain is bombarded with stimuli which are arranged into coherent principles that will be accepted by other brains, but which may or may not represent the compositional elements of the psyche. On a basic level you are observing sticks with hairs carrying gobs of colored oils being haphazardly smeared on a surface, nothing more. But if you look deeper, taking this procedure and refining it to a degree that equates to painting without thinking, then you are viewing a form of creativity that portrays imagery that is symbolic of the infantile juxtaposition of thoughts." For emphasis, he glanced at Achilles' rapidly emerging creation. "Some might categorize this as surrealism, a representation of a superior reality associated with dreams and disinterested thought. Such a representation is unconnected with cerebral mechanisms, substituting itself in place of them as a solution to the principal problems of life."

Jake found himself groping for words. "You're getting way ahead of this limited intelligence of mine," he said, examining Achilles' painting with a critical eye. "But I see nothing haphazard. If anything, there appears to be order here." He pointed to the right half of the canvas. "Those lines…they seem to be converging, as if flowing towards a single point in space…as if going to infinity but not quite getting there. And near the top…the commingling of blue and yellow splotches in the midst of a white background…they somehow suggest both dolphins and humans in a purified state."

Though Achilles had not yet completed the work, the creation seemed to convey serenity to Jake, drawing him away from the penumbra of what he would have considered rational thought. All at once he felt cleansed, as if breaking free of the chains of consciousness where confusion and chaos seemed to predominate. He was falling, then rising, manipulating his free hand as if he himself were wielding one of the brushes stroking the canvas. All at once he was suddenly seeing the painting through the eyes of Achilles. The sensation startled him, jarring him back from the edge.

"You have a keen eye," Jacob praised, sensing that Jake was teetering on the brink of something newly discovered. He had seen that same look in others. "Paintings like these are usually unfathomable to the average person simply because such individuals are attuned only to the world they perceive with their eyes. The surrealist, however, strives to turn away from the illusions constructed by their five physical senses, looking inward toward an unfiltered and largely unexplored region of the subconscious. The surrealist seeks to depict a realm purified of all the social ills plaguing the world he or she lives in, escaping to a place where consciousness is only a small part. In doing this, the surrealist attempts to unveil a superior reality, one infinitely more complex and revealing than any metaphysics."

Hercules began moving again, slowly pulling Jake and the girl counterclockwise to the next side of the raft. The painting Jake observed was different from the one Achilles' was creating, alive with color and appearing to be nearing completion. "Coral is one of our more prolific artists," Destiny explained. "She and Reef have produced more paintings than any of the others."

"How many paintings has she completed?" Jake asked.

"This one makes three hundred and twenty-four."

Jake's brow rose in astonishment. "What do you do with all of them?"

"We give them away."

"To whom?"

"To people. Mostly strangers who come to Malique wanting to be healed."

Jake digested this momentarily. "I take it there's some underlying purpose in these giveaways."

It was Jacob who gave a reply. "You might say that. Remember what I told you about mankind being insufficiently developed on the evolutionary scale to take responsibility for the planet, that the human species has not yet learned how to use the less predominant side of the brain for the benefit of the world?"

"I remember," Jake affirmed, noting that Jacob had drifted closer, his dory nudged forward by one of the other albinos not currently painting.

"And do you also remember my theory on why this new breed of dolphin has come into existence?" Jacob said, his tone oddly solemnizing.

Jake glanced over at Destiny; her gaze riveted on him as if in prelude to some new revelation. He lifted his eyes back to Jacob who was almost on top of him now. "You think they've been put here to show mankind the way to a better world."

Jacob nodded like a teacher satisfied with the answer given by one of his students. "Although I have no way of proving it, I believe these paintings can be used as one such mechanism in speeding up man's evolution toward becoming a more responsible species."

For one split second Jake thought Jacob must be mad. "How is that possible?"

"Tell me you do not feel anything when you look upon these creations," Jacob challenged. "Tell me you are not affected in some positive way."

As if to test what Jacob was saying, Jake let his eyes settle back on Coral's artwork. Almost immediately a burdensome weight seemed to lift from his inner being, making it possible for him to soar toward an infinite horizon where acts of love and kindness were in great abundance, a universe where greed and aggression did not exist. What was he feeling? Bliss? Euphoria? "It's hard to put into words, but something good seems to wash over me when I stare into these works," he found himself acknowledging. "But how can a painting induce such a reaction in a person?"

"Yes, how can it?" Jacob turned his eyes back to Coral who was focused on completing the painting. "I believe these creations somehow trigger a neurological mechanism in some people, stimulating the lesser used side of the brain, the part that is most creative, the area that is more inclined to follow a course of moral rectitude. While I cannot tell you how or why it works, I can only tell you that it works."

"Maybe these dolphins know how it works," Jake suggested.

Jacob smiled, shaking his head. "Unfortunately, they do not. It was only by chance that we learned of the strange effect these paintings have on some people. Over the years I have striven to educate these dolphins in many areas of man's accumulated knowledge, particularly the various types of art mankind has produced and treasured throughout the ages. Art, I felt, would be especially useful in giving them insight into the human psyche since nothing characterizes more fully the true nature of man than his artistic creations. Unlike most other formalized disciplines, art has remained virtually unconstrained in substance, representing a truly free expression of the beings doing the creating."

"Is surrealism their preferred mode of expression?" Jake asked.

"For the most part, yes," Jacob answered. "When I first introduced them to oil painting about seven years ago, they all began to produce works of the same general style even though each painting was unique in its own right. It was when we began giving these works away, however, that we discovered the profound effect they had on some people."

"When did you first notice this?"

"It was after several of the locals we know began to change their ways for the better. That was when they were exposed to several paintings put on permanent display in the village of Malique."

"And you think those changes were influenced by this dolphin art?" Jake said incredulously. "Isn't that stretching the envelop of speculation a bit?"

"Behavioral changes in people rarely occur on their own in an essentially unaltered environment," Jacob countered calmly, appearing amused at how Jake was handling this. "Usually it takes a rare event or the introduction of something new into their surroundings to elicit a modification in the way they act. Without elaborating on the full extent of my observations, I began to notice a relationship between these paintings and the way some people began to behave after viewing them. We now make it a priority to distribute these works among the Haitian masses living in some of the other cities in the hope of making the people more responsible in the manner they conduct themselves."

"Define what you mean when you say more responsible?"

"Contributing to the welfare of the nation, and for that matter, the world in general. Ceasing to overtax the planetary ecosystem. Cleaning up the garbage and refuse that pervades our environment, stopping the strip-mining of our remaining timberlands, and planting new trees. Helping our fellow man through hardship and difficult times. Essentially becoming environmentally and socially conscientious."

"Is that all, just demonstrating a concern for the environment and society?"

"For starters, yes."

Jake felt a need to test Jacob's convictions further. "Aren't such issues better left in the hands of government to follow through on?"

Jacob's expression abruptly hardened, hanging somewhere between a sneer and a grimace. "It is the people who must lead the way in taking responsibility for their actions, not government. History has shown that governments, all governments, sooner or later have a tendency to become corrupt and complacent, typically causing economic stagnation and social unrest. Here in Haiti that is especially true. It is the citizenry that must set an elevated moral standard, leading by example. Social cohesion must take root with respect to environmental and political issues if the planet is to survive. If we as a species are to evolve to a higher, more responsible level, the human vice of greed, the single most common disease afflicting mankind, must be diminished within the population. This vice is the remnant of the hunter-gatherer mentality that characterized the human race prior to the birth of agricultural based civilizations, when the very survival of individuals depended on their ability to obtain sources of food. In those days, an excess food supply guaranteed a continuation of their existence and a propagation of their offspring. Unfortunately, this malignant trait is still inherent in most human beings, becoming a detriment in a modern world and contributing immensely to the problems hurting the planet."

Jake continued to hold onto Hercules' dorsal fin, his mind poring over Jacob's philosophical viewpoint. "Your slant on greed is very enlightening," he admitted. "I never really thought of greed as being a disease. A moral failing, maybe, but not a disease." He decided to feel out Jacob a little more to get a better understanding of the man. "Some might argue that greed is a good thing, that it's the true driving force behind a free enterprise system, creating an economic climate that raises a society's standard of living and invoking technological breakthroughs that ultimately benefit everyone. Without a desire for monetary gain, a free enterprise system cannot flourish. In a broad sense, aren't greed and profit opposite sides of the same coin?"

Jacob took a deep breath, seeming to dissect Jake's argument. "What you say is true if exercised to a reasonable degree. But when taken to excess, greed can become a deadly mental illness that can cause severe social strife. History will attest that this often results in disastrous social upheavals and wars between nations. Did not the French and Russian Revolutions occur when the masses were driven by desperation to put an end to the extreme greed of the aristocracies oppressing and starving them? Did not the Spanish conquistadors in their fanatical search for riches and gold destroy the Tainos civilization? In an advanced stage, greed will lead to the enslavement of some human beings to do the work of others suffering from this sickness. Did not the trafficking of human slaves become one of the economic cornerstones of ancient Rome and the American Southern Confederation? This very nation emerged as a consequence of a rebellion against the greed of slavery."

Jacob suddenly smiled, replacing the gravity that was beginning to cloud his face. "Think of these paintings as a form of medicine, a potential cure for the madness brought on by excessive greed. In a way, they can be thought of as an alternate mode of healing used by these dolphins, a mode not requiring any physical contact and one that has the advantage of reaching far more people."

"Earlier you mentioned these paintings only work on some people afflicted by greed," Jake said. "Can I take it then there will be other people with this illness that cannot be cured?"

A hint of sadness manifested itself briefly in Jacob's expression. "Over the years these dolphins have healed many people suffering from a variety of illnesses, mostly physical ailments they were able to correct through direct physical contact in much the same way they healed the gunshot wound you sustained back at Navassa. Even though they know they have this ability, they have no explanation as to how it works. What they do know is that it does not work on everyone. Although I have no way of proving it, I believe most of the people they are unable to cure are truly evil individuals with dark natures. Perhaps such people are beyond help simply because deep down they are comfortable with who they are, choosing never to change their ways. It is my belief and the belief of Destiny and these dolphins that such people will remain unaffected by these paintings."

Jake swung his head back to Destiny to get a direct read on whether or not she agreed with this. The girl gave a slight nod of her head. Turning back to Jacob he said, "So through these paintings these dolphins think they can still reach significant portions of the Haitian population, suppressing greedy urges."

"Yes."

"That's a pretty tall order," Jake remarked blithely, "particularly in a country like this where people are trying to survive on a daily basis."

"Change will not come overnight. It will occur incrementally. But even that will be better than none at all."

A strange thought suddenly came to Jake. "Is greed the only human vice these paintings are capable of curtailing?"

"There is some evidence to suggest that some individuals with a propensity for violence will become less aggressive when exposed to them. In general, those affected seem to become more caring toward their fellow man, while those with dark natures appear to be immune. It might be that the type of person who is dissatisfied with their self-image will become most susceptible to these paintings."

"You mean people who perceive themselves as morally deficient or degenerate?"

"Precisely."

"What about people harboring dangerous ideologies, the kind that threaten and kill people with differing viewpoints?" Jake pressed.

"It depends," Jacob said.

"I'm not getting your drift."

"Are these people rational? Are they attempting to achieve some kind of political objective through the artful combination of violence and the promise to cease hostilities if the objective is met?"

When Jake did not immediately answer, Jacob posed the question a different way. "Is the belief in the ideology real or fantasized?"

Jake appeared completely stymied. "What's the difference?"

"Very often a real belief has a logical or scientific basis. It usually has a degree of certainty restricted by mathematics and the hard sciences, whereas a fantasized belief is irrational as judged by the hard sciences."

"I'm still not following you."

"If the violence continues even after a supposed objective is met, then the ideology has been set up to act out a fantasy. In the eyes of the people holding onto the belief, achieving the objective merely holds symbolic value." Jacob paused, waiting for Jake's response.

"Can you explain this a little more fully?"

"It is a common human weakness to exaggerate our contribution to the world, more so than the world is usually willing to acknowledge. Only through our fantasies are we able to close this gap. If the fantasy involves taking part in a revolutionary struggle against perceived oppressors, the oppressed may imagine themselves marching to the right side of history. Quite often the oppressors are fabricated to fulfill a role, becoming nothing more than props in a theatrical play staged by the fantasizer. In a fantasy ideological movement, the leader is not interested in altering the minds of the people he is fighting against. They are simply there as supernumeraries in his private psychodrama, symbolic figures set up for the sole purpose that he might act out his fantasy. The protest for him is not political in nature. It is not aimed at eliminating poverty or stopping economic imperialism. The protest is set up to make himself out to be a hero, constructed for his own edification. In such interactions the fantasist sees others as having no wills or minds of their own, caring nothing for them as individuals and casting them in roles he wishes them to play. In doing this, it never occurs to him that the other actors may be utterly failing to play the part expected of them. The fact that the fantasizer is normally surrounded by other individuals who are not fantasizing, or at least not fantasizing in the same manner, usually prevents his psychodrama from intruding into the domain of reality. But when an entire group or nation gets caught up in the fantasy, the repercussions can be disastrous to the human race. History is replete with such large-scale collective fantasies. For this to happen, however, there must first be a preexisting collective need to set the stage for such a widespread fantasy. This need arises from a conflict between a set of collective aspirations and desires, and the austere conjunctures of brutal reality. Over time, this conflict is gradually transformed into a penchant for fantasy. Hitler's fantasy of reviving German paganism in the thousand-year Reich is a classic example of this. Mussolini's aim to resurrect the ancient glory of the Roman Empire is another. Such fantasy ideologies tend to take hold of those people history has bypassed or rejected, groups that feel they are under attack from forces they claim to be more powerful than themselves but nevertheless inferior in terms of true virtue."

Once again Jake was astounded by the depth of Jacob's intellect. The man was a walking library. "How would you classify religious fanaticism aimed at murdering innocents?" he found himself asking, unable to keep the bitterness he felt out of his tone.

A shrewd gleam came into Jacob's eyes. "Religion does possess a peculiar potential for intolerance and violence. Fanaticism and strife are natural byproducts of religion simply because it deals with ultimate truths. Many philosophers find this odd since most religions are based on love. But there is a fine line separating love from hate, and when crossed it can set the stage for some of the most brutal wars man has experienced. People are more apt to go to war over religious dogma than over other issues because for most individuals it deals with the very meaning of human existence and establishes a guideline of acceptable moral benchmarks on how to live their lives. While most of the wars that plagued mankind throughout history were fought under the guise of religion, I have no doubt that many of them were shining examples of collective fantasies on a widespread scale."

Jake mused Jacob's answer before pursuing his previous question from another angle. "So, is it possible for these paintings to keep religious fanatics from killing others?" he needed to know.

"It depends how deeply they are embedded in the fantasy," Jacob said. "If they see themselves as being morally chaste in carrying out their part in the fantasy, then I doubt these paintings will affect them in any way. As I explained to you during our stroll on the beach, there is some scientific evidence that suggests the less predominant side of the human brain to be the area that gives most people a sense of spirituality, the same area these paintings may be having some kind of an influence upon. If the spiritual belief is strong enough, then it is doubtful it can be altered from an outside source."

"But what if they suspected, even to a small degree, that they were being purposely misled by the person or people inciting the movement, the religious war?"

"It would be a serious mistake for an outside observer to view the leaders of such wars as power-hungry egotists using the religion as a cynical ploy to delude the gullible masses. Such leaders can only make others get caught up in the fantasy by believing in it so intensely themselves. For most of us, beliefs are generally a passive response, formed for the purpose of better understanding the world as it is. This differs radically from the fantasist who responds to the world in an intensely active way, developing a belief that is not used for describing the world but aimed at transforming it. As such, the fantasy ideology alters the character and conduct of those holding onto it."

Jacob took a momentary break from his discourse and sighed deeply. "In a sense, a deliberate form of make-believe is erected which becomes a means for making itself real. In such a fantasy, everyone and everything becomes a stage prop."

Jake felt all the more embittered over this analysis. "Being a prop in someone else's fantasy is not a pleasant experience, especially when that someone else is trying to murder you," he said, making sure to keep his ire from showing. "Those men who attacked us last night, I suspect them to be jihadists with a mission of terror in mind."

Jacob seemed to give Jake's comment careful thought before replying. "What you are saying could very well be the case although it does not fit in well with the modus operandi of the more radical elements of Islam," he said at last.

Jake had not expected such a reply. "How so?"

"We all want to make sense of the world around us, reducing it to something we know our way around, particularly when it is acting strangely."

Jake looked at him searchingly. "You think the attack was strange? The man I captured last night has all the earmarks of a Muslim extremist."

Jacob nodded. "Yes, it certainly does appear that way, but I nevertheless find it odd. For the modern-day jihadist, there would be no glamour in attacking your vessel, especially in an out-of-the-way place like this where no media coverage would be available for broadcasting the incident. The Islamic extremists of today appear only focused on pulling off the spectacular, something specifically crafted to take root in the imagination of large populations of Muslims."

"You mean like bringing down the twin towers at the World Trade Center," Jake said.

"Exactly. Once the media got involved, bringing down the towers had an effect analogous to theater. It grabbed the audience within the Muslim world and made them feel part of the spectacle, revealing something they could easily and instantly identify."

"And what would that be?"

"Why that God was on the side of radical Islam, of course," Jacob stated breezily.

"Yes, I've heard all that before," Jake retorted, his face souring.

Jacob seemed not to notice. "In the Arab world, smaller acts of terror would have little meaning on the international stage," he rationalized. "An economic and political Goliath had to be brought down to prove beyond any doubt that God favored the extremists."

"So then what motive caused them to attack us?"

"Perhaps they wanted to hijack your vessel for some unknown purpose. After all, they did try to board it."

"True," Jake agreed, "but then they tried to ram it."

"But only after you repelled them," Jacob countered quickly. He fell into a silent interlude for several seconds before speaking again. "An attack on the heels of our earlier encounter is just too coincidental, leading me to believe a connection exists between the tuna trawler at Navassa Island and the men in the submarine."

"I did see a submarine near the island," Destiny interjected, speaking for the first time in several minutes. "The whole pod did."

Circumspection consumed Jacob's expression as he weighed this new disclosure. "Then to rule out that it was not the same one that followed us back here would be unwise," he postulated. "It only lends further support to a relationship between the tuna fishermen and the men operating the sub."

This was something Jake hadn't previously considered in spite of his conviction the sub had followed them all the way back from Navassa. "What you're suggesting is some kind of alliance between Colombians and Muslim radicals," Jake said dubiously, though not quite able to cast aside the absurdness of such a possibility. Although it seemed somewhat far-fetched, he found it difficult to dismiss such a link.

Jacob eyed Jake as if sensing his ambivalence over such a notion. "Have you ever heard of Akum's Razor?" he asked.

"You mean all things being equal, the simplest explanation usually proves to be the right one no matter how improbable it seems," Jake answered. "Yes, I-"

Jake stopped in mid-sentence as Destiny let out a small, startled cry. Almost simultaneously, several of the albinos squealed loudly and Hercules shuddered convulsively beneath him. "What is it?"

The girl suddenly flinched as if in pain, closing her eyes momentarily before opening them again. "Hermes and Aphrodite are in trouble," she said, her voice conveying distress.

Jake looked at her closely, seeing the fear taking hold of her. "How do you mean?"

Hercules flicked his powerful tail, abruptly swimming around the corner of the raft. Jake kept staring into Destiny's frightened eyes, searching for an answer. Turning his head, he followed her gaze. The albino on Coral's right was rapidly composing something, its prehensile appendages appearing like blurs as the paintbrushes held by them swept between the palettes and canvas. As if he was looking at a Polaroid photograph in the midst of development, a new image was quickly coming together, replacing the surrealistic work that had preceded it a short time earlier. As his brain interpreted the shapes swiftly taking form, he realized the new painting showed two white dolphins being netted and hauled from the water.

"We must go at once!" Destiny snapped, the urgency in her tone tugging at Jake like a hundred-ton hawser being stretched to its limit.

"Where?" Jake asked.

The girl turned her eyes back to Jake as if suddenly aware of his presence again. "Navassa Island," she said anxiously.

Chapter Sixteen: Bird of Prey

Having been given advance notice where to look, the spotter plane had been close enough to cover the distance quickly and home in on the GPS coordinates relayed to it, converging on the heading. Holding to an altitude of one thousand feet above the water, the pilot suddenly discerned movement below him in spite of the sun glare reflecting off the surface. Locking his eyes on the disturbance, a smile lit his face as he glimpsed something resembling twin alabaster torpedoes cruising side by side. The sight rather surprised him for he had only expected to find one. He didn't want to get his hopes too high, he mused wistfully, but then again, one never knew when good fortune was in the works. For the moment though, he would keep this information to himself, knowing that his partner rarely saw things optimistically the way he did.

The objects remained visible for perhaps another second before submerging, but it was enough for him to confirm their direction of travel. Banking the aircraft sharply and swooping lower, he reduced the air speed and took on a new heading, angling the plane toward a spot ahead of the creatures.

Scanning the eastern horizon briefly, he spotted the vessel that comprised the other half of his team, a high-powered 60-foot Bertram that was rapidly converging on the same general area. The boat was fast and had been specifically retrofitted for the type of work they were about to carry out. He had done this many times before but had never used the equipment he was about to deploy.

The idea had first come to him about six months ago and he had wasted no time in hiring an acoustical engineer to put together the correct combination of electronic components and hardware to bring life to the concept. Though as yet untested under actual field conditions, he was confident that the unit would in theory have the desired effect on the marine mammals he was now tracking.

Depressing the transmit button on his radio, he hailed the Bertram on an encoded, secure channel using the prearranged call signs. "This is Bird of Prey. Can you hear me, Predator?"

"Predator on the approach. You're coming in very clear, Bird of Prey. I have you in sight."

"Be advised we have acquired the target, Predator. The package is about to be dumped."

"I hope that toy of yours works," a skeptical voice grumbled. "Otherwise, this trip will have been all for nothing."

The pilot couldn't help but crack a smile, unable to share his partner's pessimism. "Well let's hope it's not," he muttered, turning his head and nodding to the two crewmen stationed further back in the cargo hold. In acknowledgment to the gesture, both crewmen disconnected the safety straps securing what he had called 'the package', a large bulky container weighing better than 1,200 pounds.

Seeing that this was done, the pilot toggled a switch on the forward console. Several seconds passed before a noticeable vibration worked its way through the controls as the cargo bay doors opened outward and caught the wind. A moment later the vibration subsided as the doors locked into a fully opened position.

Bringing the twin turboprop lower, the pilot never tired of the feel of the Casa-212. She was a sturdy fixed-wing aircraft, the type of flying machine that was exceptionally versatile. He had picked it up cheap at a government auction, knowing the plane had been confiscated from the hands of drug runners. From all outward indications, the Casa has been well maintained. With the exception of the newly installed hydraulically powered cargo bay doors positioned amidships in the lower fuselage, he had done little to modify the airplane. The bay doors had been a necessary addition. The payload was just too large and heavy to be pushed out of the plane's side door, particularly when timing of the drop was critical to the operation. The success of the venture would depend on how close he could position the unit to the creatures.

The pilot had come up with the idea for the unit from recent studies that linked whale strandings with recent improvements in active sonar systems used by the U.S. Navy. Better known as SURTASS LFA in naval circles, the low-frequency sonar acted like a powerful floodlight in an undersea environment, generating sound levels equivalent to that put out by twin-engine fighter jets. Beached whales often exhibited the damage such a barrage of sound could do, showing internal bleeding around their brains and ears. Producing as much as 215 decibels of intense sonic wave energy, a substantial body of evidence was beginning to mount showing the harm LFA systems could do to marine life. Among other things, use of such technology in the open ocean was responsible for the formation of large emboli, or gas bubbles, in the organ tissue of marine mammals.

It was this type of technology he had deemed useful, a perfect complement to his line of work. But he had no desire to inflict bodily injury on the creatures below him. His deal with the man who had hired him required they be captured unharmed if he were to be paid what amounted to five times his normal fee for the delivery of just one live specimen. The fact that there were two of these unusual white dolphins within his grasp would double his windfall. And if the client refused to cough up the full amount for a second dolphin, he was certain he could put the additional creature up for sale in other markets. Foreign governments were clamoring for dolphins they could train as military assets and, in this case, would pay an exceedingly handsome sum for such a rare animal. According to the client, these marine mammals were exceptionally intelligent and possessed a most interesting anatomical feature atypical of the average bottlenose dolphin.

The unit he was about to launch was self-contained and designed to put out only sufficient sound energy to stun the animals, disorienting them just enough for his partner to get within range to sedate and net them. To accomplish that still necessitated a substantial output of sonic energy sent out in all directions from the device to ensure that the targeted dolphins would be temporarily incapacitated. Even so, a discharge of even that amount of power would be limited and short in duration. The energy source that powered the unit consisted of fifteen lithium-ion marine batteries, all of which accounted for most of the unit's weight. An array of loudspeakers protruding from a central hub ensured that the surrounding hydrosphere would be blanketed in sound.

Cutting back on the throttle a little more, the pilot reduced his air speed further as he descended to within fifty feet of the water before leveling off. Even though the unit was enveloped in what amounted to a belt of inflated bags to both cushion it from impact during the drop and keep it from sinking, he wanted to minimize the force with which it slammed into the sea as much as possible. He and his partner had expended a sizable sum of money in developing the device, and protecting the investment was currently foremost in his mind. And if the unit performed up to his expectations, he was certain he could get at least a tenfold return on the cash he had laid out in producing it.

With his thumb planted lightly on the switch that would trigger the electronic release, he mentally counted backward as he eyed his drop zone. Three…two…one…now. "The package is away, Predator," he said loudly, his tone showing more emotion than he had intended.

"I saw it fall, Bird of Prey," the pilot's partner reported dully. "I'm heading straight for it now."

"Happy hunting, Predator. I'll stay on station to guide you to the prize. Bird of Prey signing off for now."

Reengaging more power, the pilot brought the nose of the Casa up and began to climb. As he did this, he turned anxiously in his seat to observe the expression on Hanson's face, the crewman assigned to monitor the operation of the unit. A look of intense concentration consumed the man's features as he listened intently to the sounds coming through the earphones clamped to his cranium. Several seconds passed before Hanson lifted his head to meet the pilot's eyes, his manner revealing nothing.

The pilot keyed the aircraft intercom. "Well?" he asked impatiently.

The stoicism displayed by Hanson suddenly transformed into a broad grin. "We have tone," he said jubilantly. Bringing his eyes to bear on the laptop before him, he added, "All the readings are pegged to max."

"Wonderful!" the pilot said happily, taking the plane into a moderate left bank and circling back the way they had come. "Now let's see if it does what it's supposed to do."

Looking out the side window, the pilot caught sight of the floatation bags bobbing in the distance. He visualized how the contrivance was currently working. Upon making contact with the sea, the primary component of the sonar unit was designed to fall away from the air bags, dropping fifteen feet below the ocean surface before a one-inch umbilical cable connecting it with the floats stopped its descent. Almost immediately, the device would commence emitting the low frequency sounds at the required magnitudes, jarring the senses of creatures that depended on echolocation for their survival. A transmitter with antenna positioned in the cluster of floatation bags would send out signals that indicated if the unit was functioning properly. Those were the signals both Hanson and his partner were currently monitoring. He also knew that the window of opportunity for capturing the dolphins was a small one. The amount of juice needed to generate the debilitating sound waves would quickly drain the lithium-ion battery system. Unless the second half of his team arrived in time to prevent the escape of the creatures, the animals would recover rapidly from their sound induced stupors and escape. From the few tests he had run on the device, he knew it would continue to put out sound pulses at the required level of impairment for approximately seven minutes.

Taking the plane out of its bank, he located the Bertram. Although it was still a significant distance away from the floats, it was closing the gap quickly. Nervously he studied the sea in the immediate vicinity of the sonar unit, knowing it was going to be close. A hint of something white just beneath the water suddenly caught his eye, and as he focused on the spot, he realized the pair of albino dolphins had breached less than a hundred yards from where the floats bobbed. A smile worked its way onto his face as he studied them. Both creatures appeared to be floundering on the surface in confusion, their previous direction of travel now disrupted.

As he watched the pair, a new thought struck him. Perhaps more of these white dolphins were in the area. Squinting his eyes against the harsh sun glare reflecting off the water, he looked closely for other signs that might indicate the presence of more of this rare species. Sweeping his gaze left, a fleeting glimpse of something dark and huge appeared to race below the surface. He blinked in surprise, unsure of what he was seeing, but in doing so he lost sight of the object. Banking the aircraft slightly, he tried to pick it up again. He continued to scan the water in that spot for several more seconds before giving up the attempt, realizing what he had seen could very easily have been the shadow of a passing cloud. As if to confirm this, he cast his eyes above him, noting a succession of small clouds drifting overhead. On impulse, he turned his head to the north, becoming aware of the isolated chunk of land not too far away, the lush vegetation carpeting its surface contrasting distinctly with the blue horizon. It suddenly occurred to him that the white dolphins had been holding to a heading that would have taken them to the island, but so what.

Drawing his gaze away from the remote mound of greenery, he got back to the business at hand by veering the aircraft into another bank and taking stock of the scene below him again. The creatures were still on the surface, showing little movement. Gauging the present heading of the Bertram with respect to the animals, he thought it prudent to hail his partner once more. "Bird of Prey calling Predator."

"This is Predator."

"We have quarry, Predator," he said, speaking as if savoring the words. "Two of them to be exact, chased from the depths and eagerly awaiting your arrival. Let's see if you can nab both of them. If you alter your course by two degrees to port, you'll be almost in direct line with them."

A slight pause ensued as the context of the transmission was digested. "Two of them, you say," an astounded voice suddenly shot back. "Do you mean to tell me that unit of yours actually works?"

The pilot shook his head in exasperation as he watched the boat draw closer to the targeted creatures. "Haven't I always told you to have a little faith?" he said blandly, knowing the ball was now in his partner's hands.

In spite of the confidence he tried to convey in his tone, a growing sense of urgency began to take hold of him. Anxiously he checked his watch and ran a quick mental calculation. In another three minutes the Bertram would reach its prey. That would leave an overlap of approximately thirty seconds before the batteries powering the sonic device became depleted. Already he could distinguish a pair of gunners on the vessel's bow, each man armed with an air rifle that would launch a sedation dart. Over the years, both he and his partner had learned that having a second shooter at the ready was a necessary precaution in the event that the primary shooter missed the targeted marine mammal. Inasmuch as there were now two magnificent specimens ready for capture took away this measure of assurance if they intended on snaring both creatures simultaneously. And he definitely wanted both dolphins.

Before he realized what he was doing, he keyed the radio again. "Bird of Prey to Predator."

"What is it BP?"

The pilot put just enough inflection into his voice so there was no mistaking who was in charge of the operation. "Don't screw this up!"

Chapter Seventeen: Sonic Debilitation

The sudden eruption of sound pounded Hermes and his sister like a jackhammer, sending a cascade of debilitating pain to go coursing through their bodies. Totally disoriented and blinded by the paroxysm, they were forced to surface where they floundered helplessly. Only once in his lifetime had Hermes experienced anything close to the magnitude of sonic energy that was currently slamming into them, and he knew that a passing naval ship more than seven miles away had been the cause of the emission. But this was something even more enervating, making it impossible to navigate, let alone think.

Through the blinding pain he tried in vain to locate the source of the emanation but was forced to keep his head clear of the water instead. With enormous difficulty he perceived Aphrodite doing the same. Peering about, he vaguely became aware of a flying machine high above. There was something else. A surface vessel was rapidly bearing down on them. Instinctively he knew both objects were somehow connected with the sound, and in that moment he became cognizant of the danger they represented. Though his remoteness from the main pod was substantial, he did not hesitate to send out a call of alarm through the impalpable mind link they all possessed, uncertain as to whether he would be heard. Fighting off the sonic blast as best he could, it took all his concentration to focus his thoughts on what was happening, and it was only when Aphrodite squealed out in panic that he realized the boat had come alongside them.

Looking back at his sister he could see something projecting near her blowhole, and as he reached out to remove it, a sharp sting in the vicinity of his dorsal fin made him flinch involuntarily. Within moments his pain began to subside even though the severe deluge of sound continued to pound away at him. Feeling suddenly weak and lethargic, he sensed himself beginning to sink below the surface. Forcing himself to fight back against the pull of gravity, he flicked his powerful tail, expecting to feel his body being launched high above the sea. Try as he might, his muscles failed to respond in the manner familiar to him. Torpidly, he rolled on his side, casting one eye on the vessel floating next to him. A grinning man hovered above him, wielding some kind of object. As he tried to grasp what it was, something sprang from it and abruptly expanded. Water kicked up around him, and the discomforting sensation of his body being entwined took momentary hold of his awareness. A mild weight began to tug at him, dragging him under. He tried to resist, unable to muster the energy.

With his mind strangely disconnected from his physical form, he mulled the consequences of this unanticipated circumstance objectively. Although his drowning would present certain setbacks to the project, it would by no means prevent the pod from achieving its ultimate goal. Regardless of his loss, they would go on, continuing to grow stronger in numbers. Comforted by this thought, he began to give himself to the sea. But before his head dipped below the water, another force seemed to pull at him, keeping him from sinking. Almost at the same time, the storm of sound assailing his senses seemed to taper off, quickly dwindling away to nothing. Movement caught his eye, and though restrained, he was able to turn his head just enough to distinguish the cause of it. Helplessly, he watched Aphrodite being pulled from the sea in the midst of a mesh-like netting restricting her movements. The sight seemed to galvanize him, and with a renewed effort he threw his full concentration into conveying the event to others of his kind.

Chapter Eighteen:
A Race Against Time

Jake had the Kawasaki at full throttle, squeezing every ounce of power out of the small craft as he raced over the windswept ocean at close to eighty miles per hour. Destiny clung snugly to his back, her arms clamped tightly around his waist to keep from being thrown off balance as they careened crazily over the choppy sea. Every so often they would become airborne as a foaming whitecap launched them skyward, setting the stage for a jarring impact between hull and water that threatened to eject both riders.

Gusting winds made the open Caribbean a mite rougher on this day than what Jake had seen of late, but with a quartering sea at their rear, they would make Navassa in record time. Glancing at his watch, he estimated they had already covered thirty-eight of the forty-five miles in roughly twenty-eight minutes. At any moment now, the island, and more importantly their quarry, should be coming into view. That is, if he didn't end up flipping the STX-12F under the less than ideal conditions that were at odds with their current velocity. Already they had had at least a dozen close calls upon being catapulted into the air, with the tiny bow of the Kawasaki coming dangerously close to plunging below the surface each time they landed. A high degree of risk was involved here, made all the more perilous by Hector's ingenious mechanical skills at maximizing the performance of reciprocating engines. The machine under him was even more powerful than its typical stock model due to Hector's tweaking. Jake could feel his forearms beginning to burn and cramp as he fought to keep from being dislodged from the steering bars, but he refused to let up on the gas.

When they had first left the cove, Jake had reservations about whether Destiny could take the brutal pounding she would be subjected to as the

Kawasaki sped across the open sea with its throttle wide open. But now the safety of his passenger was no longer a concern. Destiny seemed to be holding up exceptionally well to the tumultuous ride. Though the girl was tiny, he was amazed at the pressure she was able to exert as she hugged his midriff during the bumpiest moments of the precarious voyage. This he attributed to the years she had spent in riding Hercules through seas that continually offered a heavy drag against her small frame.

As Jake continued to drive the Kawasaki with reckless abandon, he contemplated the circumstances beckoning him onward. Ever since meeting up with the girl and the unusual creatures she lived with, he had felt a strong compulsion to protect them. He just couldn't explain it. Perhaps this was a way to redeem himself for his previous failure, one that perpetually haunted him. Nevertheless, he would do whatever it took to foil the abductions he had seen in the dolphin painting. His immediate objective, however, was getting there in time.

"Turn a few degrees left!" Destiny yelled in his ear. "They're on the move."

Jake did as the girl instructed, aware that such a course adjustment would actually add to their rate of travel by giving them more of a following sea. That she was able to remain in mental contact with the captured creatures and provide input on the correct heading to take was extremely valuable if they were going to track down the albino abductors, yet this ability continued to astonish him.

Destiny leaned close to his ear again. "Oh, please hurry," she urged, her voice mired in trepidation. Despite the blast of wind rushing by, Jake could tell from her tone that she had no fear for her own safety. To him, the girl was without a doubt fearless, displaying only a concern for the creatures she was trying to save. "Can you go any faster?" she pleaded.

"Only if we sprout wings," Jake muttered, pivoting his head just enough for the girl to hear. He dared not take his eyes from the sea directly ahead lest he fail to anticipate which way to lean his weight. The last thing he wanted was to upend the small craft and spill both of them into the drink. At their present speed, he knew that serious injury would result to both of them if that were to happen. Destiny was proving to be a good passenger, though, seemingly anticipating Jake's every move as she shifted her weight in perfect unison with his as he fought to keep the Kawasaki on an even keel.

"I see them," Destiny suddenly blurted, keeping only her right arm hooked around Jake's waist and pointing with the other. "There!"

Bringing his full attention back to the horizon directly in front on him, a tiny speck above the ocean abruptly caught his eye. He quickly recognized it to be a plane, and as he kept the Kawasaki heading straight for it, he was able to discern a boat over which the aircraft circled.

Jake swung his head around again. "Are you sure that's them?"

This time Destiny's voice barely carried above the blast of wind. "Hermes and Aphrodite are aboard that boat. Their presence is very strong now."

Jake nodded, leaning the waverunner a little more to port as he aimed the Kawasaki on an intercept course with the vessel. From his perspective, it seemed the boat was on a heading that would take it toward the Haitian mainland, but it was as yet too far away to be certain. Ever since they had left the cove, his mind had been groping with how he would free the captured albinos if they were fortunate enough to catch up with their abductors. He had not had time to formulate a plan. Even worse, the type of people he would be dealing with and the resources they possessed were complete unknowns. Know your enemy. That's what they had always taught him in the Seals. And yet here he was, many miles from land at a complete disadvantage.

Resorting to the use of the Kawasaki had been the only option open to them if they were going to have any chance whatsoever of saving the dolphins. Unfortunately, making immediate chase had been the main priority and there hadn't been any time to arm the waverunner in the manner of a Code One. And even if there had, the automatic weapons would have done him little good. Firing live rounds in trying to free so valuable a cargo was something that would have put the creatures at risk. The only weapon Jake currently possessed was his K-bar, tucked firmly within the sheath strapped to his calf.

Lurking in the background of Jake's thoughts was the inexorable guilt grinding away at him. If not for him, Hermes and Aphrodite would be swimming with the rest of the pod within the safe confines of the cove. After all, it was he who had suggested to the girl the importance of tracking the sub using the DBT. He had never expected two of the albinos to volunteer so readily to the task.

Swiveling his head to the side, Jake asked, "Can you tell me how many people are aboard that boat?"

Several seconds passed before Destiny replied. "Hermes has seen five men."

Jake weighed this information carefully as he kept his eyes trained on the approaching vessel. The rudiments of an idea suddenly came to him, and he explored it further. Yes, it just might work. Cutting back on the throttle, he leaned the Kawasaki hard to port, coming about by almost 180 degrees. Taking on the same heading as the boat carrying the albinos, he sped away from it. Although the distance separating them was still substantial, he increased it even more, hoping the waverunner's low profile had so far kept them from being spotted.

"What are you doing?" Destiny wailed. "Go back!"

"I have a plan," Jake shouted above the rush of wind. "Trust me on this." Opening up more distance from the oncoming vessel, he raced on for perhaps another mile before slowing and turning off the engine. Pivoting in his seat, he spun around to face the girl. "This is what I have in mind."

Maritime Law

The man piloting the Casa-212 got back on the radio, unable to keep the delight he felt out of his tone. "Nice job, Predator. You certainly have a way with dolphins." Shooting a quick glance at his fuel gauge, he added, "Time for me to head back, though. I'm close to running on fumes. See you at the dock. Bird of Prey signing off."

Bringing the aircraft out of another steep bank, he brought the plane back on a straight and level flight, setting his course for home. As he looked up from the console, his eyes were immediately drawn to the bright red plume arcing high above the sea. A second later, his partner's voice came back. "Stick around one more minute, BP, and give me a heads up on that flare. I assume you see it."

"Only a blind man would miss it," the pilot keyed back, studying the source of the flare no more than half a mile off the Bertram's bow.

Dipping the nose of the Casa, he swooped lower, getting a good look at two people waving their arms frantically as they sat aboard a small watercraft. "Looks like a man and woman on a waverunner. Probably run outta gas."

"Strange that they'd be so far from land," the pilot's partner said.

"Exactly what I'm thinking," the pilot agreed. "Give me a minute. I'm coming around for another pass." Banking hard and dropping one of the wingtips to within fifty feet of the water, he got a better look at both parties. Grinning, he keyed the radio again. "Appears to me the girl's quite a looker, Predator. Maybe you should just keep going. I'd rather you not be distracted in view of what you're carrying."

"No way, BP," the voice at the other end responded acidly. "That flare was red, signifying an emergency distress signal. Under maritime law, I have a moral and legal obligation to assist them."

"When was it you became such an upstanding mariner," the pilot quipped lightly, absolutely certain his associate had by now gotten a good look at the girl through the binoculars he kept near the helm. "Or is it more likely that ignoring a pretty face is just too much for you to handle."

A momentary silence ensued before the expected reply spilled from the radio like a swarm of angry bees pouring from a hive. "Up yours, BP. I'll drop the two of them off in Port-au-Prince."

"Suit yourself, Predator," the pilot said knowingly, well aware of the weakness his partner had for women. "See you back at the dock. Bird of Prey, flyin' away." Smiling at the cleverness of his rhyme, he gained altitude and left the stranded party of two far behind him.

Chapter Nineteen: Freeing the Dolphins

Jake caught the line thrown to him as the Bertram drew alongside the Kawasaki. Letting the small craft drift back behind the larger vessel, he read the name *Sea Lion* on the Bertram's stern. Rising conspicuously above the back deck was a pair of heavy-duty lifting davits designed for lowering and raising multi-ton loads to and from the water. Keeping his scrutiny casual, he could see the boat had been specially modified to take aboard sizable cargoes. Several crewmen milling about the deck cast curious glances at him and Destiny as they poured water over something below his line of sight. A handsome middle-aged Caucasian of medium build climbed down from the bridge and leaned over the rear transom, his eyes roaming hungrily over Destiny before sizing Jake up in the manner of an animal trainer assessing a wild beast. "Quite a bit off the beaten path, aren't you?" the man stated. "Your waverunner break down?"

"Yeah," Jake said innocently. "Just conked out on us. Would you mind giving us a tow?"

The man rested a lingering gaze on Destiny again, seeming to ignore Jake for the moment. "Tell ya what," he finally said, "if you don't mind being dropped off in Port-au-Prince, I have no problem giving you a tow."

Jake produced a false smile. "Fine by us. Would it be okay if we come aboard?"

The man looked back at Jake, his expression seeming to convey a warning. "I guess that'd be all right so long as you keep out of the way. Pull your runner up against the swim platform and watch your step." He suddenly grinned from ear to ear, displaying a set of even white teeth. "I wouldn't want this young lady to slip and fall."

Jake pulled the Kawasaki up tight against the platform, and as he did so the man climbed down and extended a hand to Destiny, helping her aboard. The hefty six-shooter holstered firmly to the man's right thigh immediately caught Jake's attention, and he recognized it to be a 0.357 magnum with a six-inch barrel. The sight of it was imposing, giving the man an air of latent deadliness that implied a lack of hesitation in using it. Pretending to be oblivious of the weapon, Jake hopped onto the platform behind Destiny, making sure the tow rope was fastened securely to one of the Bertram's stern cleats.

"Loomins the name," the man said effervescently, addressing Destiny as he continued to hold onto her hand. "Ben Loomins. And you are?"

With doe-like eyes, Destiny stared searchingly into Loomins' face longer than she should have, making Jake nervous that she would be unable to keep up the deception. From recent experience, he sensed the girl had an uncanny ability to probe down to the true nature of a person, any person. Physical contact appeared to be her primary means of doing this. And although he had seen her use this mode to heal, there seemed to be imponderable surges of energy that flowed from her touch, as if she were attuned to ferreting out the darkest and deepest secrets of a person. He wondered if she was doing this now.

It suddenly occurred to him that he'd heard of Loomins, though he had never met the man. Another name suddenly popped into his head as he searched his memory. Frank Jaffey was Loomins' associate, a pilot of colorful repute who operated mostly out of Haiti and some of the other Caribbean islands. A graduate of the U.S. Naval Academy, Jaffey had spent a good ten years as a fighter pilot, primarily flying sorties from aircraft carriers. Jake had met the man briefly in the midst of a lively poker game aboard the *USS Ticonderoga* just prior to one of his Seal missions during the invasion of Iraq. Jaffey had been extremely lucky, winning most of the hands. And although Jake had no way of proving it at the time, he had the feeling Jaffey had found an undetectable way of cheating.

"And you are?" Loomins repeated uncomfortably, his smile beginning to falter.

The word spilled demurely from the girl's mouth. "Destiny."

Jake thought it wise to intervene. "My friend warned me about taking this baby outta sight of land," he said flippantly, looking back at the Kawasaki and shaking his head.

Seemingly awakening to Destiny's companion once again, Loomins let go of the girl's hand and swung his attention back to Jake. "So why'd you do it then?" There was an edge to his tone, as if annoyed by Jake's presence.

"Oh, I don't know," Jake replied, doing his best to inject cheer into his tone. "Always did have a reckless streak, I guess." As soon as he uttered the words, he realized they weren't far from the truth. Withdrawing his eyes from the Kawasaki, he turned around to face Loomins, making sure to keep his manner jocular. It was important he play the part of the buffoon to keep Loomins lulled into complacency. The last thing he wanted was to arouse the man's suspicions. "I once tried to hitch a ride on a ten-foot tiger shark and got bitten for my trouble," he added jestfully, raising his forearm to show Loomins the prominent scar. As Loomins surveyed the old wound, Jake took the opportunity to assess the man up close. It was in his nature never to underestimate an opponent.

"Never a wise thing to do," Loomins grumbled, lifting his eyes to Jake's face. "What's your name?"

"Nick Henderson." Jake had originally planned to use another name, but something that had been nagging at him made him use the identity of Grahm's testy assistant.

"So, what was your starting point before ending up here?" Loomins asked, his gaze suddenly falling on the Kawasaki and studying it oddly.

"Southwest side of Tortuga Island," Jake stated. "Buddy of mine has an estate right there on the beach. Thought I'd do a little exploring, maybe see Navassa Island."

"You're lucky I found you," Loomins said icily, his tone chastising. "Venturing out into the open sea on a tiny craft like that is a dumb thing to do, especially when you're flirting with someone else's life besides your own. There's no telling what might have happened to this lovely young wife of yours if I hadn't come along when I did."

Jake got his first inkling of the man's subtlety. Loomins was both testing his relationship with Destiny and trying to curry favor with her by acting the part of the heroic savior. Excellent, Jake thought. The man was lowering his guard already.

Jake found it necessary to elicit a stupid lopsided grin. "Like I said, I've always had this reckless streak, but Destiny is not my wife."

Loomins' looked back at the girl with renewed interest. "My mistake," he apologized without sincerity, almost puffing up with delight. "I somehow got the impression you two were newlyweds on your honeymoon."

"No, just friends out for an afternoon spin," Jake clarified breezily.

Loomins looked back at the Kawasaki again, as if remembering something he had seen. "Why does the waverunner have those brackets up front?"

Jake had anticipated such a query. "My friend's an avid photographer. Those brackets are designed for mounting photographic equipment. You should see his house. It's alive with pictures showing tropical settings all along Tortuga and northern Haiti."

Loomins nodded as if satisfied with the explanation. "Uh huh!" Abruptly, he glanced at his watch. "I seem to be getting behind schedule. Come on back here and sit yourself down," he said, pointing to the short flight of stairs leading from the swim platform onto the Bertram's rear deck.

The girl was first up, and as Jake climbed onto the deck, he got his first glimpse of Hermes and Aphrodite. Both dolphins lay firmly strapped upon modified litters designed to restrict their movements. As Jake had hoped, Destiny said nothing.

"Interesting cargo you have there," Jake said, feigning ignorant curiosity over the creatures. "I never saw Beluga whales before."

Loomins let out a laugh filled with ridicule. "They're not Belugas, boy. Belugas are only found in cold Arctic waters. These are white bottlenose dolphins."

"I thought all dolphins were gray," Jake lied, hoping he wasn't overdoing the act.

Loomins appraised his trophies with a smug expression. "For the most part, that's true. But these babies are exceptionally rare, perhaps a brand-new species never before seen."

Jake decided to test the man. "You mean because their skin is milky white?" He had to know just how much the man knew about these creatures.

Loomins stepped over to the nearest dolphin and inclined his head. "You ever see a dolphin with one of these?" he asked, reaching down, and lifting the creature's left pectoral fin just enough to reveal a partially extended prehensile appendage protruding limply.

From the listlessness of both animals, Jake assumed they had been sedated with tranquilizers. Fighting the anger rising in him, he pretended astonishment. "Is that a hand?"

"Damned straight it's a hand," Loomins said. "Each of these dolphins has two of them."

Jake shot a quick look at Destiny to see if she was staying calm. The girl's expression remained stoic as she gazed upon the captured creatures, although he detected a slight mistiness to her eyes. "I take it you're in the business of catching live dolphins," Jake said. "What do you do with them?"

Loomins released his hold on the dolphin and stared at Jake. "I sell them," he replied irritably. Turning in annoyance, he frowned angrily at two of the closest crewmen, both of whom Jake perceived to be Haitians. "I thought I told you to keep dousing these valuable specimens with seawater," he barked furiously. "You want this hot tropical sun to raise their core body temperatures. If they're not kept cool, they'll die."

It became apparent to Jake that Loomins had a short fuse, but with the man's attention momentarily diverted, he took the opportunity to study the dolphins more closely. The eyelids of both cetaceans drooped noticeably. Hermes was the larger of the two creatures and the one Loomins had singled out to display the unusual appendage. The DBT unit that had been strapped to the albino's back was now gone, evidently removed by one of the boat's crew and stowed someplace.

Abruptly, Loomins turned back to Jake and looked at his watch again. "Try and amuse yourself for the time being," he said, seemingly gaining control of his temper for the moment, "because that's about all the conversation you'll get outta me for now. Like I told you, I've got a schedule to maintain and, unfortunately, you're holding me up."

Pointing to a large ice chest, he added, "Help yourselves to some cold beer if you're thirsty. Port-au-Prince is close to two hours away."

With that, Loomins spun around and began climbing a set of stairs leading to the bridge. As if forgetting something, he stopped and turned again. "Oh, and by the way," he said stiffly, locking eyes on Jake. "I would appreciate it if the two of you keep to the back deck and stay outta the way. Because of the potential liabilities involved, I don't usually let passengers have the run of my vessel." He paused, as if emphasizing the gravity of the request. "You never know if they'll do something dumb and get themselves hurt." Loomins let the veiled threat linger in the air a moment longer before turning and completing the climb. Ten seconds later, the boat's engine engaged noisily, and the deck shifted underfoot as they got underway.

Feeling his thirst beginning to mount, Jake stepped over to the ice chest and lifted the cover, motioning Destiny to his side as he did so. Staring at a mixed batch of canned beverages interspersed among a mass of ice cubes, he assessed their current situation. "I think they drugged the dolphins," he said guardedly. Though the decibel level emanating from the vessel's engine was sufficiently loud to keep them from being overheard, he purposely avoided exposing his face to any of the nearby deckhands lest any of them be able to read lips. "Hermes and Aphrodite don't seem right. Are you able to talk with them?"

The girl gave a slight nod of her head, keeping her face turned away from the crew as well. "Both are barely able to communicate with me. These men shot some kind of sharp projectile into them and they became very weak."

"They were probably hit with tranquilizer darts. In their current state there's a good chance they'll drown even if we're able to free them and get them back in the water."

This bit of news did not sit well with Destiny. "Is there anything you can do?"

Jake looked over at the crewmen. There were three of them. "Hermes told you he had counted five men aboard this vessel, didn't he?"

"Yes."

"Well, if his observation is correct, one man is still missing." Jake pondered this. Perhaps Loomins was not the type of man to leave anything to chance. With strangers aboard, it would be prudent to keep one man out of sight just in case the strangers had ill intentions. It was something Jake would have considered doing himself had he been in Loomins' shoes. "If we're going to do anything," he stressed, "it's crucial we find out where that fifth man is."

Destiny gazed up at him with soulful eyes. "How?"

Jake's mind moved into high gear, giving some thought to a standard military tactic used in the Seals. "We've got to create a diversion." Reaching down into the ice chest, he retrieved two Coca-colas and handed one to the girl. Popping the tab on the can he held, he took a swig. "Give me a moment to look around. There's got to be something aboard this vessel we can use."

Destiny grabbed Jake's arm. "The pod is on the way."

Jake gave this bit of news mild consideration, trying to figure what good it would do while the Bertram was underway. "You summoned them? When?"

"The moment we left the cove."

Jake gave her a bored nod, then stepped away. Making a show of stretching his arms and yawning deeply, he strolled past the deckhands, moving towards the Bertram's rear cabin. The three crewmen seemed not to notice, totally absorbed in carrying out Loomins orders. Wearing a bored expression on his face, he eyed his surroundings with a casual air. He quickly discovered that the windows to the rear cabin were tinted, obstructing his view of the cabin's interior and making him speculate whether he was currently being spied upon by the missing crewman from the other side of the glass.

A bulky object lay hidden under a heavy tarp situated to one side of the deck. Jake had noticed it earlier and had wondered what the tarp concealed. The glimmer of sunlight reflecting off something caught Jake's attention, prompting him to scrutinize the cause of it. Adjacent to the tarp, a tubular metallic barrel lay atop a pile of bunched up netting, its configuration closely resembling a handheld rocket launcher. Realizing there was something oddly familiar about what he was looking at, he studied it briefly before turning his head, mindful about drawing unwanted attention to himself. He suddenly understood how the albinos had been snared in the open ocean.

The object was a larger version of a webshot, a tool originally developed to capture wild animals without causing them injury. With a muzzle velocity of one-hundred feet per second, the device fired a net that expanded and enveloped the intended quarry, enfolding and restricting the movements of the creature unfortunate enough to be snared. Webshots had a short range, typically less than forty feet, making it necessary that the shooter get close to the target he sought to bag. The device was sometimes used by law enforcement agencies when apprehending dangerous criminals, but Seal teams had also been known to employ the system, utilizing such technology to subdue an enemy combatant without wounding them. Some webshot systems had taglines that connected the launcher with the netting so that the captive animal could be retrieved.

Jake had fired a webshot during his stint with the Seals and was familiar with its effectiveness in neutralizing opponents who could then be interrogated. The system he remembered was a single-shot launcher with a 37-millimeter bore that discharged a 12-ounce projectile, giving the device a hefty kick when fired. Based on that experience, he was certain the larger webshot would have an even more powerful recoil than its smaller cousin, particularly since it would propel a missile carrying a net capable of entrapping a creature the size of Hermes. As if to confirm this, he stole another look at the pile of netting on which the webshot sat, judging the mesh to be strong enough to capture a creature nearly twelve feet in length and weighing close to 1,000 pounds. Something else protruded from under the netting, and he scanned it fleetingly. The realization that he was looking at a webshot cartridge made his heart beat faster, and suddenly his mind scurried over the possibilities it represented.

How the men crewing the *Sea Lion* had been able to draw the albinos into the effective range of the webshot baffled Jake. On impulse, he again eyed the bulky object covered by the tarp, certain that these men had used something unique.

Turning, Jake looked back at Destiny. He was somewhat surprised to see her kneeling down between Hermes and Aphrodite, each of her hands touching the head of each creature. Even more surprising was the way the Haitian crewmen regarded her. They just stared, appearing unsure about the appropriateness of moving her out of the way. Destiny's eyes were closed in deep concentration, as if caught up in the midst of some unseen battle of the mind that required her entire focus.

With the crew's attention momentarily fixated on the girl, Jake decided it was now or never if he was going to make a move. Boldly, he stepped quickly to the door of the rear cabin and turned the knob, knowing what he would find on the other side. Closing the door behind him, he glanced to his right. Just as he had anticipated, a man wielding a carbine stood at the rear window. From the stunned expression on the man's face, Jake suspected he had been distracted in the same manner as the deckhands. Giving his opponent a fiendish grin, Jake pushed aside the rifle before it could be raised and landed a vicious kick that connected brutally with the man's stomach. With an almost imperceptible grunt, the man staggered backwards with the wind knocked from him. Following up on the attack, Jake snatched the weapon from the man's grasp and, in one smooth motion, clipped the man cleanly on the chin with the stock of the firearm. The man's body went slack almost immediately, but before his legs gave way, Jake caught him and gently lowered him to the floor. As the fallen foe lay comatose, something in the man's features made Jake do a double take. Though he was several years younger and sported a crooked nose, the man bore a striking resemblance to Ben Loomins.

Getting back to the business at hand, Jake turned and looked through the cabin's rear windows. The three deckhands were still preoccupied with the sight of Destiny kneeling between the albinos, seemingly unaware as to what had just taken place. With seasoned skill, Jake checked the carbine to see if it was loaded. Satisfied that a round was currently chambered in the weapon, he opened the cabin door and calmly sauntered back out onto the deck. One of the Haitians noticed him, abruptly going rigid when he saw the rifle pointed in his direction. Within moments, the other two men became cognizant of the threat Jake suddenly posed, and they too froze in fear. Wearing a devilish smile, Jake motioned the men over to the rear cabin where he made them lie face down on the deck.

With the crew neutralized, Jake crouched down next to Destiny. "How're our friends doing?" he asked, looking cautiously above him for any sign of Loomins. The boat's engines continued to drone on monotonously in an unaltered tempo, giving him a partial assurance that the man at the helm was currently engrossed in piloting the vessel.

As if emerging from a deep sleep, Destiny opened her eyes and gazed wearily at Jake. "Their strength is returning," she replied, her tone carrying fatigue. "I think they'll be able to swim." Both dolphins stirred as she said this, and Jake sensed the creatures were now coming out of their drug-induced stupors.

Pulling the K-Bar from its sheath, Jake sliced the leather restraints holding each albino to its litter. Hermes was the first to fully revive, and Jake watched in amazement as the male extended its prehensile appendages to their fullest and began dragging himself along the deck in a series of waddling, flopping hops. A few seconds later, Aphrodite did the same, following Hermes to the rearmost section of the deck where access to the sea was easiest. One after the other, they reached up and grabbed hold of the starboard railing, heaving themselves over the boat's side and sending out a heavy spray as they hit the water.

Stunned by the impressive spectacle, Jake had difficulty finding his voice. "I think it's time we departed the company of these fine gentlemen." Guardedly, he glanced over at the deckhands as they continued to stare in wide-eyed astonishment at what they had just witnessed.

Destiny reached out and clutched Jake by the arm. She appeared physically drained. "Wait!" she said weakly. "There's something I must do first."

Jake was mystified. "What's that?"

"A man aboard this boat is dying. I have to help him."

A frown flooded Jake's face. "How do you know that?"

"I felt his pain."

"Where is he?"

Destiny pointed to the rear cabin. "In there."

Jake had difficulty accepting this news. "If it's the man I kayoed, I only gave him a love tap."

Destiny looked up at him, her expression devoid of judgement or accusation of any kind. "I cannot leave until I help him," she insisted.

Though her voice lacked potency, Jake could feel a powerful sense of purpose underlying her conviction. Momentarily caught in the grip of indecision, he glanced cautiously toward the bridge as he listened to the beat of the engines pushing the vessel steadily onward. Up until now, everything had played out in their favor, but their mission was not yet over. From experience, he knew how quickly that could change. "Alright," he agreed. "But try to hurry."

Gesturing with the rifle for the deckhands to get to their feet, Jake herded the men into the cabin with Destiny following slowly behind him. "Stand over there!" he ordered the Haitians. "If you behave, I promise no one will get hurt."

With diminished vigor, the girl moved to where the unconscious man lay and placed a hand on his forehead. Jake could see the man's breathing was labored and that his skin had paled considerably.

"What's wrong with him?" Jake needed to know, fending off the guilt he was suddenly feeling.

Destiny did not immediately answer, letting her fingers roam languorously over the man's cranium as if searching for something. "He…he has a ruptured blood vessel," she finally replied. Her normally mellifluous voice was languid and lacking vitality.

"I caused it?"

Destiny stopped momentarily to look back at Jake, her eyes full of sympathy. "This man had a preexisting condition, a…a brain aneurysm. Any blow to the head would have triggered it." Focusing her gaze back on the man, she placed both hands on his head and closed her eyes, once again seeming to draw on some hidden force from deep within.

Jake kept his eyes on the crewmen, careful not to let his vigilance relax, but at the same time attempting to get a read on what kind of a threat they might present. From the manner in which Loomins had spoken to them, there was a good chance they would not be eager participants in trying to interfere. As he studied their faces, however, it soon became apparent they were caught up in awed fascination as they watched the girl, almost as though in worship.

Anxiety began to take hold of Jake as Destiny continued to kneel over the man. He sensed she wasn't her usual self. Even with the Islamic militant he had captured, the girl had not taken this long to heal the injury. Then it hit him. Prior to this excursion, the albinos had always assisted the girl during healings. But now she was working alone. He could see it was visibly sapping her, sucking the very life force from her body.

With sudden concern, he moved to her side as she began to slump lethargically over her patient, but as he did so the man let out a prolonged gasp. The deathly paleness that had dominated the man's pallor moments earlier abruptly vanished, and slowly his eyes fluttered dazedly open, all signs of comprehension still absent from them. In that moment, Jake was certain the man would live, that whatever infirmity had plagued him before was now completely repaired.

Jake assisted the girl to her feet, wanting only to get her back aboard the Kawasaki and put distance between them and the *Sea Lion*. But when Destiny faltered on unsteady legs, he realized she would not be able to walk. "Time to leave," he uttered, slinging her over one shoulder while maintaining his hold on the carbine. Quickly, he carried her from the cabin and moved across the back deck. He had almost reached the short flight of stairs that descended to the swim platform when the engines suddenly changed pitch, falling off sharply to an idle. Underfoot, the deck shifted as the vessel lost momentum, and with it, an angry voice bellowed. "Hold it right there or, by God, I'll shoot you where you stand!"

Jake stopped in midstride and froze.

"Drop the rifle and turn around!" Ben Loomins ordered. "Try anything and I'll blow your fucking head off."

Jake did as he was told, knowing their luck had changed for the worse.

"What'd you do with my dolphins?" Loomins yelled, his eyes seething with rage as he climbed down from the bridge. The magnum pistol he had worn was unholstered and aimed directly at Jake.

Jake knew he had to be careful how he replied. Loomins was beside himself with madness, and the wrong choice of words might put the man over the edge. With Destiny slumped over his shoulder in her current state, a remembrance of Afghanistan entered his mind, and he wondered if a similar outcome was drifting in on him with this sudden shift in the winds of fate. Overcome with these thoughts, he just stood there and said nothing as Loomins moved to within five feet of him with murder in his eyes.

Chapter Twenty: Jacob's Musings

The cove was not the same as Jacob looked out over the water. With the exception of two injured grays that were still recovering, the remainder of the pod was gone, including Destiny. This was not good, he thought. The pod had a pivotal role to play in bringing the plan to fruition, and Destiny was the catalyst that would make this possible. She was the key structural member upon which all the others balanced, the main pillar crucial to holding aloft their hopes and dreams, the very future of all life on the planet. Without her, everything would crumple and collapse under forces that were much too powerful to stop.

Jacob turned his thoughts to the man called Jake Javolyn. When he had first set eyes on him, he had been nearly certain he was looking at the man depicted in the cave painting. Never one to jump headlong to conclusions, however, he had found it necessary to test this assumption. On the ride back from Navassa he had formulated a scheme to assess Jake's moral rectitude, although Destiny had originally harbored scruples about carrying it out. Having healed Jake's arm, Destiny had already gotten a glimpse of the man's fundamental nature, and she was convinced Jake was the protector. Jacob, on the other hand, was not so quick to accept this. He had to remind the girl what a harsh mistress temptation could be, often corrupting otherwise good and noble men through the lure of incredible riches. After much urging, he had finally had his way, persuading Destiny to bring the matter to the pod's attention. It had been decided that Achilles would show Jake the *thurentra* and gauge the man's reaction to the sight of precious metals littering the base of the hybrid organism. And though Achilles had told Jake that the production of gold and platinum held no benefit, from the young albino's perspective it was not altogether a lie. Gold and platinum were most commonly used as a medium of exchange. By themselves, such commodities provided no direct benefit to those possessing them since the metals constituted neither a viable source of nourishment nor consumable energy.

Jacob nodded inwardly without any regrets at having revealed the most alluring facet of the *thurentra* to a total stranger. It had been a risk, but one worth taking. Jake Javolyn had so far demonstrated a remarkable degree of moral integrity in refraining from making off with some of the riches he had seen. That made the man altogether rare, and one to be appreciated all the more. Javolyn had something they all needed if the plan was to succeed, and that was a willingness to attack evil head-on with no misgivings about using deadly force. It was a trait they all lacked.

As he pondered such thoughts, Jacob glanced around the cove. Both Dr. Grahm and Jeffrey Parker were still busy at one end of the beach fiddling with some of the electronic gadgetry they had brought ashore. Turning his head, he caught sight of Nick Henderson donning mask, fins and snorkel, apparently preparing for a swim away from the beach. He knew what the graduate student was up to. He had seen him fin out to where the *thurentra* lay submerged earlier in the day. And although Hercules had shooed him away, he had the feeling the contentious youth had already seen the glitter of gold beneath the water. Realizing his mistake in leaving such wealth unattended, he had asked the albinos to collect the glimmering grains and hide them in the usual place. Normally they did this only once every four weeks, but one could never be overly cautious, and now they were scooping up the grains once each hour to make sure a noticeable pile did not accumulate. By his estimation, the *thurentra* was currently filtering out approximately eight pounds of highly concentrated precious metal from seawater each day. At most, Henderson would only see a few grains of the stuff settled in the sand, byproducts of the *thurentra*'s strange metabolic process.

The *thurentra*'s ability to collect such valuable elements had initially baffled Jacob when deposits of the metals first began accumulating about five years earlier. Through research, he had learned that seawater normally contained extremely small concentrations of gold in soluble form. Values ranged worldwide, with average concentrations reportedly running at approximately thirteen parts per trillion. Through

rough calculations, he had estimated the volume of seawater the hybrid organism was capable of drawing up from the deep each day, determining that the observed amounts of gold harvested would have been impossible to produce based on such negligible concentrations. The only other explanation Jacob could come up with was that the *thurentra* tentacles had worked their way into gold-enriched layers of sulfide compounds typically found at great ocean depths. He knew that the Caribbean Sea descended to a depth of four miles in the Cayman Trench whose eastern end was less than 300 kilometers from the cove's location. Continuing to delve into the subject, Jacob discovered that gold ores were often associated with sulfide deposits formed by hydrothermal vents commonly found in extremely deep regions of the sea where the earth's crustal plates were thinnest and moving apart. In such locations, superheated seawater emanating from cracks and fissures in the ocean floor dissolved minerals and metals in much higher concentrations than could occur in cold water. Upon reaching the frigid seafloor waters, dissolved precious metals and minerals precipitated out of solution, forming chimney-like vent structures, which eventually collapsed and formed again. Over long periods of time, immense mounds of these structures tended to build up, predominantly composed of iron and sulfide compounds. Sulfur-oxidizing bacteria found along these vents also had the potential of concentrating gold to even higher levels.

Although such facts lent ample support as to how the *thurentra* was able to produce such high-grade gold and platinum, Jacob failed to come up with a plausible explanation as to why the jellyfish-like creature was able to separate only these elements from the other metals and minerals, eventually bringing them to the surface waters in a purified state. Then again, finding an answer really didn't matter to him. The introduction of the precious metals into Gaia had opened new doors of possibility, both bad and good, depending on how you looked at them.

Jacob's mullings suddenly shifted to the mass genocide of the Tainos. Only a small portion of the once thriving population had survived, hidden away in the relative safety of this sanctuary long ago, of that he had no doubts. Concealed within the cave behind the falls at the far end of the cove, a mysterious linkage existed between the past and present. If word ever got out about what was produced at the bottom of the cove, he knew Gaia would be overrun with treasure hunters and soldiers of fortune, ultimately falling victim to the destructive nature of humanity's greed, something it had been spared from in earlier times, but that was mere speculation on his part. And inasmuch as he abhorred the potential harm the metal could bring to the pod, he had no choice in using it if the plan was ever to succeed. By his estimation they already had close to five tons of gold and two tons of platinum stored away within the cove and almost twice that amount at Navassa. On today's market, that equated to more than half a billion in U.S. dollars, enough to finance the future of the new species and a new beginning for Haiti. As time went on, he knew such staggering wealth would steadily increase as the *thurentra*s continued to strain more and more metal from the ocean depths.

Jacob sighed with resignation as he watched Henderson flounder out into deeper water. He had warned everyone about touching the *thurentra*. To some people, the electric shock imparted by the organism could be fatal. In some ways, the *thurentra* acted like a huge capacitor, building an electrical charge much the same way certain types of eels were able to do. Aside from manufacturing hydrogen and gold, the creature had the capacity to produce electricity, and although he had been tempted to use such free energy to light his small cabin, he had refrained from doing so to avoid becoming dependent on the use of it. For the most part, he preferred to keep living standards within the cove simple, holding comforts to a minimum. To live ascetically was in harmony with his true nature. Aside from leaving his spirit uncorrupted by outside influences, it also avoided drawing unwanted attention that might otherwise complicate and disrupt the goals he, Amphitrite, and Destiny had set for themselves.

Floating at anchor to the north side of the cove, Javolyn's vessel did little to console Jacob's misgivings about letting these strangers into his tiny kingdom. He suddenly berated himself for his possessiveness, reminding himself that Gaia was not his. Gaia was simply a concept he had rationalized through both observation and a wild stretch of the imagination. But the human mind, his mind, coupled with other unique intellects that were in some respects much more powerful than his, had fashioned possibilities that could be made real. There was a budding fantasy here, intensely envisioned and believed by those nurturing it, one that had the potential of becoming all too real in the not-too-distant future. Though beyond his understanding and control, certain things were meant to happen, the bringing together of circumstances that were rapidly providing the fuel for the fierce battle that was yet to come. Amphitrite had prophesized this. Both the stage and the props had been set, and they were about to act out their parts in the brewing storm of good versus evil that was swiftly building. But the script had not yet been set, something Amphitrite had also foretold. She had warned of the delicate balance and uncertainty woven into the cosmic structure. There would be choices to be made and actions to be carried out, with any wrong decision leading to disaster.

Jacob let his mind drift over what was at stake, instinctively knowing that taking the lead in a project of this magnitude would always be a risky endeavor, particularly when such leadership remained hidden from public scrutiny. But leaving both the dolphins and Haiti to fend for themselves was beyond consideration. He realized that he and his cousin still had another option open to them despite the distance they had so far traveled down the chosen path. Deep down, though, he understood that to retreat in pursuit of an easier life would have left him and Emmanuel devoid of all courage and ideals, something each of them would not and could not let happen no matter what the circumstances. Their course was now set, their conviction unshakable. They were going to act against tyranny, poverty, and oppression. They would strive toward making significant positive changes to a world in desperate need of it.

As Jacob reflected on these things, he wondered how Emmanuel was making out. His cousin should have been back by now from a trip to Anguilla where he had completed setting up the corporate vehicle that would carry them to their objectives. Anguilla was the ideal place for registering an international corporation, mainly because the small Caribbean island required no corporate taxes. In essence, it was the ideal tax-free haven. All of them would be shareholders in Tursiops Worldwide: Destiny, Amphitrite, Emmanuel, Lucette, and he, himself. But it was the new species of albino dolphin that would hold the major interest in the budding venture. It was a concept that had originally taken root in the albino minds some years earlier when Jacob had thought it wise to teach them everything he knew about capitalism, big business, and corporate structure. Tursiops would provide both the impetus and system required to attain their goals, and that was mainly achieving a much higher standard of living for the downtrodden masses.

Jacob smiled to himself as he thought about all the good a cash-rich corporation could do on the international level. He had to be realistic, using a practical approach to the way the modern world worked. Wielded properly, powerful corporations had clout, having the potential to manipulate heads of state and nations into serving their interests. The interests of Tursiops would remain altruistic, run by entities incapable of corruption. Tursiops would work in harmony with the ocean environment, developing and implementing alternative sources of clean renewable energy from the sea, and producing commodities that could be sold on the world market. If Tursiops worked out according to their envisioned plan, it would establish marine-based colonies all over the earth, predominantly in international waters. From an economic standpoint, it would provide vast amounts of energy and food at minimal cost to a consuming world by tapping into the oceanic reservoirs where almost limitless nutrients and previously untapped energy abounded.

Tursiops would unleash a flood tide of food, commodities, and services revolving around sea mining and mariculture, initially bringing in an estimated $12 billion a year that would ultimately enrich Haiti and other poor countries. Conceptually, here was the island nation's best hope for escape from its plight of perpetual wretchedness, an opportunity that just might steer it clear from total economic collapse. Through the production of hydrogen, magnesium, and distilled water alone, sizable revenues could be achieved that would finance the development of new technologies. Previous limits on food productivity resulting from land-based economies would be surpassed to an almost explosive degree through the use of maricultural and ocean farming, not only greatly improving the standard of living for Haiti, but for all nations of the world. Such an enterprise would provide a huge number of jobs for the poor, sprouting forth an economy of a scale never before seen. In its wake, hunger would all but vanish, with a new social structure emerging and evolving in total harmony with the planetary ecosystem. A partnership would develop between man and dolphin that would open the doors to new horizons in scientific research. Spurred on by the albino super-intelligence, the advancement of science and technology would accelerate, with meaningful breakthroughs occurring at a faster rate. In the sea colonies, crime, brutality, and social disorder would give way to intellectual, artistic, philosophical, and spiritual pursuits, setting the individual free from the lone struggle for survival that had characterized old and contemporary societies. In short, a new beginning in human evolution would commence, unrivaled by anything that had come before it. Through the combined leadership of the company's board of directors, Tursiops would empower both Haitians and cetaceans to transform their lives in a single generation.

Such thoughts tended to heighten Jacob's expectations of the future. Sometimes you had to hit rock bottom before you could begin the arduous climb back up. Here was Haiti's way out of the hole it had become mired in. If everything went to plan, no longer would it be suppressed and tortured by successive waves of domestic and international politics that washed away all hope. Innovation would pave the way for change.

Yes, Jacob reasoned, although such a grand undertaking would be immensely difficult to accomplish, it would not be unworkable. They just had to be resolute in holding onto their conviction, to keep believing the idea was possible. Over the years he had learned that anything was possible as long as you believed in it with every fiber of your being. And though it was Esmerelda who had first tried to make him understand this, it was Amphitrite who had actually made him feel the absolute power underlying it. There would be no try, no meager stab at hoping for the best, for such outlooks were too diluted in ambivalence to have any chance of success. No, the fantasy would be made altogether real by stripping away all negative leanings, all doubts. The power of their minds would work together, both human and delphine, to forge the path of their trajectories through space-time. Sentient intelligence would be used to mold the future. The mind was truly an integral part of the cosmos, and somewhere deep within this strange domain of seemingly endless chaos and swirling motes, an eerie symmetrical type of order existed that could be manipulated through conscious, and perhaps even unconscious, thought. Yes, perhaps there was a dimension where physical laws and mysticism eventually merged, intertwining and combining into a simple structure, one that determined a reality of our choosing, a place immune to the winds of chance.

Movement aboard the *Avenging Angel* caught Jacob's eye, unhinging him of these thoughts. He watched as the hulking giant, Zimbola, led the man Jake Javolyn had captured to the vessel's rear platform, apparently giving the captive a breath of fresh air. Taking a moment to study the large man, he realized how fortunate Javolyn was to have such a devoted shipmate, judging that the man's outward appearance could be somewhat misleading to anyone who did not know him. Though physically imposing and obviously possessing great strength, there was also another side to the Jamaican that somehow reminded Jacob of Hercules. Zimbola, he was certain, was one of those exceptionally rare men that would follow a person to whom they held allegiance into the very bowels of hell itself. Here was an individual who would stand steadfast behind Javolyn against all odds no matter what the circumstances, with little or no concern for his own personal safety. Unwavering loyalty, Jacob knew, was an uncommonly noble quality in human beings, a trait to be admired and treasured whenever one was fortunate enough to find it. Strangely enough, it had a tendency to show up in the most unlikely places.

Shifting his eyes to the man being led by Zimbola, Jacob became aware of the painting in the captive's hands. To the Haitian, this was not surprising. He recalled what had taken place minutes before Jake Javolyn had bolted from the cove with Destiny seated behind him on the waverunner. Javolyn had hurriedly asked Jacob if he could borrow the painting produced by Achilles. "The painting is not mine to lend," Jacob had told him with measured solemnity, already sensing what Javolyn intended to do with it. "Only Achilles can give such permission." But before Javolyn could redirect the question to the youngest member of the pod, Achilles had quickly swum over to him, holding the painting above the water. "I would be honored if you would keep this, Jay Jay," the dolphin had said, his speech coming out in a high-pitched squeal.

So, Jake Javolyn hopes to turn the Islamist by means of the albino art, Jacob thought to himself as he observed the bearded captive holding the painting in both hands. Even from where he stood, he could discern the look of deep contemplation etched on the man's face. As Jacob witnessed the scene taking place at the stern end of Javolyn's vessel, two conflicting questions struck him. If the man was truly a follower of Islam, was his faith strong enough to sustain itself in the face of the strange effect such art had on some people? Or was it that the man was simply unhappy with who he was, what he had become? Here was a test, one that might lend support to Jake Javolyn's previous assertion, though to Jacob it did not make any sense. This made him reexamine it all over again. Was the man a blind follower of distorted Islamic tenets, false doctrines concocted by militant zealots for the purpose of satisfying hate through the mass murder of innocents? Had the man actually been part of a team set on carrying out some vile deed of destruction?

Sitting down in the sand, Jacob studied Zimbola's charge at a distance with the impartial eyes of the true scientist, looking for any overt signs in the way the man was being affected by what lay on the canvas. Not having anything better to do at the moment, he continued to stare out of curiosity, trying to ignore the restless anxiety churning in the back of his mind over the fate of Hermes and Aphrodite.

Chapter Twenty-one: Raduyev's Hidden Base

The leader of the three mujahideen's continued to stare at Raduyev with those same sad eyes the Chechen well remembered. Raduyev fought back the scowl that surged up from the pit of his stomach, meeting the Pashtun's striking blue eyes with a fierce, defiant glare of his own. He would not be fooled by Sherkhan's seemingly downcast manner, knowing what lay just below the surface.

"You were late," Sherkhan stated, finally breaking the brooding silence he had manifested ever since being met at sea. Though his voice came out in a bland monotone, Raduyev sensed a subtle reprimand in the tone. "The captain of the freighter was very displeased. He did not like having to wait as long as he did for you to show up. Had you forgotten our planned rendezvous was to take place under the cover of night and not in broad daylight?"

Raduyev was not about to tolerate any criticism. "A small problem arose that delayed us," he retorted testily. "What does it matter, anyway?"

Sherkhan's eyes narrowed. "The captain risked drawing attention to his vessel," he pointed out.

"But that did not happen," Raduyev scoffed.

"A ship flying the Yemeni flag and drifting out in the middle of the Caribbean without the engines engaged is very conspicuous," Sherkhan went on blandly. "It could easily cause passing vessels or aircraft to come and see if there is a problem. We have a schedule to maintain, and you put this mission in jeopardy by exposing this submarine." Pausing, his normally morose features abruptly hardened in preparation for the words that followed. "I would like to think the right man is leading us." Letting out a seemingly bored sigh, he added, "Kalid tells me you had taken this vessel to the Haitian coast where you lost Bashir. Is this true, and if it is, for what purpose did you make this unscheduled trip?"

Raduyev shot a look of contempt at his second in command before turning his gaze back to the Pashtun. "I warn you not to insult or berate me. His Supreme Holiness, Osama Bin Laden, himself, may he live forever, has personally placed me in charge of this mission. By insulting me, you insult him."

Sherkhan touched his forehead and gave a slight bow. "Forgive me, my Muslim brother. For all eternity may you reside at the right hand of Allah in the next life that awaits you. God is great, and he will surely reward you for bearing on your shoulders this most sacred duty. As you have already proven, you are a great and noble holy warrior, one of the very strongest among us. Your skill as a fighter is fast becoming legendary, making some among us believe a man like yourself could only have been forged by the Almighty Allah to carry out his work. Guided by your hand, we will bring the Great Satan to his knees, and if God wills it, perhaps even inflict a mortal blow to Islam's greatest enemy. I, along with these two other servants of Allah, have come to aid you as was planned. We are fully prepared to follow you in fulfilling this most holy task, and if need be, to shed our blood in the sanctity of martyrdom. I only ask that you do not let personal vendettas cloud your judgement."

Raduyev glanced maliciously at Kalid once more. It was apparent Kalid had told Sherkhan everything. But the Pashtun had shown respect with his words of appeasement, and slowly, Raduyev allowed his heated glare to cool. "There is much work still needing to be done," he finally said, "considerably more than our small band can complete in so short a period of time. We will require many more strong backs if we are to meet our timetable. That is why I have arranged to have some more people brought here."

Sherkhan showed surprise. "Why was I not told of this before?"

"You had no need to know of this," Raduyev replied coldly.

"These people…they are Muslims?"

Raduyev was in no mood for any more insurrection, unable to keep the sarcasm from his voice. "I do not think you will find many people of the Islamic faith among these islanders. No, a sizable contingent of heathen infidels will be brought to us. We will use them as slaves to speed up the backbreaking labor needed to clear away large amounts of rock within these caverns."

From the Pashtun's expression, Raduyev could tell his old comrade in arms was not very comfortable with this idea. "And how will these people be brought here?" Sherkhan asked.

"They will arrive on the southern shore of this island, ferried in by boat two days from now."

"Under the cover of darkness?"

Raduyev scowled deeply, his eyes flashing with anger once again. He was growing tired of Sherkhan's questions. "We will meet them at midnight and escort them down here through the passage that extends to the island's surface." He cast his eyes to one end of the underground chamber where a string of electric lights disappeared into a narrow crevice set back in the rock. "Some of these passageways will have to be widened if we are to assemble and then lift the delivery system clear of these caves."

Sherkhan nodded with mild satisfaction, appearing quite at home in his present surroundings. With the exception of the deep pool of water dominating the center of the chamber, the place was not unlike the rocky underground fortresses he had spent so much time living in back along the Pakistani border. He let his eyes roam approvingly over the length and breadth of the cavern that housed Allah's Sword. "Osama would be pleased to see what you have already accomplished. You have chosen well in establishing such a base. From here, you will be able to carry out any number of missions undetected."

A satanic grin replaced the scowl that had been preponderating Raduyev's face, ameliorated all the more by the strange glow cast by the electric bulbs lighting the subterranean grotto. "It will be the first strike conducted from this sanctuary that will be the most important. God willing, we should be able to launch our attack on schedule."

"Then you have already located the weapon?" Sherkhan asked, his normally insipid voice feeling strangely tense within his own throat.

"Yes, the coordinates were very accurate."

Sherkhan glanced around again. "How will you bring it up? I see nothing at your disposal that can lift a weapon of that size."

Raduyev indicated the crates that were currently being removed from the sub by the other men. "That is the means by which we will lift the weapon."

Sherkhan stared blankly, not understanding Raduyev's meaning.

"I have struck an accord with others who have no love for the Great Satan," the Chechen explained. "They will provide the machinery for bringing the weapon up from the depths. The heroin you have brought will be a down payment on the use of their ship and winches. Once the bomb is recovered, the bomb will be exchanged for the remainder of the heroin aboard the Spirit of Aden."

Once again, Sherkhan's manner became uneasy. "Can these people be trusted?"

"Their very cupidity will keep their affiliation with us safe. Like most infidels, they are blinded by greed. They salivate for a continuing supply of the white heroin, which is in great demand on the black markets of America and Europe. It is these people who will give us money and other necessities in exchange for this much sought after narcotic. For the time being they will serve as an important ally, one that will increase our chances of success. These same people will provide us with the slave labor we so desperately need."

The expression on Sherkhan's face reverted back to one of melancholy. "What about the Haitian colonel? Can he be trusted to guard our secret?"

A malicious little laugh sprang from Raduyev's lips, echoing eerily within the confines of the cavern. "The man's hunger for power will keep him silent. He seeks to seize control of Haiti once the Americans are preoccupied with the death and destruction we will unleash upon them."

The Chechen smirked inwardly as he remembered the havoc created by Hurricane Katrina after it had laid waste New Orleans in 2005. Bloated by complacency and the bungling of inept bureaucrats, the United States government had been ill prepared to take on such a crisis, failing miserably in the way it had handled the devastation and chaos in the wake of the monster storm. The blow they now planned to inflict would be far worse, ultimately precipitating anarchy of apocalyptic dimensions. After that, Iran would step in, using its newly acquired nuclear capability to finish the job.

Gaining control of the glee taking hold of him, Raduyev grew serious again as he gave Sherkhan's question more thought. "You were not informed that it was the Haitian colonel who had offered us the weapon?"

Sherkhan shook his head slowly. "During the last year I have had little contact with our exalted leaders, spending most of my time eluding capture by the Americans." The Pashtun abruptly fell pensive, seeming to mull something weighing heavily on him. "So, it would appear this colonel is using us as a tool to satisfy his own ambitions, much the way we are using these infidels you speak of to bring up the weapon."

"The man's feeble grab for power is of little concern to us," Raduyev replied, punctuating it with another small laugh. His mind rested briefly on the staggering stipulations Bin Laden had agreed to in order to procure the bomb. The extent of the Colonel's greed stunned the imagination. For one, there was the down payment of $50 million in euros deposited in a discreet Cayman bank account controlled by the Colonel. Then there was the Yemeni arms dealer they had set up in Port-au-Prince to stockpile the weapons the Colonel would require. Both of these things Bin Laden had readily arranged in order to learn the bomb's location. But then there was the delicate multi-party deal Bin Laden had been able to broker with North Korea and Hezbollah in order to ensure the success of their plan, a multifaceted transaction in which the Colonel would also be a beneficiary. But Bin Laden had been getting short of funds as it was, and he had thought it economically prudent to resell the bomb to Hezbollah at an exorbitant profit, figuring Iran's scientists could get it in working order far quicker than his own people. And finally, there had been the other two items the Colonel was to receive once they had the bomb in their possession.

Raduyev dismissed these thoughts, knowing Bin Laden would be highly displeased if these last two items failed to be delivered, for they would still need the Colonel's cooperation in the aftermath of the first strike. Ever since Afghanistan had fallen, his people had needed a new country from which to operate with impunity, and Haiti was the perfect country from which to plan and execute renewed attacks against the United States.

"Let him set himself up as a king," Raduyev grunted. "Eventually we will take control of every island nation within the Caribbean, converting all those who do not oppose us to the rapture of Islam." He paused, and his face broke out in a vicious scowl. "And the ones that choose to oppose us we will crush."

For the first time since meeting up with Raduyev, Sherkhan elicited a smile. It was a smile that told Raduyev how much common ground both men shared, an expression of resolute purpose. But lurking beneath it, Raduyev sensed there was something else, something cold and calculating. He sighed inwardly, resigned to the burden of leadership. So be it, he would be careful around Sherkhan. This mission rested solely on his shoulders, and rightfully so. Sherkhan had been correct when he had fawningly stated that he, Yeslam Raduyev, had been forged by the Almighty Allah to carry out such a holy undertaking. He was by far the strongest warrior among them. And though he lacked the depth of religious conviction held by the Pashtun, it was he that would be the one to make all the decisions, the one that would alter mankind's history by paving the way for the Islamic theocracy yet to come in this part of the world. Once the Great Satan fell, all the other western nations would topple like dominos. One by one, they would come under Muslim control, falling to the dictates of Islamic law.

All at once, the thought of Javolyn squeezed in on him like an oppressive black cloud, reminding him he still had some unfinished business to take care of. The trip back from the Haitian coast had been difficult on him, and he had been forced to swallow yet another humiliating defeat at the hands of his nemesis. But it was then that he was able to piece together the circumstances that had led Javolyn to this region of the world. He had overheard tidbits of conversation between Javolyn, Daniels, and Myers during the Seal mission led by Captain Sheridan. It all made sense. Having disposed of the irksome little Jew did little to console his dissatisfaction. No matter what it took, he made himself a vow that he would not rest until he killed Javolyn. But right now he had more pressing duties that required his attention.

Reminding himself about the deal he had made with Ortega, he suddenly found solace in the edge it gave him. He thought about it some more. Maybe it was possible Javolyn could be brought to him, one way or the other. Raduyev had carried out his end of the bargain by carefully recording the location where he had last seen the strange white dolphins, the place where Bashir had disappeared. For such information,

Ortega had agreed to get him one hundred drums of desperately needed diesel fuel, some of which would be necessary to replace what he had expended in taking the sub across the Windward Passage. Ortega was a man much like himself, a man not to be denied the pleasure of revenge. But if Ortega could not get Javolyn, he just might succeed in capturing the girl that had ridden the dolphin, whoever she was. Ortega, he had guessed, had more than a simple desire for retribution regarding the girl. No, he had sensed something more. The Colombian had seemed especially interested in both the girl and the creatures she had been seen with. Yes, it just might work, he told himself. With the girl as bait, perhaps Javolyn could be lured right into his hands.

As Raduyev entertained these thoughts, he was unaware of the depraved grin that had worked itself onto his face and the strange manner in which Sherkhan was studying him. Vaguely, he became cognizant of an oddly familiar sound reverberating within the grotto, and all at once he realized it was the sound of his own laughter. This did not disturb him, for sooner or later he knew he would have his vengeance.

The Gatling Gun

Ortega climbed up to the helipad amid the *San Carlo's* superstructure, weary from the oppressive heat and humidity. It was late afternoon in the harbor of Port-au-Prince and the sun was nearing the final stages of its descent beyond the western horizon. Upon seeing Fernando still at work repairing the damaged turbine, Ortega's fatigue abruptly evaporated, replaced by a savage burst of rage. "How much longer?" he roared impatiently, the extended delay becoming unbearable.

Fernando jumped up with a start. This was the third time in the last two hours his boss had come up to take inventory of his progress. The pilot hated being in Ortega's line of fire, knowing what could happen when the man's temper flared. The fact that he was a far better pilot than Pedro did little to make him feel safe as Cardoza's lieutenant glared at him with malice in his eyes.

"Another fifteen minutes and she'll be flyable, boss," he said nervously, barely finding his voice.

"Then I'll be back up fifteen minutes from now," Ortega growled. "Have the blades spinning and be ready to go!" Turning on his heels, he started to climb back down but suddenly stopped. "Tell me, Fernando, how difficult would it be to rig this bird with an electronic Gatling gun?"

The weapon to which Ortega was referring was something Fernando had spoken of in past conversations with a few members of the *San Carlo* crew, usually over a mug of ale in some sleazy backwater cantina infesting one port of call or another. Having worked as a helicopter mechanic in the U.S. Army for more than twenty years, Fernando had considerable knowledge about mounting sophisticated weaponry to military aircraft. At the age of seventeen, he had served in Vietnam and had retrofitted Hueys and LOHs with M134 mini guns, which could spew 7.62mm rounds at a rate of up to 4,000 per minute.

"It can be done, but it'll stick out like udders on a cow on a helicopter this small. That type of gun is normally mounted on a chopper's port side and has a tendency to impart a heavy counterclockwise yaw to the aircraft when fired."

"I'll be the one to worry about that," Ortega admonished harshly. "I am making the arrangements to procure such a weapon. After what happened yesterday, I think it would be wise if we had such a capability."

"But what if we were to get boarded by the U.S. Coast Guard?" Fernando objected meekly. He knew full well the risk Ortega's suggestion posed. Once mounted to the aircraft, disconnecting such a system and effectively hiding it before it came under the scrutiny of a boarding party would be incredibly difficult.

Ortega stared back, smiling coldly. "I'm sure you'll figure out how to get around that."

Fernando felt like a trapped animal as he watched Ortega's head disappear below the platform. Almost three years had gone by since he had found employment with these people, and as he had come to learn, a group comprised of the most sadistic homicidal maniacs he had ever known. In Vietnam he had seen how the stress of battle and escalating body counts could harden most men, reducing some to what amounted to cold-blooded killers devoid of all emotion or compassion. But members of the Cardoza clan were far worse. They were a mean-spirited bunch, sharing a common passion for killing and deriving some kind of perverted joy out of the sight of suffering and death.

At the time of his recruitment by the Colombians, Fernando had been completely ignorant about the true nature of the organization, only knowing the pay was greater than anything he could ever hope to garner back in the States and that within five years he would be able to retire, living the good life on the beachfront property he would eventually purchase back in Florida. He well remembered the excitement he had felt over his good fortune when he had first found his current job, but as he recalled it now, he knew that early retirement would never be an option open to him. Ortega would see to that. It was too late for him to get out, his flying and mechanical skills much too valuable for the drug ring to let him go.

Fernando dropped his introspections and went back to work on the aircraft, realizing he had been dwelling on his current predicament way too long. But as he turned a bolt, he could not help but examine the various ways he might be able to escape the Cardoza ring for good. There was a moral decay all about him, far more encompassing and offensive to the senses than the overpowering stench of rotting fish that pervaded every corner of the vessel he was forced to live on. With one exception, he hated the miscreants who crewed the *San Carlo*. But he had managed to keep such hatred under wraps and well-guarded, not wanting to end up as shark bait or a meal for Cardoza's pet tiger back in Colombia. There was only one person aboard the ship he associated with on a regular basis, and that was Antonio, the youngest among them. Though there was a marked age difference between them, Antonio could be considered a friend. For some reason, the lad looked up to him, probably because, like him, Antonio did not share the same penchant for killing as the others had shown. Sooner or later, though, the crew's bloodlust was going to get the lad killed. The day before remained clearly etched in his mind. A stranger had nearly ended Antonio's life, a man riding a waverunner retrofitted with some unusual weaponry. And now he knew that Ortega would not rest until he found that man. With Ortega, it would become an obsession. In Southeast Asia, he had gotten a firsthand look at what an obsession could lead to if left unchecked. Usually, a lot of people died.

After turning the final bolt to the required torque, Fernando installed the safety wire that would keep the bolt from working its way loose under the high frequency vibration every component of the helicopter would be subjected to once the turbine engine was fully engaged and the aircraft was in flight. He enjoyed working with his hands, repairing damaged machinery, or building things from scratch. To his way of thinking, constructing was so much more satisfying than destroying, and he had seen enough destruction to last a lifetime.

As he completed the task, Fernando's thoughts returned to the man on the waverunner. He held no animosity toward the man, feeling only a strange kinship with him instead. It was obvious the stranger had only sought to protect the girl and dolphins, using a weird combination of weaponry to do this. Maybe this individual had been the one to configure the weaponry to the waverunner. In that thought alone, there was a common bond. And the man, no doubt, had a love of dolphins, risking his life to save the creatures. This made him diametrically different from Ortega, who he knew hated dolphins, killing them with grenades at every opportunity, or letting them get caught up in the seine net and pulled through the *San Carlo's* power block where their bodies were shredded to pulp.

Securing the engine cowling, Fernando turned his head and looked toward Haiti's capital city. Rarely did he leave the ship whenever the *San Carlo* was moored within the harbor of Port-au-Prince, knowing how unsafe the streets could be, especially after dark. From where he stood high up on the tuna trawler, he could just make out the gang-controlled slums of Cite Soleil. Much to Ortega's displeasure, they had been forced to come back here two days ahead of schedule in order to replace the destroyed runabouts. Already Pedro and several crew members had gone ashore, rowing their way into the waterfront on one of the trawler's skiffs. The Colombian crew always seemed upbeat prior to taking a shore leave here, holding a particular fondness for the place. They would be in their element. From experience, he knew they would come back to the *San Carlo* drunk and obnoxious, bragging about what they had done to some poor bastard, usually a street urchin unfortunate enough to cross paths with them.

Looking at his watch, Fernando realized the fifteen minutes given him by Ortega was almost up. Climbing into the pilot's seat of the Bell

Ranger, he flicked several switches before firing up the engine. As the power train hummed to life and gradually built to a deafening roar, he ignored the gauges lining the instrument panel, listening instead with a critical ear to the changing pitch of the overhead blades as they gained momentum. The sound of the aircraft and the vibrations coursing through it would tell him if anything was wrong. Satisfied that everything was functioning the way it should be, he scanned the various gauges as a final check, knowing precisely the readings he would see. He was not disappointed.

Ortega's Suspicion

There was something odd about the powerboat below them that made Ortega take a second look. "Take us closer to that vessel down there, but not too close," he instructed, pointing to where he was looking.

Fernando did as he was told, banking the helicopter to starboard and taking it lower. He could see the boat was headed for Port-au-Prince, and as he got closer, his eyes were immediately drawn to the small watercraft being towed behind it.

"Notice anything?" Ortega asked.

Fernando glanced sideways to read the sickening smile on the Colombian's face. Knowing it would do no good to play dumb, he told his boss what he wanted to hear. "Yeah…minus the weaponry, the watercraft being towed looks like the same one used against us yesterday."

Ortega grinned the way a man might at having just discovered a cache of diamonds. "But the boat doing the towing is very different from the one we encountered near Navassa Island," he pointed out. "Bring us lower but keep your distance. I have no wish to be fired upon like yesterday."

Dropping to within five hundred feet of the water, Fernando took the Bell Ranger in a wide circle over the vessel's wake. Two objects suddenly broke the surface, catching the eyes of both men. "Well now, this is proving to be very interesting," Ortega said. "Funny how these white dolphins keep showing up with that waverunner." Almost as soon as the

Colombian uttered the words, the albinos sounded, disappearing from sight.

Ortega fell into a protracted silence as the towing vessel picked its way through a scattered fleet of old and decrepit fishing boats. "What do you want me to do?" Fernando asked impulsively, wondering what his boss was thinking.

Several more seconds transpired as Ortega alternately shifted his gaze between the powerboat and the water to its rear. "Resume your original course," he ordered at last. "I want to be in Saint-Marc before sunset."

Relieved by Ortega's decision, Fernando brought the helicopter back on their original heading, ascending higher once again. As they climbed to altitude, Ortega periodically craned his head around to glance back at the vessel as it plied its way toward the harbor entrance. "I have seen that boat before," he muttered gruffly, almost as if talking to himself. "Finding it again should be easy."

Inwardly, Fernando shuddered at the way the words were spoken.

Chapter Twenty-two: Escape by Telekinesis

Sitting within the darkened cramped space of the storage locker, Jake continued to cradle Destiny's head in his lap. The girl was still out. Checking the luminous dial on his watch, he could tell they had been penned up this way for well over an hour. Not wanting to risk any more funny business from the two of them, Ben Loomins and his brother, Charlie, had marched Jake at gunpoint into the Bertram's forward section, locking him and Destiny in a tiny closet located in the galley. The quarters were so tight that Jake had been forced to crouch down with the girl awkwardly cradled in his arms in order for the two of them to effectively fit inside. With only a sliver of dim light finding its way through a crack in the locker door, Jake had groped around clumsily in the limited space, hoping to find something useful to extricate them from their holding cell. Handicapped by the unconscious girl pressed up snugly against him, though, he had decided to give up the attempt for the time being, seeing the futility of trying to escape with Destiny in her present condition.

Although passivity was not in Jake's nature, he had purposely avoided gambling with Destiny's life, submitting instead to the role of prisoner. Somehow, he would find a way out of this mess, but not until the girl regained consciousness. Having been forced to sit hunched forward in such a constricted manner, he could feel the muscles in his back and neck beginning to tighten up painfully. With both knees already numb from being scrunched up against the door, he exerted as much pressure against it as he could muster, hoping the wood comprising it would crack under the strain. He visualized the door in his mind's eye again, having assessed it just before being crammed into the small compartment. The door was a good two inches thick, probably consisting of solid oak, with a heavy steel bolt situated on the outside keeping it firmly secured.

From the way he was restrained, he had no room to apply even feeble leverage to force it open.

As he listened to the steady, almost hypnotic thrum of the boat's engines, something banged lightly against the Bertram's hull close to where he sat. The sound, he guessed, was the dolphins' way of letting him know they had not deserted them. Hermes and Aphrodite had been doing this periodically ever since he and the girl had been caged up.

Stroking Destiny's head with the fingertips of one hand, Jake felt her suddenly stir. "Where are we?" she asked, her voice calm and not showing any signs of the listless coma she had been in a moment earlier.

"They've got us locked away in a storage compartment. Loomins got the drop on me before I could get you off this vessel. You were out cold."

Destiny found his hand in the darkness and squeezed it. "At least we were able to free Aphrodite and Hermes," she commented, trying to rise as she said it.

"Don't try to get up," Jake warned. "It's tighter than a jammed suitcase in here."

Destiny stopped moving and remained silent for a long moment, as if letting the full magnitude of their predicament settle over her. Finally, she spoke. "The rest of the pod is here. They'll help us."

Jake stifled a laugh. "What are they going to do, come down here and open this door?"

Destiny ignored the humor. "Coral wants you to picture the mechanism that keeps this door locked."

"Why?"

"I'll explain later. Do you remember what it looks like?"

Jake was puzzled over such an odd request. "It's a sliding dead bolt that latches the door."

"Good. Now just keep thinking about it."

Having nothing better to do at the moment, Jake did as the girl asked, if only to soothe her. He visualized the bolt again, keeping it lodged firmly in his mind. The sliding mechanism was in a closed position, just the way he remembered it before it had been thrown back with a loud clank to allow them entrance to their current prison. A sudden flickering seemed to intrude its way into his thoughts. No, it was more than a flickering. He was being prodded and nudged by ethereal wisps without form or substance as he concentrated on the latch. A vision of the bolt sliding open abruptly flashed into his brain, and even before he became aware of it, the numbing pressure against his knees was swept away like a puff of air. The sudden eruption of light flooding the closet made him blink in surprise as the door suddenly swung open. Letting his eyes settle on the outer compartment, he could see that no one lurked in the dimly lit galley beyond.

Immediately stunned by what had just taken place, he looked at the girl in confusion. "How did you do that?" he gasped, mouth agape.

Rising from his lap, Destiny turned and stared down at him. "We all did it together…you and the rest of us."

Still confused, Jake could only gawk back, too tongue-tied for any more words. He tried to rise, but with all his joints now stiff from lack of movement, he had difficulty standing. He realized his legs had fallen asleep, tingling with a dull numbness. Continuing to sit, he extended his feet out in front of him, wincing with the effort. Legs, he knew, needed occasional movement if they were to remain flexible. For the blood to keep flowing, it was important the muscles were periodically stretched out. But now that circulation had been restored, the tingling in his limbs escalated rapidly to an excruciating ache. "Give me a minute to loosen up." Funny, he thought, she's been cooped up as long as I have and she's limber as a cat.

Above the steady drone of the engines, the sound of footsteps could be heard. Someone was making his way down the stairwell toward the galley. With renewed effort, Jake hobbled to his feet and pushed the door to the storage closet closed, sliding the deadbolt into place. Reaching out, he grabbed Destiny by the arm and pulled her along with him as he limped spastically through an open doorway leading to the next compartment forward of the one they were in. They had just enough time to find a place of hiding on the opposite side of the bulkhead separating the two compartments.

Jake went rigid as a voice rang out above the din of the engines. "I hope you're comfortable in there." For one fleeting moment he thought they had been discovered, but then he heard a loud banging which told him otherwise. Risking a peek around the edge of the doorway, he saw Charlie rapping a closed fist against the bolted locker door, the same carbine he had wielded earlier clutched at his side. "You were lucky to catch me off guard," Charlie went on, "but that won't happen again. I guarantee it." Turning away from the closet, Charlie opened a refrigerator and retrieved a chicken leg. Gnawing on the leg, he left the galley and went back topside.

Jake released the breath he had been holding back. "That was close."

"What now?" Destiny asked.

From the way the girl was looking up at him, Jake could tell she was expecting him to come up with another plan. Scanning their present quarters, Jake spied his K-Bar lying on a bunk behind him. Just before being jammed into the storage closet, Charlie had removed the knife from the scabbard strapped to Jake's leg and tossed it into the compartment where they now stood.

"There's got to be something down here we can use," he said, reinserting the blade back in its sheath. His legs were almost back to normal.

Destiny moved forward toward the boat's bow and opened a door. Staring over her shoulder, Jake noticed an assortment of supplies inside the compartment. A hodgepodge of coiled rope, extra anchors, rolls of netting, and small wooden crates took up most of the space. Squeezing himself into the congested room, he spied various tools attached to fixtures along each side.

He suddenly smiled as his eyes came to rest on one item in particular. Another webshot was mounted conspicuously on the wall, this one a smaller version of the one he had seen up on deck, and as he rummaged further, he quickly discovered a box of cartridges for the device.

Chapter Twenty-three:
The Webshot

Charlie Loomins was sprawled comfortably on a couch in the *Sea Lion's* rear cabin, chewing contentedly on the last morsels of meat from the chicken leg. Absentmindedly, he tossed the bone aside and let out a loud burp.

"I hope you enjoyed that."

Charlie practically leapt up from the couch at the spoken words, his brain addling in bewilderment. His brother, Ben, was currently piloting the vessel and the Haitian deckhands were not allowed in here. He scooped up the carbine lying next to him and swung the barrel toward the source, but before he could aim the weapon, Jake fired the webshot from the top of the stairwell. Twelve feet from where Charlie stood, the gas-powered gun kicked hard, discharging a compressed wad of netting at a velocity of almost one-hundred feet per second. Six feet from the launch point, the net mushroomed open, expanding to engulf its target. Finding himself suddenly entangled in the mesh, Charlie only managed a surprised grunt as he toppled to the floor with the netting contracted about him like a closed fist.

Jake was on his jailer in an instant, leaning a knee into the small of the man's back to discourage further movement. "Now I don't want to hurt you and you don't want to be hurt," he said mildly as he wrestled the carbine free of Charlie's grasp and pulled it from between the mesh. He could see the reason the gun had not discharged in the short scuffle even though Charlie's finger had been squeezing hard against the trigger. The safety was still on.

Jake handed the weapon to Destiny. "Hold onto this!" he instructed as Charlie began to squirm like a landed marlin. The man was putting up more of a fight than he had expected. "Don't make me konk you like before," Jake threatened.

"How?" Charlie whined, ignoring the threat. "How'd you get out?"

Jake pondered the question momentarily. Yeah, how? "I'll never tell," he found himself saying, forcing a hammerlock on his captive and grabbing him by the back of the belt with his free hand. "Now just behave yourself and I promise I'll try to be as gentle as possible."

Still wrapped in the net, Charlie was dragged forcefully along the floor and down the stairs. A minute later, Jake had him stowed safely away inside the same storage locker that had imprisoned him and the girl.

As Jake bolted the door, Destiny looked at him with a hint of amusement in her eyes. "What next?"

"Now we simply walk out onto the main deck and you jump overboard."

"What about you?"

"I've got to retrieve the Kawasaki. I'll catch up with you." Jake could see she didn't like this part of the plan.

Not wanting any further discussion on the matter, Jake hefted the carbine and peered through the window facing the rear deck. Having nothing else to do, the three deckhands had their backs to him as they leaned up against the stern railing. From the way they were gesticulating, they appeared to be debating something.

Seeing the opportunity before him, Jake turned to Destiny. "Stay behind me and get ready to jump!" Opening the door leading out onto the rear deck, he moved up behind the Haitians as their discussion continued. Keeping his eyes trained on the men, he pushed Destiny toward the vessel's port side. "Now go!"

Destiny climbed the railing and leapt just as the three crewmen turned. With seemingly raptured interest, they watched as the girl disappeared headlong into the sea, her arms outstretched gracefully before her in a perfect dive. Strangely, they ignored Jake, pivoting around instead to search the boat's wake for where the girl might surface. But the girl was nowhere to be seen.

Jake could not help but notice the large amount of fishing vessels dotting the sea all around him. From experience, he knew the *Sea Lion* was nearing the harbor entrance outside of Port-au-Prince. Several familiar landmarks located to the east confirmed this.

"Excuse me, gentlemen," Jake said, keeping his air casual as he walked past the deckhands and unhooked the gate leading to the swim platform. "I'll be taking my leave now."

Something in their mannerisms told Jake they would not be a threat. He moved quickly to the cleat tethering the Kawasaki and untied the line, glancing up one final time toward the bridge as he did so. Leaving the carbine on the platform, he dropped himself over the side and held onto the line. When he poked his head above the surface, the three Haitians could be seen in heated conversation again, gesturing wildly as the *Sea Lion* drew rapidly away.

Something brushed lightly against Jake's body, and an instant later the head of Achilles bobbed next to him. "Once again, you do us great honor, Jay Jay," the young albino ululated.

"Where's Destiny?" Jake asked nervously, scanning the sea all around him.

"Over here," a voice beckoned. Riding Hercules, Destiny suddenly emerged from the opposite side of the waverunner, her face lit up in a happy smile. Within moments, the remainder of the pod converged all around them, nuzzling in close to Jake and the girl.

"I think it's time we headed back," Jake said, staring hard at Destiny. "Would you like to ride with me?"

"Only if you promise not to go any faster than the pod can swim."

Jake threw her a happy grin. "You got yourself a deal."

Chapter Twenty-four: A Shocking Ordeal

Dr. Franklin Grahm knelt beside his fallen young assistant, wondering why the lad hadn't heeded the warning. As of late, Nick Henderson had become increasingly contentious and moody. The marine zoologist breathed a sigh of relief, however, when the computer whiz finally responded to the CPR administered to him by Parker. Letting out several large gasps just prior to regaining consciousness, Henderson awoke with a start and immediately expelled the water he had taken into his lungs, coughing so harshly that he vomited up his last meal in the process.

Finally catching his breath, Henderson stared up at the others hovering above him, his face a mask of confusion. "What happened?" he stammered dazedly.

Grahm took a moment to glance up at Jacob. The grizzled Haitian wore an expression that implied he had been expecting such an event. "We heard you scream, and Jacob pulled you ashore," Grahm said. "You apparently made contact with the *thurentra* and received a severe electrical shock. Can you stand?"

"I think so." With Parker assisting, Henderson staggered shakily to his feet, and as Grahm studied him, his eyes were once again drawn to the jellylike substance adhering to the grad student's forearm.

"Hold still!" Grahm ordered as he unsnapped one of the pockets on his utility belt. "I believe you have some of the *thurentra* on you."

Anger welled up in Henderson's eyes. "That thing shocked me?" The question was phrased more like an accusation, as if Grahm's explanation of what had just happened had finally sunk in.

Parker helped to immobilize Henderson's arm as Grahm scraped some of the translucent orange goo onto a small glass slide. "Jacob warned you against touching it," Grahm reminded him. "You should have listened."

"I thought it was just a ploy to keep us from seeing the-" Henderson abruptly shut up, falling silent as he suddenly became aware of Jacob standing nearby.

Parker stared sharply at him, still holding his arm. "Seeing what?"

"Nothing."

"Tell us what you saw?" Parker pressed, unwilling to let the matter go.

Henderson pulled free, almost savagely, but Grahm had already gotten enough of a sample. "There's nothing to tell."

"Go sit in the shade, Nicolas!" Grahm muttered in a soothing tone, trying to quell the brewing argument. "You need to clear your head."

"I'll do that," Henderson grumbled irritably. Turning, he strode away, seeming eager to get away from all three men.

The scientist turned to Jacob. "Once again, I must extend my apologies for the lad's impetuosity. I hope you will not consider this unfortunate event as an overstay of the hospitality you have already given us."

Jacob shrugged with indifference. "Sometimes it is best that reckless stubbornness run headlong into the very thing it had been advised against. That way we are more likely to heed future warnings."

Grahm nodded in agreement. "Perhaps it will improve his judgement as well." He indicated the glass slide he was holding. "I hope you don't mind if I analyze this?"

Jacob assessed Grahm curiously, as if seeing something he needed to examine more closely. "And if I did?"

Grahm's disappointment was evident. He had not expected this. "Why…I, uh, would respect your wishes, of course," he stuttered.

Jacob stared at the scientist a moment longer as if trying to gauge the full extent of his earnestness. "You are obviously a man driven by scientific curiosity, a man that has an insatiable need for answers." He suddenly smiled. "Please…go ahead and do what you must. I have no desire to obstruct you."

Both Grahm and Parker watched as Jacob headed off in the direction of the thatched dwellings set back from the beach. "A most interesting individual," Grahm commented. "Somehow I get the feeling a man like that could accomplish anything he put his mind to."

"I was kind of thinking the same thing," Parker agreed.

Remembering what he was holding, Grahm extended an arm to Parker. "Run this sample through the blot scanner, then send it back to Miami as soon as you're able to establish a satellite uplink. Access the DNA microarray imaging program on the Big Mac. I'd like to know how closely this matches known varieties of sea cucumbers and coelenterates."

The program to which Grahm referred was the latest version of one that had undergone modification over the last two years. It both simplified and expanded the usefulness of the older protocol of DNA microarray technology. Normally it was Henderson who handled such duties, but Parker had sufficient knowledge of the system to carry out Grahm's directive without any problems.

Parker started to walk away, but Grahm stopped him as a strange thought came to mind. "Include Natalie's genome for comparison."

A look of genuine surprise was evident on Parker's face. "You think there's a genetic relationship?"

Grahm sighed, then shrugged. "There's a mystery here, one that seems altogether impossible and yet…" He groped for the right words but couldn't find anything adequate enough to express what he was feeling. "God only knows what we'll find."

Parker studied Grahm for several seconds without speaking, then finally turned and trudged away.

Grahm watched his protégé head off to where most of their equipment had been set up to one side of the cove. He had a special fondness for Parker. The lad was bright and easy to work with. Henderson, on the other hand, had his quirks, but without him Grahm was convinced he would never have been able to develop the unique programming needed to translate delphine sounds. Unfortunately, Henderson was a rude and unruly sort, and as of late had become even more so. Perhaps he shouldn't have brought him along.

There was something else about the youth that had begun to peck away at the back of his mind. Was it betrayal? Too many recent coincidences made it difficult to shed his suspicions. And he noticed that Henderson had never really developed a close attachment to Natalie the way he and Parker had. Intentionally, he let his thoughts shy off in another direction, ashamed of himself for considering the possibility that Henderson couldn't be trusted.

Almost by reflex, he glanced over at the cove's entrance. Still no sign of the pod. He was worried about the fate of the two captured dolphins, knowing what could happen to these incredibly intelligent beings if they fell into the wrong hands. They were not meant to be isolated from their own kind, to be penned up in some laboratory far from the sea. Here among these people, the creatures were treated with love and a deep abiding respect.

In the midst of these mullings, the girl came to mind. Already he had developed a strong affection for her. If he had had a daughter, he would have wanted her to be just like Destiny. The thought sent an unexpected surge of yearning through him. The same haunting image that had plagued him all these years suddenly popped into his head. His wife, Harriet, had been pregnant at the time she disappeared. Had she given birth, the child would have been Destiny's age.

Longing for the woman he loved, Grahm wandered aimlessly along the beach, unable to enjoy the magical spell of the place Jacob called Gaia. The nostalgia he felt was a gruff reminder of what had happened so many years ago, and as he wallowed helplessly in its grip, he realized how cowardly he was. Yes, he finally admitted to himself, failing to face the truth was a form of cowardice, wasn't it? By coming here first instead of diving down to explore what remained of the vessel his wife had used to sail the Caribbean had only tended to reveal his utter gutlessness. Was he truly afraid of what he might discover? After all these years, he still couldn't bring himself to accept her loss, knowing that some small part of him actually believed she had not really perished.

With great difficulty, he stopped berating himself. He knew he was torn between two conflicting choices. There was still a mystery he had to unravel about this place, so much more he needed to learn about these magnificent white creatures and their interaction with the girl who rode and communicated with them through some unknown mind link. Destiny was altogether special, someone he felt inexplicably drawn to. Without knowing why, he felt a deep sense of loss with the girl now gone, and he would not leave until she returned safely. But he also had another need, one that required he go back to Navassa Island to locate the sunken sloop. Burdened by this impasse, he knew he had to satisfy both needs very soon. Like a man trapped in a stupor, he continued to roam the beach without purpose, every so often gazing haplessly toward where the dolphins would re-enter the cove.

No Longer Fearful

An evening twilight was rapidly falling upon Saint-Marc, bathing the old fortress that sat above the town in an eerie reddish backwash of glowing incandescence. Somewhere in the distance, the sound of an approaching whirlybird grew gradually in volume, slowly drowning out the low rhythmic beat of reggae emanating from one of the taverns farther back along the waterfront. Like a gnat emerging out of the southwestern horizon, the aircraft took on size and form as it rushed toward the small group of men tracking it. Circling once, it descended swiftly, taking on a heading that would bring it to a lesser used area of the docks. The Bell Ranger flared sharply, throwing up a cloud of dust that partially obscured the setting sun. Hovering briefly, it settled down gingerly on one of the run-down wharves, almost as if testing the aging timbers that would support it.

Dabbing the sweat from his brow, Hennington stood back far enough from the savage blades to avoid the storm of grit that was cast in all directions. Wearily, he watched as Ortega climbed out of the cockpit and came toward him, the man's head lowered forward like the oncoming prow of a ship as he moved under the whirling rotor. Unlike all his previous meetings with the Colombian, the sight did not elicit the same level of fear in the broker. Ever since leaving the mambo he had felt cleansed, purged of the guilt he had unknowingly carried up to then. His own reckless greed, he had come to realize, had been the cause of this guilt. But because a great burden had been lifted, he was no longer afraid.

Stepping forward to meet Ortega, Hennington left his bodyguards standing farther back, not wanting them to hear what would be said. As always, he could see the threat of violence in Ortega's eyes as the man first looked at him before shifting his gaze to Ternier's thugs.

"This had better be important," Ortega grunted with impatience, speaking in Spanish as he always did when the two men spoke. "Did you forget about our little arrangement? Never call me on my satellite phone unless absolutely necessary. This is the second time you contacted me in the last day."

"It is imperative I get back to Port-au-Prince tonight."

Ortega appeared shocked at Hennington's audacity. He suddenly gave the impression of a volcano ready to erupt. "Do you think I am a taxi service?" he snarled.

Hennington spoke fast, trying to pacify the Colombian's soaring anger. "The Colonel will not provide you with the people you requested unless you fly me back at once," he lied. "He has some important business to discuss with me and suggested I contact you to help me out."

For one fleeting moment, Hennington expected Ortega to strike him. Slowly, the pent-up rage emblazoned on his face began to ease. "There is only room enough for two more aboard this bird," he growled, looking beyond the broker at the three Haitians.

"Then only one of these men will accompany me," Hennington replied.

Ortega reached out and grabbed Hennington by the forearm, making the broker flinch in pain at the strength of grip. The message was clear, reaffirming just who was in charge here. "You have not forgotten about the weapon I asked for?"

Hennington had not forgotten. He had made the appropriate arrangements earlier the day before, several hours before being sent by Ternier to go to Malique. "You will have it by tomorrow."

"You are certain of this?" The Colombian applied more pressure, but Hennington sucked up the pain, refusing to give Ortega the satisfaction of seeing him squirm. "I would hate to be disappointed."

"My contact is very reliable."

A cruel smile affixed itself to Ortega's face. "Bueno. Muy Bueno." He kept the grip of steel locked firmly in place a moment longer before letting go.

Hennington managed to keep his face expressionless as the blood returned to his fingers. "Walter McPherson has arrived in Port-au-Prince. He is eager to take delivery of the frozen dolphin carcasses."

"He understands this will be strictly a cash transaction?"

"He understands perfectly."

Cardoza's lieutenant appeared pleased. "Life is good." As an afterthought, he looked down at Hennington's legs. "I noticed you are no longer limping, my fat friend. You are healing much more quickly than I would have thought possible. Perhaps I went too easy on you." He stared for another moment before placing a hand on Hennington's shoulder and moving him toward the helicopter. "Come! The Colonel awaits you."

Looking over his shoulder, Hennington motioned the leader of Ternier's thugs to follow. He smiled inwardly at his own deception. Before Ortega had arrived here, he had stressed to the leader how upset Ternier would be if the Colonel were denied the immediate delivery of the medallion by the fastest means possible. The other two men would therefore have to make the cumbersome journey back to Port-au-Prince without them.

Instinctively, Hennington ducked down as the chopper blades began to crank faster overhead. Walking was definitely easier now. He could even walk stooped over like he was currently doing without his knee bothering him. Much to his amazement, his painful limp had all but vanished soon after leaving the mambo, and he no longer moved like a cripple.

Climbing aboard the aircraft, he now understood beyond a shadow of a doubt that the mambo had seen something in him that he had been blind to all these years. Oddly, he remembered most of the things she had said. It was true, he had continued to travel the same path over and over again, and in the process, had been constantly disappointed where he had ended up. Somehow the woman had made him see something he had failed to see all his life. Happiness could only come from deep within, that it could not be bought or sold like much of the merchandise and services he provided. For some people, they had to be comfortable with their self-image before they could develop a true joy for life. He was now curious to discover who he actually was, hopeful that deep down he was not really a coward, that there existed at least a shred of courage within him. And though there was misery all about him, self-fulfillment might be possible if he no longer strived for the false gold. Perhaps there was a chance for him after all.

As he buckled himself in, Hennington shifted his thoughts back to the strange images that had flashed through his mind when the mambo had placed her hand upon his head. Even as the helicopter began to rise and gain speed, those same images continued to stay with him, blocking out all sensation of the darkening ocean flitting swiftly by below.

Chapter Twenty-five: Return to the Cove

With Destiny sitting behind him on the waverunner and the rest of the pod leading the way, Jake finally entered the cove late into the evening under another gibbous moon. Rather than have Zimbola lower the docking chute on the *Angel's* stern, he decided to leave the Kawasaki tied up alongside the trawler for the time being. Having not had anything to eat since noon, he was now ravenous, wanting only to get something in his stomach. Unfortunately, Zimbola, Phillipe and Hector had other ideas, eager to get an account of the day's events. Not wanting to disappoint them, Jake gave them a brief recount of what had happened, deciding to leave out how the lock to the storage closet had been opened.

Destiny had soon disappeared, wanting to attend to the two recovering gray bottlenose dolphins. Jake's plan to have a quick meal in the *Angel's* galley was quickly aborted when Achilles suddenly chittered noisily off the vessel's larboard side. "Jacob invites everyone to dinner, Jay Jay," the albino trilled. "Will you be coming ashore?"

"Will Destiny be there?"

"Yes, Jay Jay."

"Then tell Jacob I accept his invitation."

Jake watched as the juvenile turned and swam toward the shore. The brazier Jacob had grilled fish on the night before was already burning brightly, occasionally outlining several figures moving about close to its flickering glow. Breathing deeply, he took in the rich fragrance hanging in the air, wondering what it would be like to spend his remaining years in such a place. There was life here, pulsing and vibrant, ceaselessly rapturous to the spirit.

Turning, Jake noticed Zimbola hovering nearby. "How's our captive doing?"

The giant cocked his head, scratching his huge cranium and smiling oddly. "I do not know what to make of it, but he has been staring at that painting like a starry-eyed puppy all day. He will not put it down."

"Has he given you any more trouble?"

"No…there must be strange magic in that painting to make him behave like that. I think the white witch-"

Zimby abruptly caught himself, seeing the frown that immediately clouded Jake's face. "Perhaps the girl did something to him during her healing ritual."

News of the man's docility was not altogether unexpected by Jake. He, himself, had experienced the strange power of the dolphin art. On impulse, a wild thought came to him. "Bring him ashore, Zimby. I'd like him to eat with the rest of us."

Zimbola nodded impassively, showing no surprise. Having spent most of the day keeping an eye on the prisoner, Jake knew his friend would have voiced an objection if he thought the man was still potentially dangerous or could not be controlled. "That may not be so bad an idea," the Jamaican concurred.

Going below deck to his stateroom, Jake retrieved his satellite phone and put in a call to Mat Daniels. He would have placed a call to him earlier, but recent mitigating circumstances had forestalled him from doing so. Mat picked up on the fourth ring.

"Daniels at your service."

"What's cooking, buddy? It's Jake."

"What happened to you? I've been waiting for your call all day."

"Don't ask, it's a long story."

"Will I be getting the present you spoke of anytime soon?"

Jake remained silent for several seconds as he contemplated a decision. "Sorry to disappoint you, pal, but I seem to have lost the package. I do have one piece of intel that may interest you, though."

"Speak to me."

"If I were you, I'd keep my eyes on the lookout for a hundred-foot sub. There's one roaming the waters between Haiti and Navassa Island."

"You saw it."

"With my own two eyes."

Mat waited for Jake to say more, then grew impatient. "Come on, fella, you're holding back on me. I know you have more to tell."

"Sorry, old buddy. That's all I can give you right now. I'll be in touch as soon as I find out more. Gotta run."

"Jake!" Mat shouted, catching Jake before he could end the call.

"Yeah."

"Take good care of yourself."

Jake could not help but smile. "You know what your problem is, Mat?"

"What?"

"You worry too much."

Five minutes later, Jake waded ashore, having taken a much needed invigorating swim from the *Angel* to the beach. Turning to look back at the *Angel*, he could discern movement on the water as the other members of his crew were currently taking the skiff to join him. Facing the fire again, he saw Grahm coming over to greet him.

Grahm extended a hand. "Let me congratulate you for what you did today, lad."

Reluctantly, Jake clasped the proffered hand. Praise such as this made him feel uneasy. "I only gave Destiny assistance. She was really the one who made the rescue possible."

"You're much too modest. From what Jacob tells me, you did a lot more than just assist." Grahm turned his head toward the water. "The youngest member of the pod seems to be very fond of you."

Jake followed his stare, seeing Achilles watching him. "Sorry I wasn't able to recover the DBT," he said, eager to change the subject. "Those dolphin hunters probably still have it."

"That's quite all right, my lad. I brought a few more along on this trip."

Jake thought it appropriate to pursue another topic. "Did your assistant have any luck in identifying that freighter the sub met?"

"As a matter of fact, he did. *Spirit of Aden* was the name on that ship."

"What about its registry? Were you able to get a view of the flag it flew?"

"Yes. I didn't recognize it, so I consulted Jacob. The man is a walking encyclopedia. He identified it as a Yemeni flag." Grahm scrutinized Jake's expression in the glow of the brazier. "You look troubled."

Jake looked on as the skiff from the *Angel* neared the beach. He could see it was being nudged along by two albinos, although he couldn't tell which two. "Nothing to concern yourself about," he said, showing Grahm a smile and turning him in the direction of the fire. "What say we eat? I'm starving."

As they walked toward the fire, Jake sensed Grahm had something else to talk about. "Would you mind if we delayed that trip to Navassa Island until the day after tomorrow?" the scientist asked, his tone bordering on embarrassment. "I know our original business arrangement hinged on only chartering your boat for a period of three days at most, but unfortunately the funds I have available will be inadequate to cover anything more than that." Grahm paused, his discomfiture growing heavy. "If there's-"

Jake cut him off. "Don't give it another thought. I'll take you to Navassa day after tomorrow and hopefully we'll find your boat. We'll work out the tab later. After what's happened the last two days, I'm going to need a full day of rest anyway." He glanced around for Destiny as he spoke, locating the silhouette of her petite form sitting on a rock next to Jacob as the Haitian grilled fish steaks on the brazier. From the aroma wafting off the fire he could tell they were having grouper again, and his stomach began to churn hungrily in anticipation.

Breaking away from the scientist, Jake stepped over to Jacob and exchanged a few pleasantries before squatting down beside the girl. "How is Thetis and the other gray doing?" he said softly. With the exception of the waterfall's dull roar in the background, all was quiet and he did not want to disturb the ambiance of the evening.

A gentle wash of light from the grill spilled briefly off Destiny's brown eyes as she turned her head. She watched as Zimbola led the man she had healed the day before to the edge of the gathering. "Both should make a full recovery by tomorrow," she said in a lackluster tone.

Perplexed by the girl's unexpected sullenness, Jake groped for words. "That's good," he managed, trying his best to brighten her mood. "I'm sure that will make Achilles feel a whole lot better."

Destiny did not respond, keeping her gaze focused elsewhere.

Up close, Jake could see she was preoccupied with something weighing heavily upon her. "What's wrong?"

"I discussed with Jacob what Hermes and Aphrodite told me. He thinks a special type of sonar was used to stun them."

Destiny's statement brought to mind something Jake had been taught during BUD/S training. Working underwater when military sonar was activated was dangerous. A ship's sonar could be lethal to a diver at close range. It only stood to reason that sonar emissions of a lesser potency would temporarily disable a living organism rather than kill it.

Jake thought back to the vessel they had escaped. There had been something aboard it covered by a tarp. "Remember the plane we saw circling the *Sea Lion*?" he said.

Destiny nodded.

"I think that plane was acting as a spotter to direct Loomins to the dolphins. If the plane dropped such a sonar device near the dolphins, it would explain why they were captured so easily."

It seemed more logical to Jake that the plane would carry such technology rather than the boat, owing to its greater speed and spotting ability. Ben Loomins wanted the dolphins essentially unharmed if the creatures were to have any saleable value. One possible way to accomplish this might very well involve the use of sonar of sufficient magnitude to temporarily incapacitate but not cause injury. The device that sent out the emissions would have to be dropped almost on top of the creatures before they could race away beyond its limited effective range. Had the Bertram been the carrier of such a contrivance, he doubted it would have been able to get close enough to debilitate them. The crew of the *Sea Lion* would simply complete the capture by first sedating and then netting the stunned albinos. Hauling aboard the sonar emitter would be the crew's final task before getting underway.

"Has this ever happened to any of the albinos before?" Jake asked curiously.

The question caused Destiny's eyes to well up. "Never."

"Then I have to assume Ben Loomins and his brother may have come up with a new way of capturing dolphins in the wild."

Jake expelled a long breath laced with frustration. The girl was hopelessly naïve. Glancing toward the water, he could just make out several albinos staring in his direction. "I think it would be wise to have the pod stay clear of Navassa Island for the time being. Loomins will most likely revisit the place where the albinos were last spotted."

The suggestion seemed to startle the girl and she looked away. Her reply was barely audible. "That's not possible!"

Jake was momentarily speechless. He could see no reason why members of the pod would have a need to venture out into the open sea. Everything they required was close at hand right here in the cove. An abundant food supply was readily available. The large holding pen Jacob had built at the cove's northern end was kept well stocked with fish. He started to open his mouth, but before any words could be uttered, a shadow fell across him that was followed by a light touch on his shoulder.

"Let us take a stroll together, Mr. Javolyn," a voice interceded. The tone was low, affable.

Jake was surprised to see Jacob standing over him. From the way Destiny's mentor hovered, he had the impression the man had overheard the last part of the conversation.

"If you please," the Haitian persisted. "I have a few things to discuss with you."

Rising to his feet, Jake glanced back down at the girl, unable to grasp what she had meant. Why was it not possible? Vaguely aware that Grahm was now manning the brazier, he let Jacob guide him away from the others milling about the fire. He assumed the man needed to converse in private.

Jacob led Jake leisurely along the water's edge, seeming to mull what he was going to say. Jake waited patiently for him to speak as they continued to walk slowly in the direction of the waterfall.

"A lot has happened in the past several days," Jacob finally began. "Two days ago, you were a complete stranger to Destiny, a person with untested qualities." He sighed deeply, as if culling out the appropriate words. "But now you seem to have been accepted by the pod, a man who they are able to trust. This comes as a great surprise to me, because they are creatures that do not readily surrender trust."

Jake abruptly stopped and stared at Jacob. "What about you? Am I someone you think you can trust?" He took it for granted that Jacob had seen the painting on the wall of the cave, but still he felt compelled to ask.

Jacob smiled elusively. "You saw the gold! You were not tempted by it?"

The directness of the question caused Jake to flounder like a man having his legs swept out from under him in a sudden rush of whitewater. It took him several moments to regain his footing. "You set me up?" he sputtered incredulously.

Jacob shrugged without pleasure. "Yes…admittedly it was a test of sorts, a way of determining the kind of person you are."

The stirrings of indignation welled up from the pit of Jake's stomach. "Did I pass?"

"That depends on how you answer the question." Jacob studied him as though Jake were under a microscope. "Does the fact that so much wealth lies within these waters tempt you in any way?"

The pique Jake was feeling slowly abated, giving way to tolerance. Try as he might, he couldn't fault Jacob for testing him in light of what the lure of gold had done to both men and entire nations throughout history. The desire to satisfy greed spawned temptation. Greed was an inborn part of human nature, one of humanity's ugly imperfections firmly rooted in most people. It was a stubborn trait, often acting like a persistent virus that would not go away, sometimes lying dormant just below the surface for long periods before recurring to manifest its wicked symptoms. It was a vice that many human beings had to deal with in their own way. Those who failed to conquer it usually ended up being enslaved by it, sentenced to a life of chronic wickedness.

Without knowing why, Jake's pending business arrangement recently negotiated with Hennington took hold of his thoughts, and he found it necessary to gaze deep within himself, searching an array of feelings. Hennington had given him an opening, and the temptation to capitalize on it had quickly consumed him. An exorbitant pile of potential cash had been intentionally dangled before him, and like a drooling hyena hungering for a meal he had automatically reached for it, but then demanded more. Undeniably, he had been enticed by the promise of easy money for the delivery of something entirely unknown, tossing good judgement to the four winds. Did putting the squeeze on a greedy man also constitute a form of greed, or was it simply another form of survival?

In asking himself these questions, Jake felt the first tendrils of guilt wending their way into his conscience. He tried rationalizing it, attempting to resolve the conflict, but soon realized he was at a moral crossroad without direction. Rarely did he indulge in self-analysis, but then again, Jacob was asking him to look for flaws in his own moral convictions. Was it possible for a person to actually evaluate their own probity with any degree of honesty? Strangely, Jacob's query caused him to reflect on why he had come to Haiti in the first place.

Instinctively, Jake voiced the only answer that was within him. "You don't have to worry about me. Your gold will remain safe." With heartfelt sincerity, he knew he was being truthful.

Jacob held his gaze a brief moment longer before turning his head to look back at the fire. "We, who reside in Gaia, live a simple existence. In a place such as this, we have no need of gold." He let out an audible breath. "The precious metals will serve a useful purpose, however."

Jake was suddenly inquisitive. Though he had only known Jacob a short time, everything the man did seemed to have an objective. "What kind of purpose?"

Jacob wheeled slowly about to face him again. "As I explained to you earlier today, nature has a way of recruiting the very sentience she has created to fulfill certain goals that will benefit her. There is much more going on about you that you could not possibly know, things that will eventually become clear to you if you should ever decide to keep more lasting company with these wonderful creatures." For emphasis, Jacob glanced over at the small pack of albinos shadowing them just off the beach.

With his thoughts racing on ahead, Jake tried to find meaning in Jacob's carefully contrived wording. Lasting company? Where's he going with this? Unexpectedly, the abstruse things Destiny had said the night before flashed in his mind's eye like a burst of lightning, intensely bright and blinding. "Thetis begs you to reconsider. Failing to bond with Achilles will place the pod in immediate danger, setting it on an irreversible course of imminent doom. She believes there is still hope, but only if you remain linked to Achilles. Without this link the pod will cease to exist." Oddly, he had not forgotten the words, although he was still unable to fathom their full implication.

Jake suddenly latched onto the very thing that had puzzled him a little while ago. "Why is it necessary for these dolphins to go near Navassa Island?"

In the moonlight, Jacob's expression became somber, and Jake could see he was having difficulty answering. Jake had to wait only a moment longer before the Haitian's response came tumbling out. "The *thurentra* you saw is not the only one. There are others."

The revelation hit Jake with the abruptness of a spotlight suddenly turned on to illuminate the contents of a dark basement. At least he could now begin to connect a few of the dots. "And those others are at Navassa?"

Jacob gave an affirmative nod.

Reading the Haitian's demeanor, Jake now sensed a subtle change in the man. The wall of hermetic guardedness that always seemed to reside just below the surface was now being lowered, albeit very slowly. Perhaps Jacob would trust him after all. "I assume they're able to produce precious metals like the one in this cove."

"Some of them, yes, but not all."

"You mean they're not all alike?"

"Some of them would surprise you." Jacob smiled as if the memory of how the unusual organisms had come into existence was a constant source of wonder to him.

"I take it, then, that members of the pod make periodic visits to Navassa to harvest the gold and platinum."

A strange gleam came into Jacob's eyes, one that Jake perceived as amusement. "Among other things," the Haitian volunteered. "Some of the *thurentras* also produce magnesium in great quantities."

"Magnesium, huh!" The mention of the metal caused Jake to think about the diversified uses the element had around the world. A huge demand currently existed for its lightweight, high-strength properties, making the metal a prime feature in all types of structural components. "Do you do anything with it?"

Jacob's cryptic smile broadened. "Oh, yes." He started to amble down the beach again, now seemingly very comfortable with Jake's presence. "Dr. Grahm has informed me that you will be taking him back to Navassa Island two days from now. Achilles can show you some of the other *thurentras* if you would like to see them."

The onset of frustration suddenly enfolded Jake, tightening around him like a boa constrictor. The perils that obviously existed around Navassa were all too real. The possibility of danger still lurked there in the form of Colombian tuna fishermen, militant Islamics, and dolphin hunters. "I don't think it would be wise for any of the pod to venture anywhere near that island for a while," he grumbled, aware of the tenseness his own voice held.

A deep weariness suddenly replaced the smile Jacob had been wearing. "Sometimes you have to keep going, no matter what the risks. A crucial mission is at stake here."

Once again, Jake was bewildered. "What do you mean, mission?"

Jacob stopped walking and sat down in the sand, lapsing into an annoying silence.

To Jake, the Haitian's laconic manner was becoming tiresome. Unlike the expansive individual he had conversed with earlier on, the man sitting before him now seemed to have fallen into a state of taciturn withdrawal. He wished Jacob would stop beating around the bush and get to the point. With growing frustration, he sat down beside him, expecting him to at least offer more.

A passing cloud abruptly eclipsed the moon, turning the water darker as Jacob swiveled his head to scrutinize Jake up close. In the darkness, his face became unreadable. "A plan has been devised that may ultimately save the planet," he finally said.

Jake stared dumbly. "A plan? What kind of plan?"

Slowly, Jacob began to explain, and as he did, Jake's eyes widened in astonishment. As Jacob talked, the words continued to pour out faster and faster, leaving Jake nearly spellbound. He quickly gathered that Jacob had finally decided to trust him completely, not holding back on anything. Over the next hour he listened with rapt attention, no longer noticing his famishing hunger clamoring to be satisfied.

Chapter Twenty-six: Change for the Better

When Jake came back to the fire, Destiny was immediately at his side, giving him a heaping plate of grouper fillets and a stein of fresh water. The girl watched as he wolfed down the food like a ravenous animal.

"Far and away, this has to be the tastiest grouper I've ever eaten," Jake said, washing down the last morsel and smacking his lips.

Destiny looked at him intently. "You understand now why members of the pod must go to Navassa Island?"

"They must be very noble creatures to risk their lives this way." Jake glanced around at the shadowy figures still lingering nearby, his eyes searching the duskiness before settling on the person he perceived to be Nick Henderson. Jacob had told him about the grad student's mishap. "Do they really think the human race is worth saving?"

"The ability to change lies deep within all of us," Destiny replied.

"If that's true, why isn't everyone making a conscious effort to change for the better?"

The girl turned her head, her gaze singling out one of the men in the limited light. Jake saw she was looking at his captive. The man sat quietly next to Zimbola, staring passively out over the water. "People sometimes need help," Destiny clarified.

"I suppose you're referring to the albino art?"

"The art has its uses, yes. But acts of kindness and compassion can also go a long way in making a difference."

Jake let a small, amused laugh fly from his lips. "I hope you're not going to suggest we turn the other cheek and kiss the people trying to kill us." Indicating the creatures still partly visible out on the water, he quickly added, "These dolphins have got to learn to fight back when they're attacked."

Destiny had no response.

Jake's thoughts raced back to Navassa, remembering the incredible leap one of the albinos had executed in intercepting a grenade intended for the *Angel*. Though the creature had flipped the small bomb back toward the helicopter with near miss results, he could not help but wonder if the dolphin had had the option of destroying the aircraft had it wanted to. "Have any of these creatures ever actually fought back?" As soon as he uttered the words, he knew they had flown from his mouth a little too vehemently. He realized the warrior in him was talking.

The girl dropped her eyes to the ground, idly digging her toes in the sand. "Striking back in anger is not in their nature. They are incapable of aggression."

Jake fought back his rising frustration. "Then their passivity against assault will become a major liability, making their task all the more difficult. Perhaps none of them will even survive in attempting to carry out this plan."

"They are aware of the risks," Destiny replied, the words spilling out swiftly.

Jake pointed to the Islamic that had tried to kill him. "You see the man you healed. There are many people in the world just like him who are intent on killing people just like us. In order to survive, we have no choice but to fight back."

"But you chose not to kill him," Destiny countered softly.

In Jake's mind, a replay of the underwater fight with the man flashed before him as if he were viewing a movie. He had gone for a killing strike with the bang stick and the man's elbow had unexpectedly gotten in the way. "Only pure luck saved him," Jake shot back.

Destiny searched his face with gentle eyes and her riposte was mellifluous. "You could have let him drown or die from his wound, but you didn't. Instead, you chose to let me heal his injury. Even now you let him come ashore to eat with the rest of us."

Jake found himself unable to find any words as he stared back at the girl.

The girl held his gaze for an extended moment before looking toward the captive again. "I have spoken to him, and he has asked for our forgiveness."

"He what?" Jake blurted, completely dumbfounded.

Destiny smiled disarmingly. "His name is Bashir!"

Chapter Twenty-seven: Metamorphosis

Bashir continued to stare out over the water, marveling at its muted shimmering surface. There was something sublime about the wavering light, a harmonic balance between beauty, serenity, and… something else. It mystified him, oddly reminding him of the painting with its…its…he couldn't seem to put his finger on it. It lay just beyond the fringes of his comprehension. Casting off the frustration, he exhaled slowly, depleting his lungs before refilling them with the scented air. With his mind now relaxed, he refocused his eyes once more on the water. The feeling assaulted him again, the potency of both starlight and moonglow merging smoothly to produce a symphonic interplay of fascinating oscillations, both past and present. Yes, it was all there before him, a magical cosmic dance that enlivened the spirit. And hidden within it, a universal truth that could not be denied. It existed on its own, far from the bounds of religious doctrine.

In the midst of his spell, discrepant movement amid the glimmerings made him break from his reverie. He looked closely, perceiving it was well beyond where a gentle rise of wavelets lapped soothingly against the sandy shore. They were watching him again. For the moment, the mysterious white creatures had made him a subject of interest, seeming to probe his inner being from where they floated. He sat transfixed, feeling an abnormal calmness suddenly wash over him. With the hulking giant sitting close at hand, he should have felt threatened, but strangely he did not. Unaccustomed to such peace and tranquility, his thoughts began to drift over distant memories, recollections he now viewed as abhorrently unpleasant. For perhaps the first time in his life, he was seeing things clearly, unobstructed by circumstance and dogmatic teachings. Yes, the hate had blinded him, taking away his ability to think.

He tried putting it all into perspective. Hadn't he changed in the last eight hours? No, that wasn't quite right. More likely he had found his true self, a unique part of him buried deep that was incapable of change.

Orphaned at an early age, Bashir had grown up in the midst of wretched poverty in the slums of Beit Lahiya on the Gaza Strip, the youngest of six brothers. Though he barely remembered the woman who had birthed him, he knew she was the reason five of her oldest sons had blown themselves up on suicide missions. This desire for martyrdom had been incessantly encouraged within his family, so strong was his mother's hatred of the Jews, and it was this intense loathing that had caused her to finally take her own life as a way of killing Israelis.

By the time he was twelve, he had been recruited into the ranks of Hamas, enjoying a certain amount of prestige through the ultimate sacrifices of his mother and brothers. The Hamas leadership had become both surrogate mother and father to him, brimming with the word of God and the certainty of their cause. Yes, he had to admit to himself, the Palestinians were most likely the first terrorist people on earth. Over time, Hamas had spread its deadly preachings, steadily gaining support until it had finally taken over the reins of power in a country besieged with struggle. Winning a stunning landslide victory in a democratic election held in Palestine a little more than a year ago, the militant ruling party had provided additional glue for unifying the various Islamic radical groups into a loose coalition. Hezbollah, Al Qaeda, Islamic Jihad, and a host of others were now further emboldened to pursue their objectives within the region. Militant Islam had grown stronger, taking another step forward in its hate-filled agenda aimed at destroying Israel and establishing a Muslim caliphate all over the world.

Caught up in the fervor of jihad, Bashir had nearly let himself follow in the footsteps of his mother and brothers. He had come close to submitting to the will of Muslim mentors much older and wiser than he. Gleefully, they had smuggled him into Tel Aviv laden with a belt of high explosives hidden on his body, expecting him to spackle the walls of a certain restaurant with infidel flesh. At the time, he had perceived himself as being well prepared for martyrdom, ready to claim his place in paradise by carrying out the task assigned him. At the last minute, however, he had removed the bomb and fled, somehow finding his way beyond the Israeli border into Jordan. Journeying to the port city of Al Aquabah, he had managed to get work aboard a tramp steamer bound for Bandar-e Abbas, Iran. From there he eventually wound up in Pakistan. Ashamed of his cowardice, he had avowed before Allah to atone for his failure. As if in divine answer, he had chanced into the man called Kalid and confessed his sin. It was Kalid who had recruited him into the brotherhood of Al Qaeda.

In joining Al Qaeda, he had been a fool. Only now did he grasp the fact he had been sightless, for he knew the leadership of Hamas had considered Bin Laden's agenda to be far too destructive even for their own slaughterhouse sensibilities.

As he pondered his past, he could not refute the constant indoctrination of outrage they had instilled in him. But now all he could see were a faction of Muslim supremacists forcing their dictates upon others. The painting had gently compelled him to look deep inside himself, making him realize that he did not want to kill innocents after all. With this discovery, one overriding question kept plaguing him: Was it truly the will of God that all non-Muslims be killed for their blasphemous existence?

The answer rang loud and clear within him. No!

Such an idea now seemed completely and irrevocably inane, totally repulsive to his sensibilities. His newfound insight pointed to one conclusion, and one conclusion only, that the purity of Islam had been infected with an ugly malignancy, a moral corruption. The Muslim religion had been contaminated by the aspirations of men like Bin Laden and Raduyev, men who preyed on the blood of innocents. This was not and could not be God's way by any rational stretch of the imagination. The Islamic militant's justification for jihad had been grossly distorted. Using violence as a vehicle of expression was simply not God's way. He did not need the Koran to tell him this, for the Koran was merely based on a collection of words open to interpretation and often misused by biased minds. Rather it was an absolute sense emanating from somewhere deep within him that imparted such a conviction, something that simply was and could not be soiled by anything pernicious.

On impulse, Bashir turned and looked back at the girl. It was she and the creatures that had provided him with this insight, the instruments by which he could see himself for what he truly was. The painting had only been a means of conveyance, a tool, but the essence of both the girl and the dolphins had been firmly embedded within the depicted forms and texture. These divine angelic beings have shown me the way.

With his thoughts meandering over these things, he was suddenly caught in the grip of a sudden realization, giving him a premonition of horrific destruction yet to come. Undeniably, he had been part of the plan, but now he had to make amends, certain he would be unfit for paradise if he did not. I must do what I can to stop this insanity, he swore to himself.

Wondering what he could possibly do, several voices seemed to vibrate all at once in the depths of his soul. We will help you! They chimed in unison.

The inner voices spoke to him again, and Bashir suddenly knew the angels of Allah would take him to the place he had to go.

Missing

Without any words being said for the moment, Jake and Destiny ambled toward the falls, leaving the company of those still gathered around the fire. Sensing something was wrong, Jake studied the girl out of the corner of one eye, not wanting to be overly intrusive. For the second time this evening she appeared lost in thought, as if deeply preoccupied with something. He started to open his mouth to say something, but the sound of loping footsteps approaching from the rear made him turn. Out of the darkness, Phillipe raced forward to meet him.

"Bashir is gone!" the boy shouted breathlessly.

Jake's face immediately clouded. "Gone?"

"Yes, he is missing. Zimby looks for him."

Chapter Twenty-eight: Bashir's Mission

Late into the evening, Amphitrite walked out on the deserted pier. Jimenez, one of the local fishermen who often assisted her, was at her side, while Athena and several albinos were nearby in the water below. With little breeze to disturb the array of berthed fishing boats tied up against the timber structure, the dock was eerily quiet. Coming slowly toward her, she could discern a trail of luminescence on the ocean surface as something neared the platform on which she stood. Within moments, the imposing bulk of Hercules came alongside the pier, a man clinging to the dolphin's dorsal fin. Apollo and Artemis arrived a few seconds later, silently poking their heads above the water and staring wordlessly up at the woman.

Amphitrite turned to Jimenez. "Please help this man up the ladder," she said, making the request in English and talking loud enough for the clinging man to hear.

The Haitian fisherman climbed down and offered a hand to the stranger, helping him onto the wooden rungs.

Slowly, the man climbed up onto the platform, his silhouette appearing to scrutinize Amphitrite with uncertainty. "Who are you?" he asked, water dripping from his body. With the subdued glow of moonlight at the stranger's back, it did little to show his face.

"My identity is of no importance at this moment," Amphitrite replied calmly. She studied the man closely as though she might learn something new. She had heard the voiceless call and knew that the man before her had slipped unseen from the cove, aided by the others. "I am told you have journeyed up a poorly chosen path and that you wish to retrace your footsteps in order to stop something terrible from happening. Is this correct?"

The man looked back down at the creature that had carried him here, but Hercules was gone. In the darkness, his shroud of perplexity seemed to thicken as he turned again to face Amphitrite. "Will you take offense if I ask you to lower the veil covering your face?" There was apology in his tone.

The question amused Amphitrite. From the others, she had already learned a few things about the man. "In the culture from which you come, I thought it was unacceptable for a woman to reveal her face?"

Even in the dim light, the stranger's mannerism suggested surprise. "I am a long way from such a place."

Amphitrite lowered the shawl slowly to her shoulders, keeping her face to the moon.

A startled intake of breath was heard as the man stared. "I see another angel…an angel who looks very much like the one that healed me."

Amphitrite smiled. "The person you speak of is my daughter, Destiny."

"Destiny has shown me much kindness," the man responded, his voice containing awe.

"Yes, I know," Amphitrite said, keeping the smile in place. "She tells me your name is Bashir." She hesitated briefly. "Before I can help you, Bashir, it is important that I place my hand on your head."

"There is no need of that," Bashir answered. "I am fully recovered from my injury."

"You may have other injuries that you are not yet aware of." Amphitrite was not referring to any impairments of the flesh.

"Very well," Bashir said, the words coming out in a sigh. "I suppose an angel can see many things."

Amphitrite raised her left hand and planted it softly on Bashir's forehead, closing her eyes as she did so. Probing by this method did not always work, and for the moment she saw nothing. Through her daughter and the others, she had learned about the man's capture by the one who had helped Destiny rescue the dolphins. In healing Bashir's wound, the pod had gained only partial insight into the man's fundamental nature, knowing he had been part of some unknown objective in the Caribbean. And though an indistinct wickedness seemed to surround that objective, the man himself seemed to be more of a victim rather than an evildoer. Yes, she had known of these things beforehand through the ethereal flickers that often flitted in and out of her consciousness like the delicate songbirds fluttering weightless about the cove.

The vision that suddenly came to her, however, pierced her mind like a cold dagger, making her cringe. For what seemed like an eternity, she bore up to it, assaying the full context of what she was seeing. Finally, with knees quaking, she withdrew her hand.

Turning, Amphitrite locked eyes with Jimenez. "This man must be delivered to Navassa Island tonight. Will you take him there?"

Jimenez nodded, more than happy to oblige.

Amphitrite turned back to Bashir. "I bade you a safe and successful voyage, Bashir," she offered, still reeling from what she had seen. "God go with you!"

"Two of his angels have already helped me," Bashir said earnestly. "I am sure he will continue to guide me."

Amphitrite stood still, watching the two men climb down into Jimenez's boat. She continued to stand there long after the boat had disappeared into the night. Over and over, one thought kept echoing in her brain. So, it begins!

Chapter Twenty-nine: The Amulet

The Colonel's eyes bulged in disbelief, wondering if the trinket's authenticity was for real. He had never expected Hennington to actually bring him back the medallion, only that the broker return with news of the cheval and the valuable talisman it possessed. "Am I to understand she simply handed this over to you?"

No emotion of any kind showed on Hennington's face. "She did."

The old scar on Ternier's jaw tingled at the memory of the accursed thing that had taken the form of a white woman. It didn't make sense to him. Why? Why would she give it up so readily? The thought tormented him, thundering through his mind as he paced around his office like a caged lion waiting to be fed.

Ternier halted abruptly. Unless?

He recalled the amulet's searing heat the last time he had clutched it. The pain had been agonizing. His mother, Erzulie, had suffered a similar fate when her hands had bled painfully upon holding the ancient object so long ago.

Suspiciously, Ternier eyed the trinket in Hennington's hand as if it were a vial of poison. "You may place the object on my desk," he instructed curtly. He would not repeat his past mistake. With hands clasped stiffly behind him, he resumed his pacing, once more projecting the rigid bearing that was so much a part of him. "And what did you learn about Ronaldo Trebek?" he said, changing the subject.

"Other than the fact that he still lives in Malique, there is not much to tell."

"I assume you spoke to him?"

"Yes. The man prefers to spend his days as a simple fisherman."

Ternier mulled this, finding it difficult to believe. He hadn't yet decided what to do about his former accomplice. The fact that Trebek had knowledge of the hydrogen bomb might possibly compromise the grand plan he had devised, and that was not good.

The Colonel turned his eyes back to Hennington. The broker's mannerism struck him as odd. There was something different about the way he spoke and carried himself. "You have nothing else to tell me?" he asked, regarding the man closely.

The broker met Ternier's stare with uncharacteristic calmness. "Malique is only reachable by boat, seaplane or helicopter these days. The road that used to lead there has remained blocked by a mudslide that occurred many years ago."

The reference made Ternier grimace inwardly, yet another reminder of the cheval's strange power. In response, his eyes were again drawn to the amulet, now lying innocently on his desk. Surely she will be powerless without it!

An overwhelming desire to be alone suddenly came over Ternier as he thought about the cheval. He needed time to think without any distractions. Stepping back to his desk, he sat down heavily, casting his eyes back on Hennington. "Leave me!" he ordered.

Hennington rose from the chair he had been sitting in but stopped short of moving any further. "The *San Carlo* is back in the harbor."

Ternier's eyes were drawn to the amulet once again, and for the moment he ignored Hennington.

Not getting a response, Hennington rephrased the declaration. "Sebastian Ortega has arrived back in Port-au-Prince with his flagship."

The Colonel stared blankly at the amulet. "I am well aware of that," he said, the words uttered dully. The sight of the trinket continued to hold his attention. "She comes back earlier than expected."

"Ortega would like to take delivery of the merchandise a day earlier than planned."

Ternier looked up sharply in annoyance, his eyes suddenly coming alive with a flaming, hypnotic vehemence. "Leave me!" he hissed, waving the broker away as if he were some form of loathsome vermin. "I will contact you when I am ready and not until then."

For one brief moment before turning to leave, Hennington met Ternier's withering gaze, and in that moment Ternier could not detect the slightest trace of timidity in the man. Could it be that the cheval has done something to him? The thought disturbed him to no end. People without fear could not be controlled. Perhaps it will be necessary to take him before my mother again.

After Hennington had left, Ternier focused all his attention back on the amulet. Cautiously, he extended a hand to touch it, but held back, startled that his hand was shaking. For several minutes, he sat and stared, trying to overcome the fear gripping him. I will not let her do this to me! He scolded himself. Maddened with rage, he poked the trinket gingerly with a finger, withdrawing his hand even more quickly. He felt no heat. Emboldened, he touched the charm again, holding his finger against it a little longer this time. There was no pain. Warily he covered the amulet with his palm, noticing how cool it felt. With unrestrained glee, he snatched it from the desk, caressing it lovingly as one thought raced through his mind. My future is now assured.

Chapter Thirty: Accusations

Walter McPherson was in no mood to accept failure, especially after following Grahm and his two assistants to this godforsaken place. Everything he had ever heard about Haiti's economic plight had been confirmed by his own eyes. He found it difficult to believe this land had once been the richest country in the western hemisphere. But after getting a taste of the island nation's people and infrastructure, he now understood why it was by far the poorest. Port-au-Prince was a virtual slum, a hopeless haven of unimaginable poverty and squalor. Port-a-Potty would have been a name more befitting, he thought as he recalled the taxi ride from the airport that had taken him here to the La Casa Grande where he was currently staying.

With the hotel located in Petitionville, supposedly the city's richest suburb, he had endured an unpleasant and bumpy ride over a barely passable road that looked like a semi-dry riverbed strewn with deep ruts and potholes. Burning tires interspersed among a seemingly endless succession of dilapidated shacks off to both sides of the road had further downgraded the dismal journey. The cab he had ridden in had not been much better and had only tended to intensify his discomfiture with the gloom all about him. A dented, rusting hulk with blown springs, it jarred him to the teeth each time it met another discontinuity in the surface upon which it rode. On top of that, the vehicle was missing a functioning horn, taillights, windshield wipers, spare tire, mirrors, and a host of other essential safety features. On the way in, swarms of emaciated, sunken-eyed beggars had surrounded the car yelling, "Blanc! Blanc!" either hustling prostitutes or demanding money.

Reputed to be one of the few prestigious hotels adorning the outskirts of the city, he found the La Casa Grande to be a major anticlimax. Adding to his woes, his room was currently without running water. After being subjected to several discreet knocks on his door since arriving, he had finally learned to ignore the solicitations of sleazy prostitutes looking for an easy mark. And once again, the leaky air conditioner was not working.

It was late at night, and with the exception of a lit taper casting eerie shadows on the walls, the room was bathed in an ominous gloaming. The electricity had cut out again, making him glance longingly out the room's window overlooking the hotel's center court. Glowing softly in the darkness, a line of burning candles outlined the sunken bar situated in the swimming pool, their minuscule flames reflecting off the water that beckoned invitingly. When he had first arrived here, an artificial waterfall spilling profusely into the pool had given him a false impression of the place. But without power, the plummeting stream had ceased flowing, driving home the condition of his oppressive surroundings. Every so often, a rising crescendo of shouting from the hotel's casino intruded rudely into his quarters, a stark reminder that the establishment's clientele would not be discouraged from laying down bets.

With his clothes rapidly becoming damp with sweat, he was in no mood to be confronted with yet another disappointment. He had expected more from Frank Jaffey, a man who had distinguished himself in the U.S. Navy as an exceptional fighter pilot. "You're telling me you bagged two specimens, then lost them," he blurted angrily, his tone on the verge of a shriek. He shook his head in disbelief. "You actually had them aboard your vessel and somehow you lost them."

Jaffey looked over at Ben Loomins, impaling his partner with a vicious glare. "Unfortunately, yes. We had 'em, but then they escaped."

McPherson affixed both men with a glare of his own. "You mind elaborating?"

Jaffey shot another venomous look at Loomins. "Yeah, explain to the captain how you managed to blow such an incredible catch."

Loomins shrugged helplessly, clearing his throat as he did so. "Everything went perfect until we picked up two people adrift on a waverunner."

"We?" Jaffey grumbled, his eyebrows rising in protest. "Don't make me a party to your screw-up, asshole. You took it upon yourself to take aboard two strangers."

"They appeared innocent enough," Loomins sputtered. "They were stranded on a waverunner dead in the water. What was I supposed to do, just leave 'em and keep going on my merry way? Maritime law requires I lend assistance."

"Bullshit!" Jaffey shot back. "You picked them up because you saw a pretty face."

McPherson was bewildered. "One of the people was a girl?"

"Yeah," Jaffey confirmed. "Ben, here, is a real sucker when it comes to women. He can't help himself."

Loomins' face reddened with both anger and embarrassment. "I had the situation under control. I locked up the two of them in a storage locker. Somehow, they found a way to get out."

"What good did that do?" Jaffey snarled. "The damage had already been done."

McPherson looked from one to the other in confusion, his fuse rapidly shortening. "Two people sabotaged the operation?" Is that what they were telling him?

Jaffey nodded contemptuously. "They freed the creatures…right under the nose of my vigilant partner, here."

"Screw you!" Loomins snapped.

McPherson was at the end of his rope. "Stop this blame game and tell me what happened," he spat heatedly. "In good faith I advanced the two of you $80,000 to bag me a specimen, so I'd like to know precisely how these dolphins managed to slip from your grasp."

Loomins shook his head in frustration. "The girl's boyfriend cut the restraining straps holding down the dolphins. They were able to walk themselves across the deck on those hands of theirs and pull themselves over the railing."

McPherson's jaw dropped. "You saw this?"

"No, but the deckhands did. I was up on the bridge piloting the boat."

"I thought your plan was to tranquilize them before hauling them aboard," McPherson reminded him.

"They were tranquilized!" Loomins argued.

"Apparently not enough."

"There was enough sedative in those darts to take down a rhino," Loomins persisted. "I checked the dosages myself."

McPherson paused, looking doubtful. For several seconds he pondered what Loomins was telling him before riveting the man with an accusing stare. "Wasn't that rather stupid to leave these people with the run of the boat?" he admonished. "Nobody tried to stop them from freeing the dolphins?"

Loomins fidgeted nervously. "My brother was keeping an eye on them," he muttered.

McPherson let out a reproachful laugh. "A lot of good that did."

"The girl's boyfriend sucker-punched Charlie while he was watching the girl. She was doing something to the dolphins."

"Like what?"

"I don't know. I wasn't present to see for myself."

"What about your deckhands? They just stood there?"

"The guy had taken Charlie's rifle and kept them away. That's when he cut the dolphins loose."

McPherson scoffed derisively. "And I suppose that's when these creatures just got up and left."

"Yes." Loomins uttered the word as if he found this hard to believe himself.

"So what happened next?"

"The girl revived my brother who was still out cold." Loomins was speaking rapidly now. "According to the deckhands, she seemed to do the same thing to him that she did to the dolphins. Charlie used to be a professional fighter but came away from the sport with a glass jaw. The doctors said he had a non-operable brain aneurysm. Any blow to the head could prove fatal to him."

"What did this girl actually do?"

"Not much of anything other than place her hands on his head."

"But you didn't see her do this."

"No. I was told that when Charlie started to come to, the girl collapsed. Her boyfriend was in the process of moving her back aboard their waverunner when I caught them. That's when I decided to lock them up in the storage locker."

McPherson stood motionless for a long moment, trying to make sense of this strange sequence of events. "If he was attempting to get back on the waverunner, I have to assume it was still operable. I take it you never checked to see if it would run." The look he gave Loomins was devoid of all respect. "You were set up. This whole story about a waverunner on the fritz was simply a ploy to get aboard your vessel. Those people had to have known in advance what you were carrying."

Ben Loomins appeared crestfallen, holding his tongue.

"Did you notice any other vessels in the vicinity while capturing the dolphins?"

"None."

McPherson turned to Jaffey. "What about aircraft?"

"The sky was clear," Jaffey stated.

"And that waverunner was nowhere in sight at the time?"

Both men shook their head.

McPherson eyed each man coldly. "Just look at the facts, gentlemen. Those people had one objective, and one objective only. And that was to free the dolphins. Somehow, they had advance knowledge of the capture and came up with a plan to get aboard your vessel." He paused, throwing a sideways glance at both men. "That is, unless this whole story you're giving me is all horseshit. Perhaps you want to keep these dolphins for yourselves. Maybe you think you can get a better price elsewhere."

Both Jaffey and Loomins bridled at the suggestion. "Once we make a deal, we stick by it," Jaffey growled, suddenly looking like he would have no misgivings about striking McPherson. "I'm no longer in the military, Captain. You're not speaking to some low-ranking midshipman trying to pull the wool over the eyes of the big brass. You better think twice before you throw any more wild accusations around like that."

McPherson gazed back, unruffled. "So then how did these people manage to free themselves from their confinement?" he finally asked, his tone mocking.

Jaffey glanced at his partner. "I don't know!" Loomins said peevishly. "It's been driving me crazy how they managed to escape from that locker. It should have been impossible. A heavy dead bolt locked them in there. They somehow found a way to slide it open from the inside."

"And when they got out?"

"They found one of the netting devices we keep aboard and caught Charlie by surprise in the boat's salon. They snared him with the webshot and locked him away in the same storage locker. After that, the girl jumped overboard and her boyfriend retrieved his waverunner. I wasn't aware of the escape until I got back in the harbor."

"I assume your deckhands saw both of them leave but failed to alert you at the time?"

Loomins reddened with embarrassment again. "Yeah… they witnessed the whole thing but didn't try to stop them. These Haitians who work for me are a superstitious lot. A belief in voodoo runs deep in these islanders. They referred to the girl as a white witch. They were fearful of bringing misfortune on themselves had they alerted me right away."

"Why would they call this girl a white witch?"

Loomins shrugged. "Who knows? I can't even begin to imagine how their minds work. But from what they told me, there's more of these white dolphins than just the two we captured."

McPherson perked up suddenly. "What do you mean?"

Loomins smiled thinly. "My crewmen counted at least nine of those creatures trailing behind the boat while we were underway. After the girl jumped overboard, they spotted her riding the largest among them."

McPherson turned and looked back at the swimming pool, a heavy trickle of sweat pouring from his brow. He wondered how much longer he would be able to endure a hellhole like this. He should have been rewarded for his troubles in coming here by now, flying back to the states in Frank Jaffey's Casa-212 with the prizes he had come to retrieve. This sudden revelation, however, had sparked a new set of possibilities into the scheme of things. Perhaps he would walk away with much more than he had originally anticipated.

Spinning around, he gaffed Jaffey with a penetrating stare. "If there's that many of this unknown species, then you and your partner should have no trouble getting a chance to redeem yourselves."

"Where do we look?" Jaffey said testily. "Do you think all these dolphins have emitters strapped to their bodies? Ben removed the one we found on the male during the capture. Without a signal to home in on, it'd be like looking for a needle in a haystack."

McPherson smiled bitterly. "Gentlemen…one thing I've learned is that when in doubt, go back to the point of origination."

"What are you getting at?" Ben asked.

"The plan is simple," McPherson said. "Go back to where you bagged the dolphins and see if you spot any more."

Jaffey nodded. "I suppose what you're suggesting is as good as any other plan." He hesitated, appearing to give the idea some thought. "All right…we'll give it a shot."

An angry scowl abruptly crossed Loomins' face. "If I ever get my hands on Nick Henderson, he'll wish he never poked his nose into our business."

McPherson gaped at Loomins as if the man had backhanded him squarely across the mouth. "Who?"

Chapter Thirty-one: Telepathic Mind-link

Jake Javolyn kicked his way deeper through the murk, carried along by a strong current. The poor visibility surprised him, and he wondered if a storm had passed this way in the last several hours. Indistinct shapes suddenly materialized below him, and as his eyes penetrated the gloom, he started to make out ridges of jutting coral parading by in the midst of a white sandy plain. Although he was fairly deep, perhaps sixty feet below the surface, he felt no escalating pressure, nor a desire to breathe. The thought that this was rather strange ran briefly through his mind. He had been down for some time now without a tank of air to sustain him.

Letting the current take him, he glided effortlessly above a forest of calcareous growths, noticing how bleached and lifeless the formations were. Instinctively, he knew the coral had been dead for many years now, killed off by runaway pollution. The sight failed to disturb him as the flow of water swept him on. He had long since grown used to seeing such sterile habitats while conducting many similar explorations up and down the Haitian coastline, all of them with the same objective. There was a plus side to such barren desolation that would make his search easier, however, and that lay in the unchanging nature of the rocky structures. Without living polyps to generate new growth, the shape of dead coral would remain relatively constant for many years to come, wearing away only gradually through the grinding turbulence of storm-tossed seas.

Something abruptly caught his eye as he looked on, and as he stared, the silhouette of a lone human hovered in the distance ahead, unaffected by the strength of the current. The figure motioned to him, pointing below at something for him to see. Swept closer, he glimpsed the thing being indicated. It was a gargantuan sea turtle, etiolated and unmoving, its broad concave shell stretched out before him.

No! That wasn't what he was seeing at all. Rather, it was a formation of bleached brain coral that had the configuration of a sea turtle. Dumbstruck, he gazed in wonder as a sense of elation quickly engulfed him. The very thing he had been searching for all these months finally lay before him. With a little luck, his quest would soon end.

Looking up, he started to wave his thanks to the lone figure, but the figure was gone. Turning, he glanced about in confusion, wondering what had become of the stranger. But deep down he knew it had not been a stranger. With a start, he gazed in all directions again. It had been Myers. But that was impossible. Myers was dead.

An overwhelming need for air took hold of him, and with sudden alarm he realized he had been down far too long. Fighting back the temptation to breathe, he placed his fins on the formation beneath him, preparing to push off hard and launch himself toward atmosphere high above. But something had hold of his ankles and he could not move. A wave of horror ran through him as he looked down. The diver that had almost got him the night before was back, holding fast to his legs. He tried to kick away, but he was now physically spent and his legs failed to respond. With choking awareness, a wash of water flooded his lungs, and with strangling brutality, a cold blackness rushed in on him.

Jay Jay! A voice cried out from across the galaxy. *Jay Jay!* The cry was closer this time, accompanied by a heavy thud. *I know the location of the turtle coral. I will show you where it is if you wish to go there.* In moments, the nightmare receded into nothingness as Jake found himself back in his quarters, the last tendrils of sleep ebbing away quickly. Another thud landed on the *Angel's* hull, and he lifted the curtain from the window to investigate. Achilles was there, the dolphin's dark orbs scrutinizing him through the Plexiglas.

Rubbing the sleep from his eyes, Jake climbed out of bed. The thought that Bashir had disappeared the night before rushed in on him, and he tried to postulate where the man might have gone. Maybe he... *I can help you find the turtle, Jay Jay.* Jake stopped short, glancing about him. The cabin was empty.

Scratching his head, he wondered if he was still dreaming. Though it had come to him as a barely perceptible whisper, he had distinctly heard a voice. *Am I losing my sanity?*

No, you are perfectly sane, the voice answered. *And you are no longer dreaming.*

What's going on?

Another thump sounded against the hull. *Look out the window, Jay Jay!*

Jake glanced out the window, only to see Achilles again.

The young albino stared back with that permanent smile of his. *I am not currently phonating, Jay Jay. You have become attuned to projected thoughts emanating from me. I was able to see your dream, Jay Jay. You have been searching for that particular formation for some time now without any success. I can bring you to the turtle. I know where it is!*

Jake could only stare back in amazement, wondering if this, too, was another part of the dream as well. Maybe he would find himself waking up at any moment.

Chapter Thirty-two: Erzulie's Chamber

The skulls stacked against the wall behind Erzulie grinned hideously in the dimly lit chamber as Colonel Ternier laid the amulet down before her. "I believe this is bona fide, mother," he said, reading the wary look on her face.

Erzulie examined the trinket carefully, not yet willing to make contact with it. As if to neutralize any lurking spells, she reached into one of the many glass jars on the table before her and sprinkled some powder upon the object, chanting a repetitive phrase incomprehensible to Ternier. The chanting went on for nearly a minute before a startled gasp escaped her. The talisman began to give off an eerie red aura, the scant light reflecting dully off Erzulie's face and imparting an expression not much different from the skulls.

"What do you think, mother?" Ternier asked, unable to contain himself any longer. He had never grown used to these mystic rituals.

As if in answer, an inhuman bloodcurdling scream pierced the air within the chamber, emanating from one of the torture cells further back in the prison. Ternier listened, enraptured, glad that the chamber's steel door was still ajar so as not to impede the cries of a tormented soul. The sound of agony always pleased him. For several seconds, he wallowed glaze-eyed in the shriek before it finally trailed away into a hopeless wail.

Erzulie's eyes and mouth appeared to retract into broadening, blackened hollows under the feeble emission radiating from the amulet. "You have done well, my son. Nothing can oppose us now!"

An upwelling of immense satisfaction rose up from Ternier's loins and worked its way onto his countenance. "I have another surprise for you, mother."

Erzulie looked up to scrutinize her son more fully, the pits within her face widening even more. "Yes, my son?"

"I have apprehended Emmanuel Baptiste."

Erzulie glanced back down, the glow from the amulet now appearing stronger and changing over to a deep blood-red. "This charm has the power of the rada contained within it," she said, her voice gravelly and filled with emotion. "The cheval gave it up because she and all those she protects have fallen out of favor with the rada. The amulet would have been useless in her hands, maybe even a danger to her." Placing her gaze back on her son, she asked, "When and where did you catch Baptiste?"

"Less than two hours ago at the airport. Baptiste was disembarking from a flight originating out of Anguilla. One of my people working in customs recognized him even though the man was traveling under an assumed name."

Erzulie seemed to smile, though her features continued to be obscured in shadow. "Already the power held within the charm manifests itself. It tells me the rada now favor us." Lifting the amulet, she placed the chain attached to it around her neck, letting the ancient piece of jewelry dangle between her shriveled breasts where it glowed even brighter. "With this behind you, you will be unstoppable, my son. The power you now enjoy will be but nothing compared to that which awaits you." She paused, seeming to savor the feel of the object against her chest. "Where is Baptiste being held?"

"He is in this very prison. Would you like me to bring him to you?"

"Not just yet, my son. I will need time to meditate. There are other considerations more pressing at the moment."

"I assume you are referring to Malique, mother?"

Erzulie turned her face up to Ternier again, her expression appearing even more skull-like than before. "The fulfillment of revenge is not much different than harvesting fruit. The taste grows sweeter as the fruit ripens."

The Colonel was used to his mother speaking in metaphors. She had always talked this way, and Malique was the fruit to which she referred. Their intended raid on the village many years ago had left a bitter taste in both their mouths because the fruit had not sufficiently ripened. But Malique was now ripe for the plucking, and the analogy made him anticipate the potential sweetness all the more.

Yes, he would honor Ortega's request, and the tiny fishing village would provide the needed bodies. It would be easier this way, allowing him to avoid accounting for too many missing prison inmates. A few prisoners disappearing every so often was one thing, but to have nearly two dozen vanish all at once left him exposed to possible repercussions by an assortment of human rights groups, and even worse, incarceration by The Hague. With United Nations troops still in Haiti, it was important he evade bringing such attention to himself. But then again, the day when such accountability would not matter anymore was fast approaching.

"I will make the necessary arrangements, mother," Ternier said.

Erzulie rested her gaze on the amulet once more. The talisman continued to glow with a strange ominous intensity.

Chapter Thirty-three: Treasure Found

Jake held on tight as Hermes towed him along, his mind feasting on several concerns. One of those concerns was Bashir's sudden disappearance the night before. Deep down he had the feeling the pod had something to do with it but decided to keep the matter to himself. It was a beautiful Caribbean morning with near-flat seas, and he had no desire to break the spell. Several others had accompanied him on the outing, including Destiny, Hercules, and Aphrodite, Hermes twin sister. With Achilles out in front of the small contingent and leading the way, they had left the cove and were currently traveling south toward a place called the Devil's Horn, a distance of roughly four miles down the coast.

Originally, Achilles had wanted to be Jake's mode of transport, but because Hermes was bigger and more powerful than the juvenile albino, the pod had thought it best to have one of the adults do the pulling rather than have the smallest member of the group run the risk of fatiguing himself. From what Jake was seeing, however, the adult consensus was off the mark, for the young dolphin appeared to be bursting with energy. Every so often along the way, Achilles would execute a series of acrobatic flips, soaring high into the air each time. On several of the aerial maneuvers, Jake could have sworn the juvenile had reached a height of close to sixty feet above the water, turning five and sometimes six complete somersaults during each leap.

In watching these antics, Jake wondered whether the young albino was just happy or simply showing off. Either way, he was justifiably impressed with the athletic prowess displayed by Achilles. But he still remained no less than astounded by what had happened earlier. Even now, his brain continued to reel over the mind link he had attained with the juvenile. How the cetacean had been able to read his mind, he could not even begin to fathom. And though the mental union had not lasted long, he was beginning to have a clue as to what bonding meant. Try as he might, though, he had not been able to reestablish a mental link with the juvenile since the mind-boggling event.

As they continued to make their way south, Jake turned his head to espy Destiny and her mount. To Jake, the girl was a sight to behold as she rode Hercules, her long dark mane trailing behind her and glistening like burnished coal under the morning sun. Once again, she was outfitted in that all-white wet suit which fit her body like a second skin. Destiny was truly in her element as she hunched forward atop the huge albino bull, the same dive mask he had seen before strapped snugly against her face. Periodically, the girl would glance in his direction and throw him a warm smile, seemingly glad about his presence.

As it was, Jake was eager to discover the location of the turtle-like formation, something that had eluded him for a long time now. Without words having been spoken, Achilles had claimed to know where it was. For this jaunt, he had opted to keep his choice of equipment simple, wearing only a shorty wet suit, mask, fins, snorkel, and his trusty K-bar, preferring to leave the waverunner behind and ride Hermes instead. The supposedly short trip was to be nothing more than a brief reconnaissance to confirm if the calcareous structure was the one he had been searching for.

Several times during the excursion, Jake had tried to ride Hermes in the same manner exhibited by Destiny astride her own mount, but finally gave up the attempt. Destiny, it seemed, had a riding technique all her own, naturally conjoining with Hercules as if both beings were actually one. In watching her, Jake could not help dispel the impression that Hercules had been created for this very purpose. Whereas the girl sat just forward of the giant's dorsal fin and held onto straps specifically designed for looping around the creature's pectoral flippers, Jake was forced to grip his own mount's dorsal fin, letting his body trail back as the bottlenose switchbacked through the sea.

Hermes was a powerful animal, and as Jake was towed onward, he was struck by the idea that here was a newly evolved sentience whose mind was likely even more powerful than its body. Some of the things Grahm had told him during the initial voyage to Navassa Island jumped to the forefront of his thoughts. Cetaceans had developed intelligences at least equal if not greater to that of the Homo sapien, having inhabited the planet far longer than man. Grahm had explained to him that without hands for building machinery, the forerunners of this creature could only develop inwardly, possessing thoughts and cultures far different from that of its human counterpart. But something had now changed, something both extraordinary and wonderful. Equipped with digital extremities in combination with an intellect that showed every indication of being superior to man's, the emergence of this newcomer on the planetary scene opened a whole new frontier to all types of possibilities, possibilities that were confided to him by Jacob last night. And from what he'd already seen, it was very probable that the creature to which he clung also possessed both telepathic and telekinetic abilities. Yes, he concluded, it was quite possible this species was one up on man in every way. Convinced of this, he felt honored that he had been accepted by these amazing beings.

With such thoughts dominating his awareness, Jake did not realize Hermes had stopped moving. Looking around, he now saw that the jutting headland known as the Devil's Horn lay directly to the east. Almost immediately, Hercules swam alongside Jake so that Destiny could speak to him.

Hiking the dive mask to her forehead, she indicated the area over which they floated. "The formation is directly below us."

"How deep?" Jake asked.

Destiny paused, apparently consulting with the others in the silent mode of communication she used. "About twelve meters," she finally replied.

Jake adjusted his dive mask in preparation for descending, but Hermes did not move.

"Achilles will take you down, Jay Jay," Destiny said.

Jake nodded, noticing the juvenile was suddenly beside him. Hyperventilating for several seconds, he filled his lungs to capacity and grabbed hold of Achilles' dorsal fin. Abruptly Achilles dove.

Just as Jake had experienced in the dream, he felt the strength of the current as he descended. Visibility was not particularly good in this locale, perhaps a step down from what was typical in most undersea habitats along the Haitian coast. The water carried a lot of suspended sediment, and he could see no more than forty feet through the murk. This was understandable, considering the proximity of a small river discharging on the southern side of the Horn. He had taken the time to look at a map of the area just before coming here, noting the river winding its way down from the higher elevations to the east.

The pressure built rapidly as Achilles arrowed for the bottom, and Jake's ears popped as he swallowed to relieve the escalating discomfiture on his eardrums. Within moments, ridges of coral suddenly sprang into view as the juvenile maintained a purposeful heading. All at once the young dolphin stopped flicking its tail, taking on a lazy glide that brought it over a lower portion of the reef, giving Jake the opportunity to let his eyes adjust to the size and shape of the rocky formation below him. Achilles made three full circuits around the structure, allowing Jake ample time to take in the sight.

A gigantic sea turtle lay sprawled out on a bed of white sand, its broad heart-shaped carapace bleached a pale brown and extending a full ten meters in length. From above, Jake was amazed at the anatomical correctness of the formation. It appeared to match perfectly the physical characteristics of a real sea turtle, exhibiting four flipper-like legs, a tail, and a bulbous head that jutted ostensibly from beneath the shell in all the right places.

As if knowing Jake had seen enough, Achilles dipped lower, dropping below the edge of the turtle's convex shell. Beneath this level the coral was substantially recessed, and as Jake's eyes adapted to the reduced light, he could see that the carapace of the formation overhung a pedestal of rock that formed the base of the structure. From this perspective, the coral outcropping gave the appearance of a giant mushroom. Two lone spider crabs, their shells encrusted in brown algae, scuttled out of his way as he let go of Achilles and slipped under the umbrella of coral. Swimming beneath the overhang and making one full lap around the center column, Jake gauged the distance between the sandy bottom and the underside of the shell to be fairly uniform, about four feet in height all the way around. One area back toward the turtle's tail contained a significant buildup of calcareous rubble. It was here that he focused his efforts, moving aside small chunks of rock.

The available light dimmed further as Jake began to work, making him glance briefly behind him to investigate the cause. Congregated together, Destiny and all four albinos hovered suspended just below the edge of the overhang. Overcome by curiosity, they peered in at him. Turning back to the task at hand, Jake resumed his labors and dug deeper, displacing several larger coral fragments before his hands encountered something incongruous with the rubble. Running his fingers along it, he felt a flat surface. Encouraged, he cleared away more rock. Some kind of a metallic box, possibly aluminum, sat embedded among the loose stone.

Working more quickly now, Jake uncovered the front face of two more boxes, each face about two feet wide by eighteen inches high. Extending an arm, he managed to get a hand behind a corner of one of the boxes. Although the confined space afforded him little in the way of leverage, he positioned his body as best he could to exert as much force as possible. The box barely budged, its contents apparently quite weighty.

With lungs now burning, Jake made a decision, and that was to bury the boxes once again. Quickly, he pushed rubble back in front of the containers and withdrew from the rocky enclosure. Achilles was standing by to take him to the surface, and upon gripping the juvenile's dorsal fin, Jake was whisked swiftly to the air above.

Inhaling ponderously upon gaining atmosphere, Jake eased his aching lungs. He looked at his dive watch, realizing he had been down nearly four and a half minutes. Turning his eyes toward the land, he took a moment to study the shoreline, gauging his current position with respect to several conspicuous landmarks along the headland. From where he floated, he guessed he was approximately a quarter mile directly off the rocky promontory.

"There is no need for you to memorize where you are, Jay Jay," Achilles ululated, as if reading Jake's mind. "When you wish to return here, I will take you."

Jake took in the words, growing used to the way Achilles always seemed to be one step ahead of him. "I'll remember that Achilles." Pivoting his head, he noticed Destiny sitting atop Hercules close behind him. Though he half expected her to ask about the boxes, the girl sat quietly, leisurely stroking the giant albino's head.

"You're probably wondering what those boxes contain," Jake huffed, continuing to breath heavily from the lengthy dive.

Destiny smiled lazily. Though she had been submerged as long as Jake, she showed not the slightest sign of strain. "I have been brought up to respect the privacy of others," she said softly. "Hopefully your search is now at an end and you will find peace within yourself."

Jake had not expected such a reply. "But you were down there watching me," he panted, continuing to breathe heavily. "You're not curious about why I came here?"

"I was only concerned for your safety. It is normal for every member of the pod to look out for one another. These waters off the Horn can be dangerous."

As his oxygen debt diminished, Jake's breathing began to slow perceptibly. "I need to confirm what's in those boxes, but not now," he offered. "When the time is right, I'll come back here with the *Angel* and bring up what's down there."

"When that time comes, we'll be ready to help if you need us."

Jake nodded. "I just might take you up on that offer." He looked north. "What say we head back? I've seen all I need for now."

Achilles gave Jake just enough time to lower his face mask and insert the snorkel in his mouth before flicking his tail hard and taking off in the direction of the cove. It soon became evident that the young albino would not be denied towing him on the return trip.

Chapter Thirty-four: DNA Confirmed

Though things like this no longer surprised him, Grahm nevertheless continued to stare in wonder at the data displayed on the laptop screen. Everything Jacob had claimed about the *thurentra* was proving to be true. The Big Mac in Miami had done its job, identifying a genetic marker common to both the hybrid organism residing on the cove floor and a species of sea cucumber found in Caribbean waters. What was even more interesting was the discovery of a second DNA sequence within the *thurentra* that inferred a match with a fragment of Natalie's genome.

Grahm turned to Parker. "You're certain Big Mac scanned the genome of every known variety of coelenterate."

Parker gave a lackluster nod. "Yep. Probably came close to burning out her circuits with the survey she made. It was quite extensive."

Frustration showed on Grahm's features. The face of his long-departed wife suddenly loomed in his mind's eye. Had she still been alive, she might have provided valuable insight in the search. "Then it's got to be a species of coelenterate never before catalogued."

"Assuming it actually belongs to the coelenterate phylum," Parker was quick to point out. "I only instructed Big Mac to focus on the coelenterates."

Grahm shifted his eyes to the inverted funnel positioned above the water where the *thurentra* lay. "It stands to reason a life form capable of transforming or mutating other organisms into newly evolved creatures has never before been catalogued. Jacob's description of the organism fits that of a jellyfish, and right now, that's what I'm sticking with."

Parker whistled. "So you think this unknown variety of jellyfish is a genetic cousin of Natalie's and the other pod members."

Grahm scratched his beard. "It certainly seems to look that way."

"This trip isn't over yet," Parker said. "Who knows…maybe we'll get lucky and find this jellyfish before we're done."

"Perhaps," Grahm agreed tiredly. He sank down on a nearby flat-topped rock and rubbed his eyes. He was a scientist and men of his profession needed proof to corroborate observations simply because things weren't always what they appeared to be. Here was at least an inkling of evidence backing up how the *thurentra* came into being. Dispelling the skepticism he had felt over the merging of a sea cucumber and an unknown form of jellyfish was not easy for him. A discovery like this was unprecedented in the history of biological research. Newly evolved organisms were just not produced in the manner Jacob had described. And yet he could not reject the supporting evidence, though of and by itself it was not conclusive. Such thoughts caused his mind to explore another possibility.

Was Jacob's application of the Gaia Theory so absurd after all? Had Mother Nature actually come up with a remedy for neutralizing man's destructive nature, of putting mankind back on the right track? Grahm's eyes locked on several white fins cleaving the water in the vicinity of the waterfall. And if such a divine purpose were truly in the works, maybe these dolphins had been specifically created to fulfill a certain role.

Caught up in this idea, Grahm explored it further. If allowed to propagate and multiply, who knew what achievements this new breed might accomplish? With prehensile digits they could build machines, but in so doing mankind might perceive them as a threat. In the laboratory, he had seen with his own eyes how quickly Natalie could take a complex pipe puzzle, disassemble it, and then put it back together in no time flat. Then there was the Rubik's Cube. Natalie had solved it easily, no matter how randomly it was reset each time. If an albino could do that, then designing and fabricating new types of machinery and electronic gadgetry was more than likely only a step away in their technological advancement.

Back in Miami, Grahm had been astounded to discover that Natalie had already known how to play chess. Even Nick Henderson, an exceptional player in his own right, had been no match for the female dolphin. This recollection brought a humorous smile to Grahm's face, for he knew that Henderson had considered each of Natalie's three victories to be nothing more than flukes. Following the third loss, Henderson had refused to play anymore.

Grahm mulled this over. Only now did he fully comprehend the extent of Henderson's bias. His young assistant exemplified humanity's narcissistic need to believe man to be the preeminent thinker, doer, and feeler on the planet. Henderson was a perfect example of man's self-perceived superiority over all other living species, even in light of the fact that the brain size of some cetaceans had grown equal to and then surpassed the size of modern man's some thirty million years ago. The current Tursiops truncatus alone, Grahm knew, had been around on the order of fifteen million years with a brain size on a par with the present-day Homo sapien. Without prehensile extremities with which to develop a written language, however, it only stood to reason that delphine history would be stored away in such large brains, passed down from generation to generation. If that were true, the knowledge locked away in those minds would be vast.

As one of the foremost delphinologists on the planet, Grahm understood that past increases in brain sizes of both humans and cetaceans indicated a rising curve of further evolution in the cranial capacity of the two species. But it was the cetacea that still held a sizable lead. With a mass of 9,000 grams, the brain of a forty-ton sperm whale was six times heavier than that of a human. Even so, the consensus among most scientists was to place these brains in a category below man's, rationalizing that large bodies required large brains to control their behavior. They also argued that since larger-brained cetaceans had no hands, they had no need to develop intelligence. But Grahm's opinion went counter to such reasoning, holding to the belief that cut off from the need for building, for food preservation and preparation, and for external forms of transportation, cetaceans in all probability had highly advanced ethics and laws, developed over eons and passed on to succeeding generations. Despite having no direct experience of living in the sea, man still insisted upon imposing the criteria for intelligence relating to cetaceans, refusing to see that some of those large brains were actually superior to human brains in unique and different ways.

In working with dolphins over the years, Grahm had become more than convinced they harbored a complex inner reality quite different from that of man. With dolphins, group survival took precedence over individual members. Necessities for survival took in the group as a whole, with sick or grieving pod members cared for by the healthier animals. However, when such care put the survival of the group in jeopardy, the injured member would voluntarily commit suicide by simply ceasing to breathe.

Perhaps the most notable cetacean ethic was their special regard for man. Generally speaking and with few exceptions, dolphins and whales appeared to avoid injuring a human, even under extreme degrees of provocation. And although Grahm had no way of proving it, he suspected that cetaceans viewed man as an incredibly dangerous species in concert. Even with incomplete knowledge about man, contacts at sea with members of the human race often revealed to cetacea how harmful mankind could be, not only to the environment but to all life in the hydrosphere. Experiences with whaling and tuna fleets alone were good enough examples of the detriment man posed. Factor in massive oil spills, the effects of ship's sonar, undersea explosions, widespread pollution of the oceans, and naval warfare, and cetaceans had enough fragmentary knowledge about the nature of the human race to know that man could easily wipe them out if he so chose.

Grahm turned his eyes in another direction. Henderson was at it again, snorkeling around the *thurentra* like a bloodhound on the scent of elusive quarry. There was something unusual going on out there to arouse the lad's curiosity, of that he was certain. His young assistant had grown increasingly withdrawn over the past forty-eight hours, appearing to be preoccupied with the hybrid organism. But whatever was sparking his interest he was keeping to himself.

In the last several days, Grahm had seen a different side to Henderson, and he didn't like what he was seeing. Although the grad student had always been a bit cantankerous and surly, those traits had become far more pronounced as of late. Among other things, Henderson was proving himself to be a racist, showing an open hostility and disrespect towards Jacob. It was now apparent Henderson had preconceived notions about how these islanders should act and behave, and Jacob was not conforming to the image Henderson had expected of him.

Henderson was being stubborn. He had put reason aside, wanting to delude himself into believing all Haitians were illiterate and ignorant. As smart as the lad was with computers, Henderson refused to accept the premise that no race, culture, or ethnic group held a monopoly on intelligence and that exceptional intellect could spring up from any quarter in the human species.

Unconscious of his own action, Grahm shook his head as he continued to watch his stubborn assistant fin around the *thurentra*, wondering if Henderson would be foolish enough to get himself zapped a second time. Serves him right if he does.

Movement at the cove entrance abruptly caught Grahm's eye, and he realized Javolyn and the girl had returned with four of the albinos. The sight brought a smile to his face, particularly that of the girl. And while he had no idea why, a feeling of joy seemed to take hold of him every time he set eyes on her. Strangely, it warmed him to see Destiny in Jake's company. The two seemed right together. Even stranger was how natural it appeared for both of them to be whisked along by the albino dolphins.

Grahm felt a tinge of envy as the group turned toward the beach, wishing he, too, could share such a bond with these noble creatures. The way they had taken to Javolyn in so short a time still continued to puzzle him, but then again, maybe they could sense certain qualities in the makeup of an individual that determined the full measure of their interaction with that person. He couldn't even begin to imagine what kind of thoughts pulsed through those marvelous brains. With fifteen million years of advanced evolutionary development already behind the Tursiops' neurological hardware, he had to assume their view of the universe and existence itself had to be worlds apart from that of human perception. But then enhance those brains further through a mysterious event that had all the earmarks of an evolutionary jump, an elevated sentience had emerged with immeasurable mental capabilities, giving it a potential that now dwarfed man's.

As Grahm watched the group work its way toward the beach, he realized it would take more than his remaining years to fully grasp the underlying philosophies of these newcomers to the planet.

Chapter Thirty-five: A Harsh Contradiction

Bashir worked his way down through the fissures in the rock, slowly making his way toward the subterranean grotto. The fisherman called Jimenez had dropped him off on the southern side of the island just before dawn, leaving him with a small sack of cornmeal, a flask of freshwater, and half a dozen mangos for sustenance. Finding the concealed entrance that would lead him to the hidden submarine pen had not been easy, and he had wasted many hours groping his way through the objectionable thickets that overgrew the karst before stumbling upon the opening. His knowledge of its exact location relative to other topographic features had been rather obscure. Unlike Yeslam and some of the others in the team, he had had far less opportunity to venture out onto the island's upper plateau.

His body ached in various places, the result of having to travel on foot over jagged bedrock that riddled the island's interior. The sun had not yet arisen by the time he had first gained the island's upper terrace, and in the dim twilight he had misjudged a small but craggy pocket overgrown with cacti. The ensuing spill he had taken had left him bruised and bleeding in several places, and irksome quills of cactus had broken off in his hip. And coming into contact with the poisonwood trees that abounded over the rough terrain had only added to his discomfort, for his skin now itched wildly where rashes had broken out. He didn't care. He would do what he could to put a stop to this madness.

A strange detachment from what he was doing seemed to urge him onward, all the while his mind vaguely aware he had no actual plan to follow. Still, he continued to follow the passageway, descending deeper through the honeycombed rock that comprised the island's substrata. A series of electric bulbs strung out along the power cable that wound its way toward the underground stronghold provided ample light as he labored his way lower. Already he could hear the generator to which the cable was attached, the sound of it reaching his ears in a barely audible hum.

As Bashir descended lower, he thought about the man in charge of this operation. From his association with Yeslam Raduyev, he had learned the Chechen was actually the nephew of the infamous Shamil Basayev, a fanatical Muslim fundamentalist who had been killed more than a year earlier. Basayev had been a rebel warlord and the most wanted man in Russia. Through sheer audacity, Basayev was responsible for more high-profile acts of terrorism than any other Chechen. In a bid to rid Chechnya of Russian domination, Basayev had been reputed to have allied himself to Al Qaeda, purchasing nuclear weapons for Bin Laden in three former Soviet states – Turkmenistan, Ukraine, and Kazakhstan. Rumor had it that those weapons were a mix of suitcase and tactical warhead bombs.

Regarded as little more than a foot soldier by his superiors, Bashir had not been privy to many of the details of his group's mission, although he had learned enough to fill in some of the missing tidbits of information concerning the operation. Raduyev was the youngest of seven nuclear experts that worked for Bin Laden, all of them Central Asian Muslims. In an attempt to secure a lasting alliance with Al Qaeda, Basayev had offered up his nephew as part of a long-term scheme that had the potential of bringing down the country Bin Laden deemed the Great Satan. Blond-haired Chechens were much sought after by Bin Laden, owing to the reduced scrutiny such individuals would draw upon themselves. Initially, Yeslam had been planted as a one-man cell, thereby minimizing contacts until certain objectives could be achieved. Through carefully forged documents, Raduyev had gained entrance into the United States where he had first earned a degree in nuclear engineering before seeking admission to Navy Seal training. Knowledge of military techniques used by the Seals would be invaluable to the plan, which would involve clandestine undertakings at sea.

Bashir occupied himself with such thoughts as he inched his way down to the final turn in the winding passageway where it gave way to the subterranean grotto. Above the soft drone of the generator, voices could be heard. With great caution, he poked his head around the last barrier of rock, his eyes falling on two nearby figures with their backs to him.

"... very soon." It was Raduyev talking.

"I am still uneasy about bringing these infidels here," the other man said. "Down one man already, it will be difficult to control so many people in these constricted caverns."

The voice of the second speaker caught Bashir by surprise. Although he had known three other militants would be joining up with Raduyev, he hadn't been informed that one of them would be Gullu Sherkhan.

"You are beginning to sound like a woman more and more each day," Raduyev chided. "We will need a large labor force to widen the tunnels if our plan is to succeed."

Bashir found it difficult to believe Sherkhan's apparent calmness in the face of such open admonishment. Back in Afghanistan, an underlying friction had always existed between the two men, but now something had changed.

"Where will these people sleep?" Sherkhan said evenly, choosing to ignore the insult. "There is little room down here for so many."

"We will keep them working around the clock in the tunnels above," Raduyev snapped. "They will have little time for rest. We will push them hard, dividing ourselves up in shifts to oversee and ensure their efforts."

Sherkhan shrugged resignedly. "What about tools? Even among us, we don't have enough to go around."

Raduyev shifted around to glare at the Pashtun, and Bashir barely managed to pull his head back in time to keep from being seen. "More tools will be brought to us when the labor force arrives. I have already arranged for that."

"What about food?" Sherkhan pressed. "These people will require nourishment if we expect them to keep working. I have examined our stockpile of food and fresh water. Our supply is too limited to give any of it away."

Raduyev's response came back as a snarl. "Feeding these islanders does not concern me. We will use them until they can no longer serve us."

Bashir remained hidden, daring not to sneak another peek as he eavesdropped, but no further conversation ensued. He waited another minute before sidling his head around the bend in the rock, only to discover both men were now gone. He was still unsure of his next move, mulling over what he had just learned. This was something else he had been in the dark about.

Apparently Raduyev had made a deal to have people abducted and brought to this place for the sole purpose of performing slave labor. The most startling aspect of the plan was the manner in which those people would be treated. The idea caused Bashir to take a hard look at himself, making him realize what kind of a monster he might have become if not for the way fate had interceded to take him into the hands of those angelic beings. They had rescued him from defiling his soul forever, opening him up to reveal the person he truly was. Men like Raduyev were brutal and evil to the core. Raduyev was incapable of showing someone the mercy and compassion the captain of the *Avenging Angel* had given him. He found it hard to believe he had looked up to the Chechen before his capture. The one they called Jay Jay had treated him kindly. Even though his captor had had every right to let him die, the man had instead chosen to have his wound tended. On top of that, he had fed him and brought him ashore to eat with the others.

It was these thoughts that further galvanized Bashir, causing him to see the utter contradiction an individual like Raduyev represented. Here was a man whose fundamental faith was at irreconcilable odds with sober logic. More than ever now, he knew that Raduyev had to be stopped, and with renewed conviction he suddenly became cognizant of what he must do next.

To find out what happens next in this on-going saga, read Part 3 of the Dolphin Riders Series - The Girl Who Rode Dolphins, 3rd Edition Retribution.

Acknowledgments

No one deserves more credit for their support in the writing of this tale than my wife and soul mate, Harriet, my biggest fan. Her indomitable spirit and encouragement was indispensable in keeping me focused on completing a work that could have otherwise gone unfinished, a story that could have conceivably transpired in an alternate universe closely paralleling our own. As the novel progressed, it was always a delight to gauge her reaction, which was never disappointing as I read proceeding entries to her over breakfast each and every Saturday morning.

But the thing that finally compelled me to actually write it was the way Harriet was able to cope with her illness. Harriet is tough as nails and since the year 2000 she's been battling CML - chronic myeloid leukemia - and so far she's put up one hell of a valiant fight, absolutely refusing to yield to what most doctors would describe as a devastating, life-threatening malady. Thus, she made up her mind long ago to live out a normal existence, avoiding hospitals completely and refraining from seeing doctors as much as possible. Consequently, it was her grit and determination that inspired me to take pen to paper and flesh out an adventure imbued with these admirable qualities of the spirit. In its basic subliminal form, I wanted to honor her with something unique, essentially a literary work that came from the deepest part of me, something only I could give her, but something which would reflect her iron will and indomitable strength. This is initially mirrored in the book's opening scene where we find a woman adrift and marooned in a thunderous, tumultuous sea. She is alone and clinging to a piece of flotsam, and the reader finds the woman to be pregnant. By all rights, she should accept her fate and succumb to the elements, but she continues to fight on in the face of overwhelming odds, clinging to life, and refusing to quit until she has nothing left within her to resist the battering forces of a sea gone mad. Later in the book we learn the woman survives with the help of a dolphin and that her name is Harriet Grahm. And although she has no recollection of her former life, she ends up taking on a new identity, becoming Amphitrite, one of the cornerstone characters of the story. During her ordeal at sea, something incredible has happened to Amphitrite, and her failure to remember her past has somehow given her the power to glimpse the future. Henceforth, she becomes an arrant believer in this power and what the future holds, convinced her visions are real, and it is this ability that spills over and infects the reader to make the story palpable and real.

Writing the novel was a labor of love that took four years to complete. In creating it, I had to constantly challenge myself to come up with new ideas, not always knowing where the story was headed since some of the characters within the developing plot started taking on a life of their own. I only knew I wanted to take the reader on a journey to high adventure, an escape from the often mundane routines of everyday life most of us encounter, and in adhering to this I kept imagining what I'd like to see on the big screen if the novel was ever made into a blockbuster movie. My heartfelt appreciation also goes out to my daughter, Melissa, for her added encouragement to keep me moving forward with this project. And I certainly would be remiss if I left out her three little progenies, Troy Jacob, Solomon, and the latest addition to the family, Jayna Jocelynne, each of whom provided me with the personality traits and inspiration to create the mischievous impish characters which have now come alive to play an integral part within the sequel to this tale.

And lastly, I want to thank my sister, Barbara, for showing an enthusiastic interest in my creativity. Whenever she picked up the uncompleted manuscript, she always seemed to have trouble putting it down, totally absorbed and fascinated by the plot's intrigue and explosiveness.

About the Author

Michael J. Ganas is a licensed professional engineer. Following a stint in the U.S. Army, he earned a degree in civil engineering from Cornell University. Shortly thereafter, his love of the sea prompted him to pursue a career as a deep-sea commercial diver, heading a wide array of marine construction projects. This eventually led him into his current occupation, which takes on the challenges of civil engineering in underwater environments. Having published over twenty technical articles involving marine engineering, he decided on writing his first novel, an epic action adventure titled ***The Girl Who Rode Dolphins***, which eventually merited seven literary awards and has since been subdivided into the first three books of the on-going ***Dolphin Riders*** book series. ***Gaia's Heartbeat*** is the second book in the series.

www.ingramcontent.com/pod-product-compliance
Lightning Source LLC
LaVergne TN
LVHW020703110826
845149LV00012B/2085

9781966191063